THE TWO GUARDIANS

MORE WILDSIDE CLASSICS

THE TWO GUARDIANS

CHARLOTTE M. YONGE

WILDSIDE PRESS

THE TWO GUARDIANS

This edition published 2005 by Wildside Press, LLC.
www.wildsidepress.com

PREFACE.

In putting forth another work, the Author is anxious to say a few words on the design of these stories; not with a view to obviate criticism, but in hopes of pointing to the moral, which has been thought not sufficiently evident, perhaps because it has been desired to convey, rather than directly inculcate it.

Throughout these tales the plan has been to present a picture of ordinary life, with its small daily events, its pleasures, and its trials, so as to draw out its capabilities of being turned to the best account. Great events, such as befall only a few, are thus excluded, and in the hope of helping to present a clue, by example, to the perplexities of daily life, the incidents, which render a story exciting, have been sacrificed, and the attempt has been to make the interest of the books depend on character painting.

Each has been written with the wish to illustrate some principle which may be called the key note. "Abbeychurch" is intended to show the need of self-control and the evil of conceit in different manifestations; according to the various characters, "Scenes and Characters" was meant to exemplify the effects of being guided by mere feeling, set in contrast with strict adherence to duty. In "Henrietta's Wish" the opposition is between wilfulness and submission — filial submission as required, in the young people, and that of which it is a commencement as well as a type, as instanced in Mrs. Frederick Langford. The design of the "Castle Builders" is to show the instability and dissatisfaction of mind occasioned by the want of a practical, obedient course of daily life; with an especial view to the consequences of not seeking strength and assistance in the appointed means of grace.

And as the very opposite to Emmeline's feeble character, the heroine of the present story is intended to set forth the manner in which a Christian may contend with and conquer this world, living in it but not of it, and rendering it a means of self-renunciation. It is therefore purposely that the end presents no great event, and leaves Marian unrecompensed save by the effects her consistent well doing has produced on her companions. Any other compensation would render her self-sacrifice incomplete, and make her no longer invisibly above the world.

October 14th, 1852.

CHAPTER I.

"With fearless pride I say
That she is healthful, fleet, and strong
And down the rocks will leap along,
Like rivulets in May."

WORDSWORTH.

Along a beautiful Devonshire lane, with banks of rock over-
hung by tall bowery hedges, rode a lively and merry pair, now
laughing and talking, now summoning by call or whistle the span-
iel that ran by their side, or careered through the fields within the
hedge.

The younger was a maiden of about twelve years old, in a long
black and white plaid riding-skirt, over a pink gingham frock, and
her dark hair hidden beneath a little cap furnished with a long
green veil, which was allowed to stream behind her in the wind,
instead of affording the intended shelter to a complexion already a
shade or two darkened by the summer sun, but with little colour
in the cheeks; and what there was, only the pale pink glow like a
wild rose, called up for the moment by warmth and exercise, and
soon to pass away. Still there was no appearance of want of health;
the skin was of a clear, soft, fresh shade of brown; the large dark
eyes, in spite of all their depth of melancholy softness, had the
wild, untamed animation of a mountaineer; the face and form
were full of free life and vigour, as she sat erect and perfectly at
ease on her spirited little bay pony, which at times seemed so lively
that it might have been matter of surprise to a stranger that so
young a horsewoman should be trusted on its back.

Her companion was a youth some ten or eleven years her
senior, possessing a handsome set of regular features, with a good
deal of family likeness to hers; dark eyes and hair, and a figure
which, though slight, was rather too tall to look suitable to the
small, stout, strong pony which carried him and his numerous
equipments, consisting of a long rod-case, a fishing-basket
and landing-net, in accordance with the lines of artificial flies
wreathed round his straw hat, and the various oddly contrived
pockets of his grey shooting-coat.

In the distance at the end of the lane there appeared two
walking figures. "Mrs. Wortley!" exclaimed the young lady.

"No, surely not out so soon!" was the answer. "She is in the
depth of lessons."

"No, but Edmund, it is, look, and Agnes too! There, Ranger

has better eyes than you; he is racing to them."

"Well, I acknowledge my mistake," said Edmund, drawing up his rein as they came upon the pair, — a pleasing lady, and a pretty blue-eyed girl of fourteen. "I did not believe my eyes, Mrs. Wortley, though Marian tried to persuade me. I thought you were always reading Italian at this time in the morning, Agnes".

"And I thought you were reading Phædrus with Gerald," said Mrs. Wortley.

"Ay," said Agnes, "we did not know what to make of you coming up the lane; you with your lance there, like the Red Cross Knight himself, and Marian with her palfry for Una."

"The knight must have borrowed the dwarf's ass," said Edmund, laughing, and putting his lance in rest.

"And where have you been, then, at this portentous time of day, Agnes?" asked Marian.

"We heard a report of Betty Lapthorn's child having another fit," said Agnes, "and set off to see; but it turned out to be a false alarm. And now we are going up to the Manor House to ask Lady Arundel if she has any arrowroot for it, for ours is all used up."

"Shall we find her at leisure?" added Mrs. Wortley.

"Yes," said Marian. "Gerald has finished his lessons by this time. Mamma thought it would be too far for him to go with us, and besides he frightens the fish."

"Which you are in too good training to do, Marian," said Mrs. Wortley. "And how is your papa today?"

"Oh, it is a good day," said Marian: "he was up before we set off."

"Down stairs? For perhaps we had better not go now, just after he is tired with coming down," said Mrs. Wortley. "Now, Mr. Arundel, you will tell me honestly, and this arrowroot will do just as well another time; or if Marian will carry home the message —"

"Well," said Edmund, smiling, "to give you a proof of my sincerity, I think you had better perhaps go rather later in the day. My uncle very unnecessarily hurried himself, thinking that he was keeping me waiting to help him down stairs, and I thought he seemed rather tired; but he will be very glad to see you in the afternoon. Indeed, he would be very glad now, only you asked me as a question of prudence."

"Don't make civil speeches at the end to spoil just such a reply as I wanted," said Mrs. Wortley. "I am afraid you do not think Sir Edmund much better since you were last at home."

Edmund shook his head. "If he has not lost ground, it is well," said he, "and I think at least there is less pain."

"Well, I will not keep you any longer," said Mrs. Wortley; "good-bye, and good sport to you."

And with a wave of the hand on rode the two cousins, Edmund and Marian Arundel.

"What an excellent thing it is for the village that those Wortleys are come!" said Edmund.

"Yes; now that mamma cannot attend much to the school and poor people, I don't know what we should do without them. How different it was in old Mr. May's time! I hope we shall get the Church set to rights now, when papa is well enough to attend to it."

"It is high time, certainly," said Edmund; "our Church is almost a disgrace to us, especially with the Arundel aisle, to show what our ancestors did."

"No, not quite to us," said Marian; "you know papa would have done it all long ago, if the idea had not vexed poor old Mr. May so much. But Ranger! Ranger! where is Ranger, Edmund?"

Edmund whistled, and presently, with whirring, rushing wing, there flew over the hedge beside them a covey of partridges, followed by Ranger's eager bark. Marian's pony started, danced, and capered; Edmund watched her with considerable anxiety, but she reined it in with a steady, dexterous, though not a strong hand, kept her seat well, and rode on in triumph, while Edmund exclaimed, "Capital, Marian!" Then looking back, "What a shot that was!" he added in a sort of parenthesis, continuing, "I am proud, Mayflower is not a bit too much for you now, though I think we must have given her up if you had had another tumble."

"Oh, no, no, I do so delight in Mayflower, pretty creature!" said Marian, patting her neck. "I like to feel that the creature I ride is alive — not an old slug, like that animal which you are upon, Edmund."

"That is decidedly ungrateful of you, Marian, when you learnt to ride upon this identical slug, and owe the safety of your neck to its quiet propensities. Now take care down this stony hill; hold her up well — that is right."

Care was certainly needed as they descended the steep hill side; the road, or rather pathway, cut out between high, steep, limestone rocks, and here and there even bare of earth. Any one but a native would have trembled at such a descent but though the cousins paid attention to their progress, they had no doubts or alarms. At the bottom a clear sparkling stream traversed the road, where, for the convenience of foot passengers, a huge flat stone had been thrown across from one high bank to the other, so as to form a romantic bridge. Marian, however, did not avail herself of it, but rode gallantly through the shallow water, only looking back at it to observe to Edmund, "We must make a sketch of that some day or other."

"I am afraid we cannot get far enough off," said Edmund, "to make a good drawing of it. Too many things go to the making of the picturesque."

"Yes, I know, but that is what I never can understand. I see by woeful experience that what is pretty in itself will not make a pretty drawing, and everyone says so; but I never could find out why."

"Perhaps because we cannot represent it adequately."

"Yes, but there is another puzzle; you sometimes see an exact representation, which is not really a picture at all. Don't you know that thing that the man who came to the door did of our house, — the trees all green, and the sky all blue, and the moors all purple?"

"As like as it can stare; yes, I know."

"Well, why does that not satisfy us? why is it not a picture?"

"Because it stares, I suppose. Why does not that picture of my aunt at Mrs. Week's cottage satisfy you as well as the chalk sketch in the dining-room?"

"Because it has none of herself — her spirit."

"Well, I should say that nature has a self and a spirit which must be caught, or else the Chinese would be the greatest artists on the face of the earth."

"Yes, but why does an archway, or two trees standing up so as to enclose the landscape, or — or any of those things that do to put in the foreground, why do they enable you to make a picture, to catch this self and spirit."

"Make the phial to enclose the genie," said Edmund. "Abstruse questions, Marian; but perhaps it is because they contract the space, so as to bring it more to the level of our capacity, make it less grand, and more what we can get into keeping. To be sure, he would be a presumptuous man who tried to make an exact likeness of that," he added, as they reached the top of the hill, and found themselves on an open common, with here and there a mass of rock peeping up, but for the most part covered with purple heath and short furze, through which Ranger coursed, barking joyously. The view was splendid, on one side the moors rising one behind the other, till they faded in grey distance, each crowned with a fantastic pile of rocks, one in the form of a castle, another of a cathedral, another of a huge crouching lion, all known to the two cousins by name, and owned as familiar friends.

On the other side, between two hills, each surmounted by its own rocky crest, lay nestled in woods the grey Church tower and cottages of the village of Fern Torr; and far away stretched the rich landscape of field, wood, and pasture, ending at length in the blue line of horizon, where sky and sea seemed to join.

"Beautiful! how clear!" was all Marian's exclamation, though she drew up her horse and gazed with eager eyes, and a deep feeling of the loveliness of the scene, but with scarcely a remark. There was something in the sight which made her heart too full for words.

After a time of delighted contemplation, Ranger was summoned from a close investigation of a rabbit-hole, and turning into a cart track, the cousins rode down the side of the hill, where presently appeared an orchard full of gnarled old apple trees, covered with fruit of all shades of red, yellow, and green. A little further on were the large stone barns, and picturesque looking house, which enclosed a farm-yard strewn with heaps of straw, in which pigs, poultry, and red cows were enjoying themselves. The gate was opened by a wild-looking cow-boy, who very respectfully touched his cap; and at the house door appeared a nice elderly looking old fashioned farmer's wife, who came forward to meet them with bright looks of cordiality, and kindly greetings to Master Edmund and Miss Marian.

"Thank you, thank you, Mrs. Cornthwayte," said Edmund, as he held Marian's pony; "we are come to ask if you will give our ponies stable room for a couple of hours, while we go fishing up the river."

"O yes, certainly, sir, but won't you come in a little while and rest? it is a long walk for Miss Marian."

They did comply with her invitation so far as to enter the large clean kitchen; the kitchen for show, that is to say, with the sanded floor, the bunch of evergreens in the covered kitchen-range, the dark old fashioned clock, the bright range of crockery, and well polished oaken table; and there, while Marian laid aside her riding-skirt, the good woman commenced her anxious inquiries for Sir Edmund.

"Pretty much the same as usual, thank you," said Edmund.

"No better, then, sir? Ah! I was afraid how it was; it is so long since I have seen him at church, and he used to come sometimes last summer: and my husband said when he saw him last week about the rent, he was so fallen away that he would hardly have known him."

"It has been a very long illness," said Edmund.

"Yes, sir; I do wish we could see him about among us again, speaking as cheerful as he used."

"Why he is very cheerful now, Mrs. Cornthwayte," said Edmund. "No one who only heard him talk would guess how much he has to suffer."

Mrs. Cornthwayte shook her head with a sort of gesture of compassionate admiration, and presently added,

"But do you think he gets better on the whole, Master Edmund? Do the doctors say there is much likelihood of his being well again, and coming among us?"

Edmund looked down and did not reply very readily. "I am afraid we must not hope for that; we must be satisfied as long as he does not lose ground, and I certainly think he has had less pain of late."

A little more conversation passed between Edmund and the good wife, and a few words from Marian; after which they set off across one or two fields towards the place of their destination, Marian carrying her little sketching-basket in silence for some distance, until she suddenly exclaimed, "Edmund, is papa really getting worse?"

"Why should you think so, Marian?"

"I don't know, only from what you say when people inquire after him; and sometimes when I come to think about it, I believe he can do less than last year. He gets up later, and does not go out so often, and now you say he will never get quite well, and I always thought he would."

"No, I am afraid there is no likelihood of that, Marian: the doctors say he may be much better, but never quite well."

"But do you think he is better?"

"He has had less suffering of late, certainly, and so far we must be thankful; but, as you say, Marian, I am afraid he is weaker than last time I was at home, and I thought him much altered when I came. Still I do not think him materially worse, and I believe I might have thought him improved, if I had been here all the winter."

Marian became silent again, for her disposition was not to express her feelings readily, and besides, she was young enough to be able to put aside anxiety which, perhaps, she did not fully comprehend. It was the ordinary state of things for her father to be unwell, and his illness scarcely weighed upon her spirits, especially on a holiday and day of pleasure like the present; for though she often shared Edmund's walks and rides, a long expedition like this was an unusual treat.

After traversing several fields, they entered a winding path through a copse, which, descending a steep hill side, conducted them at length to the verge of a clear stream, which danced over or round the numerous rocks which obstructed its passage, making a pleasant, rippling sound. Here and there under the overhanging trees were deep quiet pools, where the water, of clear transparent brown color, contained numbers of little trout, the object of Edmund's pursuit. But more frequently the water splashed, dashed, and brawled along its rocky way, at the bottom of the narrow wooded ravine in which the valley ended. It was indeed a beautiful scene, with the sun glancing on the green of the trees and the bright sparkling water; and Marian could scarcely restrain her exclamations of delight, out of consideration for the silence required by her cousin's sport. She helped him to put his rod together, and arrange his reel, with the dexterity of one who well understood the matter; and then sat down under a fern-covered rock with a book in her hand, whilst he commenced his fishing. As he slowly proceeded up the stream, she changed her place so as to follow him at a distance; now and then making expeditions into the wood at the side of the hill to study some remarkable rock, some tree of peculiar form, or to gather a handsome fern-leaf, or nodding fox-glove with its purple bells. Or the little sketch-book came out, and she caught the form of the rock with a few strokes of bold outline and firm shading, with more power over her soft pencil than is usual at her age, though her foliage was not of the most perfect description. Her own occupations did not, however, prevent her from observing all her cousin's proceedings; she knew whenever he captured a trout, she was at hand to offer help when his hook, was caught in a bramble, and took full and complete interest in the sport.

At last, after a successful fishing up the glen, they arrived at a place where the ravine was suddenly closed in by a perpendicular rock of about twenty feet in height, down which the water fell with its full proportion of foam and spray, forming a cascade which Marian thought "magnificent," — Edmund, "very pretty."

"Edmund, I am afraid the Lake country has spoilt you for Devonshire. I wish they had never sent your regiment to the north!"

"That would not prevent the falls in Westmoreland from being twice the height of this."

"It would prevent you from saying that here it is not as beautiful as any thing can be."

"And nothing short of that will satisfy you. You had better

stand in a narrow pass, and challenge every passer-by to battle in defence of the beauty of Fern Torr."

"I don't care about every body; but you, Edmund, ought to be more dutiful to your own home."

"You are exclusive, Marian; but come," and he stuck his rod into the ground, "let us have some of your sandwiches."

"Not till you confess that you like Fern Torr better than all the fine places that you ever saw."

"Liking with all one's heart is one thing, admiring above all others is another, as you will find when you have seen more of the world, Marian."

"I am sure I shall never think so."

While this contest was going on, Marian had unpacked some sandwiches and biscuits, and they sat down to eat them with the appetite due to such a walk. Then came a conversation, in which Marian submitted to hear something of the beauties of the Lakes, in the shape of a comment on the "Bridal of Triermain," which she had brought with her; next an attempt at sketching the cascade, in which Edmund was successful enough to make Marian much discontented with her own performance, and declare that she was tired of sitting still, and had a great mind to try to climb up the rocks by the side of the fall. She was light, active, and well able to scramble, and with a little help here and there from her cousin's strong hand, the top was merrily gained; and springing along from rock to rock, they traced the windings of the stream even to the end of the copse and the opening of the moor. It was a great achievement for Marian, for even Edmund had only once been this way before when out shooting. She would fain have mounted to the top of a peak which bounded her view, but being assured that she would only find Alps on Alps arise, she submitted to Edmund's judgment, and consented to retrace her steps, through wood and wild, to Mrs. Cornthwayte's, where they found a feast prepared for them of saffron buns, Devonshire cream, and cyder. Then mounting their steeds, and releasing Ranger from durance in the stable, they rode homewards for about three miles, when they entered the village in the valley at the foot of the steep rocky hill, from which it was named Fern Torr. Excepting the bare rugged summit, this hill was well covered with wood, and opposite to it rose more gently another elevation, divided into fields and meadows. The little old Church, with its square tower, and the neat vicarage beside it, were the only buildings above the rank of cottages, of which some twenty stood irregularly ranged in their gardens and orchards, along the banks of the bright little stream which bounded the road, at present scarcely large enough to afford swimming space for the numerous ducks that paddled in it; but the width of its stony bed, and the large span of the one-arched bridge that traversed it, showing what was its breadth and strength in the winter floods.

A little beyond this bridge was a wicket gate, leading to a path up the wooded height; and Edmund at this moment seeing a boy in a stable jacket, asked Marian if he should not let him lead the ponies round by the drive, while they walked up the steps. She readily agreed, and Edmund helping her to dismount, they took their way up the path, which after a very short interval led to a steep flight of steps, cut out in the face of the limestone rock, and ascending through ferns, mountain-ash, and rhododendrons for about fifty or sixty feet, when it was concluded by what might be called either a broad terrace or narrow lawn, upon which stood a house irregularly built of the rough stone of the country, and covered with luxuriant myrtles and magnolias. Immediately behind, the ground again rose so precipitously, that scarcely could coign of vantage be won for the garden, on a succession of narrow shelves or ledges, which had a peculiarly beautiful effect, adorned, as they were, with gay flowers, and looking, as Edmund was wont to say, as gorgeous and as deficient in perspective as an old piece of tapestry.

"There is papa out of doors," exclaimed Marian, as she emerged upon the lawn, and ran eagerly up to a Bath chair, in which was seated a gentleman whose face and form showed too certain tokens of long and wasting illness. He held out his hand to her, saying, "Well, Marian, good sport, I hope, and no more tumbles from Mayflower."

"Marian sits like a heroine," said Edmund, coming up; "I am glad to see you out."

"It is such a fine evening that I was tempted to come and see the magnolia that you have all been boasting of: and really it is worth seeing. Those white blossoms are magnificent."

"But where is mamma?" asked Marian.

"Carried off by Gerald, to say whether he may have a superannuated sea kale pot for some purpose best known to himself, in his desert island. They will be here again in another minute. There, thank you, Edmund, that is enough," he added, as his nephew drew his chair out of a streak of sunshine which had just come over him. "Now, how far have you been? I hope you have seen the cascade, Marian?"

"O yes, papa, and scrambled up the side of it too. I had no idea of any thing so beautiful," said Marian. "The spray was so white and glancing. Oh! I wish I could tell you one half of the beauty of it."

"I remember well the delight of the first discovery of it," said Sir Edmund, "when I was a mere boy, and found my way there by chance, as I was shooting. I came up the glen, and suddenly found myself in the midst of this beautiful glade, with the waterfall glancing white in the sun."

"I wish we could transplant it," said Edmund; "but after all, perhaps its being so remote and inaccessible is one of its great charms. Ah! young monkey, is it you?" added he, as Gerald, a merry bright-eyed boy of seven years old, came rushing from behind and commenced a romping attack upon him. "Take care, not such a disturbance close to papa."

"O mamma, we have had the most delightful day!" cried Marian, springing to the side of her mother, who now came forward from the kitchen garden, and whose fair and gentle, but careworn, anxious face, lighted up with a bright sweet smile, as she observed the glow on her daughter's usually pale cheek, and the light that danced in her dark brown eye.

"I'm glad you have had such a pleasant day, my dear," said she. "It is very kind in Edmund to be troubled with such a wild goose."

"Wild geese are very good things in their way," said Edmund; "water and land, precipice and moor, 'tis all the same to them."

"And when will you take me, Edmund?" asked Gerald.

"When you have learnt to comport yourself with as much discretion as Marian, master," said Edmund, sitting down on the grass, and rolling the kicking, struggling boy over and over, while Marian stood by her papa, showing him her sketches, and delighted by hearing him recognize the different spots. "How can you remember them so well, papa," said she, "when it is so very long since you saw them?"

"That is the very reason," he answered, "we do not so much dwell on what is constantly before us as when we have long lost sight of it. To be confined to the house for a few years is an excellent receipt for appreciating nature."

"Yes, because it must make you wish for it so much," said Marian sadly.

"Not exactly," said her father. "You cannot guess the pleasure it has often given me to recall those scenes, and to hear you talk of them; just as your mamma likes to hear of Oakworthy."

"Certainly," said Lady Arundel. "I have remembered much at poor old Oakworthy that I never thought of remarking at the time

I was there. Even flaws in the glass, and cracks in the ceiling have returned upon me, and especially since the house has been pulled down."

"I cannot think how the natives of an old house can wilfully destroy all their old associations, their heirloooms," said Edmund.

"Sometimes they have none," said his aunt.

"Ay," said Sir Edmund, "when Gerald brings home a fine wife from far away, see what she will say to all our dark passages and corner cupboards, and steps up and steps down."

"Oh! I shall not be able to bear her if she does not like them," cried Marian.

"I suppose that was the case with Mrs. Lyddell," added Sir Edmund, "that she discovered the deficiencies of the old house, as well as brought wherewith to remedy them. He does not look like a man given to change."

"He has no such feeling for association as these people," said Lady Arundel, pointing to Edmund and Marian; "he felt his position, in the country raised by her fortune, and was glad to use any means of adding to his consequence."

"I should like to see more of them. I wish we could ask them to stay here," said Sir Edmund, with something like a sigh. "But come, had we not better go in? The hungry fishers look quite ready for tea."

CHAPTER II.

"And now I set thee down to try
How thou canst walk alone."

Lyra Innocentium.

Scarcely eight months had passed since the last recorded conversation, when Marian, in a dress of deep mourning, was
slowly pacing the garden paths, her eyes fixed on the ground, and
an expression of thoughtful sadness on her face. Heavy indeed
had been the strokes that had fallen upon her. Before the last summer had closed, the long sufferings of her father had been termi-
nated by one of the violent attacks, which had often been expected
to be fatal. Nor was this all that she had to mourn. With winter had
come severe colds and coughs; Lady Arundel was seized with an
inflammation of the chest, her constitution had been much enfee-
bled by watching, anxiety, and grief, and in a very few days her
children were orphans.

It was the day following the funeral. Mrs. Wortley was staying
in the house, as were also the two guardians of the young Sir
Gerald Arundel and his sister. These were Mr. Lyddell, a relation
of Lady Arundel; and our former acquaintance, Edmund Arundel, in whom, young as he was, his uncle had placed full confidence. He had in fact been entirely brought up by Sir Edmund,
and knew no other home than Fern Torr, having been sent thither
an orphan in earliest childhood. His uncle and aunt had supplied
the place of parents, and had been well rewarded for all they had
done for him, by his consistent well doing and completely filial
affection for them.

Marian was startled from her musings by his voice close at
hand, saying, "All alone, Marian?"

"Gerald is with Jemmy Wortley, somewhere," she replied,
"and I begged Mrs. Wortley and Agnes to go down the village and
leave me alone. I have been very busy all the morning, and my
head feels quite confused with thoughts!"

"I am glad to have found you," said Edmund. "I have seen so
little of you since I have been here."

"Yes, you have been always with Mr. Lyddell. When does he
go?"

"Tomorrow morning."

"And you stay longer, I hope?"

"Only till Monday; I wish it was possible to stay longer, but it
is something to have a Sunday to spend here."

"And then I am afraid it will be a long time before we see you again."

"I hope not; if you are in London, it will be always easier to meet."

"In London! Ah! that reminds me I wanted to ask you what I am to say to Selina Marchmont. I have a very kind letter from her, asking us to come to stay with her directly, and hoping that it may be arranged for us to live with them."

"Ah! I have a letter from her husband to the same effect," said Edmund. "It really is very kind and friendly in them."

"Exceedingly," said Marian. "Will you read her letter, and tell me how I am to answer her!"

"As to the visit, that depends upon what you like to do yourself. I should think that you would prefer staying with the Wortleys, since they are so kind as to receive you."

"You don't mean," exclaimed Marian, eagerly, "staying with them for ever!"

Edmund shook his head. "No, Marian, I fear that cannot be."

"Then it is as I feared," sighed Marian. "I wonder how it is that I have thought so much about myself; but it would come into my head, what was to become of us, and I was very much afraid of living with the Lyddells; but still there was a little glimmering of hope that you might be able to manage to leave us with the Wortleys."

"I heartily wish I could," said Edmund, "but it is out of my power. My uncle —"

"Surely papa did not wish us to live with the Lyddells?" cried Marian.

"I do not think he contemplated your living any where but at home."

"But the Vicarage is more like home than any other place could ever be," pleaded Marian, "and papa did not like the Lyddells nearly so well as the Wortleys."

"We must abide by his arrangements, rather than our own notions of his wishes," said Edmund. "Indeed, I know that he thought Mr. Lyddell a very sensible man."

"Then poor Gerald is to grow up away from his own home, and never see the dear old moors! But if we cannot stay here, I had rather be with Selina. She is so fond of Gerald, and she knows what home was, and she knew and loved — them. And we should not meet so many strangers. Only think what numbers of Lyddells there are! Boys to make Gerald rude, and girls, and a governess — all strangers. And they go to London!" concluded poor Marian, reaching the climax of her terrors. "O Edmund, can you do nothing for us?"

"You certainly do not embellish matters in anticipation. You will find them very different from what you expect — even London itself, which, by the by, you would have to endure even if you were with Selina, whom I suspect to be rather too fine and fashionable a lady for such a homely little Devonshire girl."

"That Mrs. Lyddell will be. She is a very gay person, and they have quantities of company. O Edmund!"

"The quantities of company," replied her cousin, "will interfere with you far less in your schoolroom with the Miss Lyddells, than alone with my Lady Marchmont, where, at your unrecognized age, you would be in rather an awkward situation."

"Or I could go to Torquay, to old Aunt Jessie?"

"Aunt Jessie would not be much obliged for the proposal of giving her such a charge."

"But I should take care of her, and make her life less dismal and lonely."

"That may be very well some years hence, when you are your own mistress: but at present I believe the trouble and change of habits which having you with her would occasion, would not be compensated by all your attention and kindness. Have you written to her yet?"

"No, I do not know how, and I hoped it was one of the letters that you undertook for me."

"I think I ought not to relieve you of that. Aunt Jessie is your nearest relation; I am sure this has been a great blow to her, and that it has cost her much effort to write to you herself. You must not turn her letter over to me, like a mere complimentary condolence."

"Very well," said Marian, with a sigh, "though I cannot guess what I shall say. And about Selina?"

"You had better write and tell her how you are situated, and I will do the same to Lord Marchmont."

"And when must we go to the Lyddells? I thought he meant more than mere civility, when he spoke of Oakworthy this morning, at breakfast."

"He spoke of taking you back to London immediately, but I persuaded him to wait till they go into Wiltshire, so you need not be rooted up from Fern Torr just yet."

"Thank you, that is a great reprieve."

"And do not make up your mind beforehand to be unhappy at Oakworthy. Very likely you will take root there, and wonder you ever shrank from being transplanted to your new home."

"Never! never! it is cruel to say that any place but this can be like home! And you, Edmund, what shall you do, where shall you go, when you have leave of absence?"

"I shall never ask for it," said he with an effort, while his eye fell on the window of the room which had been his own for so many years, and the thought crossed him, "Mine no more." It had been his home, as fully as that of his two cousins, but now it was nothing to him; and while they had each other to cling to, he stood in the world a lonely man.

Marian perceived his emotion, but rather than seem to notice it, she assumed a sort of gaiety. "I'll tell you, Edmund. You shall marry a very nice wife, and take some delightful little house somewhere hereabouts, and we will come and stay with you till Gerald is of age."

"Which he will be long before I have either house or wife," said Edmund, in the same tone, "but mind, Marian, it is a bargain, unless you grow so fond of the Lyddells as to retract."

"Impossible."

"Well, I will not strengthen your prejudices by contending with them."

"Prejudice! to say that I can never be as happy anywhere as at my own dear home! To say that I cannot bear strangers!"

"If they were to remain strangers for all the years that you are likely to spend with them, there might be something in that. But I see you cannot bear to be told that you can ever be happy again, so I will not say so any more, especially as I must finish my letters."

"And I will try to write mine," said Marian with a sigh, as she reached the door, and went up to take off her bonnet.

Edmund lingered for a moment in the hall, and there was met by Mrs. Wortley, who said she was glad to see that he had been out, for he was looking pale and harassed. "I did not go out for any pleasant purpose," said he. "I had to pronounce sentence on poor Marian."

"Is it finally settled?" said Mrs. Wortley. "We still had hopes of keeping her."

"Sir Gerald and Miss Arundel are of too much distinction in Mr. Lyddell's eyes to be left to their best friends," said Edmund. "It was hard to persuade him not to take possession directly, on the plea of change being good for their spirits."

"It is very kind of you to put off the evil day," said Mrs. Wortley; "it will be a grievous parting for poor Agnes."

"A grievous business for every one," said Edmund.

"How? Do not you think well of Mr. and Mrs. Lyddell?"

"I know my uncle never thought of these poor children's living with them. He thought Mr. Lyddell a good man of business, but neither he nor my aunt ever dreamed of such a home for them."

"Would they have preferred Lady Marchmont's? Marian is very fond of her, and was much gratified by a very nice affectionate letter that she received this morning."

"Yes, but I am glad she is out of the question. It is offering a great deal both on her part and her husband's to take charge of these two, but it would never do. She is almost a child herself, — a bride and beauty under twenty, — excessively admired, very likely to have her head turned. No, it would be too absurd. All her kindness, amiability, desire to make Marian her friend and companion, would only serve to do harm."

"Yes, you are right; yet I cannot help half wishing it could be, if it was only to save poor Marian her terrors of going among strangers."

"I know exactly how it will be," said Edmund. "She will shut herself up in a double proof case of shyness and reserve. They will never understand her, nor she them."

"But that cannot go on for ever."

"No; and perhaps it might be better if it could."

"Well, but do you really know anything against them? He seems inclined to be very kind and considerate."

"Electioneering courtesy," said Edmund. "But now you begin to question me, I cannot say that my — my mistrust shall I call it — or aversion? is much better founded than the prejudices I have been scolding poor Marian for. Perhaps it is only that I am jealous of them, and cannot think any one out of Fern Torr worthy to bring up my uncle's children. All I know of them is, that Mrs. Lyddell was heiress to a rich banker, she goes out a good deal in London, and the only time that I met her I thought her clever and agreeable. In their own county I believe she is just what a popular member's wife should be — I don't mean popular in the sense of radical. I think I have heard too something about the eldest son not turning out well; but altogether, you see, I have not grounds enough to justify any opposition to their desire of having the children."

"How are they as to Church principles?"

"That I really cannot tell. I should think they troubled themselves very little about the matter, and would only dislike any thing strong either way. If my aunt had but been able to make some arrangement! No doubt it was upon her mind when she asked so often for me!"

"Yes, but there is this comfort," said Mrs. Wortley, seeing him much troubled, "that she did not seem to make herself anxious and restless on their account. She trusted them, and so may we."

"Yes, that is all that one can come to," said Edmund, sighing deeply. "But Gerald! One pities Marian the most now, but it is a more serious matter for him."

"Gerald will be more in your power than his sister," said Mrs. Wortley.

"As if that was much comfort," said Edmund, half smiling, then again sighing, "when even for my own concerns I miss my uncle's advice at every turn. And probably I may have to go on foreign service next year."

"Then he will be at school."

"Yes. He was not to have gone till he was ten years old, but I shall try to hasten it now. He must go with his sister to Oakworthy though, for to begin without him there would be complete desolation in her eyes."

Here the conversation was concluded by Marian's coming down to write her painfully composed letters. That to her cousin, Lady Marchmont, who, as Selina Grenville, had been a frequent and favourite visitor at the manor, ran glibly enough off the pen, and the two or three quiet tears that blotted the paper, fell from a feeling of affection rather than of regret; but the letter to old Mrs. Jessie Arundel, her great aunt, and one or two others which Edmund had desired her to write, were works of time. Marian's feelings were seldom freely expressed even to those whom she loved best, and to write down expressions of grief, affection, or gratitude, as a matter of course, was positively repugnant to her.

The great work was not finished till late, and then came in Gerald and Agnes, and the tea drinking among themselves was rendered cheerful by Agnes' anticipations of pleasure in their going the next day to the parsonage for a long visit. Gerald began to play with her, and soon got into quite high spirits, and Marian herself had smiled, nay, almost laughed, before the gentlemen came in from the dining room, when the presence of Mr. Lyddell cast over her a cloud of dull dread and silence, so that she did not through the rest of the evening raise her head three inches from her book.

Yet as Mrs. Wortley had said, Mr. Lyddell was evidently inclined to be kind to her and her brother. He patted Gerald on the head as he wished him good night, and said good-naturedly to

Marian that she must be great friends with his girls, Caroline and Clara.

Marian tried to look civil, but could not find an answer both sincere and polite, and Mrs. Wortley, speaking for her, asked if they were nearly of the same age as she was.

"Well, I can't exactly tell," said Mr. Lyddell. "I should think she was between them. You are thirteen, aren't you, Marian? Well, Caroline may be a couple of years older, and Clara — I know her birthday was the other day, for I had to make her a present, — but how old she was I can't exactly recollect, whether it was twelve or thirteen. So you see you will not want for companions at Oakworthy, and you will be as happy there as your poor mamma used to be in the old house. Many was the laugh she has had there with my poor sister, and now they are both gone — well, there, I did not mean to overset you, — but —"

Marian could not bear it. She could talk of her mother to Mrs. Wortley, Agnes, or Edmund, with complete composure, but she could not bear Mr. Lyddell's hearty voice trying, as she thought, at sentiment, and forcing the subject upon her, and without a word or a look she hurried out of the room, and did not come back all the evening. Agnes followed her, and pitied her, and thought Mr. Lyddell should have said nothing of the kind, and sat down over the fire with her in her own room to read hymns.

The next day Mr. Lyddell left Fern Torr, and Marian was so glad to gee him depart as to be able to endure much better his invitations to Oakworthy. That same day Marian and Gerald went to the parsonage, and Edmund, after spending a quiet Sunday at Fern Torr, bade them farewell on the Monday morning.

CHAPTER III.

"Where once we dwelt our name is heard no more,
Children not thine 'may tread' my nurseryfloor."
                                        COWPER.

The way of life at Fern Torr parsonage was so quiet as to afford few subjects for narration. Mrs. Wortley was a gentle, sensible person, very fond of Marian and Gerald, both for their own sake and their mother's, and to be with her was to them as like being at home as anything could be. Agnes was quite wrapped up in her friend, whom she pitied so heartily, and was to lose so soon. She had known no troubles except through Marian, she reverenced Marian's griefs, and in her respect for them was inclined to spoil her not a little. Then, through nothing against the Lyddells had ever been said to Agnes, she had caught all Marian's prejudiced dislike to them, and sometimes in lively exaggeration, sometimes in grave condolence, talked of them "as these horrid people."

Marian felt every day was precious as it passed, and the time seemed to her far less than two months, when one day there arrived a letter from Mrs. Lyddell to announce that the family were about to leave London, and in the course of a week Mr. Lyddell would come to fetch her and Gerald to Oakworthy.

The letter was kindly expressed, but this was lost upon Marian in the pain its purport gave her, and the difficulty of composing an answer. She chose her smallest sheet of writing-paper with the deepest black edge, wrote as widely as she could, and used the longest words, but with all Mrs. Wortley's suggestions, she could not eke out what she had to say beyond the first page. She would not even send her love to her cousins, for she said she could have no particular affection for them, and to express any pleasure in the prospect of seeing so many strangers would be an actual untruth.

What a week was that which followed! Marian loved her home with that enthusiasm which especially belongs to the inhabitants of mountainous districts, and still more acutely did she feel the separation from all that reminded her of her parents. If she had not had Gerald to go with her she did not know how she could have borne it, but Gerald, her own beautiful brother, with his chestnut curls, dark bright eyes, sweet temper, and great cleverness and goodness, he must be a comfort to her wherever she was. Gerald was one of those children who seem to have a peculiar atmosphere of bright grace and goodness around them, who make beautiful earnest sayings in their simplicity which are treasured up by their friends, who, while regarding them with joy and something like veneration, watch them likewise with fear and trembling. Thus had his mother looked upon Gerald, and thus in some degree did Mrs. Wortley; but Marian had nothing but pride, joy, and confidence in him, unalloyed save now and then by the secret, half superstitious fear that such goodness might mark him for early death.

By Marian's own especial desire, she went to almost every cottage to take leave, but all she could do was to stand with her head averted and her lips compressed, while Mrs. Wortley spoke for her. Her next task was to look over the boxes and drawers at the manor house, in case it should be let; for no one else could be trusted to decide what hoards of highly prized trifles should be locked up, and what must be thrown away. She alone could choose the little keepsakes to be given to old servants and village friends, and she must select what she would take to Oakworthy.

She stood lingering before each picture, viewing the old familiar furniture with loving eyes, and sighing at the thought that strangers would alter the arrangements, look carelessly or critically on her father's portrait, think her wild garden a collection of weeds, and root up the flowering fern which Edmund had helped her to transplant. She went into her own room, and felt almost ready to hate the person who might occupy it; she lay down on the bed, and looking up at the same branch of lime tree, and the same piece of sky which had met her eyes every morning, she mused there till she was roused by hearing Gerald's voice very loud in the nursery. Hastening thither, she found him insisting that his collection of stones and spars was much too precious to mend the roads with, as their maid Saunders proposed, and Agnes settling the matter satisfactorily by offering to take them to adorn a certain den in the vicarage garden with. The ponies were to be turned out to grass, the rabbits were bestowed on James Wortley, and Ranger was to be kept at the vicarage till Edmund could come and fetch him, together with his books, which Marian had to look out, and she found it a service of difficulty, since "Edmund Gerald" could scarcely be said to answer the purpose of a proper name in the Arundel family.

The last day at home arrived, the eve of S. James. Marian went to prepare her class at the weekly school, resolved to do just as usual to the last. She had to read them the conversation on S. James's Day in "Fasts and Festivals," but she could hardly get through with it, the separation between early friends reminded her so much of herself and Agnes, and then the comparison of the two roads, one in burning and scorching sunshine, the other in the cool fresh shade, almost overset her, for though she could not tell why, she chose to be persuaded that the first must be hers. But they both ended in the same place. She felt tears coming into her eyes, but she kept them down, and went on reading in a steady monotonous voice, as if the meaning was nothing to her; she asked the children questions in a dry, grave, matter-of-fact way, as if she had not the slightest interest in them or in the subject, though her heart was full of affection to the dullest and roughest among them, and when she went away, her nod, and "well, good morning," to the school mistress were several shades further from warmth than usual.

All the way back from the school she was eagerly telling Agnes exactly the point where she left each child in her class, and begging her to say the kind things which she meant to have said to Grace Knight, the mistress.

Agnes laughed and said, "I hope she will take my word for it all. Why could you not speak to her? At least I thought you were not afraid of her."

"I don't know," said Marian. "I thought I could, but it is very odd. You see, Agnes, how it is; the more I care, the more I can't speak, and I can't help it."

"Well, don't be unhappy about it," said Agnes. "I know what you mean, and am ready to take you as you are, and if other people don't, it is their own fault."

Agnes was rather too fond of Marian to be exactly right here, for it was not at all a good thing that she should be encouraged in a reserve which led her not always to do as she would be done by.

The two girls came in, lingered in each other's rooms while they dressed, and at last were called down stairs by Mrs. Wortley, who was ready to finish with them the last chapter of the book they had been reading aloud together. Gerald sat in the window, his friend Jemmy hanging over him, and the two together composing a marvellous battlepiece, in which Gerald drew horses, men, cannon, and arrows, and Jemmy, like a small Homer, suggested the various frightful wounds they should be receiving, and the attitudes in which they should fall. The general, with a tremendous Turkish sabre, an immense cocked hat, and a horse with very stiff legs, was just being represented receiving an unfortunate-looking prisoner, considerably spotted with vermillion paint, when a sound of wheels was heard, and both boys starting up, exclaimed, "Here he comes!"

He, as Marian knew full well, was Mr. Lyddell; and a chilliness came over her as he entered, tall, broad, ruddy, treading heavily, and speaking loudly: and Gerald pressed close to her, squeezing her hand so tight that she could hardly withdraw it to shake hands with her guardian. With one hand he held her cold reluctant fingers, with the other gave Gerald's head a patronizing pat. "Well, my dears, how d'ye do? quite well? and ready to start with me tomorrow? That is right. Caroline and Clara have had their heads full of nothing but you this long time — only wanted to have come with me."

Here Marian succeeded in drawing back her hand, and retreated to the window; Gerald was creeping after her, but Mr. Lyddell laid hold of his chin, and drew him back, saying. "What, shy, my man? we shall cure you at Oakworthy My boys will give you no peace if they see you getting into your sister's pocket."

Gerald disengaged himself, and made a rapid retreat. It was a long time before he again appeared, and when Mrs. the housekeeper at the Manor House, came down in the course of the evening to say good-bye, she said, "And ma'am, where do you think I found that dear child, Sir Gerald, not two hours ago?" She wiped away a gush of tears, and went on. "I thought I heard a noise in the drilling room, and went to see, and there, ma'am, was the dear little fellow lying on the floor, the bare boards, for the carpet is taken up, you know, Miss Marian, before his papa's picture, crying and sobbing as if his heart would break. But as soon as I opened the door, and he saw me, he snatched up his hat, and jumped out at the open window, which he had come in by, I suppose, for I never heard him open the door."

Marian, after her usual fashion, had no reply, but it was pleasant to her to think of what had taken place, since Gerald had not in general shown much concern at the leaving home.

They all met at breakfast next morning; Marian, was firmly determined against crying, and by dint of squeezing up her lips, and not uttering a word, succeeded in keeping her resolution; but poor Agnes could eat no breakfast, and did nothing but cry, till Mr. Lyddell, by saying that her tears were a great honour both to herself and Marian, entirely checked them.

"I hope," said Mr. Wortley, "that Mrs. Lyddell will not be very strict in inquiring into the quantity of Marian's idle correspondence. The friends there mean to console themselves with multitudes of letters."

"Oh, certainly, certainly," said Mr. Lyddell. "Old friends for ever! So mind, Marian, I mean to be very angry if you forget to write to Miss Wortley."

"Thank you," said Marian, knowing that she was saying something silly, and trying to smile.

"Come, then," said Mr. Lyddell, "thank your friends once more for their kindness, and let us be going."

Thanks from Marian were out of the question, and she tried to get out of hearing of the sentences beginning, "I am sure we shall always be sensible," "Nothing could be kinder," which her guardian was pouring out. She moved with Agnes to the door: the summer sky was deeply blue, without a cloud, the fresh green branches of the trees stood up against it as if bathed in light, the flower beds were glowing with gay blossoms, Gerald and Jemmy were playing with Ranger under the verandah, and the Church bells rang cheerfully for morning service, but alas! at the gate was the carriage, Saunders sitting sobbing on the outside, and David Chapple, Mr. Wortley's man, standing on one leg on the step talking to her. Near at hand was the gardener from the Manor House, waiting with his hands full of Miss Arundel's favourite flowers, and there stood old Betty Lapthorn and her grandchild, Gerald's nurse who had married, and the old man to whom the children had so often carried the remains of their dinner; all the school children too, and Grace in the middle of them, waiting for the last view of Miss Arundel and little Sir Gerald.

Mr. Lyddell finished his acknowledgments, and Marian and her brother received an embrace and good-bye from their friends, David jumped down and shut the door, Saunders sobbed aloud, there was another good-bye from each of the Wortleys, and a hearty response from Gerald, Mr. Lyddell called out, "All right," and away they went.

On went the carriage, past the Church, with its open door and pealing bell, the rocky steps up to the Manor House, nestled in the shrubs, the well known trees, the herds of longhorned, red cattle, the grey stone cottages, and the women and tiny children at the doors, the ford through the sparkling shallow brook, the hill with the great limestone quarry, the kiln so like a castle, the river and its bridge of one narrow, high pitched, ivy grown arch, the great rod rock, remembered as having been the limit of papa's last drive, the farm house in the winding valley beyond, with its sloping orchard and home field, the last building in the parish. They drove through the little market town, slowly wound up the heights beyond, looked down into the broad, beautiful space where the river Exe winds its blue course amid wood, field, and castled hill, descended, losing sight of the last of the Torrs, glanced at Exeter and its Cathedral, arrived at the station, and there, while waiting hand in hand on the platform, gazing at the carriage, and starting at each puff, snort, cough, and shriek of the engines, Marian and Gerald did indeed feel themselves severed from the home of their childhood.

It was not till the afternoon that they left the railroad, and then they had a two hours' drive through a country which Marian found very unlike her own: the bleak, bare downs of Wiltshire, low green hills rising endlessly one after the other, the white road visible far away before them, the chalk pits white and cold, a few whitey brown ponds now and then, and at long intervals a farm house, looking as if it had been set down there by mistake, and did not like it, carts full of chalk, and flocks of sheep the chief moving objects they met, and not many of them.

Marian sighed, yawned, and looked at Gerald many a time before they at length came to a small, very neat-looking town, where the houses stood far back from the street, and had broad clean pavement in front of them. "This is Oakworthy," said Mr. Lyddell, and Marian looked with interest. The church was just outside the town, white, and clean looking, like everything else, and with a spire. That was all she could see, for they drove on by the side of a long park wall, enclosing a fir plantation. The gate of a pretty lodge was thrown back, and they entered upon a gravelled carriage-road, which, after some windings, led to a large house, built of white brick, regular and substantial. They stopped under the portico at the door, and Mr. Lyddell, as he handed Marian out of the carriage, exclaimed, "Welcome to Oakworthy Park!"

It seemed to Marian that there was a whole crowd waiting for her in the hall, and she had received at least three kisses before she had time to look around her, and perceive that this formidable troop consisted of a tall, fresh-coloured lady, two girls, and two little boys. Each of the girls eagerly grasped one of her hands, and drew her into the drawing-room, exclaiming, "I am glad you are come!" Here were two more strangers, youths of the age at which their juniors call them men, and their seniors, boys. They did not trouble the guests with any particular demonstrations of welcome, only shaking hands with them carelessly, and after another moment or two Marian found herself sitting on a chair, very stiffly and upright, while Gerald stood about two feet from her, afraid of a second accusation of getting into her pocket, looking down, and twisting the handles of her basket.

"Lionel, Johnny," said Mrs. Lyddell, "have you nothing to say to your cousin? Come here, my dear, and tell me, were you very sorry to leave Fern Torr?"

Gerald coloured and looked at his sister, who replied by a hesitating, faltering, "Yes, very."

"Ah! yes, I see," said Mrs. Lyddell, "but you will soon be at home here. It shall not be my fault or your cousins' if you are not, — eh, Caroline?"

"Indeed it shall not," returned Caroline, again taking Marian's hand, at first pressing it cordially, but letting it go on feeling the limp, passive fingers, which were too shy and frightened to return the pressure.

Mr. Lyddell came in, and while his wife was engaged in speaking to him, Marian had time to make her observations, for the chilling embarrassment of her manner had repelled the attentions of her cousins. Though she had never seen them before, she knew enough about them to be able to fit the names to the persons she saw before her, and make a few conjectures as to how she would like them.

That youth in the odd-looking, rough, shapeless coat, yet with a certain expensive, fashionable air about the rest of his dress, who stood leaning against the chimney-piece in a nonchalant attitude, was her eldest cousin, Elliot Lyddell. The other, a great contrast in appearance, small, slender, and pale, with near-sighted spectacles over his weak, light grey eyes, dressed with scrupulous precision and quietness, who had retreated to the other end of the room and taken up a book, was Walter. The elder girl, Caroline, was about fifteen, a very pleasing likeness of her mother, with a brilliant complexion, bright blue eyes, and a remarkably lively and pleasant smile, which Marian was so much taken with, that she wished she could have found something to say, but the dress and air both gave her the appearance of being older than Agnes, and thus made Marian feel as if she was a great way above and beyond her. The other sister had a fair, pretty face, much more childish, with beautiful glossy light hair, and something sweet and gentle in her expression, and Marian felt warmly towards her because she was her mother's god-child, and bore the same name.

The younger boys, Lionel and John, were nice-looking little fellows of nine and seven. They had drawn towards Walter, gazing all the time at Gerald, and all parties were rejoiced when Mrs. Lyddell, after a few more attempts at conversation, proposed to take the guests to their rooms.

With a light, quick step, she led the way up two staircases and a long passage, to a good-sized, comfortable room intended for

Marian, while Gerald's was just opposite. With a civil welcome to Saunders, kind hopes that Marian would make herself at home, and information that dinner would he ready at seven, she left the room, and Saunders proceeded with the young lady's toilette. Gerald stood gazing from the window at the trees and little glimpse of the town in the distance. He said little, and seemed rather forlorn till leave was given him to unpack some goods which he could not easily damage. Just as Marian was dressed, there was a knock at the door, and without waiting for an answer, Caroline and Clara entered, the former saying, "I hope you find everything comfortable: you see we make you quite at home, and stand on no ceremony."

It was pleasantly said, but Marian only gave a constrained smile, and answered, "Thank you," in such an awkward, cold way, that Caroline was thrown back. Her sister, only conscious of freedom from the restraints of the drawing-room, began exclaiming in short sentences, "O what a pretty basket! so you have out your work already! what a lovely pattern! how quick you have been in dressing! we came to see how you were getting on. O what is this pretty box? do let me see."

"A work-box," said Marian, by no means disposed to turn out all the small treasures it contained for Clara's inspection. — Caroline perceived this, and said with a little reproof to Clara,

"You curious child! Perhaps Marian would like to come and see the schoolroom before going down."

"Oh, yes," said Clara; "you must come. You have not seen Miss Morley yet, — our governess, — poor, unfortunate, faithful Morley, as we always call her."

This manner of mentioning the governess, and before Saunders too, greatly surprised Marian, and she felt little inclination to face another stranger; but she could think of no valid objection, and allowed herself and Gerald to be conducted down one of the flights of stairs into a passage less decorated than the rest of the house. Clara threw open a door, calling out, "Here they are!" and Marian found herself in the presence of a little, nicely dressed lady, who looked very little older than Caroline, and had a very good-natured face. Coming forward with a smile, she said, "Miss Arundel, I believe. I hope you are quite well, and not tired. Sir Gerald, how d'ye do? We shall be good friends, I am sure."

Gerald shook hands, and Marian thought she ought to do so too; but it had not been her first impulse, and it was too late, so she only made a stiff bend of head and knee. Clara, happily unconscious of the embarrassment with which Marian had infected

Caroline, went on talking fast and freely:

"So, you see, this is the schoolroom. There is Caroline's desk, and here is mine; and we have made room for you here. I suppose you have a desk. And here are all our books, and our chiffonnière; Caroline has one side and I the other. Oh, I must show you my last birthday presents. Ah! aren't we lucky to have got such a nice view of the terrace and the portico from here! We can always see the people coming to dinner, and when the gentlemen go out riding, it is such fun, and —"

"My dear Clara," interposed Miss Morley, seeing Marian's bewildered looks, "your cousin is not used to such a chatterbox. I assure you, Miss Arundel, that Clara has been quite wild for the last week with the prospect of seeing you. I have actually not known what to do with her."

Marian gave one of her awkward smiles, and said nothing.

"You left Devonshire this morning, I think?" said Miss Morley.

"Yes, we did."

"Fern Torr is in a very beautiful part of the country, is it not?"

"Yes, very."

They were getting on at this rate when Mrs. Lyddell came in, and took Marian and Gerald down to the drawing-room with her, as it was almost dinner time. No sooner had the door closed behind them, than governess and pupils at once exclaimed, "How pale!" "how shy!" "how awkward!"

"I dare say that is only shyness," said Caroline, "but I must say I never saw anything so stiff and chilly."

"Yes, that she is," said Clara, "but it's only shyness; I am sure she is a dear girl. But how white she is! I thought she would have been pretty, because they say the Arundels are all so handsome."

"She has fine eyes," said Miss Motley; "and that dear little Sir Gerald, I am sure we shall all be in love with him."

"Well, I hope we may get on better in time," said Caroline, taking up a book, and settling herself in a most luxurious attitude in spite of the unaccommodating furniture of the schoolroom.

Marian recovered a little at dinner, and was not quite so monosyllabic in her replies. Her netting was a great resource when she went into the drawing-room after dinner, and she began to feel a little less rigid and confused, made some progress in acquaintance with Clara, and when she went to bed was not without hopes of, in time, liking both her and Caroline very much.

CHAPTER IV.

"A place where others are at home,
But all are strange to me."
$\qquad$ *Lyra Innocentium.*

Marian began the next morning by wondering what a Sunday at Oakworthy would be like, but she was glad the formidable first meeting was over, and greeted Gerald cheerfully when he came into the room.

After a few minutes a bell rang, and Marian, thinking it must be for family prayers, hastened into the passage, wondering at herself for not having asked last night where she was to go. She was glad to meet Caroline coming out of her room, and after quickly exchanging a "good morning," she said, "Was that the bell for prayers?"

"No, it was for the servants' breakfast," said Caroline "and for ours in the schoolroom too."

"But don't you have prayers in the morning?" said Gerald,

"No," answered Caroline gravely.

"Why not," the little boy was beginning but Marian pressed his hand to check him, shocked herself, and sorry for Caroline's sake that the question had been asked.

Caroline spoke rather hurriedly, "I wish we could, but you see papa is out so often, and there are so many people staying here sometimes: and in London, papa is so late at the House — it is very unlucky, but it would not do, it is all so irregular."

"What?" said Clara, hopping down stairs behind them. "O, about prayers! We have not had any in the school room since Miss Cameron's time."

"Miss Cameron used to read a chapter and pray with us afterwards," said Caroline; "but when she was gone, mamma said she did not like the book she used."

"Besides, it was three quarters out of her own head, and that wasn't fair, for she used to go on such a monstrous time," said Clara.

"Hush, Clara," said her sister, "and mamma has never found a book she does think quite fit."

"There's the Prayer Book," said Gerald.

"O that is only for Church," said Clara, opening the school-room door; "O she is not here! Later than ever. Well, Marian, what do you think of her?"

"Of whom?" asked Marian.

"Of poor unfortunate faithful Morley," said Clara.

"You call her so after Queen Anne?"

"Yes," said Caroline, "and you will see how well the name suits her when you are fully initiated."

"But does she like it?"

"Like it?" and Clara fell into a violent fit of laughing, calling out to Lionel, who just then came in, "Here is Marian asking if we call Miss Morley 'poor unfortunate' whenever we speak to her."

"She is coming," said Lionel, and Clara sunk her boisterous laughter into a titter, evident enough to occasion Miss Morley to ask what made them so merry, but the only answer she received was from Lionel, "Something funny," and then both he and Clara burst out again into laughter, his open, and hers smothered.

Marian looked amazed. "Ah! you are not used to such ways," said the governess; "Clara and Lionel are sometimes sad creatures."

Breakfast took a very long time, and before it was quite over, Mrs. Lyddell came in, spoke in her rapid, good-natured tone to Marian and Gerald, and remarked rather sharply to Miss Morley that she thought they grew later and later every Sunday. Nevertheless, no one went on at all the faster after she was gone. Miss Morley continued her talk with Caroline and Clara about some young friends of theirs in London, and Lionel and Johnny went on playing tricks with their bread and butter, accompanied by a sort of secret teasing of Clara. Nothing brought them absolutely to a conclusion till one of the servants appeared in order to take away the things, and unceremoniously bore away John's last piece of bread and cup of tea.

Johnny looked up at the man and made a face at him; Miss Morley shook her head, and Caroline said, "How can you be so naughty, Johnny? it serves you quite right, and I only wish it happened every morning."

"Come, Gerald, and see the ponies," said Lionel.

"My dears," said Miss Morley, "you know your mamma never likes you to go out before Church especially to the stables; you only get hot, and you make us late with waiting for you."

"Nobody asked you to wait for us," said John. "Come, Gerald."

"No, I see Sir Gerald is a good little boy, and is coming steadily with us," said Miss Morley.

"Yes, Gerald, do," said Marian.

"There will be plenty of time by and by," said Gerald, sitting down again.

"O very well," said John. "Well, if you won't, I will; I want to see Elliot's colt come in from exercising, and he will be sure to be there himself now."

Lionel and Johnny ran off, Caroline looked distressed, and went out into the passage leaving the door open. Walter was coming along it, and as she met him, she said, "Walter, the boys are off to the stable again; we shall have just such a fuss as we had last Sunday if you cannot stop them. Is Elliot there again?"

"I am afraid he is," said Walter.

"Then there is no chance!" said Caroline, retreating; but at that moment Lionel and John came clattering down from their own distant abode at the top of the house. "Who likes to walk with me through, the plantations to Church?" said Walter; "I was coming to ask if you liked to show that way to Gerald."

Lionel and John, who had a real respect for Walter, thought it best to keep silence on their disobedient designs, and accept the kind offer. Gerald gladly joined them, and off they set. Miss Morley, Caroline, and Clara, had all gone different ways, and Marian remained, leaning her forehead against the window, thinking what her own dear Sunday-school class were doing at Fern Torr, and feeling very disconsolate. She had stood in this manner for some minutes when Clara came to tell her it was time to prepare for Church, followed her to her room, and contrived to make more remarks on her dress than Marian could have thought could possibly have been bestowed on a plain black crape bonnet and mantle.

Through all the rather long walk, Clara still kept close to her, telling who every one was, and talking incessantly, till she felt almost confused, and longed for the quietness of the church. Mr. Lyddell's pew was a high, square box, curtained round, with a table and a stove, so that she hardly felt as if she was in church, and she was surprised not to see Elliot Lyddell there.

They had to walk quickly back after the service, dine hurriedly, and then set off again for the afternoon service. Miss Morley sighed, and said that the second long hot walk almost killed her, and she went so slowly that the schoolroom party all came in late. They found no one in the pew but Mrs. Lyndell and Walter, and Marian once more sighed and wondered.

On coming home, Miss Morley went in to rest, but as it was now cool and pleasant, her pupils stayed out a little longer to show the park and garden. They were very desirous of making the Arundels admire all they saw, and Lionel and John were continually asking, "Have you anything like that at Fern Torr?"

Gerald, jealous for the honor of home, was magnificent in his descriptions, and unconscious that he was talking rhodomontade. According to him, his park took in a whole mountain, his house was quite as large and much handsomer than Mr. Lyddell's, the garden was like the hanging gardens of Babylon, and green-houses were never wanted there, for "all sorts of things" would grow in the open air. His cousins were so amazed that they would hardly attend to Marian's explanations, and thought her description of the myrtle, which reached to the top of the house, as fabulous as his hanging gardens.

"And, Marian, what do you think of this place?" asked Clara.

After some pressing, the following reply was extracted: — "It is so shut in with fir-trees, but I suppose you want them to hide the town, and there is nothing to see if they were away."

"O Marian!" said Caroline, "when we showed you the beautiful view over the high gate."

"But there was no hill, and no wood, and no water."

"Did you not see Oakworthy Hill?"

"That tame green thing!" said Marian.

"The truth is," said Johnny, "that she likes it the best all the time, only she won't own it."

"Nonsense, Johnny," replied Lionel, "every one likes their own home best, and I like Marian for not pretending to be polite and nonsensical."

"And I tell you," said Gerald, "that you never saw anything so good as my Manor house in your whole life."

Here they went in, and Marian gently said to Gerald as they came into her room, "I wish you would not say *my*, Gerald, it seems like boasting. My park — my house —"

Gerald hung his head, and the colour came deeply into his cheeks. "Marian," said he, "you know how I wish it wasn't mine now," and the tears were in his eyes. "But they boast over me, and they ought not, for I'm Sir —"

"Oh! hush, Gerald. You used never to like to hear yourself called so, because it put you in mind — . Yes, I know they boast; but this is not the way to stop them, it only makes them go on; and what does it signify to you? it does not make this place really better than home."

"Yes, but I want them to know it."

"But you should not want to set yourself up above them. If you don't answer, and, let them say what nonsense they please, it would be the best way, and the right way, and so you would humble yourself, which is what we must all do Gerald."

Gerald was silenced, but looked dissatisfied; however, there was no more time to talk, for Clara came to say that tea was almost ready, and Marian rang for Saunders. Gerald looked as if he was meditating when first they sat down to tea, and after some little time he abruptly began, "I don't like your church at all. It is just like a room, and nobody makes any noise."

"Nobody makes any noise," repeated Caroline, smiling; "is that Fern Torr fashion?"

"I do not mean exactly a noise," said Gerald, "but people read their verse of the psalm, and say Amen, and all that, quite loud. They don't leave it all to the clerk in his odd voice."

Lionel mimicked the clerk so drolly, that in spite of "Don't, my dear," and "O! Lionel," nobody could help laughing; and Johnny added an imitation of the clerk at their church in London. After the mirth was over, Gerald went on, "Why does not every one say Amen here?"

"Like so many charity children," said Lionel, with a nasal drawl.

"No, indeed!" cried Gerald, indignantly; "Edmund does it, and everybody."

"Everybody! as if you could tell, who never went to church in your life, except at that little poky place," said Johnny,

Gerald's colour rose, but Marian's eye met his, and he remembered what she had said, and answered quietly, "I don't know whether Fern Torr is poky, but it is a place where people are taught to behave well."

"Capital, Gerald, excellent!" cried Caroline, laughing heartily, "that is a hit, Lionel, for you!" while Gerald looked round him, amazed at the applause with which his speech, made in all simplicity, was received.

As soon as tea was over, Miss Morley called Lionel and John to repeat the Catechism, and added doubtfully, "Perhaps Sir Gerald would rather wait for next Sunday."

"O no, thank you," said Marian, "we always say it."

"You need not, Marian," said Caroline, "we never do, only it would be so troublesome for the boys to have to learn it at school."

"I should like to say it if Miss Morley has no objection," said Marian.

"Oh! yes, certainly," was the answer. "See, Lionel, there is an example for you."

Marian and Gerald stood upright, with their hands behind them, just as they had stood every Sunday since they could speak; Lionel was astride on the music stool, spinning round and round, and Johnny balancing himself with one leg on the floor, and one hand on the window sill. When the first question was asked, the grave voice that replied, "Edmund Gerald," was drowned in a loud shout —

> "*Jack Lyddell, Jack Lyddell,*
> *Shall play on the fiddle*" —

evidently an old worn out joke, brought to life again in the hope of making the grave cousins laugh, instead of which they stood aghast. Miss Morley only said imploringly, "Now, Johnny, my dear boy, *do*," and proceeded to the next question. Throughout the two boys were careless and painfully irreverent, and the governess, annoyed and ashamed, hurried on as fast as she could, in order to put an end to the unpleasant scene. When it was over she greatly admired the correctness of Gerald's answers, seeming to think it extraordinary that he should not have made a single mistake; whereas Marian would have been surprised if he had. Gerald whispered to his sister as they went down to the drawing-room, "Would it not be fun to see what Mr. Wortley would say to Lionel and Johnny, if he had them in his class?"

On Monday, Marian and Gerald began to fall into the habits of the place, and to learn the ways of their cousins, though it was many years before they could be said really to understand them.

Of their guardian himself, they found they should see very little, for their four schoolroom companions, his own children, had but little intercourse with him. Sometimes, indeed, Johnny, who enjoyed the privileges of the youngest, would make a descent upon him, and obtain some pleasure or some present, or at least a game of play; and sometimes Lionel fell into great disgrace, and was brought to him for reproof, but Caroline and Clara only saw him now and then in the evening, and never seemed to look to him as the friend and approver that Marian thought all fathers were. As to Miss Morley, she had only spoken twice to him since she had been in the house.

Mrs. Lyddell seemed supreme in everything at home. She was quick, active, and clever, an excellent manager, nor was she otherwise than very kind in word and deed; and Marian could by no means understand the cause of the mixture of dread and repugnance with which she regarded her. Perhaps it was, that though not harsh, her manner wanted gentleness; her tones were not soft, and she would cut off answers before they were half finished. Her bright, clear, cold, blue eye had little of sympathy in it, and every look and tone showed that she expected implicit obedience, to commands, which were far from unpleasant in themselves, though rendered ungracious by the want of softness and mildness with which they were given. Marian often wondered, apart from the principle, how her cousins, and even Miss Morley, could venture to disregard orders given in that decided manner; but she soon perceived that they trusted to Mrs. Lyddell's multifarious occupations, which kept her from knowing all their proceedings with exactness, and left them a good deal at liberty.

Marian was disposed to like Miss Morley, with her gentle voice and kind manner, but she was much surprised at her letting things go on among her pupils, which she must have known to be wrong in themselves, as well as against express commands of Mrs. Lyddell. Once or twice when she heard her talking to Clara, she said to herself, "Would not mamma say that was silly?" but at any rate it was a great thing to have a person of whom she was not in the least shy or afraid, and who set her quite at her ease in the schoolroom.

The first business on Monday morning, after the little boys had gone off for two hours to a tutor, was an examination into Marian's attainments, beginning with French and Italian reading and translation, in which she acquitted herself very well till Mrs. Lyddell came in, and put her in such a state of trepidation that she no longer knew what she was about. In truth, Marian's education had been rather irregular in consequence of her father's illness, and its effect had been to give her a general cultivation of mind, and appreciation of excellence, to train her to do her best, and fed an eagerness for information, but without instructing her in that routine of knowledge for which Mrs. Lyddell and Miss Morley looked. She was not ready in answering questions, even upon what she knew perfectly well; she had no tables of names and dates at finger's ends, and when she saw that every one thought her backward and ignorant, the feeling that she was not doing justice to her mamma's teaching added to her confusion, her mistakes and puzzles increased, and at last she was almost ready to cry. At that moment Caroline said, "Mamma, you have not seen Marian's drawings yet. Do fetch them, Marian."

The drawings served in some degree to save Marian in the opinion; at least, of Miss Morley: for an artist-like hand and eye were almost an inheritance in the Arundel family, and teaching her had been a great amusement to Sir Edmund. Miss Morley and Caroline thought her drawings wonderful; but Mrs. Lyddell, who had never learnt to draw, was, as Marian quickly perceived, unable to distinguish the merits from the faults, and was only commending them in order to reassure her. Her music was the next subject of inquiry, and here again she did not shine, for practising had been out of the question during the last two years of her father's life; but as she could not bear to offer this as an excuse, she only said she knew she could hardly play at all, but she hoped to improve. To her great relief, Mrs. Lyddell did not stay to listen to her performance, but went away, leaving her to Miss Morley, who found something to commend in her taste and touch.

When the business of learning actually commenced, Marian grew more prosperous; for she had the good custom of giving her whole attention, and learnt therefore fast and correctly. Her exercise was very well done; her arithmetic, in which Edmund had helped her, was almost beyond Miss Morley's knowledge; and she was quite at home in the history they were reading aloud. Moreover, when they came to talk of what they had read, it proved that Marian was well acquainted with many books which were still only names to Caroline; and when Gerald came in with his books, his reference to her showed that she knew as much Latin as he did.

They dined in the schoolroom at half-past one, then took a walk on the long, dull, white road, and came back at a little past four; after which the girls had each to practise for an hour, to look over some lessons for the next day, and to dress; but all the rest of their time was at their own disposal. There was to be a dinner-party that evening, and Clara advised her not to dress till after tea. "For we don't go down till after dinner," said she, "and I don't like to miss seeing the people come. Gerald, you had better get ready, though, for you boys always go down before."

"Must I?" said Gerald.

"O yes, that we must!" said Lionel; "and you will see how Johnny there likes to be petted by all the old ladies, and called their pretty dear."

Johnny rushed upon his brother, and there was a skirmish between them, during which Miss Morley vainly exclaimed by turns, "Now Lionel!" and "Now Johnny!" It ended by John's beginning to cry, Lionel laughing at him, and declaring that he had done nothing to hurt him, and both walking off rather sullenly to dress for the evening. Gerald was bent on the same errand; and no sooner was he gone than Miss Morley, Caroline, and Clara all broke out into loud praises of him. He was so docile, he shut the door so gently, he seemed so very clever. He had quite won Miss Morley's heart by running back to the schoolroom to fetch her parasol for her when she found she had left it behind; Caroline admired him for being so merry and playful without rudeness, and Clara chimed in with them both. All expressed wonder at not finding him a spoiled child; and this, though the praises gratified Marian greatly, rather offended her in her secret soul; and she wondered too that Caroline and Clara seemed disposed to make the very worst of their own little brothers, so as to set off Gerald's perfections by force of contrast.

Mrs. Lyddell came in while they were still talking. She was beautifully dressed, and looked very handsome, and, in Marian's eyes, very formidable; but she sat down and joined heartily in the praises of Gerald, till Marian thought, "What could they have expected poor Gerald to be, if they are so amazed at finding him the dear good little fellow he is!" It was in fact true that he was an agreeable surprise, for as an only son — a great treasure — and coming so early to his title, he was exactly the child whom all would have presumed most likely to be spoiled; and his ready obedience struck the Lyddells as no less unusual than those habits in which he had been trained, in consequence of the necessity of stillness during Sir Edmund's long illness. It was more natural to him to shut the door quietly than to bang it, to speak than to shout, and to amuse himself tranquilly in the house than to make a great uproar. He was courteous, too, and obliging; and though Lionel and Johnny were in consequence inclined to regard him as a "carpet knight so trim," the ladies fully appreciated these good qualities. Mrs. Lyddell perhaps made the more of her satisfaction, because she was conscious of not liking his sister's stiff, formal, frightened manners.

Mrs. Lyddell waited till the boys came from dressing, and took them all three down with her. Clara sat down in the window-seat to watch the arrivals, as soon as she had recovered from her amazement at hearing that Marian had not been in a house with a dinner-party since Gerald was born. "Is it possible!" she went on saying, and then bursting into a laugh, till Caroline said sharply, "How can you be so silly, Clara! you know the reason perfectly well."

"But it is so odd," continued Clara. "Why, we are never a week without a party, and sometimes two!"

"Hush," said Caroline, "or I shall never finish my Italian."

The little boys came up to tea; Gerald would not make much answer when Clara asked if the ladies had talked to him, but Johnny looked cross, and Lionel reported "it was because his nose was put out of joint." Coming up to Marian, to whom he seemed to have taken a fancy, Lionel further explained confidentially how all the ladies made a fuss with Johnny, and admired his yellow curls, and called him the rose-bud, and all sorts of stuff; and how Johnny liked to go down in his fine crimson velvet, and show off, and have all his nonsense praised, "And the pretty dear is so jealous," said Lionel, "that he can't bear any one to say one word to poor me — oh no!"

"Why, do you wish for them to do so?" said Marian.

"Oh no, not I — I never did; and I'm glad I'm grown too big and ugly for them. I always get as near Elliot as I can and try to hear if they are saying any thing about the hunt; and the ladies never trouble their heads about what is good for any thing, so they never talk to me."

"That is no great compliment to Gerald," said Marian.

"Ah! you'll soon see. If there is any fun in him, they will soon cast him off; but now he is new, and he has not found them out yet, and they *do* dearly like to say Sir Gerald; so Johnny is regularly thrown out, and that is what makes him look sulky."

"Well, but it is using him very ill to desert him for Gerald," said Marian.

"Oh, they won't desert him. They like mamma's good dinners too well for that; only Johnny can't bear any one else to be taken notice of. Trust the county member's son for their making much of him."

"But that applies to you too, Lionel."

"Ay, and I could soon get their civility if I cared for it," said Lionel grandly. "But I know well enough what it is worth. Why, there is Walter, who is the best of us all — nobody cares one straw for him, except Caroline and —"

"And you?" asked Marian.

"Why — why — yes, if he was not so much of a parson already."

"Oh, Lionel!" said Marian, shocked; and he turned it rather hastily into "I mean, he is not up to any thing; he does not shoot, and he does not care for dogs, or horses; nothing but books for ever."

A summons to the tea-table put an end to Lionel's communications, which had so amazed Marian that she could do nothing but ponder on them all the time that Clara would leave her in quiet.

The going into the drawing-room was to her a most awful affair; and Saunders seemed to be very anxious about it, brushing and settling her hair, and arranging the plain black frock, as if she would never have done; seeming, too, not a little worried by Clara, who chose to look on at all her proceedings. At last it was over Marian wished Gerald good night, and descended with her two cousins and Miss Morley. Caroline and Clara were in blue, Miss Morley in white; and as they entered just opposite to a long pier glass, Marian thought that with her white face, straight dark hair, and deep mourning dress, she looked like a blot between them, and wished to shrink out of sight, instead of being conspicuous in blackness.

The ladies came in a few minutes after, and Caroline and Clara went forward, shaking hands, smiling, and replying in a way which was by no means forward, and with ease that to Marian was marvellous. If people would but be kind enough not to look at her! But Mrs. Lyddell was a great deal too civil for that too come to pass, and presently Marian was called and introduced to two ladies. She was seated between them, and they began talking to her in a patronising manner; telling her they remembered her dear mamma at her age; saying that they had seen her brother, and congratulating her on having two such delightful companions as the Miss Lyddells. Then they asked about Devonshire; and as Marian's cold short replies let every subject fall to the ground in a moment, they proceeded to inquire whether she could play. Truth required her to confess that she could, a very little; and then they begged to hear her. Poor Marian! this was too much. She felt as if she was in a horrible mist, and drawing up her head as she always did in embarrassment, she repeated, "Indeed, indeed I cannot!" protestations which her tormentors would not believe, and which grew every moment more ungracious, as, to augment her distress, she saw that Mrs. Lyddell was observing her. At the moment when she was looking most upright and rigid, Caroline came to her relief. The same request had just been made to her, and she came to propose to Marian to join in the one thing she knew she could play — a duet which she had that morning been practising with Clara. It was very kind, and Marian knew it; for Caroline had said that she never liked that duet, and was heartily tired of it; but all the acknowledgement her strange bashfulness would allow her to make was a grateful look, and a whisper, "Oh, thank you!"

Afterwards one of the young lively visitors sang, and Marian, who had never heard much music, was quite delighted; her stiff company-face relaxed, a tear came to her eyes, and she sat with parted lips, forgetting all her fears and all the party till the singing was over, and Caroline touched her, and told her it was bed-time. Marian wondered to see how well Caroline and Clara managed to escape without being observed; but she marvelled at their going to bed so much as if it was a thing of course to have no "good night" from father or mother. When they were outside the door, in the hall, Marian, her heart still full of the music, could not help exclaiming, "How beautiful!"

"What? Miss Bernard's singing?" said Clara. "I declare, Caroline, Marian was very nearly crying! I saw you were, Marian."

"She does sing very nicely," said Caroline, "but that song does not suit her voice. It is too high."

"And she makes faces," said Clara, "she strains her throat; and she has such great fingers — I could never cry at Miss Bernard's singing, I am sure."

Marian did not like this. "Good night," said she, abruptly.

"You are not vexed, are you?" said Clara, kindly. "I did not think you would mind my noticing your crying. Don't be angry, Marian."

"Oh, no, I am not at all angry," said Marian, trying to speak with ease, but she did not succeed well. Her "good nights," had in them a tone as if she was annoyed, as in fact she was; though not at all in the way Clara supposed. She did not care for the notice of her tears, but she said to herself, "This is what Edmund calls destroying the illusion. If they would but have let me go to bed with the spell of that song resting on me!"

She sighed with a feeling of relief and yet of weariness as she came into her own room, and found Saunders there. Saunders looked rather melancholy, but said nothing for the first two or three minutes; then as she combed Marian's hair straight over her face, she began, "I hope you enjoyed yourself, Miss Marian?"

"Oh, Saunders," said Marian, "I'm very tired; I don't think I shall ever enjoy myself anywhere but at home."

"Ah — hem — ah," coughed Saunders, solemnly; then, after waiting for some observation from Marian, and hearing only a long yawn and a sigh, she went on. "Prettily different is this place from home."

"Indeed it is," said Marian, from her heart.

"Such finery as I never thought to see below stairs, Miss Marian. I am sure the Manor House was a pattern to all the country round for comfort for the servants, and I should know something about it; but here — such a number of them, such eating and drinking all day long, and the very kitchen maids in such bonnets and flowers on Sundays, as would perfectly have shocked Mrs. White. And they are so ignorant. Fancy, Miss Marian, that fine gentleman the butler declaring he could not understand me, and that I spoke with a foreign accent! I speak French indeed!"

"But, Saunders," said Marian, rather diverted, "you do speak Devonshire a little."

"Well, Miss Marian, perhaps I may; I only know 'tisn't for them to boast, for they speak so funny I can't hardly make them out; and with my own ears I have heard that same Mr. Perkins himself calling you Miss Harundel. But that is not all. Why, not half of them ever go to church on a Sunday; and as to Mrs. Mitten, the housekeeper, not a bit does she care whether they do or not; and no wonder, when Mr. Lyddell himself never goes in the afternoon, and has gentlemen to speak to him. And then down at the stables — 'tis a pretty set of drinking, good-for-nothing fellows there. I hope from my heart Sir Gerald won't be for getting down there among them; but they say Master Lionel and Master John are always there. And that Mr. Elliot —"

In this manner Saunders discoursed all the while she was putting Marian to bed. Both she and her young lady wore doing what had much better have been let alone. Saunders had no business to carry complaints and gossip, Marian ought not to have listened to them; but the truth was that Saunders was an old attached confidential servant, who had come to Oakworthy, more because she could not bear to let her young master and mistress go entirely alone and unfriended among strangers, than because it would be prudent to save a little more before becoming Mrs. David Chapple. Fern Torr was absolute perfection in her eyes; and had the household at Oakworthy been of superior excellence, she would have found fault with everything in which it differed from the Manor House. Her heart was full; and to Miss Marian, her young lady, a Fern Torrite, a Devonian like herself, she must needs pour it out, where she had no other friend. On the other hand, Saunders was still in Marian's eyes a superior person — an authority — one whom she could never dream of keeping in order, or restraining; and here a friend, a counsellor, the only person, except Gerald, who had known the dear home.

So a foundation was laid for confidences from Saunders, which were not likely to improve Marian's contentment. When she had bidden her maid good night, and sat thinking before she knelt down to say her prayers, she felt bewildered; her head seemed giddy with the strangeness of this new world; she knew not what in it was right and what was wrong; all that she knew was, that she felt lonely and dreary, and as if it could never be home. Her heart seemed to reach out for her mother's embrace and support, and then Marian sank down on her knees, rested her face on her arms, and while the tears began to flow, she murmured, "OUR FATHER, Which art in heaven."

Soon after, her weary head was on her pillow, and the dim grey light of the summer night showed the quiet peace and calmness that had settled on her sleeping face.

CHAPTER V.

"That is not home where, day by day,
I wear the busy hours away."

In a short time, Marian had settled into her place at Oak Worthy, lost some part of her shyness towards the inhabitants, and arrived at the terms which seemed likely to continue between her and her cousins.

There was much that was very excellent about Caroline Lyddell; she had warm feeling, an amiable and obliging disposition, and great sweetness of temper; and when first Marian arrived she intended to do all in her power to make her at home, and be like a sister to her. But she did not understand reserve; and before Marian had got over her first shyness and awkwardness, Caroline felt herself repulsed, and ceased to make demonstrations of affection which met with no better response. Marian made none on her side; and so the two cousins remained very obliging and courteous to each other, but nothing more.

Clara had begun by making herself Marian's inseparable companion in rather a teasing manner, caressing her continually, and always wanting to do whatever she was doing; but as novelty was the great charm in Clara's eyes, and as she met with no very warm return to her endearments, all this soon wore off; and though she always came to Marian whenever she had any bit of news to tell, — though she often confided to her little complaints of the boys or Miss Morley, — this was no great compliment, for she would have done the same to anything that had ears. Her talk was no longer, as it had been at first, exclusively for Marian; and this wag rather a relief, for it was not at all like the talk Marian was used to with Agnes or with Edmund.

Young and unformed as Marian was, it would be hard to believe how much, without knowing it, she missed the intercourse with superior minds, to which she had been accustomed. It was just as her eye was dissatisfied with the round green chalk hills, instead of the rocks and streams of her own dear home; or as she felt weary of the straight, formal walks she now took, instead of her dear old rambles,

> *"Over bank and over brae,*
> *Where the copsewood is the greenest,*
> *Where the fountain glistens sheenest,*
> *Where the lady-fern grows strongest,*

Where the morning dew lies longest."

Edmund's high spirits, Agnes' playful glee, — how delightful they were! and though Marian often laughed now, it was not as she had laughed at home. Then, too, she grew shy of making remarks, or asking questions, when Clara had nothing to say but "How odd!" or Miss Morley would give some matter-of-fact answer, generally either quite beside the point, or else what Marian knew before. Caroline understood what she meant, and would take up the subject, but not always in a satisfactory manner; for she and Marian always seemed to have quite opposite ways of viewing every thing. Each felt that the other had more serious thoughts and principles than most of those around them, but yet their likings and dislikings were very different in the matter of books. "Anna Ross" was almost the only one of Caroline's favourites that Marian cordially liked; and this, as Caroline suspected, might he owing to a certain analogy between Anna's situation and her own, by no means flattering to the Lyddell family. It was wonderful how many were the disparities of tastes, views, and opinions between them; but the root of these differences seemed undiscoverable, since Marian would not or could not argue, replied to all objections with a dry, short, "I don't know," and adhered unalterably to her own way of thinking.

Miss Morley settled the matter by pronouncing that Sir Edmund and Lady Arundel must have been very narrow-minded people; and this judgment was so admired by Caroline and Clara, that it was sure to be brought forward as conclusive, whenever Marian was the subject of conversation. At last Lionel broke in one day, "Stuff! Marian is a good, sensible, downright girl, and it is my belief that all that you mean by narrow-mindedness is that she cares for what is right, and nothing else."

"How much you know about it, Lionel!" said Clara, laughing; but Caroline answered in earnest, "There is reason in what you say, Lionel — Marian does care for what is right; but the question is, whether her views of it are not narrow?"

"The narrower the better, say I," said Lionel, as he plaited his whip-lash.

"Strait is the gate, and narrow is the way, that leadeth unto life," came into Caroline's head, and she stood thoughtful. Clara exclaimed, "Well done, Lionel! I wonder what he'll say next to defend his dear Marian."

"I know what I mean well enough," said Lionel. "I suppose you call it being broad-minded to trace your drawings through against the window, when mamma goes on telling you not. Better have her narrow mind, say I."

"Then why don't you," said Clara, "instead of going down to the stables for ever with that man of Elliot's that mamma said you were never to speak to?"

Lionel whisked his whip-lash before Clara's eyes, so as to make her wink. "I did not say I was good myself;" said he; "I said Marian was." And he ran out of the room.

Clara laughed at Lionel's admiration of Marian, which had begun to be a joke in the schoolroom; but Caroline, as she practised her music, thought a good deal over the conversation. "Is a narrow mind really a fear of doing wrong?" was a question she asked herself several times; and then she thought of all the things she had heard called narrow-minded and scrupulous in Marian or others, but she soon found herself lost in a mist, and wished she could talk it over with her former governess, Miss Cameron. As to what Lionel had said about the drawing, she was conscious she was very wrong; her mamma had called it an idle practice to trace the outline through against the glass, and had forbidden it; but a difficulty had soon brought her back to the window-pane, exclaiming, "Just for this one thing, I am sure mamma would not object."

"If Miss Cameron had been here, it would not have happened," said Caroline to herself with a sigh, and for a few days she kept away from the window; but another difficulty occurred, again she yielded to the temptation, and whoa she heard her mother's step in the passage, hurried back to her desk with guilty precipitation. A few days after, Clara was actually caught in the fact by Mrs. Lyddell, and then Miss Morley began making an excuse, evidently quite as much out of kindness to herself as to her pupil. Marian looked up in surprise, with a wondering, inquiring expression in her eyes. They were cast down the instant the governess turned towards her; but Miss Morley always felt abashed, by meeting that look of astonishment, which awoke in her a sensation of self-reproach such as she had seldom known before.

Miss Morley was a little afraid of Marian's eyes, though not of her in any other respect; nor did she like her much better than Caroline did, though she gave her much less trouble than any of her other pupils, except Caroline. Those questions and observations puzzled her, and she thought the poor child had been reading books beyond her years — it was such a great disadvantage to be an only daughter. Besides, she really believed Marian Arundel had no affection for any one, — no warmth of feeling; she would ten times prefer a less diligent and more troublesome pupil, in whom she could take some interest, and who showed some affection, to one so steady and correct in behaviour, without the frank openness of heart which was so delightful. To make up, however, for this general want of liking for poor Marian, on the other hand, every one was fond of Gerald. His behaviour in the schoolroom was so very nice and good, and out of doors his climbing, running, and riding were no less admired by his contemporaries. Now and then, indeed, a dispute arose between him and the other two boys, when Gerald criticised, and declared that "Edmund and everybody" thought as he did; or when he would try to outdo the sporting exploits reported of Elliot, by Edmund's shooting at Fern Torr. One day there was a very serious quarrel, Gerald having taken up the cause of an unfortunate frog, which Lionel and Johnny were proposing to hunt, by rolling their marbles at it.

Gerald declared they should not, that frogs were harmless, innocent creatures, and that Edmund and everybody liked them. This only made Lionel and Johnny more determined; partly from the absurdity of Gerald's appeal, and partly for the sake of mischief; and Gerald was overpowered, unable to save his protégé, and obliged to witness its cruel death. He burst into tears, and then, came the accusation of crying for a frog. Poor little boy, he burst away from his tormentors, and never stopped till, he was safe in his sister's room pouring out his grief to her and Saunders (for it was her dressing-time), and comforted by their sympathising horror and pity.

Saunders said it gave her a turn, and Marian's feelings were much of the same nature. She could not have thought it of Lionel. He was, indeed, reckless and unruly; by reputation *the* naughty one of the set; but Marian had often thought that much of Johnny's misbehaviour was unjustly charged on him, and there was an honesty about him, together with a cordiality towards herself, which made her like him. And that he should have been wantonly cruel!

She comforted Gerald as well as she could, and they went back to the schoolroom together. Lionel, as he often did, brought her a knot in a piece of string to be untied; she felt almost ready to shrink from him, as capable of such a deed, and gave it back to him after untying it, without a word. Lionel stood leaning against the shutter looking at her for some minutes, while she fetched her books, and sat down to learn her lessons. Tea came in; and while there was something of a bustle, and all the others were talking, and engaged in different ways, Lionel crossed over to her and said in a low voice, "So Gerald has made you angry with me?"

"No; but Lionel, I could not have thought you would have done such a thing."

"'Twas only a frog," said Lionel; "besides, I only did it to tease Gerald."

"I do not see that that makes it any better," said Marian, gravely.

"Why, Gerald was so ridiculous, to say Edmund and everybody liked frogs; but I didn't — I only mean that, if he had not made a fuss, I would never have hurt the frog, and I did not mean to kill it as it was; so never mind, Marian. I'll tell you what, Marian," added he, sinking his voice, "I'd rather Caroline and Clara, and poor unfortunate into the bargain, scolded me till they were black in the face, than that you looked at me as you did just now."

"Did I?" said Marian, rather alarmed. "I am sure I did not know I looked anyhow."

"Didn't you, though? It is just the way you look at poor unfortunate when she sports her humbug."

"Hush, Lionel! this will never do. You know you ought not to talk in that way," said Marian, rising to put an end to the conversation.

"But we have made it up?" said Lionel, holding her dress.

"Yes, yes," said Marian hastily, and with full forgiveness in look and tone. As she took her place at the tea-table, she wondered within herself what was the matter with her eyes to cause such remarks, and still more why she could not help liking Lionel so much the best of her cousins, in spite of all the naughtiness of word and deed, which shocked her so much.

The nest day she was walking in the garden with Clara, when Gerald came running up, with an entreaty that she would come and have a game at cricket with him and Lionel. Clara exclaimed, laughed, and stared in amazement.

"She plays famously," said Gerald; "she, and Agnes, and I, beat all the other Wortleys one day last summer. Come, Marian, don't say no; we have not had a game for a very long time."

"Who is playing?" asked Marian.

"Only Lionel and me; Johnny is out with Mrs. Lyddell Come, we want you very much indeed; there's a good girl."

To Clara's astonishment and Lionel's admiration, Marian complied; and though, of course, no great cricketer, her skill was sufficient to make her a prodigy in their eyes. But the game was brought to a sudden conclusion by Miss Morley, who, seeing them from the window, came out very much shocked, and gave the girls a lecture on decorum, which Marian felt almost as an insult.

When they went in, Gerald told Saunders the whole adventure; and she, who at Fern Torr had been inclined to the same opinion as Miss Morley, and had often sighed and declared it to be unlike young ladies when Marian and Agnes had played, now agreed with him that it was very hard on Miss Marian not to have a little exercise, lamented that she should always be cooped up in the schoolroom, and declared that there could be no harm in playing with such a little boy as Master Lionel.

The most unpleasant result was, that Miss Morley and the cousins took an impression that Agnes Wortley must be a vulgar romp, and were inclined to think her an unsuitable friend for Marian. Their curiosity was excited by the frequent letters between the two friends. Marian always read those which she received with the utmost eagerness, hardly ever telling any part of their contents, but keeping them to be enjoyed with Gerald in her own room; and half her leisure moments were employed in filling fat, black-edged envelopes, which were sent off at least as often as once a week.

"I wonder what she says about us!" said Clara, one day.

"I don't think it would suit you," said Caroline; "I should not think she painted us *couleur de rose.*"

"Except Lionel," said Clara, "if their admiration is mutual. But, by the by, Miss Morley, why do you not desire to see her letters? You always look at mine."

"She is not quite in the same situation," said Miss Morley.

"But could not you?" continued Clara. "It would be very entertaining only to look for once."

"And I think it would be only proper," said Caroline. "Who knows what she may say of us to these dear friends of hers?"

The subject was not allowed to drop; the girls' curiosity led them to find numerous reasons why their cousin's correspondence should not pass without examination, and Miss Morley found she must either endure their importunity, or yield to it. She was driven to choose the part of the oppressor; and one day, when Clara had been tormenting her more than usual, she addressed Marian, who was folding up a letter. "I think," said she, speaking in a timid, deprecating tone — "I think, Marian, if you please, it might be as well, perhaps, if I were sometimes to look over your letters; it has always been the custom here."

Then; was no encouragement to proceed in the look of blank amazement with which Marian replied, "Edmund Arundel and Mr. Lyddell both approve of my writing to Agnes Wortley."

"Ah!" interposed Clara; "but did they mean that your letters should never be looked over?"

"I heard nothing about it," said Marian.

"Miss Cameron always looked over mine," said Caroline.

"I will ask Mr. Lyddell himself as soon as he comes home," said Marian, determinedly.

There was a pause, but Caroline and Clara did not look satisfied. Miss Morley knew they would leave her no peace if she desisted, and she went on, — "I wish I could sometimes see a proof of willingness to yield."

Marian was out of patience, and putting her letter into the desk, locked it up; and Caroline laughingly remarked, "Really, there must be some treason in that letter!" If the observation had been taken as it was meant, all would have been well; but Marian bit her lip with an air that convinced the sisters that Caroline had hit the mark; and their glances stimulated Miss Morley to say, as decidedly as she could, "Marian, your present conduct convinces me that it is desirable that I should see that letter."

Marian's dark eyes gave one indignant flash, as she proudly drew up her head, opened her desk, laid her letter on the table before Miss Morley, and slowly walked out of the room; but as soon as she had shut the door, she ran at full speed along the passage to her own room, where, throwing herself on the bed, she gave way to a fit of violent weeping, and sobs which shook her whole frame. Proud, passionate feelings at first almost choked her, and soon these were followed by a flood of the bitter tears of loneliness and bereavement. "Who would have dared insult her thus, had her father and mother been living?" and for a minute her agony for their loss was more intense than it had ever been. Gradually, "the turbid waters brightening as they ran," became soothing, as she dwelt on the sweet, holy memory of her parents, and wholesome as she mourned over her fit of pride and anger. But for what were they accountable, whose selfish weakness and thoughtless curiosity had caused the orphan's tears to flow?

Caroline had not seen those flashing eyes without an instant perception of the injustice of the accusation. Her half-jesting speech had led the matter much further than she had intended; and alarmed at the consequences, she ran after her cousin to entreat her pardon; but Marian, unconscious of all save the tumult within herself, hurried on too fast to be overtaken, and just as

Caroline reached her door, had shut it fast, and drawn the bolt, and a gentle knock and low call of "Marian, dear Marian," were lost in the first burst of sobs. Caroline, baffled and offended, turned away with feelings even more painful than hers; and too proud to repeat the call, walked up and down, waiting till the door should be opened, to assure her cousin that nothing should induce her to touch the letter, and to beg her forgiveness; but as minutes passed away in silence, she grew tired of waiting, thought Marian sullen and passionate, and at length, returned to the schoolroom. As soon as she entered, Clara exclaimed, "O Caroline, only think, how odd —"

"I don't want to hear anything about it," said Caroline, sitting down to the piano; "I wish we had never thought of it."

She began, playing with all her might, but gradually she abated her vehemence, as she caught a few sounds of a conversation between Clara and Miss Morley. At last she turned round, asking, "What? who is his godfather?"

"Mr. Arundel, 'Edmund and every body,' you know," answered Clara. "I never heard anything like it. Only fancy his hearing that boy say his catechism!"

"What? I don't understand," said Caroline; "Mr. Arundel and Gerald! Nonsense! He can't be his godfather. Mamma said he was only four-and-twenty, and Gerald is almost nine."

"Here is Marian's authority for it," said Clara; "and certainly those Arundels are a curious family."

"Mr. Arundel is the next heir, is he not?" inquired Miss Morley.

"Yes," said Caroline; "I heard mamma telling old Mrs. Graves the whole story. His father and mother both died when he was very young, Sir Edmund brought him up entirely, and every one looked upon him as the heir till Gerald was born; and a groat disappointment it must have been, for now he has next to nothing. But they all were just as fond of each other as before; and it does seem very strange that Sir Edmund should have made him their guardian, at his age, when there was Lord Marchmont, who is their cousin, too."

"I dare say," said Clara, as if a most brilliant thought had struck her, "I dare say there is a family compact, such as one reads of in books, that he is to marry Marian."

"My dear Clara!" said Miss Morley laughing, "How should such a notion come into your little head?"

"Now see if it is not so!" said Clara; "I do believe she is in love with him already, and he is coming to see her."

"Is he?" cried Caroline, "I am very curious to sec him. Mamma says he is very handsome, and quite a distinguished looking person. When does he come?"

"You had better read," said Clara; "I can tell you that there are wonderful things in the letter."

Curiosity again asserted its power, and Caroline yielded. The letter had been opened, and it would not signify if one more person looked at it. She took it, and read eagerly and stealthily, starting at every sound.

"My dear Agnes — I hope you and Jemmy are getting on well in your solitude without the schoolboys. Tell Charles, when you write, that a gentleman staying here caught a trout last week that weighed three pounds, but I believe that those which are caught in these rivers taste of mud, and are not nearly so good as our own. I was very much afraid that Gerald would go to school this summer, but now Mrs. Lyddell has heard that it was settled that he should not go till he was ten, and it is arranged for him to stay till next year, when I hope he will be happier than Charles was at first. You asked after his drawing, so I have put in the last scrap I met with, and in case you should not be able to find out what it is meant for, I must inform you that it is the dog springing on the young Buecleuch. The other day he sent Edmund a letter in hieroglyphics, with pictures instead of nouns, and Edmund answered it in the same way with funny little clever drawings throughout. His regiment is going abroad nest spring, he thinks, to the Cape, but he has promised to come and see us first, and thinks of going home to see about his things. Thank Mrs. Wortley for being so kind as to scold me for not dating my letters. I shall not be likely to forget the date of this on September 30th, for Mr. Lyddell has just paid me my first quarter's allowance, and I am frightened to think how large it is; ten pounds a quarter only for my dress, and I am to have more when I am seventeen. So matters can go on more as they used in the parish. Will you be so kind as to pay this quarter's schooling for Amy Lapthorn and Honor Weeks and Mary Daw, and find out what clothes they want, and if Susan Grey has not a new bonnet, give her one, and a flannel petticoat for old Betty, and if any body else wants anything else let me know, and pay up for all the children that dear mamma used to put into the penny club, and send me word what it comes to, and I will send the money when Edmund comes to pay his visit. I suppose the apples are gathered by this time; you cannot think how I miss the golden and red piles under the trees, and the droning of the old cyder press. And do those beautiful Red Admiral butterflies come in the crowds they did last year to the heaps of apples in our orchard? Do you remember how we counted five that all came and sat on your pink frock while we were watching them?

"Will Mr. Wortley be kind enough to tell me of some book of questions on the Catechism, more advanced than the one he gave me? I suppose we ought to go on with the Catechism, till we are confirmed, and so Gerald and I always go through a section every Sunday, taking the book by turns, and he knows our old one perfectly. He is so good and steady about it that I quite wonder, considering that there is no authority to keep him up to it, but he is very anxious to stand a good examination when his godfather comes, and Edmund is sure to ask hard questions. And Gerald has never missed since we have been here, getting up in time to come and read the Psalms with me before breakfast, and really I think that is exceedingly good of him; but I have come to the end of my paper, so goodbye. "Your affectionate

"MARIAN C. ARUNDEL."

Caroline's cheeks glowed as she read, both with shame at her own proceedings, and with respect for her narrow-minded cousin; but she had no opportunity for making remarks, for just as she had finished the letter, and folded it up again, the boys were heard coming in. The first thing Gerald said was, "So Marian has not sent her letter; I will run down with it, or it will be too late."

"It is not sealed," said Clara.

"Clara looks as if she had been peeping," said Johnny.

"I should like to see any one peep into Marian's letters," said Gerald, taking it up, and carrying it away with him.

Lionel stood with his eyes fixed on Clara. "I do believe it is true then!" said he, laying hold of Clara's arm; "I have a great mind to say I'll never speak to you again, Clara. Peeping into people's letters. Why, you ought to be hooted through the town!"

The boys looked nearly ready to put the hooting into effect, but Clara answered angrily, "Peeping! I have been doing no such thing! Don't be so rude, Lionel."

"That is humbug," said Lionel; "you have been looking impudently, if you have not been peeping slyly."

"Lionel, you are a very naughty boy indeed!" said Clara, almost crying; "I have done just as Miss Morley and Caroline have been doing; Miss Morley always looks over —"

"Let who will do it," said Lionel, "it is an impudent, ungentlemanlike thing, that you all ought to be ashamed of. I declare papa shall hear of it."

"Lionel, do you know what you are saying?" said Caroline.

"This is sadly naughty!" feebly murmured Miss Morley.

"Lionel, mamma will be very angry," said Clara.

"I don't care," said Lionel loudly and vehemently; "I know that you all ought to be ashamed of yourselves, every one of you. Why, if you were boys you would never hold up your heads again; but girls can do anything, and that is the reason they have no shame."

"Hush! Lionel, dear Lionel!" said Caroline, coming to him persuasively, but he shook her off:

"I want none of your *dears*," said he; "ask Marian's pardon, not mine."

He turned his back, and took up a book. The girls dared say no more to him; Miss Morley very nearly cried as she thought how impossible it was for women to manage great boys. She ought to complain of his rudeness, but the explanation of what gave rise to it was impossible, and so, poor woman, she thought herself too good-natured.

Gerald, in the meantime, had gone to his sister's room, where he called hastily on finding the door fastened. She opened it, and he eagerly asked what was the matter.

"Never mind," said Marian; "thank you for remembering my letter. Will you fetch the sealing wax out of —"

"Well, but what is the matter?"

"Nothing that signifies; never mind."

"But I do mind, I can't bear for you to cry. You know I can't, so don't begin again," added he, as his affectionate tones made her lip quiver, and her eyes fill with tears.

"But, Gerald, pray get the wax, or — . But no, no," added she hurriedly, "do not, I will not touch it, till —"

"Till when?" asked Gerald; "I wish you would tell me how they have been vexing you. I am sure they hare, for they all looked guilty. Poor Marian!" He put his arm round her neck, and drew her cheek to his. Who could withstand such a brother? Marian whispered. "Only — but don't make a fuss — only Miss Morley made me show her my letter."

He started from her, and broke forth into a torrent of indignation; and it was not quickly that she succeeded in getting him to listen to her entreaties that he would not tell any one.

"What do you mean to do?" said he. "O I will write such a letter to Edmund, in hopes she will ask to see it. But she won't venture on mine. Shall I tell Edmund?"

"No, no, Gerald, you do nothing; pray don't say anything. I will speak to Mr. Lyddell, for it was he who gave me leave."

"And I hope he will give poor unfortunate a good rowing. Won't it be fun?"

"Now, Gerald, pray don't say such things, or I shall be sorry I told you. I dare say she thought it was right."

"Stuff and nonsense! Right indeed! I hope Mr. Lyddell will give it to her well!"

"If I may not write without having my letters read, I am sure I shall never be able to write at all!"

"And when shall you speak? Luckily there is no company tonight, and I hope I shall be there to hear."

"No, you will not; I shall wait till you are gone to bed, for I am sure Lionel and Johnny ought to know nothing about it. I believe I had better not have told you; but, Gerald, you are all I have, and I can't help telling you everything."

"Of course, Marian, so you ought, for let them laugh at me as they will, I always tell you everything. And won't it be nice when I am grown up, and we can get away from them all, and live at home together, and I go out shooting every day, and you and Ranger stand at the top of the steps to watch me? For Ranger will be too old to go out shooting by that time."

In the midst of this picture of rural felicity, Saunders came to tell Marian that it was time to dress.

When she returned to the schoolroom, Caroline would have given anything not to have read the letter; she was too sure that there was nothing wrong in it, and she could not show the trust in her cousin which would have enabled her to speak freely, and say she was very sorry for her speech and meant nothing by it; nor did she wish to revive the subject before Lionel, whose indignation would be still more unpleasant in Marian's own presence. She therefore said nothing, and on the other hand Marian felt awkward and constrained; Lionel was secretly ashamed of his own improper behaviour to Miss Morley, and well knowing that he should never dare to perform his threat of telling his father, put on a surly kind of demeanour, quite as uncivil to Marian as to anyone else; and but that Clara never minded anything, and that Johnny knew and cared little about the matter, their tea that evening would have been wonderfully unsociable. Gerald had not much to say, but the bent of his thoughts was evident enough when his ever-busy pencil produced the sketch of a cat pricking her paw by patting a hedgehog rolled up in a ball.

Neither Miss Morley nor her pupils ever expected to hear more of the letter, for they knew perfectly well that what Lionel had said was but a threat, for the appeal direct to Mr. or Mrs. Lyddell was a thing never thought of at Oakworthy. Marian had, however, made up her mind; her anxiety overpowered her shyness; she knew that Mr. Lyddell was the proper person, and perhaps the fact was that she was less afraid of him than of his wife. So, though she resisted all the glances cast at her by Gerald, whenever he thought he saw a good opportunity for her, and waited till all the three little boys had gone to bed, she by no means gave up her purpose. It was time for her too, to wish good night; and while her heart beat fast, she said, "Mr. Lyddell, you gave me leave to write to Agnes Wortley. Was it on condition of my letters being looked over?"

"Who meddles with your letters?" said Mr. Lyddell, much surprised.

Caroline, having helped to get her governess into the scrape, thought it but fair to say what she could for her, and answered, "Miss Morley thought that you and mamma would wish it."

"By no means," said Mr. Lyddell, turning to Marian, "I have the highest opinion of Mr. and Mrs. Wortley, the very highest; I wish your correspondence to be perfectly free."

"Thank you," said Marian. "Good night!" and away she went, to tell Gerald how it had passed; and he, who had been lying awake in expectation, was much disappointed to hear no more than this.

As soon as she was gone, Mrs. Lyddell exclaimed, "What could have given Miss Morley reason to think that her letters were to be inspected? Really, Miss Morley must have some courage! I should be sorry to be the person to make the request."

"Ah! Marian was very angry indeed," said Clara; "quite in a passion."

"Very proper," said Mr. Lyddell. "A spirited thing. She is a girl of sense."

Mrs. Lyddell let the matter drop with the girls, but going to the schoolroom, she inquired into it more fully, and found that by poor unfortunate faithful Morley's own account, she had allowed herself to be made the tool of the curiosity of Caroline and Clara. She spoke severely, and Miss Morley had displeasure to endure, which was considerably more disagreeable than all Clara's importunities could have been.

However, the next morning it appeared as if the whole affair was forgotten by all parties; Marian win just as usual, and so were her cousins; but, in secret, Caroline felt guilty, and held her in higher estimation since she had seen the contents of the letter, which, as she could perceive, Marian might well be doubly unwilling to show; she wished that Marian would but be as open to her as she was to Agnes, but this unfortunate business seemed like another great bar to their ever being really intimate, and she did not know how to surmount it.

These reflections were shortly after driven out of Caroline's head by a severe fit of toothache, which for three days made her unfit for anything but to sit by the fire reading idle books. Mrs. Lyddell proposed to take her to Salisbury to consult a dentist, and Lionel was supposed likewise to require inspection. Then, turning to Marian, Mrs. Lyddell said, "This is not the pleasantest kind of expedition, but perhaps you may like to see Salisbury, and I think your bonnet wants renewing."

"Thank you," said Marian, pleased with the Invitation. "I shall be very glad to go; I believe my teeth ought to be looked at. The dentist at Exeter said last winter that they were crowded and ought to be watched."

"Very well," said Mrs. Lyddell, "we will see what Mr. Polkinghorn says."

"Polkinghorn," said Marian, as Mrs. Lyddell left the room; "that is a Devonshire name."

"You are very welcome to him, I am sure," said Caroline; "I wish the trade was abolished."

"What cowards girls are!" said Lionel.

"Let us see how boys behave before we say anything against girls," was Marian's answer.

"Shan't you scream?" said Lionel.

"Of course she will not," said Caroline, "unless with joy at meeting a Devonshire man."

Marian laughed, and Lionel began an exhilarating story about an unfortunate who was strapped to the dentist's chair, dragged nine times round the room, and finally had his jaw broken.

Marian enjoyed her drive to Salisbury, though it added to her contempt for Wiltshire scenery, by showing her more and more of desolate down. She watched the tall Cathedral spire from far in the distance, peering up among the hills like a picture more than a reality, and she admired the green meadows and quiet vale where the town stands. Poor Caroline was taken up with dreadful anticipations of Mr. Pokingtooth, as Lionel called him, and when arrived at his clamber of torture, hung back, so as to allow Marian to be the first victim. The result of the examination was, that it would be better; though not absolutely necessary, that a certain double tooth should be extracted, and Mr. Polkinghorn, left the room in search of an instrument.

"So you think it ought to go?" sighed Marian.

"I should say so," said Mrs. Lyddell, "but you may decide for yourself."

Marian covered her face with her hands, and considered. The dentist returned; she laid back her head and opened her mouth, and the tooth was drawn. Caroline and Lionel escaped more easily, and they left the dentist's. Mrs. Lyddell said something in commendation of Marian's courage, and asked if she would like to see the Cathedral, an offer which she gladly accepted, expecting to go to the service, as the bells now began to ring; but she was disappointed, for Mrs. Lyddell said, "Ah! I had forgotten the hour. We must do our commissions first, and be at the Cathedral before the doors are shut." Marian did not venture to express her wishes, but she thought of the days when attending the Cathedral service had been the crowning pleasure of a drive to Exeter, and in dwelling on the recollection, she spent the attention which Mrs. Lyddell expected her to bestow on her new bonnet.

Their business did not occupy them very long, and they entered the Cathedral before the anthem was over; but Marian felt that it was not fitting to loiter about the nave while worship was going on within the choir; and the uncomfortable feeling occupied her so much, that she could hardly look at the fair clustered columns and graceful arches, and seemed scarcely to know or care for the gallant William Longsword, when led to the side of his mail-clad, cross-legged effigy. The deep notes of the organ, which delighted Caroline, gave her a sense of shame; and even when the service was over, and they entered the choir, these thoughts had not so passed away as to enable her to give full admiration to the exquisite leafy capitals and taper arcades of the Lady Chapel. Perhaps, too, there was a little perverseness in her inability to think that this Cathedral surpassed that of Exeter.

She thanked Mrs. Lyddell rather stiffly, as she thought to herself, "I did not reckon upon this!" and they set out on their homeward drive. Caroline looked thoughtful, and did not say much, Lionel fell asleep, and Mrs. Lyddell, after a few not very successful attempts at talking to Marian, took out her bills, and began to look over them and to reckon. Marian sat looking out of the window, lost in a vision of the hills, woods, and streams of Fern Torr, which lasted till they had reached home.

Such an expedition was so uncommon an event in the lives of the inhabitants of the schoolroom, that those who stayed at home were as excited about it as those who went, and a full and particular account was expected of all they had seen and all they had done. Caroline and Lionel both seemed to think Marian a perfect miracle of courage in voluntarily consenting to lose a tooth.

"And I am sure," said Caroline as they sat at tea, "I cannot now understand what made you have it done."

"To oblige a countryman," said Marian laughing.

"Well, but what was your real reason?" persisted Caroline.

"Mrs. Lyddell thought it best, and so did the dentist," said Marian.

"O," said Caroline, "he only said so because it was his trade."

"Then how could Mrs. Lyddell depend on him?" said Marian, gravely.

"Dentists never are to be depended on," said Caroline; "they only try to fill their own pockets like other people."

"You forget," said Lionel, "Devonshire men are not like other people."

"O yes, I beg their pardon," said Caroline, while every one laughed except Gerald; who thought the praise only their due.

"But why did you have it done?" said Clara, returning to the charge; "I am sure I never would."

"Yes, but Marian is not you," said Lionel.

"You would have disobeyed no one," said Caroline.

"I do not know," said Marian, thinking of one whom she would have disobeyed by showing weakness.

"Then did you think it wrong not to have that tooth drawn?" said Caroline.

"I do not know."

"Did you think it right to have it done?"

"I do not know, unless that I did not like it."

"Do you mean to say that not liking a thing makes it right?" exclaimed Clara.

"Very often," said Marian.

"Miss Morley, now is not that Popish?" cried Clara.

"Perhaps your cousin can explain herself," said Miss Morley.

"Yes, do," said Caroline, "you must tell us what you mean."

"I don't know," was Marian's first answer; but while uttering the reply, the real reason arranged itself in words; and finding she must speak clearly, she said, "Self-denial is always best, and in a doubtful case, the most disagreeable is always the safest."

Miss Morley said that Marian was right in many instances, but that this was not a universal rule, and so the conversation ended.

CHAPTER VI.

"O Brignal banks are fresh and fair,
And Greta woods are green;
I'd rather rove with Edmund there,
Than reign our English queen."

ROKEBY.

Winter came, and with it the time fixed for that farewell visit from Edmund Arundel, to which Marian and Gerald had long looked forward. Marian was becoming very anxious for it on Gerald's account, for she was beginning to feel that he was not quite the same child as when he first arrived at Oakworthy. He was less under control, less readily obedient to Miss Morley, less inclined to quote Edmund upon all occasions, more sensible of his own consequence, and more apt to visit that forbidden ground, the stables.

She longed for Edmund's coming, trusting to him to set everything right, and to explain to her the marvels of this strange new world.

Several gentlemen were staying in the house, and there was to be a dinner party on the day when he was expected, so that she thought the best chance of seeing him would be to stay in the garden with Gerald, while the others took their walk, so that she might be at hand on his arrival. Clara, though by no means wanted, chose to stay also, and the two girls walked up and down the terrace together.

"It is so very odd," said Clara "that you should care about such a great old cousin."

"He is only twenty-four," answered Marian.

"But he must have been grown up ever since you remember."

"Yes, but he is so kind. He used to carry us about and play with us when we were quite little children, and since I have been older he has made me almost a companion. He taught me to ride, and trained my bay pony, my beautiful Mayflower, and read with me, and helped me in my music and drawing."

"That is more than Elliot would do for us, if he could," said Clara. "It is very dull to have no one to care about our lessons, but to be shut up in the schoolroom for ever with poor unfortunate."

Marian did not choose to say how fully she assented to this complaint, but happiness had opened her heart, and she went on, — "I have had so many delightful walks with him through the beautiful wood full of rocks, and out upon the moor. O, Clara, you cannot think what it is to sit upon one of those rocks, all covered with moss and lichen, and the ferns growing in every cleft and cranny, and the beautiful little ivy-leafed campanula wreathing itself about the moss, and such a soft, free, delicious air blowing all around. And Edmund and I used to take out a book, and read and sketch so delightfully there!"

"Do you know, Marian," said Clara mysteriously, "I have heard some one say — I will not tell you who — that it is a wonder that Mr. Arundel is so fond of you, of Gerald, at least, for if it was not for him, he would have had Fern Torr, and have been Sir Edmund."

"But why should he not be fond of Gerald?"

"Really, Marian, you are a very funny person in some things," exclaimed Clara. "To think of your not being able to guess that!"

Here Mrs. Lyddell interrupted them by calling from the window to ask why they were staying in the garden?

"We were waiting to see Mr. Arundel, mamma," answered Clara.

"I think," said Mrs. Lyddell, "that as I am going out, it is not quite *the thing* for you young ladies to wait to receive a gentleman in my absence. You had better overtake the others. Marian will see Mr. Arundel in the evening."

"How cross!" exclaimed Clara, as soon as they were out of hearing. "Now we have to go along that horrid, stupid path that poor unfortunate is so fond of! If mamma had to go there herself, she would know what a nuisance it is!"

Marian was silent, because she was too much annoyed to speak properly of Mrs. Lyddell, whose interference seemed to her a needless piece of unkindness. At home she would have thought it strange not to hasten to greet cousin Edmund, and she feared he would think she neglected him, yet she could not, in Clara's presence, leave a message for him with her brother. Gerald begged her to remain, but she replied, with, a short, blunt "I can't," and set off with Clara, feeling provoked with everybody. In process of time she recovered candour enough to acknowledge to herself that Mrs. Lyddell was right as far as Clara was concerned, but the struggle kept her silent, her cousin thought her sulky, and the walk was not agreeable.

Gerald did not as usual attend her toilette, but as she passed along the passage on her way to the schoolroom, she heard sounds in the hall so like home that her heart bounded, Gerald's voice and Edmund's in reply! She could not help opening the door which separated the grand staircase from the schoolroom passage, the voice sounded plainer, she looked over the balusters, and saw — yes, actually saw Edmund, the top of his black head was just below her. Should she call? Should she run halfway down stairs, and just exchange one greeting unrestrainedly? But no; her heart beat so fast as to take away her breath, and that gave her time for recollection: Mrs. Lyddell might not think it proper, it would be meeting him in an underhand way, and that would never do!

Marian turned back, shut the door of communication, and in the next moment was in the schoolroom. When Gerald came up to tea, he was in the wildest spirit; making fun, romping with Lionel and John, and putting everything in such an uproar that it was quite a relief when the time came for going down to the drawing-room.

Now, Marian's great fear was that the gentlemen would be cruel enough to stay in the dining-room till after half-past nine, when she would be obliged to go to bed. She could hardly speak to anybody, she shrank away, as near the door as she dared, and half sprang up every time it opened, then sat down ashamed of herself, and disappointed to see only the servants with coffee and tea.

At last, the fatal time had all but come, when the black figures of the gentlemen entered one after the other, Marian scarcely venturing to look at them, and overpowered with a double access of fright and shyness, which chained her to her seat, and her eyes to the ground. But now — Edmund's hand was grasping hers, Edmund was by her side, his voice was saying, "Well, Marian, how are you?"

She looked up at him for one moment, then on the ground again, without speaking.

"Oakworthy has put no colour in your cheeks," said he. "Are you quite well?"

"Quite, thank you," said she, almost as shortly and coldly as if she had been answering Mrs. Lyddell.

"When did you hear from home?"

"Yesterday," said she, speaking more readily. "Agnes always writes once a week. When do you go there?"

"Next week, when I leave this place."

"You come from the Marchmonts, don't you?"

"Yes, Selina sends you her love, and all manner of kind messages. She hopes to see you in London after Easter."

"O dear! There is Mrs. Lyddell looking at me, and I see Caroline is gone! Good night, Edmund."

"So soon? I hoped to have seen more of you today; I came early on purpose."

"I thought so, but they would not let me stay at home."

"I understand. Don't squeeze up your lips and look woeful. I knew how it was. Good night."

Marian walked slowly up stairs, sighing as she went, and looked into Gerald's room. He was awake, and called out, "Well, Marian, are you not glad he has come?"

"O yes, very," returned Marian, in a tone of little gladness; "I hope you will be very happy with him."

"Why not you?"

"It will be all disappointment," she answered in a choking voice, as, sheltered by the darkness, she knelt down by Gerald's bed, and burst into tears. "It will all be like today."

"No, it shall not!" cried Gerald; "I will tell Edmund all about it, and he shall send them all to the right about! I can't think why you did not tell Mrs. Lyddell that you always stay at home for Edmund."

"Miss Arundel," said Saunders, at the door, "do you know that it is half an hour later than usual?"

The next morning Marian awoke with brighter spirits. It was possible that she might accomplish one walk with him, and Gerald was sure of being constantly at his side, which was the great point. At any rate, she could not be very unhappy while he was in the house.

She heard nothing of him all the morning, but, just as the schoolroom dinner was over, in came Mrs. Lyddell, and with her Edmund himself, to the great surprise of all the inhabitants. Marian looked very happy, but said very little, while there was some talk with Miss Morley, and then Edmund asked if she had no drawings to show him. She brought out her portfolio, and felt it like old times when he observed on her improved shading, or criticised the hardness of her distant hills, while Miss Morley wondered at his taste and science. It was delightful to find that she and Gerald were really to take a walk with him by themselves. She almost flew to fetch her walking dress, and soon the three were on their way together.

There was a great quantity of home news to be talked over, for Edmund had not heard half so often nor so minutely as Marian, and he had to be told how Charles Wortley got on at his new school, that Ranger had been lost for a day and a half, and many pieces of the same kind of intelligence, of which the most important was that Farmer Bright's widow had given up the hill farm, and his nephew wanted to take it, but Mr. Wortley hoped that this would not be allowed, as he was a dissenter.

"Indeed!" said Edmund; "I wonder Carter did not mention that."

"Had you heard this before?" said Marian; "I thought it news."

"Most of it is," said Edmund, "but not about the farm. The letting it is part of my business here, but I did not know of this man's dissent. Your correspondence has done good service."

"I am sure it is my great delight," said Marian; "I do not know what I should do without hearing from Agnes. I think I have learnt to prize her more since I have known other people."

"You don't find the Miss Lyddells quite as formidable as you expected though?" said Edmund; "the eldest has a nice open, countenance."

"We get on very well," said Marian. "Caroline is so good-tempered and clever, and Lionel is delightful."

"O, Edmund," interposed Gerald, "Lionel and I had such fun the other day. We caught the old donkey and blindfolded it with our handkerchiefs, and let it loose, and if you could but have seen how it kicked up its heels —"

They went on with the history of adventures of the same description, enjoying themselves exceedingly, and when Marian went in, she was much pleased to find how favourable an impression Edmund had made on her companions, although some of their commendations greatly surprised her; Miss Morley pronouncing that he had in the greatest degree an *air distingue*, and was a remarkably fashionable young man. Marian could endure the *air distingue*, but could hardly swallow the fashionable young man, an expression which only conveyed to her mind the idea of Elliot Lyddell and his moustached friends. However, she knew it was meant for high praise, and her present amiable fit was strong enough to prevent her from taking it as an insult.

The next day was Sunday, and she provokingly missed Edmund three times, in the walks to and from church, he being monopolized by "some stupid person," who had far less right to him than she had; but at last, when she had been completely worried and vexed with her succession of disappointments, and had come into what Lionel would have emphatically called "a state of mind," Edmund contrived to come to her before going in doors, and asked if she could not take a few turns with him on the terrace. She came gladly, and yet hardly with full delight, for the irritation of the continually recurring disappointments through the whole day, still had its influence on her spirits, and she did not at first speak. "Where is Gerald?" asked Edmund.

"I don't know; somewhere with the boys," said Marian, disconsolately.

"Well, why not?" said Edmund laughing.

"I don't know," said Marian.

"That is a meditative 'I don't know,' which conveys more than meets the ear."

"I don't know whether — I mean I don't think it does Gerald any good."

"It? — what?"

"I don't know," repeated Marian in a tone which to any one else would have appeared sullen.

"I should like to arrive at your meaning, Marian. Are you not happy about Gerald!"

"I don't know," said Marian; but Edmund, convinced that all was not right, was resolved to penetrate these determined professions of ignorance.

"Is Gerald under Miss Morley?" he asked.

"Yes, during most of the day. They all say he is very good."

"And does not that satisfy you?"

"I don't know."

Edmund perceived that the subject of her brother was too near her heart to be easily approached, and resolved to change his tone.

"How have you been getting on?" he asked. "Does learning flourish under the present dynasty?"

"I don't know," replied Marian for the seventh time, but she did not as usual stop there, and continued, "they think one knows nothing unless one has learnt all manner of dates, and latitudes, and such things. Not one of them knew Orion when they saw him in the sky, and yet even Clara thought me dreadfully stupid because I could not find out on the globe the altitude of Beta in Serpentarius, at New Orleans, at three o'clock in the morning."

Edmund could not help laughing at her half-complaining, half-humorous tone, and this encouraged her to proceed.

"In history they don't care whether a man is good or bad; they only care when he lived. O Edmund, the lists of names and dates, kings and Roman emperors — ."

"Metals, semi-metals, and distinguished philosophers," said Edmund; and Marian, who in days of old had read "Mansfield Park," laughed as she used to do at home.

"Exactly," said she, "O, Edmund, it is very different learning from what it used to be. All lesson and no thinking, no explaining, no letting one make out more about the interesting places. I wanted the other day to look out in some history book to find whether Rinaldo in Tasso was a real man, but nobody would care about it; and as to the books, all the real good *grown-up* ones are down in Mr. Lyddell's library, where no one can get at them."

"Does not Miss Lyddell enter into these things?"

"O yes, Caroline does, a great deal more than Miss Morley; but I don't know — I never can get on with Caroline —"

Marian had now gone on to the moment when her heart was ready to be open, and the whole story, so long laid up for Edmund, began to be poured forth; while he, anxious to hear all, and more sympathizing than he was willing to show himself, only put in a word or two here and there, so as to sustain the narration. Everything was told, how Clara was frivolous and wearisome; how Caroline was cold, incomprehensible, and unsympathetic; how unjust and weak Miss Morley was; how sharp, hasty, and unmotherly she found Mrs. Lyddell; and then, growing more eager, Marian, with tears springing to her eyes, told of the harm the influence of Oakworthy was doing Gerald; his love of the stables, and Saunders' opinion of the company he was likely to meet there. This led her to more of Saunders' communications about the general arrangement of the house, and the want of really earnest care for what is right; further still to what Saunders had told of Elliot and his ways, which were such as to shock her excessively, and yet she had herself heard Mr. Lyddell say that he was a fine spirited fellow!

Edmund was not sorry to find that he had but small space in which to give the reply for which Marian was eagerly looking. He avoided the main subject, and spoke directly to a point on which his little cousin was certainly wrong. "Well, Marian, who would have thought of your taking to gossiping with servants?" Then, as she looked down, too much ashamed to speak, he added, "I suppose poor Saunders has not sought for charms at Oakworthy any more than you have."

"Indeed I do not think I tried to make the worst of it when I came."

"Is that a confession that you are doing so now?"

"I do not know."

"Then let us see if you will give the same account tomorrow; I shall ask you whenever I see you particularly amiable. And now I think I have kept you out quite late enough."

The next day was very pleasant, bright, and frosty; Marian, from having relieved her heart, felt more free and happy, and her lessons went off quickly and smoothly. All went well, even though

Edmund was obliged to go and call on a friend at Salisbury instead of coming to walk with her. Her walk with Miss Morley and her cousins was prosperous and pleasant; the boys ran races, and Marian and Clara were allowed to join them without a remonstrance. Marian was running and laughing most joyously, when she was stopped by hearing a horse's feet near her, and looking round saw Edmund returning from his ride. "May I keep her out a little longer?" said he to Miss Morley, as he jumped off his horse, and Marian came to his side. Miss Morley returned a ready assent, and after disposing of the horse, the two cousins walked on happily together, she telling him some pleasant histories of Gerald and the other little boys, and lamenting the loss that Lionel would be when he went to school. After they had talked over Salisbury Cathedral, and Marian had heard with great interest of Edmund's late employments in Scotland, and all he was to do and see in Africa, and saying much about that never-ending subject, Fern Torr, Edmund thought her so cheerful that he said, "Well, may I venture to ask your opinion of the people here?"

"I don't know," said Marian, who was so much ashamed of the accusation of gossiping with Saunders as to be willing to pass over all that had been founded on her information, "perhaps I did say too much yesterday, and yet I do not know I am sure I should never have chosen them for friends."

"Perhaps they would return that compliment."

"Then you really think it is my own fault?"

"No;" (Edmund tried hard to prevent his "no" from being too emphatic, and forced himself to go on thus) "I do not suppose it is entirely your fault, but at the same time you do not strike me as a person likely to make friends easily."

"O, Edmund, I could never bring myself to kiss, and say 'dearest' and 'darling,' and all that, like Clara."

"There is the thing," said Edmund; "not that it is wrong to dislike it, not that I could ever imagine your doing any thing like it;" and, indeed, the idea seemed so preposterous, that both the cousins laughed; "but the disposition is not one likely to be over and above prepossessing to strangers."

"You mean that I am disagreeable?"

"No, far from it. I only mean that you are chilly, and make almost all who come near you the same towards you."

"I cannot help it," said Marian.

"Yes, you could in time, if you did not fairly freeze yourself by constant dwelling on their worst points. Make the best of them with all your might, and you will soon learn to like them better."

"But if the things are so, Edmund, how can I see them otherwise?"

"Don't look out for them, and be glad of every excuse for disliking the people. Don't fancy harshness and unkindness where no one intends it. I am quite sure that Mr. Lyddell wishes to give you every advantage, and that Mrs. Lyddell thinks she treats you like her own child."

"I don't think I should like to be her own child," said Marian. "It is true that she is the same with me as with them, but —"

"Poor Marian," said Edmund, kindly, "you have been used to such gentleness at home, that no wonder the world seems hard and unkind to you. But I did not mean to make you cry; you know you must rough it, and bravely too."

"Never mind my crying," said Marian, struggling to speak; "it is nothing, but I cannot help it. It is so very long since any one has known what I meant."

Edmund could not trust himself to speak, so full was he of affectionate compassion for her, and of indignation against the Lyddells, when these few words revealed to him all her loneliness; and they walked on for a considerable distance in silence, till, with a sudden change of tone, he asked if she had had any riding since she came to Oakworthy.

"O no, I have not been on horseback once. What a treat a good canter on Mayflower would be!"

"I suspect one victory over her would put you in spirits to be amiable for a month," said Edmund.

"Dear old Mayflower!" said Marian. "How delightful that day was when she first came home, and we took that very long ride to the Eastcombe!"

Edmund and Marian fell into a line of reminiscences which enlivened them both, and she went in-doors in a cheerful mood, while he seriously took the riding into consideration; knowing, as he did, that her mother had thought a great deal of out-of-door exercise desirable for her, and guessing that her want of spirits might very probably arise from want of the air and freedom to which she had always been accustomed. The result of his meditations was, that the next morning she was delighted by Gerald's rushing into the school-room, calling out, "Put on your habit, Marian; make haste and put on your habit. You are to have my pony, and I am to have Lionel's, and Edmund is to have Sorell, and we are all to ride together to Chalk Down!"

How fast Marian obeyed the summons may well be believed; and though Gerald's pony was not comparable to Mayflower, it was much to feel herself again in the saddle, with the fresh wind breathing on her checks, and Edmund by her side. Par and joyously did they ride; so far, that Gerald was tired into unusual sleepiness all the evening; but Marian was but the fresher and brighter, full of life and merriment, which quite surprised her cousins.

But visits, alas! are fleeting things, and Edmund's last day at Oakworthy came only too soon. Precious as it was, it was for the most part devoted to business with Mr. Lyddell, though he sent Marian a message that he hoped for a walk with her and her brother in the afternoon.

The hour came, but not the man; and while Caroline and Clara went out with Miss Morley, Marian sat down with a book to wait for him. In about an hour's time the boys came to tell her they were going to the pond with Walter.

"O Gerald, won't you wait for Edmund?"

"I have waited till I am tired. I cannot stay in this whole afternoon, and I do not think he will come this age."

"He is shut up in the study with papa," said Lionel; "I heard their voices very loud, as if they were in *such* a rage."

"I wish I could see them," said Johnny, "it would be such fun."

Away ran the boys, leaving Marian in a state of wonder and anxiety, but still confident that Edmund would not forget her. She put on her walking dress, and sat down to her book again, but still she was left to wait. The winter twilight commenced, and still no Edmund; steps approached, but not the right ones; and in came the walking party, with a general exclamation of "Poor Marian! what, still waiting?" Miss Morley advised her to take a few turns on the terrace, instead of practising that horrid Mozart. Marian disconsolately went down stairs, looking wistfully at the library door as she went past it, and, at a funeral pace, promenaded along the terrace. As she passed beneath the window of Caroline's room, a head was popped out, and a voice sang —

"So, sir, you're come at last, I thought you'd come no more, I've waited with my bonnet on from one till half-past four! You know I sit alone —"

At that moment, Edmund himself was seen advancing from the door; the song ended in a scream of laughter and dismay, and the window was hastily shut. Edmund smiled a little, but very little, and said, "True enough, I am afraid I have used you very ill."

"Tiresome affairs," said Marian, looking up into his harassed face. "I hope they have not made your head ache?"

"I have been worried, but it is not the fault of the affairs, I wish you had not lost your walk," added he abruptly, beginning to stride on so fast that she could scarcely keep up with him, and apparently forgetting her presence entirely in his own engrossing thoughts. She watched him intently as she toiled to keep by his side, longing, but not daring, to inquire what was the matter. At last he broke out into a muttered exclamation, "destitute of all principle! all labour in vain!"

"What — how — Mr. Lyddell?"

"This whole day have I been at it, trying to bring him to reason about that farm!"

"What? Did he wish the Dissenter to have it?"

"He saw no objection — treated all I said as the merest moonshine!"

"What? all the annoyance to the Wortleys, and the mischief to the poor people!" exclaimed Marian, "Why, we should have a meeting-house!"

"Nothing more likely, in the Manor field, and fifty pounds subscribed — all for the sake of toleration and Gerald's interests."

"You don't mean that he has done it?" said Marian, alarmed, and not quite understanding Edmund's tone of irony, "Cannot you prevent it?"

"I have prevented It; I said that, with my knowledge of my uncle's intentions, I could never feel justified in consenting to sign the lease."

"And that puts a stop to it? Oh, I am very glad. But I suppose he was very angry?"

"I never saw a man more so. He said he had no notion of sacrificing Gerald's interest to party feeling."

"How could it be for Gerald's interest to bring Dissenters to Fern Torr? I am sure it would be very disagreeable. I thought it, was quite wrong to have any dealings with them."

"He has been popularity-hunting too long to have many scruples on that score."

Marian could not help triumphing. "Well, Edmund, I am glad you have come to my opinion at last. I knew you would not like the Lyddells when you knew them better."

"I never was much smitten with them," said Edmund, abruptly, as if affronted at the imputation of having liked them.

"But Edmund," cried Marian, standing still in the extremity of her amazement, "what have you been about all this time? Have you not been telling me it is all my own fault that I do not get on with them?"

He was silent for a little while; and then turning round halfway, as people do when much diverted, he broke out into a hearty fit of laughter. "It is plain," said he, at last, "that nature never designed me for a young lady's counsellor."

"What do you mean, Edmund?"

"I suspect I have done mischief," said Edmund, after a little consideration, "and I believe all that remains to be done is to tell you all, and come down from my character of Mentor, which certainly I have not fulfilled particularly well."

"I am sure I do not understand you," said Marian.

"Well, then," said Edmund, speaking in a more free and unembarrassed tone than he had used since he had been at Oakworthy, "this is the fact of the matter, as Mrs. Cornthwayte would say, Marian. I always thought it very unlucky that you were obliged to live here; but as it could not be helped, and I really knew nothing against the Lyddells, there was no use in honing and moaning about it beforehand, so I tried to make the best of it. Well, I came here, and found things as bad as I expected, and was very glad to find you steady in the principles we learnt at home. Still, I thought you deficient in kindly feeling towards them, and inclined to give way to repining and discontent, and I think you allowed I was not far wrong. Today, I must allow, I was off my guard, and have made a complete mess of all my prudence."

"O, I am very glad of it," said Marian. "I understand you now, and you are much more like yourself."

"Yes, it was a very unsuccessful attempt," said Edmund, again laughing at himself, "and I am very glad it is over; for I have been obliged to be the high and mighty guardian all this time, and I am very tired of it;" and he yawned.

"Then you don't like them any better than I do," repeated Marian, in a tone of heartfelt satisfaction.

"Stop, stop, stop; don't think that cousin Edmund means to give you leave to begin hating them."

"Hating them? O no! but now you will tell me what I ought to do, since there is no possibility of getting away from them."

"No, there is no possibility," said Edmund, considering; "I could not ask the Marchmonts again, though they did make the offer in the first fulness of their hearts. Besides, there are objections; I should not feel satisfied to trust you to so giddy a head as Selina's. No, Marian, it cannot be helped; so let us come to an understanding about these same Lyddells."

"Well, then, why is it that we do not do better? I know there are faults on my side; but what are the faults on theirs?"

"Marian, I believe the fault to be that they do not look beyond this present life," said Edmund, in a grave, low tone.

Marian thought a little while, and then said, "Caroline does, but I see what you mean with the others."

"Then your conduct should be a witness of your better principles," said Edmund. "You may stand on very high ground, and it entirely depends on yourself whether you maintain that position, or sink down to their level."

"O, but that is awful!" cried Marian; and then in a tone of still greater dismay, "and Gerald? O, Edmund, what is to become of him?"

"I must trust him to you, Marian."

"To me!"

"You have great influence over him, and that, rightly used, may be his safeguard. Many a man has owed everything to a sister's influence." Then, as Marian's eye glistened with somewhat of tender joy and yet of fear, he went on, "But take care; if you deteriorate, he will be in great danger; and, on the other hand, beware of obstinacy and rigidity in trifles — you know what I mean — which might make goodness distasteful to him."

"O, worse and worse, Edmund! What is to be done? If I can do him so much harm, I know I can do him very little good; and what will it be when he is older, and will depend less on what I say?"

"He will always depend more on what you *do* than on what you say."

"But what can I do? all the schoolboy temptations that I know nothing about. And Elliot — O, Edmund! think of Elliot, and say if it is not dreadful that Mr. Lyddell should have the management of our own Gerald? Papa never could have known —"

"I think, while he is still so young, that there is not much harm to be apprehended from that quarter," said Edmund; "afterwards, I believe I may promise you that he shall not be left entirely to Oakworthy training."

"And," said Marian, "could you not make him promise to keep away from the stables? Those men — and their language — could you not, Edmund?"

"I could, but I would not," said Edmund. "I had rather that, if he transgresses, he should not break his word as well as run into temptation. There is no such moral crime in going down to the stables, as should make us willing to oblige him to take a vow against it."

"Would it not keep him out of temptation?"

"Only by substituting another temptation," said Edmund. "No, Marian; a boy must be governed by principles, and not by promises."

"Principles — people are always talking of them, but I don't half understand what they are," said Marian.

"The Creed and the Ten Commandments are what I call principles," said Edmund.

"But those are promises, Edmund."

"You are right, Marian; but they are not promises to man."

"I could do better if I had any one to watch me, or care about me," said Marian.

Edmund's face was full of sadness. "We — I mean you, are alone indeed, Marian; but, depend upon it, it is for the best. We might be tempted not to look high enough, and you have to take heed to yourself for Gerald's sake."

"I do just sometimes feel as I ought," said Marian; "but it is by fits and starts. O, Edmund, I would give anything that you were not going."

"It is too late now," said Edmund, "and there are many reasons which convince me that I ought not to exchange. In a year or two, when I have my promotion, I hope to return, and then, Marian, I shall find you a finished young lady."

Marian shuddered.

"Poor child," said Edmund, laughing.

"And you are going home," said Marian, enviously.

"Home, yes," said Edmund, in a tone which seemed as if he did not think himself an object of envy.

"Yes, the hills and woods," said Marian, "and the Wortleys."

"Yes, I am very glad to go," said Edmund. "Certainly even the being hackneyed cannot spoil the beauty or the force of those lines of Gray's."

"What, you mean, 'Ah! happy hills; ah! pleasing shade?'"

"Yes," said Edmund, sighing and musing for some minutes before he again spoke, and then it was very earnestly. "Marian, you must not go wrong, Gerald must not — with such parents as yours —" Marian did not answer, for she could not; and presently he added, "It does seem strange that such care as my uncle's should have been given to me, and then his own boy left thus. But, Marian, you must watch him, you must guard him. If you are in real difficulty or doubt how to act, you have the Wortleys; and if you see anything about which you are seriously uneasy with regard to him, write to me, and I will do my utmost, little as that is."

"Yes, yes, I am glad to be sure of it," said Marian.

"Well, I am glad to have had this talk," said Edmund. "I did you injustice, Marian; you are fit to be treated as a friend: but you must forgive me, for it cost me a good deal to try to be wise with you."

"I think you have seemed much wiser since you left it off," said Marian, "Somehow, though I was glad to hear you, it did not comfort me or set me to rights before."

Edmund and Marian could have gone on for hours longer, but it was already quite dark; and the sound of Elliot's whistle approaching warned them that one was coming who would little understand their friendship, — why the soldier should loiter with the little girl, or why the young girl should cling to the side of her elder cousin. They went in-doors, and hastened different ways; they saw each other again, but only in full assembly of the rest of the family. And at last, soon after breakfast the nest morning, Marian stood in the hall, watching Edmund drive from the door; and while her face was cold, pale, and still as ever, her heart throbbed violently, and her throat felt as if she was ready to choke. She heard of him at Fern Torr, she heard of him at Portsmouth, she heard of his embarkation; and many and many a lonely moment was filled up with tears of storm and tempest; of fever and climate, of the lion and of the Caffre.

CHAPTER VII.

"Child of the town! for thee, alas!
Glad nature spreads nor tree or grass;
Birds build no nests, nor in the sun
Glad streams come singing as they run.
Thy paths are paved for five long miles,
Thy groves and hills are peaks and tiles,
Thy fragrant air is yon thick smoke,
Which shrouds thee like a mourning cloak."
                    ALAN CUNNINGHAM.

And so Edmund was gone! But he had bequeathed to Marian a purpose and an object, which gave her a spirit to try hard and feel out a way for herself in this confused tangle of a world around, her. She was happier, though perhaps more anxious; for now it was not mere vague dislike and discontent, but a clearer perception both of the temptations around and of the battle required of her.

In January the whole family went to London, the object of many of Marian's terrors. Caroline and Clara were both sorry to go, and the boys lamented exceedingly; Lionel saying it was very hard that the last two months before his going to school should be spent boxed up there, with nothing to do. Indeed the life of the schoolroom party was here more monotonous than that at Oakworthy; for besides the constant regularity of lessons, there was now no variety in the walks; they only paced round the square, or on fine days went as far as the park.

And then there were the masters! Marian was in a state of great fear, under the anticipation of her first lessons from them; but the reality proved much better than she had expected. To be sure, she disliked the dancing with all her heart, and made no great figure in music; but people were patient with her, and that was a great comfort; and then she thoroughly liked and enjoyed the lessons in languages and in drawing. There were further advantages in the London life, upon which she had not calculated, for here she was nobody, less noticed than Caroline, seldom summoned to see visitors, and, when she went into the drawing-room, allowed to remain in the back-ground as much as she pleased; so that, though her eye pined for green trees and purple hills, and her ear was wearied with the never-ceasing sound of wheels, London so far exceeded her expectations, that she wrote to Agnes, that, "if there were no smoke, and no fog, and no streets, and no people, there would be no great harm in it, especially if there was anything for the boys to do."

The boys were certainly to be pitied; in a house smaller than Oakworthy, and without the occupations out of doors to which they had been accustomed, edicts of silence were more ineffectual than ever, and yawns became painfully frequent. Every one's temper fell into an uncomfortable state of annoyance and irritation; Miss Morley, instead of her usual quiet, piteous way of reproving, was fretful; Caroline was sharp; Clara sometimes rude like the boys, sometimes cross with them; even Marian was now and then tormented into a loss of temper, when there was no obtaining the quiet which she, more than the others, needed in order to learn a lesson properly. Each day Lionel grew more unruly, chiefly from the want of occupation, leading the other two along with him; and each day the female portion of the party grew more inclined to fretfulness, as they felt their own helplessness. It even came to consultations between Miss Morley and Caroline whether they must not really tell of the boys: but the evil day was always put off till "next time."

Gerald was riotous when Lionel and John made him so, but not often on his own account; and he had more resources of his own than they had. His drawing was a great amusement to him, though rather in a perverse way; for he would not be induced to take lessons of the master, seldom drew at the right time, or in the right place, and frequently in the wrong ones.

"I never can learn except when I am drawing," he said, and his slate was often so filled with designs, that the sums were jostled into the narrowest possible space, while his Latin grammar was similarly adorned. There sat the Muse in full beauty, enthroned upon Parnassus, close to *musa musæ; magister* had a wig, and *dominus* a great rod; while the extraordinary physiognomies round *facies faciei* would have been worthy of any collection of caricatures. Moreover the illustrations of the verb *amo* commemorated the gentleman who was married on Sunday, killed his wife on Wednesday, and at the preter-pluperfect tense was hanged on Saturday. Other devices were scattered along the margin, and peeped out of every nook — old men's heads, dogs, hunters, knights, omnibuses; and the habit of drawing so grew upon him, that when he was going to read any book where scribbling was insufferable, Marian generally took the precaution of putting all pencils out of reach.

She often warned him to take care of the school-room Atlas; but, incited by Lionel, he could not resist the temptation of putting a pipe in the mouth of the Britannia who sat in a corner of the map of England. This pipe she carefully rubbed out, but not till it had received from the others a sort of applause which he took as encouragement to repeat the offence; and when next Marian looked at Britannia, she found the pipe restored, and a cocked hat on the lion's head. Again there was much merriment; and though Miss Morley, more than once, told Gerald this would never do, and he really must not, she could not help laughing so much, that he never quite believed her to be in earnest, and proceeded to people the world with inhabitants by no means proportioned to the size of their countries. John-o'-Groat and his seven brothers took possession of their house, Turks paraded in the Mediterranean, and in the large empty space in the heart of Africa, Baron Munchausen caused the lion to leap down the crocodile's throat.

It was about this time that Marian was one day summoned to the drawing-room at an unusual time, and found Mr. and Mrs. Lyddell both there looking exceedingly gracious. "Here is a present for you, Marian," said the former, putting into her hands a large thin parcel.

"For me! O thank you!" said Marian, too much surprised and embarrassed to make much of her thanks; nor did her wonder diminish as, unfolding the paper, she beheld a blue watered silk binding, richly embossed, with the title of "The Wreath of Beauty," and soon there lay before her, in all the smoothness of India paper and mezzotint, a portrait, beneath which she read the name of Selina, Viscountess Marchmont.

"Selina!" repeated she, in the extremity of her amazement.

"Yes," said Mr. Lyddell, resting there in expectation of renewed and eager acknowledgements; but all he received was this — "Can that be Selina?"

"It is said to be a very good likeness," said Mrs. Lyddell.

"O!" cried Marian, and there she checked herself.

"Mr. Lyddell was quite struck with the resemblance to you," added Mrs. Lyddell.

The astonishment of Marian's glance was greater than ever, but here she bethought herself that Mr. Lyddell had intended to give her great pleasure, and that she was very ungrateful; whereupon the room seemed to swim round with her in her embarrassment, and with a great effort she stammered out something about his being very kind, and her being very much obliged to him; and then, perceiving that she ought to add more, in order to satisfy that judge of politeness, Mrs. Lyddell, she said that it was a long time since she had seen Lady Marchmont, and that she could not so well judge of the likeness; and then she bore it away to sigh and wonder over it unrestrainedly with Gerald.

No wonder the Lyddells were surprised, for Lady Marchmont's portrait was incomparably the most beautiful in the book; the classical regularity of the features, the perfect form of nose and chin, the lovely lip, and the undulating line of the hair, all were exquisite; the turn of the long neck, the *pose* of the tall graceful figure, and the simple elegance of the dress, were such as to call for great admiration. But all that Marian saw was an affectation in that twisted position, — a straining round of the eyes, and a kind of determination at archness of expression in the mouth. Where was the merry, artless, sweet-looking Selina she remembered, whose yet unformed though very pretty features had faded from her memory, and left only the lively, good-natured expression which, here she sought in vain?

"O Selina, Selina, can you be like this'?" exclaimed she; "and to think of their saying I am like it! I am sure I hope one is as true as the other."

Gerald drew his face into a horrible caricature of the expression in the portrait, and set his sister laughing.

"I hope I shall never see her If she has grown like it," said she, sighing.

"I should take the stick to her if she was," said Gerald.

"I am afraid it must be too true," said Marian, "or she would never allow herself to be posted up in this absurd way. I wonder Lord Marchmont allows it!"

"I'll tell you, Marian," said the sympathising Gerald, "if I had ten beauties for my wife —"

"Ten beauties! O, Gerald!"

"Well, one ten times as beautiful as Selina, I mean; I would cure her of vanity well; for I would tell her that, if she chose to have her picture drawn in this Book of Beauty, it should only be with a ring through her nose, and two stars tattooed on her cheeks."

"And a very good plan too," said Marian, laughing; "but I am afraid poor Selina cannot be in such good hands. See, here are the impertinent people writing verses about her, as if they had any business to ask her what she is thinking about. Listen, Gerald; did you ever hear such stuff?"

> *"Lady, why that radiant smile,*
> *Matching with that pensive brow,*
> *Like sunbeams on some mountain pile*
> *Glowing on solemn heights of snow?*

"Lady, why that glance of thought,
Joined to that arch lip of mirth,
Like shade by fleecy cloudlet brought
Over some paradise of earth?

"Yea, thou may'st smile, the world for thee
Is opening all its fairest bowers;
Yet in that earnest face I see
These may not claim thy dearest hours.

"But for thy brow, thy smile we deem
The gladsome mirth of fairy sprite;
But for thy smile, thy mien would seem
Some angel's from the world of light.

"Yet laughing lip and thoughtful brow
Are depths and gleams of mortal life;
Angel and fay, of us art thou,
Then art a woman and a wife!"

"What would they have her to be? a husband?" said Gerald.

Here Caroline and Clara came hastily in, eager to see the portrait and read the verses, and very far were they from being able to imagine why she did not like the portrait. Caroline owned that there might be a little affectation, but she thought the beauty very considerable; and as to Clara, she was in raptures, saying she never *did* see any one half so lovely. And as to the verses, they were the sweetest things she ever read; and she carried them off to show to Miss Morley, who fully sympathised with her. Marian found no one to share her opinion but Gerald and Lionel, and their criticisms were unsparingly extended to Lady Marchmont's features, as well as her expression, "Such mincing lips! such untidy hair! Hollo! who has given her a black eye?" till they had not left her a single beauty.

Marian hoped the subject was quite forgotten, when she had hidden away the book under all her others: but the nest time there was a dinner-party, Mrs. Lyddell desired her to fetch it, to show to some one who knew Lady Marchmont. She took it up stairs again us soon as she could, but again and again was she obliged to bring it, and condemned to hear it talked over and admired. One day when she was going wearily and reluctantly up stairs, she was arrested by a call from Lionel, who was creeping up outside the balusters in a fashion which had no recommendation but its extreme difficulty and danger.

"Eh, Marian, what, going after beauty again?"

"I wish it was Beauty and the Beast," said Marian, disconsolately. "There are different tastes in the world, that is certain; but don't break that neck of yours, Lionel."

Lionel replied by letting go with one hand and brandishing that and his foot over the giddy space below. Marian frowned and squeezed up her lips, but did not speak till it pleased him to draw himself in again, and throw himself over the balusters before her, saying, "That is a reward for you, Marian; Clara would have screeched."

The next time Marian was desired to fetch the book, it was for a morning visitor, — a broad, stately, pompous old lady, who had had the pleasure of meeting Lady Marchmont, and thought Miss Arundel very like her.

"Are you going after beauty?" said Lionel, again meeting Marian on the stairs.

"Yes," said Marian, with a sigh.

"Well, I hope she will be pleased, that's all," said Lionel.

Marian thought there was a meaning in this speech, but she was in haste, and without considering it, ran down stairs again. As she was opening the drawing-room door, she saw Gerald on the top of the stairs, calling to her, "Marian, have you that book? O, wait —"

"I cannot come now, Gerald," said she, entering the room, and shutting the door after her. She laid the book on the table, and the page was opened.

"O beautiful!" exclaimed the old lady, "How exact a likeness!"

"Why, Marian!" broke involuntarily from Mrs. Lyddell, and Marian, looking at the print, could, in spite of her dismay, hardly keep from laughing; for the elegant Lady Marchmont now appeared decorated with a huge pair of mustachios, an elaborate jewelled ring in the nose, and a wavy star on each cheek, and in the middle of the forehead; while over the balustrade on which she was leaning there peeped a monster with grotesque eyes, a pair of twisted horns, a parrot's beak, vulture's claws, and a scaly tail stretching away in complicated spires far into the distance. No one could for a moment doubt that this was Gerald's work, and Marian felt sure that he had been thereto incited by Lionel. Extreme was her consternation at the thought of the displeasure which he had incurred; but in the mean time there was something very amusing in the sight of the old lady beginning to perceive that something was wrong, and yet not able to make it out, and not choosing to own her difficulties. Mrs. Lyddell, though vexed and angry, carried it off very well. "Ah! some mischief of the boys," said she, decidedly. "I am afraid it is not fit to be seen." And so saying, she closed the book, and changed the conversation.

As soon as the visitor had taken leave, the scene was changed; Mrs. Lyddell walked hastily to the table, threw open the book, and began to examine into the degree of damage it had suffered. "I suppose you know nothing of this, Marian?" said she, surveying her with one of her quickest and most formidable glances.

"O no," said Marian; "I am sure I am very sorry."

"Well, I must inquire about it," said Mrs. Lyddell, taking up the book, and hastening towards the school-room, followed by poor Marian, trembling with all her heart for her brother, and somewhat for Lionel, even though she could not help being angry with him for having got Gerald into such a scrape.

There stood the boys, looking partly exulting, partly frightened; Lionel a little more of the first, Gerald a little more of the second; for this was Gerald's first desperate piece of mischief, whereas Lionel had survived many such. Besides, Gerald's handiwork was too evident to be mistaken, while his companion's part in the folly could be known to no one; and though it might be guessed at by Marian, Lionel thought she might be trusted.

The book was spread upon the table, and the expressions of horror from the three ladies of the school-room were as strong as could reasonably be expected.

"Indeed," pleaded Miss Morley, in her deplorable tone, "I am continually ordering Sir Gerald not to scribble in books, but he never will obey."

"That is not true!" cried Gerald, in a loud, startling voice.

"Gerald," said Mrs. Lyddell, "that is no proper manner of speaking; you have behaved very ill already — do not add to your fault. Before any more is said, beg Miss Morley's pardon."

There was a silence, and she repeated, "I desire that you will ask Miss Morley's pardon directly — still silent? what is the meaning of this?"

Gerald stood bolt upright, and very rigid; poor Marian glancing appealingly, first at him, then at Mrs. Lyddell, then at Miss Morley, all equally without effect. She saw it all — that he might have been brought to own that be had done wrong about this individual case; but that the sweeping accusation of disobeying orders, which, as they all knew, were never given with anything like decision, had roused a proud, determined sense of injustice, and that he was ready to suffer anything rather than apologise. She was wild to speak, to do something; yet what could she attempt?

Mrs. Lyddell would not begin upon the book-scribbling subject till she had conquered the spirit of defiance, and continued to insist on his begging Miss Morley's pardon; but the more she ordered, the more determined he grew. There he stood, his proud, dark eye fixed on a picture on the wall, his lip curled with a sort of disdain, and an expression in his whole motionless figure that, had his cause but been good, would have been resolution, whereas it now was only indomitable self-will and pride.

At any rate, it was an expression that showed that he was not to be conquered by woman, though he might have been won over by her: and Mrs. Lyddell had tact enough to give up the battle without owning herself defeated, and without further discussion said, "Go to your own room, Gerald; I shall give you time to reflect and get the better of your obstinacy. You may come here again when you are ready to ask Miss Morley to forgive you for your very improper conduct towards her."

Without turning to the right or left, — without one look towards his sister, Gerald walked out of the room, and even shut the door after him gently. Poor Marian, who could guess all that she felt?

"This is very extraordinary," said Mrs. Lyddell, "so well-behaved a boy as he is in general."

"Ah! boys of his age always get quite beyond ladies' management," said Miss Morley.

"Such determined obstinacy!" said Mrs. Lyddell.

"Perhaps he did not understand you," said Marian, unable to keep from saying something, though she could not in her agitation think of anything to the purpose.

"Understand? that is nonsense, Marian. What was there to understand? He spoke very improperly, find I desire him to apologise; and if he is obstinate, it is very wrong of you to defend him."

Marian was silenced, though her heart was swelling and her temples throbbing. In another minute Mrs. Lyddell was summoned to some more company, and Marian had nothing worse to hear than her companions' commiseration for the book, and declarations that India rubber would do it no good.

The afternoon passed away, and nothing was heard of Gerald: indeed, Marian understood him well enough to expect that nothing would be heard. As she was on her way to her own room, looking wistfully at his door, Lionel overtook her; and thumping her hard on the back, exclaimed, "Isn't it a jolly beast, Marian?"

"O, Lionel, it was very naughty of you. How could you make

Gerald behave so ill?"

"Never mind, Marian, he will get out of it soon enough. Come, don't be savage; we did it all for your good."

"My good! how can you talk such nonsense?"

"Why, I'll bet you anything you like, that mamma will never be for having the little beastie down to show the company."

Marian half smiled; it was pleasant to find that, towards her at least, the boys' intention had been anything but unkind, but still she hardly knew how to be placable with Lionel when he had led her brother into mischief, and then left him to bear all the blame.

"It was very wrong," she repeated.

"Come, don't be cross, Marian. You don't mean that you really cared for that trumpery picture?"

"I did not care for it so much," said she, "but it was a valuable book, and it was very kind of your papa to give it to me, so I was sorry to have it spoilt."

"Won't it rub out?" said Lionel.

"No, of course not."

"I thought pencil always did."

"And then, Lionel, why could you not have thought what disgrace you were leading Gerald into?"

"You don't think, Marian, I was going to be shabby enough to leave Gerald alone in the scrape? No, if I do, I'll give you leave to tell of me or do whatever you please; but you see now he is not in disgrace for drawing that pretty little beast, but for giving poor unfortunate a bit of his mind, so what use would there be in my putting my neck into the noose before my time? No, if Gerald is the fellow I take him for, and stands out about begging her pardon, the whole business of the book will blow over, and we shall hear no more of it."

Marian shook her head. "O, Lionel, if you would only think whether a thing is right before you do it!"

"How can you wish me to be so stupid, Marian?"

"I am sure, Lionel, the funniest, merriest people that I know, think most about what is right."

"Well, that may do in Devonshire perhaps," said Lionel, stretching himself, "but it won't here except with you. Indeed there is nobody else that I know of that does make such a fuss about right and wrong, except Walter, and he hasn't got an atom of fun to bless himself with."

"But, Lionel, what good will all the fun in the world do us when we come to die?" said Marian, whispering.

The boy looked full at her, but would not show that he felt any force in her words. "I don't mean to die just yet," he said, and by way of escaping from the subject he mounted on the balusters, and was sliding down as he had often done before, when by some hitch or some slip he lost his balance, and slid down without the power to stop himself. Marian thought him gone, and with suspended breath stood, in an agony of horror, listening for his fall on the stones of the hall far beneath; but the next moment she saw that he had been stopped by the turn of the staircase, and the instinct of self-preservation had made him cling fast to the rail with both hands, though he was unable to recover his footing on the narrow ledge of the steps beyond it. She did not scream or call, she ran down to the landing place — how she did it she knew not — but she threw her arms round him and succeeded in lifting and dragging him over the rail, which was not very high, till he stood on the safe side of the balusters, Her heart beat, her head swam, and she was obliged to sit down on the step and pant for breath; Lionel leant against the wall, for his nerve was not restored for a moment or two, after his really frightful peril. Not a word was spoken, and perhaps it was better that none should pass between them. Mr. Lyddell's step was heard ascending, and they both hurried away as fast as they could.

No one was told of the adventure, it was not Marian's part to speak of it, if indeed she *could* have done so, and it did not appear that Lionel chose to mention it. Perhaps it was that he did not like to enter upon it seriously, and it had been too much of an answer to his light speech to be made a laughing matter. At any rate he was silent, and Marian was very glad of it.

Mr. Lyddell was coming up to visit the prisoner and try if he could bring him to reason, but it soon transpired that all his attempts had been in vain, even though he came to a threat that unless Gerald made his submission before the next day was at an end, he should be sent to school with Lionel at the end of another fortnight.

Marian's distress increased, she was equally wretched at her brother's increasing misbehaviour and at its punishment, It was provoking to see Johnny walking about in all the grandeur and self-consequence of being quite out of the scrape, and evidently rejoicing that Gerald was in it; it was provoking to hear Miss Morley and the girls wondering, even Saunders' pity was provoking, and there was nothing that gave her the least comfort but the perception that Lionel was certainly graver and more subdued.

She was allowed to go to her brother for a little while that evening, with some hope that she might prevail with him. She found him leaning against the window in the failing light, listlessly watching the horses and grooms in the mews, which his high window overlooked. He turned his head as she came in, but without speaking, and then looked back at the window, till she came up to him, put her arm round his neck and turned his face towards her. It was a sullen, dogged countenance, such as she had seldom or never seen him wear before.

"Gerald, dear Gerald, what is the meaning of this? You never used to behave so?"

"I never was served so before," muttered he.

"You have drawn it on yourself. Why will you not submit and ask her pardon?"

"What should I ask pardon for? I said nothing but the truth."

"How can you say so. Gerald? Did you not know that you ought not to scribble in books? Can you say that Miss Morley has not often spoken to you about the Atlas?"

"If you call 'O Sir Gerald!' and 'O you sad boy,' desiring me in a rational way, I don't," said Gerald, imitating the tones, "laughing and letting me go on; I thought she liked it."

"Now seriously, Gerald."

"Well, I mean that she did not care. If people tell me a thing they should make me mind them."

"You should mind without being made, Gerald.

"I would if I thought them in earnest. But now, Marian, was it not a horrid shame of her to speak just as if I had been always disobeying her on purpose, making Mrs. Lyddell go into a rage with me for what was entirely her own fault?"

"No, no, Gerald, you cannot say it was her fault that you spoilt the picture."

"I think she ought to beg my pardon for telling such stories about me," repeated Gerald sullenly.

"Recollect yourself, Gerald, you know she meant that she had put you in mind that you ought not; and don't you think that, true or not, your speech was very rude?"

"If I was to beg her pardon it would mean that she spoke the truth, which she did not, for she never took any pains to prevent me from drawing in the map-book, or any where else."

"It would not mean any such thing if you were to say, 'Miss Morley, I misunderstood you, and I am sorry I was so rude.' I am sure you must be sorry for that, for it was not at all like a gentleman. Will you come and say so?"

"You're like the rest," mumbled Gerald, turning his back

upon her, and sitting like a stock.

"Don't you think it would be the best way? Would it not make you happier? O what is the use of being obstinate and disobedient? Think of going to school in disgrace. O! Gerald, Gerald, what is to be done?"

Still she spoke with earnest pauses and anxious looks, but without the least effect, and at last she said, "Well, Gerald, I must go, and very much grieved I am. How would dear mamma like to see her little boy going on in this way?"

She went to the door and looked back again there, and beheld Gerald, with his hands over his face, striving to suppress a burst of sobbing. She sprung to him, and would have thrown her arms round his neck, but he pushed her off roughly, and with strong effort, drove back the tears, and put on an iron face again. Again she entreated, but he would not open his lips or give the least sign of listening, or of attending to any persuasion, and she was obliged to leave him at last without hope of subduing his obstinacy. How far he was now from being the gentle, good child that he once had been! and by whose fault was it? Her spirit burned with indignation against those who, as she thought, had worked the change, and O! where was the influence from which Edmund hoped so much?

The next day was long and miserable, for Gerald gave no sign of yielding, but remained shut up in his room, maintaining an absolute silence, when, at different times, Mrs. Lyddell went to visit him, and assure him that Mr. Lyddell was fixed in his determination to send him to school if he did not yield before the time of grace was up.

The time of grace was at an end the next morning, and at nine o'clock, Gerald was summoned to the dining-room, where Mr. and Mrs. Lyddell were at breakfast. He wanted to carry it off with a high hand, but his long day of solitude had dulled him, and he looked pale and weary.

"Gerald," said Mrs. Lyddell, "I am sorry you have so persisted in your misbehaviour to oblige us to punish you, as we threatened to do. Are you now willing to own that you did wrong?"

"I ought not to have spoilt the book," said Gerald boldly, "and I was rude to Miss Morley."

"There is a brave boy," said Mr. Lyddell, very much relieved. "Well, Gerald, I am glad you have given in at last; I hate obstinacy, as I told you yesterday, but that is over, and we will say no more about it; only you know we told you that you should be sent to school, and we must keep our word."

"Yes," said Gerald, trying not to let a muscle of his face relax; though now the die was cast, his consternation at the thought of school was considerable.

"Well, you may go," said Mr. Lyddell, "and remember that obstinacy must be got out of a boy some way or other."

Gerald went, and soon entered the schoolroom, where he walked up to Miss Morley, saying, "I am sorry I was rude to you the day before yesterday."

"Ah! Sir Gerald, I was sure your better sense — your generous spirit — but I hope your submission — I hope Mr. Lyddell forgives — overlooks —"

"I am to go to school when Lionel does, if that is what you mean," replied Gerald, and then he came up to his sister, and looked earnestly, yet with an inquiring shyness into her face. Marian might have been hopeful, for his manner showed that it was for her opinion that he really cared; but she was sad and unhappy at seeing his pride still so far from being subdued, and though her heart yearned towards him, she shook her head and looked coldly away from him to her book.

Gerald was chilled and went back to Lionel, who had plenty of ready sympathy for him; a story half caught from his mamma's report, half guessed at, that the old lady had looked full at the beast's curly tail, and had said she had never seen anything so like Lady Marchmont; the assertion of his own certainty that Gerald would never give in nor own that poor unfortunate had spoken the truth, and Gerald felt triumphant, as if his self-will had been something heroic, and his imprisonment and going to school a martyrdom. It did not last, Gerald's nature was gentle and retiring; he dreaded strangers, and his heart sank when he thought of school. He wanted his sister to comfort him, but he would soon be out of her reach. No Marian — all boys — all strange, and there was no help for it now. Gerald rested his forehead against the window and gulped down rising tears. But when he found himself on the point of being left alone with Marian, his pride rose, and he would not confess that he had been wrong or that he was unhappy, so he ran down stairs to find the other boys and to get out of her way.

So it went on, Marian was very unhappy at this loss of his confidence; but the more she attempted to talk to him, the more he avoided her, being resolved not to show how great his dislike and dread of school was.

"Gerald," said Lionel, the last day before they were to go, "I have been thinking I should like to give Marian something instead of that book."

"So should I," said Gerald, delighted with the idea, for he was feeling all the time that he was vexing his sister, and wishing to do something by way of compensation.

"I did not mean you," said Lionel, "for it — for you would never have been sharp enough to think of the beast for yourself. I only told you because you could tell me what she would like best. Papa has just given me a sovereign."

"He has given me another," said Gerald, "and we will put them together, and do it handsomely."

"Well, what shall it be? Not that stupid book over again."

"O no, no, she has had enough of that already, and there are plenty of other books that she wants."

"No, don't let it be a book," said Lionel; "I can't think how anybody can like reading, when they can help it."

"Well, I do like some reading, when it is a shipwreck, or a famous bloody battle," said Gerald.

"Yes, but then it makes one's eyes ache so."

"It does not mine."

"Well, if I go on long it always makes mine ache," said Lionel. "And don't the letters look green and dance about, when you read by candle light?"

"No," said Gerald. "How funny that is, Lionel. But I'll tell you what, we will get Walter to take us out, and we shall be sure to see something famous, in some shop-window or other."

Walter was at home for the Easter vacation, and under his protection the boys were allowed to go out. Very patient he was, and wisely did he give his counsel in the important choice which, if left to the boys themselves, might probably have been really something famous. Marian would have been grateful to him, had she known all that he averted from her, a stuffed fox, an immense pebble brooch, a pair of slippers covered with sportive demons. At every shop which furnished guns, knives, or fishing tackle, they stopped and lamented that she was not a boy, there was nothing in the world fit for girls; they tried a bazaar, and pronounced everything trumpery, and Walter was beginning to get into despair, when at last Lionel came to a stop before a print shop, calling out, "Hollo, Gerald, here's Beauty and the Beast itself!"

It was the beautiful engraving from Raphael's picture of

> Saint Margaret in meekness treading
> Upon the dragon 'neath her spreading.

and Walter, rejoicing that their choice was likely to fall on anything which a young lady might be so glad to possess, conducted them into the shop, and gave all the desired assistance in effecting the purchase. It was a fine impression, and the price was so high as to leave the boys' finances at rather a low ebb; but Walter, in his secret soul, thought this by no means to be regretted, since it was much better for them that it should be generously spent at once in this manner, than that it should be frittered away in the unaccountable and vain manner in which he had usually seen schoolboys' money wasted.

So S. Margaret was bought and rolled up, and so afraid were the boys that she should not be rightly sent home, that they insisted on carrying her themselves, and almost quarrelled as to which should have the first turn.

Marian, on coming into her room, found both the boys on the top of the chest of drawers, trying to pin the print up against the wall, and though her arrival caused them some discomfiture, it was on the whole a fortunate circumstance, since it saved the corners from extensive damage.

"O Lionel! O Gerald! how beautiful! how very nice! What a lovely face! Is it really for me? How I do thank you, but I am afraid you have spent all your money."

"It is a better Beauty and the Beast than the old one," said Gerald, "Isn't it, Marian?"

"A better beauty, but not a better beast," said Lionel.

"It is very beautiful indeed," said Marian; "I shall get a frame for it, and it will always put me in mind of you both."

"Yes, you will always think of me when you look at the beauty," said Lionel, "and of Gerald when you look at the beast."

"S. Margaret and the dragon! I wish I knew the story," said Marian; "but I suppose it is an allegory like that of S. George. How good and innocent she looks! Yes, see, Gerald, she is walking pure and white through the park forest, and conquering the dragon. You see the palm in the hand for victory. So innocent and so fearless."

"I thought it would be one of those funny Roman Catholic stories, like what Caroline was reading one day," said Lionel.

"I don't like making fun of those," said Marian. "They often mean a great deal, if you don't laugh at them, and tell them properly. I am sure this print is to put us in mind of how we are to overcome temptation, and I do like it very much. Thank you both."

Lionel was here called away, but Gerald remained, and proceeded to a more minute examination of the beauties of the print, of which he was very proud.

"O, Gerald, dear, if we could be like it," said Marian.

"Like it? That you'll never be, Marian; your hair is too black."

"Yes, but like it within. Pure and clear from sin in the midst of a bad world. I shall look at it and think of that very often, and you must think too, Gerald."

"I mean to be good at school," said Gerald.

And leaning against his sister, he let her talk to him as in times of old, advising him with all her might, for he really liked it, and was comfortable in having it so, though he would have been ashamed to own that he did. Her advice was at once childish and wise; sometimes sensible, sometimes impracticable. Let any sister of fourteen think what counsel she would give a brother of nine if he would but listen to her, and she will have a very fair idea of it. Gerald listened and promised earnestly, and she thought, hoped, and trusted that his promises would be kept: she reminded him of all that could strengthen his resolution, and talked of the holidays with what cheer she might. She had copied out a morning and evening prayer from her own treasured book, rather than give him such another, because she thought he would perhaps heed them more in her handwriting, and she now gave them to him, folded up in a neat little silk case, which he could keep without observation. How she put her arm round him and pressed him towards her as she gave them into his hand, and felt that she was doing what her mother would have done, so earnestly, so tearfully, so much more impressively. O was she watching them now?

The brother and sister were interrupted at last, and called down to tea. The evening passed away heavily, spent as it was for the most part in the drawing-room; and the last thing before the boys went to bed, Lionel pushing Gerald roughly off, held Marian fast by the hand, and whispered in her ear, "I say — you've written out something for Gerald."

"Yes," she answered, horrified that he should have found it out.

"Would you mind doing it for me? Don't tell any one."

Was not this a pleasure? Marian sat up in her dressing-gown that night to write the prayers in her very clearest writing, for she knew Lionel never liked to read what was not large and clear, and she guessed that late in the evening, after all his lessons, he would have too many "green and blue monsters," as he used to call them, before his eyes, to be willing to give them more work than he could possibly help. She thought her mamma would have been very uneasy if she had heard of those green and blue monsters, and she wondered whether Mrs. Lyddell knew or cared about them, but Lionel was one of the least regarded of the family, and nobody but Johnny ever thought it worth while to make a trifling complaint to her. It was far worse that Lionel should be left to obtain a form of private prayer by such a chance as this. Alas! alas for them all! She was too unhappy to think more of Lionel, and in the midst of earnest prayers for Gerald, she cried herself asleep.

Poor child, she was too miserable all the next day to give us any pleasure in contemplating her.

CHAPTER VIII.

"Too soon the happy child
His nook of homeward thought will change;
For life's seducing wild;
Too son his altered day-dreams show
This earth a boundless space,
With sunbright pleasures to and fro,
Coursing in joyous race."
                                        Christian Year.

A couple of weeks had passed away, and Marian was beginning to feel rather more accustomed to the absence of Gerald and Lionel, and to find pleasure in the letters which spoke of her brother taking a good place, and from which it did not appear that he disliked school so much as she had feared. Still she could not but miss him grievously, and feel the want of some one to cling to her, bring his troubles to her, and watch for moments of private conference. Her days seemed to follow each other without animation or interest; and if it had not been for some of her lessons, and for his letters and Agnes Wortley's, she felt as if she could have done nothing but yawn till the holidays.

One day, as the young ladies were returning from a walk in the park, they saw a carriage standing at their own door, — too frequent an occurrence, as Marian thought, to call for such warm interest as Clara expressed. Yet even Marian grew eager when she heard her cousins exclaim that there was a coronet on it, — a Viscount's coronet. They were now close to the house, just about to ring, when the door opened, the visitor came out, and at that moment Marian sprang forward with a joyful face, but without a word. The lady held out both hands, and standing on the top of the steps of the door, she drew Marian up to her, and kissed her on each cheek with great eagerness, completely regardless of the spectators.

"Marian, dear little Marian herself! I was afraid I had quite missed you, though I waited as long as I could. You look like your own self, little pale cheeks! Well, I must not stay; I have arranged with Mrs. Lyddell for you to spend tomorrow with me. I will send the carriage for you, and you know how much I have to show you — my husband and my son! You will come, Marian? Not a word? Ah! your own way. Good-bye; you will find your tongue tomorrow. Good-bye."

She let go the hands and sprang into the carriage, giving a

smile and nod as she drove off, that filled Marian's soul, almost to overflowing, with a rush of memories. It was as if she was no longer standing on the hard steps, with black streets, and tall, dingy yellow houses bounding her view, and carriages thundering in her ears; no longer lonely among numbers, but as if she was on the bright green grass-plat by the Manor-House door, the myrtles and sycamore nodding round her; the shadows of the clouds chasing each other in purple spots over the moors; her father at the window; her mother, Gerald, Edmund, Agnes, all standing round; that sweet voice, with, that same bright smile, that same arch little nod, repeating the "good-bye," and speaking of meeting next year; and Marian herself thinking how very long a year would be. And now two years had passed since that time, and such years! How much older Marian felt! But there was Selina — Selina herself, not the Beauty — that was enough for joy!

Marian was roused from her dream by exclamations of delight and admiration from her cousins, "How very beautiful!" "O, I never saw anything so lovely!" "Marian, how could you say that she was not like her picture?"

"I don't know," said Marian, gradually waking from her trance.

"Don't you think her the most beautiful creature you ever saw?"

"I don't know."

"Don't know!" cried Caroline, impatiently. "Do you know whether your head is on or not?"

"I don't — nonsense," said Marian, laughing heartily, "The fact was, I never had time to look or think whether she was pretty; I only saw she was just like herself."

"Well, Marian; so you met her?" said Mrs. Lyddell's voice in its most delighted tone, at the top of the stairs. "I never saw a more charming person. So very handsome, and so elegant, and so very agreeable. You have heard of her invitation?"

"Yes; thank you for letting me go," said Marian.

"O yes, of course! I am delighted that you should have the advantage of such an acquaintance. I hope it will be quite an intimacy. I am sure whenever — Well, certainly, I never met with anything more fascinating. She spoke of you with such affection, my dear; I am sure she must be the most delightful person!"

Marian was not suffered to proceed up stairs till she had been told all the particulars of Lady Marchmont's visit, and had answered many questions respecting her; and, when she went up to the school-room, it was the same thing. The party there seemed to look upon their good fortune, in having had a sight of her, something as if they had seen the Queen, or "the Duke;" and it was with a sort of awe that Clara pronounced the words "Lady Marchmont," as she talked over every particular of her dress and deportment.

All this in some degree perplexed Marian. Titled ladies were by no means unusual among Mrs. Lyddell's visitors, and did not create anything like this sensation; and she had not been used at home to hear Selina Grenville talked of as anything more than a wild, gay-tempered girl, whose character for wisdom did not stand very high. To be sure she was now married, and that might make a difference; but then Edmund had since spoken of her as giddy, and as if he had not the highest idea of her discretion. Moreover, it struck Marian herself that she had spoken of her husband and child just as if they were two playthings, to be shown off. Of course that was only in fun, but Marian's was the time of life to have great ideas of the requisite gravity of demeanour in a married woman. Altogether, much as she loved Selina, and clever and engaging as she thought her, it astonished her not a little to find that the relationship conferred upon herself such distinction in the eyes of her cousins; and she spent the evening and the next morning alternately in speculations of this kind, hopes of a home-like day, and fears that Selina after all might prove the affected Vis-countess of the Wreath of Beauty.

The time came, the carriage was sent punctually, and in due time Marian was being marshalled up the broad staircase by the tall servants, in all the trepidation of making her first visit in state on her own account, and feeling at every step as if she was getting further into the Wreath of Beauty. Across a great drawing-room, — such a beautiful grand room, — a folding door is opened; "Miss Arundel" is announced, and there she stands in all her stiffness.

There was a little table near the fire, and beside it sat Lady Marchmont, writing notes, in the plainest and most becoming of morning dresses, — a sort of brown holland looking thing, with a plain, stiff, white collar, and a dark blue ribbon, her only orna-ment, except one large gold bracelet. Her hair was twisted in glossy sunny waves behind her ear, as in some Greek statues; her blue eyes were bright and lustrous, and nothing was ever clearer and more delicate than the slight tinge of red on her cheeks. Lord Marchmont was standing leaning on the mantelshelf, apparently in consultation with her.

As soon as Marian entered, Selina's pen was thrown down,

and she flew forward, throwing her arms round her little cousin, and kissing her repeatedly. Then, her arm round Marian's neck, and her hand on her shoulder, she led her towards Lord Marchmont, who stepped forward to receive her, saying, "Yes, here she is, here is your little cousin; and hero, Marian, here is your great cousin. Now I would give five shillings to know what you think of each other."

"I suppose one part of that pleasure will only be deferred till I am out of the room," said Lord Marchmont, as he shook hands with Marian in a kind, cordial, cousinly manner. He was a brown, strong-featured man of three or four and thirty, hardly young enough, and far from handsome enough, in Marian's very youthful eyes, to be suited to his wife, but very sensible and good-natured looking.

"No, Marian is a safe person, and will get no further than 'I don't know;' at least if she is the Marian I take her for," said Lady Marchmont.

"Very prudent," was his answer, smiling at Marian; and then, in compassion to her confusion, gathering up his papers, and pre-paring to depart.

"Are you going?" said his wife. "Well, I do you the justice to say that, under the circumstances, it is the wisest proceeding in your power; for I shall not get three words out of Marian all the time you are here."

After a few more words of consultation on their own affairs, he left the room, and then Selina caught hold of Marian again, and said she must have a thorough good look at her all over, to see how much of dear old Fern Torr she had brought with her.

Selina Grenville was the youngest daughter of a sister of Sir Edmund Arundel, who had, like the rest of her family, died early. She had been a good deal abroad with her father and a married sister. Her uncommon beauty and engaging manners gained her, when she was little more than eighteen, the affection of Lord Marchmont, a more distant connection of the Arundel family; and happily for Selina, she appreciated him sufficiently to return his love so thoroughly, as to lay aside all the little coquetries which had hitherto been the delight of her life; and to devote herself to him even as he deserved.

It might have been that the poem had said too much in pro-nouncing her to be a woman as well as a wife; for Selina Marchmont was almost as much of a child as Selina Grenville had been, and only now and then did those deeper shades of thought pass over her face, which showed how much soul there was within her as yet only half developed. Her manners were almost more playful than suited her position, though they became her perfectly; her husband delighted in them; but it was this that had given her grave and saddened cousin, Edmund, an impression that her sense was not of a high order.

She was very warm-hearted. She had been exceedingly attached to her uncle and aunt at Fern Torr; and now it seemed as if she could never fondle Marian enough. The first thing was to show her baby, but she premised that she did not expect Marian to go into raptures about him; she never did expect any one to like babies. "In fact, Marian," she whispered, "don't betray me, but I am a wee bit afraid of him myself. It is such a very little live thing, and that nurse of his never will let me have any comfort with him, and never will trust me to get acquainted with him in a *tête-à-tête*, poor little man! O, here he comes! the Honourable William James Bertram Marchmont — his name nearly as long as himself."

In came a broad, tall, dignified nurse, large enough to have made at least four Selinas, carrying a small bundle of long white robes. Selina took the little bundle in her arms rather timidly, and held it for Marian to see. Pew babies were ever looked at more silently; he was a small, but pretty, healthy-looking child of between two and three months old, — a very wax doll of a baby, with little round mottled arms moving about, and tiny hands flourishing helplessly, he looked just fit for his mamma. She held him with the fond, proud, almost over care with which little girls take for a moment some new brother or sister; and as she gazed upon him without a word, the earnest intensity of expression gathered upon her beautiful face. After about five minutes thus spent, she roused herself, and began gaily to tell Marian not to trouble herself to seek for a likeness in him to anybody, or to say anything so wild as that he in the least resembled her or his papa; and then she nodded and smiled at him, and seemed as if she would have talked to him and played with him, if his nurse had not been standing close by all the time, looking as if she was being defrauded of her property.

"It is time Master Marchmont should be taken out before the sun goes off, my Lady," said she, authoritatively.

"Very well, I suppose he must," said Selina, reluctantly giving him back again after a timid kiss.

"There goes my lady nurse and her child," said she with a sigh, hidden even from herself by a laugh. "I am sure he seems a great deal more hers than mine; but there, I should never know what to do with him. Come, Marian, now for all about yourself, my poor child. How do they use you?"

Much indeed there was to hear; and much to tell on either side, and scarcely for a moment did the two cousins cease from talking as they sat together in the morning, and drove together in the afternoon. Selina was one of those people who have a wonderful power of dispelling reserve, chiefly by their own frankness; and when she had told Marian all the history of her first sight of Lord Marchmont, and the whole courtship, and all that she had thought "so very noble" in him, and tried to make her understand how very happy she was, Marian's heart was open in her turn. Not the depths of it, — not such things as by a great effort she had told to Edmund, and might possibly tell to Mrs. Wortley, but much more than she could ever have said to any one else; and free and abundant was the sympathy and pity she received, — pity even beyond what she thought she deserved. She was surprised to observe that Selina spoke of the Lyddells with a sort of contempt, as if they were wanting in refinement; whereas she herself had never thought of their being otherwise than lady-like, and certainly very fashionable; but she supposed Lady Marchmont knew best, and was pleased to find herself considered superior. Gerald was of course one of their subjects of conversation, and gradually Marian, with her strict regard to truth, from a little unguardedness, found herself involved in a tangle from which there was no escape, without telling the whole story of the Wreath of Beauty.

She need not have been afraid; Selina laughed as if nothing would ever make her cease, and insisted on Marian's bringing the portrait the next time she came to visit her. She vowed that she would patronise Lionel for ever for his cleverness; and when Marian looked sorrowful about the consequences, she told her that it was much better for Gerald to be at school, and she was very glad he was gone; and then she patted Marian's shoulder, and begged that she would not think her very cruel for saying so.

Marian was very glad to be able to acquit her of vanity, when she heard the history of the insertion of the engraving, which had been entreated for by persons whom Lord Marchmont did not like to disoblige. The engraving both he and Selina disliked very much; and when Marian saw the original portrait, she perceived that the affectation did not reside there, for it was very beautiful, and the only fault to be found with it was chiefly attributable to the fact that miniatures always make people look so pretty, that this did not give the idea of a person so surpassingly lovely as Selina.

Lord Marchmont came in several times to speak to his wife, but Marian did not see much of him till dinner-time, and then she liked him very much. He was certainly rather a grave person, and she wondered to see how Selina could be so merry with him; but he was evidently amused, and Marian had yet to learn how a clever and much occupied man likes nonsense to be talked to him and before him in his hours of relaxation. He behaved to Marian herself very kindly, and just as if she was a grown-up person, — a treat which she had scarcely enjoyed since she left Fern Torr; and though she was silent, as usual when with strangers, it was with no uncomfortable shyness: she was more at ease already with him than with Mr. Lyddell.

Selina told him the history of Gerald's works of art in so droll a manner, that Marian herself saw it in a much funnier aspect than she had ever done before. He was much diverted, and turning to Marian, said, with seriousness that would have alarmed her, but for Selina's laughter, and a certain sub-smile about the corners of his mouth, that he hoped he was not to take the Beast as anything personal. Selina told him that she wanted him to convince Marian that it was a very good thing for Gerald to be sent to school, and he set to work to do so in earnest with much kindness, and by asking sundry questions about her brother's attainments and tastes, he so won her, that she was ready to do him the honour of acknowledging him as one of her own cousins.

The evening came too soon to an end, though the carriage had not been ordered to take Marian home, till ten o'clock. It had all been like one dream of brightness, and Marian, when she awoke the next morning, could hardly believe that it was the truth that she had enjoyed herself so much, and that a house containing such happiness for her could be in London or so near her.

The schoolroom looked very black and dull after the bright little sitting-room where she had parted with Selina; the lessons were wearisome, her companions more uncongenial than ever; she felt actually cross at the examination to which Clara subjected her about every trifle she could think of, in the house of Marchmont. She could have talked of its delights if there had been anybody to care about them in her own way, but that was the great if of Marian's life. She was conscious that her day's pleasure had unhinged her, and made her present tasks unusually distasteful, and she thought it the fault of the Lyddells, and in a great fit of repining blamed Edmund for injustice to Selina in not letting her house be their home. Her great hope was of another day there, the only thing that seemed to give a brightness to her life, and she looked forward to an intercourse between Lady Marchmont and Mrs. Lyddell, which would produce continual meetings.

However, time passed on, and she did not see Selina. Mrs. Lyddell took her when she went to return the visit, but Lady Marchmont was not at home. It was not till after more than a fortnight that she received a little note from her, saying that they were going to a show of flowers, and would send for Marian to go with them.

There was quite a commotion in the house on the occasion; not that all were not willing that Marian should go, but that Mrs. Lyddell thought her dress not at all fit; the plain straw bonnet which Marian *would* buy, in spite of all that could be said to the contrary, and that old black silk dress which did very well just for going to Church in, with a governess, but —

Mrs. Lyddell and Saunders were for once in their lives agreed; and Marian, who thought her money would have served her this time to fulfil her grand scheme of buying Tytler's History of Scotland, was overpowered, and obliged to let them have their will, and wear it outside her head, in white silk; instead of inside, in Robert Bruce's wanderings.

She was quite ready, in new bonnet and mantle, by the time Lady Marchmont's carriage was at the door, and very happy she was to find herself by her side again. Perhaps there was a little consciousness of newness in the manner in which she wore them, for Lady Marchmont remarked upon them, and said that they were very pretty, as in fact they were. Marian looked disconsolate, and Selina laughingly asked why. She told her former wishes, and was further laughed at, or rather Mrs. Lyddell was. Selina said the old bonnet would have done just as well; "it was so like such people to smarten up for a great occasion."

Such people! Marian wondered again, and disliked her white bonnet more than ever, resolving for the future to trust her own taste. She soon forgot all this, however, in the pleasure of seeing green grass and trees, and the beautiful, most beautiful flowers, with their delicious perfume. This was real delight, such as she had never imagined before, and she thought she could have studied the wonderful forms of those tropical plants for ever, if it had not been for the crowds of people, and for a little awe of Lord Marchmont, who had given her his arm, and who did not seem to know or care much even for the dove orchis or the zebra-striped pitcher-plant. She wished she could turn him into Edmund, and looked at every plant which she fancied a native of the Cape, almost as kindly as if it had been a primrose of Fern Torr.

It was another delightful day. Marian went back with her friends, and sat by while Selina was dressed for an evening party, heard a description of her home in the country, and gave a very unflattering one of Oakworthy, gained somehow or other a renewed impression of her own superiority to the Lyddells, and went home to indulge in another fit of discontent.

Such were Marian's visits to Lady Marchmont, and such their effect. Mrs. Lyddell did much indeed that was calculated to give strength to the feeling by the evident pride which she took in Marian's familiarity with Lady Marchmont, and even in the cold, distant, formal civility with which she herself was treated.

There was danger around Marian which she did not understand, the world was tempting her in a different way. She disliked what she saw among the Lyddells too much to find their worldly tastes and tempers infectious, but her intercourse with Selina was a temptation in a new form. She loved Selina so heartily as to see with her eyes, and be led by her in opinions: especially when these were of a kind according with her own character. It was from her that Marian imbibed the idea that she was to be pitied for living in her present home, not because Mrs. Lyddell's mind was set on earth and earthly things, but because she did not belong to those elite circles which Marian learnt to believe her own proper place. Edmund had told her she might stand on high ground, and she believed him, but was this such high ground as he meant? The danger did not strike Marian, because it did not seem to her like pride, since the distinction, whatever it was, did not consist in rank; she would have had a horror of valuing herself on being a baronet's daughter, but this more subtle difference flattered her more refined feelings of vanity; and though she was far from being conscious of it, greatly influenced her frame of mind, and her conduct towards her cousins. It was not without reason now that Caroline thought her proud.

It must not, however, be supposed that this was Marian's abiding frame of mind; it was rather the temper which was infused into her by each successive visit to Selina during the next three years. Of course, every time it was renewed, it was also strengthened, but it was chiefly her London disposition, and used in great degree to go off when she was taken up with the interests of Oakworthy, and removed from the neighbourhood of Lady Marchmont.

Oakworthy was so preferable to London, except so far as that she was there out of Selina's reach, that she began to have a kindness for it. She knew some of the poor people there, in whom Caroline had kept up an interest ever since Miss Cameron's time; the smoky streets of London had taught her to prize the free air and green turf of the Downs; and, thanks to Edmund, her own dear Mayflower awaited her there, and she enjoyed many a canter with Caroline and Walter. She began for the first time to become acquainted with the latter, and to learn to look upon him with high esteem, but to obtain a knowledge of him was a very difficult matter. He was naturally diffident and bashful, and his spirits were not high; he had been thrown more and more into himself by his mother's hastiness of manner and his father's neglect. His principles were high and true, his conduct excellent, and as he had never given any cause for anxiety, he was almost always overlooked by the whole family. Nor was he clever, and the consciousness of this added to his timidity, which being unfortunately physical as well as mental, caused him to be universally looked down upon by his brothers. Even Marian began to share the feeling when she saw him turn pale and start back from the verge of a precipitous chalk pit where she could stand in perfect indifference, and when she heard him aver his preference for quiet horses. Mayflower's caperings were to him and Caroline so shocking, and it appeared to them so improper that she should be allowed to mount such an animal, that but for her complete ease, her delight in the creature's spirit, and her earnest entreaties, a complaint against Mayflower would certainly have been preferred to the authorities.

In spite of all this, there was satisfaction in talking to Walter, for he saw things as Marian did, right and wrong were his first thoughts, and his right and wrong were the same as hers. This was worth a great deal to her, though she was often provoked with him for want of boldness in condemnation. A man grown up could, she thought, do so much to set things to rights, if he would but speak out openly, and remonstrate, but Walter shrank from interfering in any way; it seemed to cost him an effort even to agree with Marian's censure. Yes, she thought, as she stood looking at the print of S. Margaret, Walter might pass by the dragon, nay, fight his own battle with it, but he would never tread it manfully under, so that it might not rise to hurt others. He might mourn for the sins around him, but would he ever correct them? Marian thought if she was a man, a man almost twenty, destined to be a clergyman, she had it in her soul to have done great things; then she would not be shy, for she should feel it her duty to speak.

In the meantime, Marian had a trouble of her own, a sore place in her heart, and in its tenderest spot, for Gerald was the cause. The first holidays had been all she could desire; he was affectionate, open, full of talk about home and Edmund, with the best of characters; and with the exception of all the other boys being "fellows" and nameless, there was nothing like reserve about him; but the next time, he had not been three days in the house, before she perceived that the cloud had come down again, which had darkened the last few weeks before his going to school. He avoided being alone with her, he would not let her ask him questions, he talked as if he despised his governors and teachers, and regarded rules as things made to be eluded. His master's letter did not give a satisfactory account of him, and when Marian tried to fish out something about his goings on from Lionel, she met with impenetrable silence, Lionel himself seemed to be going through school pretty much in the same way, with fits and starts of goodness, and longer intervals of idleness, but he made his eyes a reason, or an excuse, for not doing more. They were large, bright, blue, expressive eyes, and it was hard to believe them in fault, but strong sunshine or much reading by candle-light always brought the green and purple monsters, and sometimes a degree of inflammation. It was said that he must be careful of them, and how much of his idleness was necessary, how much was shirking, was a question for his own conscience.

Every time Gerald came home, Marian saw something more that pained her. There was the want of confidence that grew more evident every time, though it was by no means want of affection; it was vain to try to keep him away from the stables; he read books on Sunday which she did not approve, she did not think he wrote to Edmund, and what made her more uneasy than all was, that Elliot was becoming the great authority with him. Elliot had begun to take a sort of distant patronising notice of hint, which seemed to give him great pleasure, and which Marian who every year had reason to think worse of Elliot, considered very dangerous. She could not bear to see Gerald search through, the newspapers for the racing intelligence, and to see him orating scientifically to Lionel and Johnny about the points of the horses; she did not like to see him talking to the gamekeepers, and set her face, more than was perhaps prudent, against all the field sports which were likely to lead him into Elliot's society.

In her zeal against this danger, she forgot how keen a sportsman Edmund himself was, and spoke as if she thought these amusements wrong altogether, and to be avoided, and this, together with the example of Walter, gave Gerald a very undesirable idea of the dulness of being steady and well conducted. That he spent more money than was good for him, was also an idea of hers gathered from chance observations of her own, and unguarded words of the other boys; but this was one of the points on which his reserve was the strictest, and she only could be anxious in ignorance. The holidays, anticipated with delight, ended in pain, though still she cherished a hope that what alarmed her might be boyish thoughtlessness of no importance in itself, and only magnified by her fears.

She was encouraged in this by finding that Lord Marchmont, when he saw him once in London, thought him a very fine, promising boy, and that Mr. and Mrs. Lyddell did not seem to see anything seriously amiss. But then Lord Marchmont had not seen enough of him to be able to judge, and would not have told her even if he had thought there probably was anything wrong; and she could not trust to Mr. and Mrs. Lyddell. It was very painful to imagine herself unjust to her only brother, and she drove the fears away; but back they would always come, every time Gerald was at home, and every time she looked and longed in vain for a letter from him.

Thus passed, as has already been said, three years, spent for the most part without event. Caroline, at eighteen, was introduced; but though her evenings were given to company, her mornings were still spent in the schoolroom, of which indeed she was the chief brightness. Marian, though she had the offer of coming out at the same time, was very glad to embrace the alternative of waiting another year. She was now a little past her seventeenth birthday, which emancipated her from being absolutely Miss Morley's pupil. She breakfasted with the rest of the family, dined with them when there was not a large party, learnt more of masters, and studied more on her own account than she had ever done before; and only depended on Miss Morley and Clara for companionship in walking and meals, when Caroline was otherwise engaged.

She was more with the Marchmonts than ever during this spring. She rode with them, kept Selina company when her husband went out without her; went about with her wherever a girl of woman's height, though not yet come out, could be taken; and was almost always at any of her dinners or evening parties, where she could have the pleasure of seeing anything that was distinguished. It was a very pleasant life; for she was new to the liberty of being loosed from schoolroom restraints, and at the same time the restraints and duties of society had not laid hold upon her. Among Selina's friends she was not expected to talk, and could listen in peace to the conversation of the very superior men Lord Marchmont brought around him; or if she chanced to exchange a few words with any of them, she remembered it afterwards as a distinction. Selina, with all the homage paid to her beauty, her rank, her fascination of manner, and her husband's situation, was made much of by all, and was able to avoid being bored, without affronting any one; and a spoilt child of fashion herself, in her generosity and affection, she made Marian partake her pleasures, and avoid annoyances as far as she could, like herself. It was a pleasant life, and Marian thoroughly enjoyed it but was it a safe one?

CHAPTER IX.

"So too may soothing Hope thy leave enjoy,
Sweet visions of long severed hearts to frame;
Though absence may impair or cares annoy,
Some constant mind may draw us still the same."
                                                    Christian Year.

"**H**ere are two letters for you, Marian," said Mrs. Lyddell, meeting the girls as they came in from a walk; "Lady Marchmont's servant left this note."

"An invitation to dinner for this evening," said Marian opening it; "ah! I knew they were to have a party; 'just recollected that Lady Julia Faulkner used to know Fern Torr, and I must have you to meet her, if it is not a great bore.'"

"Then, my dear, had you not better send an answer? James can take it directly."

"No, no, thank you; the carriage will call at seven. Who can this Lady Julia be? But —" by this time Marian had arrived at her other letter, and, with a sudden start and scream of joy, she exclaimed, "They are coming!"

"Coming? Who?" asked Caroline.

"Agnes — and Mr. and Mrs. Wortley! O! All coming to stay with their friends in Cadogan Place. I shall see them at any time I please."

"I am very glad of it," said Caroline.

"Tell them that their earliest engagement must be to us," said Mrs. Lyddell. "When do you expect them?"

"Next week, next week itself," cried Marian, "to stay a whole fortnight, or perhaps three weeks. Mr. Wortley has business which will occupy him —"

Few faces ever expressed more joy than Marian's in the prospect of a meeting with these dearest of friends; Mrs. Lyddell and Caroline smiled at her joy as she flew out of the room to make Saunders a partaker in her pleasure.

"Strange girl," said Caroline; "so cold to some, so warm to others; I shall be glad to see these incomparable Wortleys."

"So shall I," said Mrs. Lyddell; "but I expect that Marian's opinion of them will soon alter, she has now become used to such different society. However we must be very civil to them, be they what they may."

In the meantime Marian penned a letter to Agnes, in terms of delight and affection twenty times warmer than any which had ever passed her lips, and then resigned herself to Saunders' hands to be dressed, without much free will on her own part; too excited to read as usual during the operation, sometimes talking, sometimes trying to imagine Agnes in London, a conjunction which seemed to her almost impossible.

The carriage came for her, and in due time she was entering the great drawing-room, where Selina, looking prettier than ever in her evening dress, sat reading a novel and awaiting her guests.

"O Selina, only think," she began; "the Wortleys are coming!"

"What say you? Why, Marian, you are in a wild state. Who are coming?"

"The Wortleys, Selina, my own Agnes."

"O, your old clergyman's daughter! You constant little dove, you don't mean that you have kept up that romantic friendship all these years?"

"Why, Selina!"

"Yes, yes, I remember all about them now: the daughter was your great friend."

"She was more yours," said Marian, "when you were at Fern Torr, because you were more nearly the same age. Don't you remember how you used to whisper under the sycamore tree, and send me out of the way?"

"Poor little Marian! Well, those were merry times, and I rather think your Agnes promised to be very pretty."

"And shall not you be glad to see her?"

"When do they come?"

"Next Monday, to — Cadogan Place."

"Close to you. Well, that is lucky; but now, my dear, if you can come down from the clouds for a moment, I want to tell you about Lady Julia."

"Who is she?" said Marian, bringing back her attention with an effort.

"A tiresome woman," whispered Selina, with a sort of affectation of confidence; "but the fact is, Lord Marchmont used to know her husband, or his father, or his great grandfather, sometime in the dark ages, and so be wants me to make much of her. She is one of the people that it is real toil to make talk for; but by good fortune I remembered that I had heard some legend about her once knowing my uncles, and so I thought that a cross-examination of you about Gerald and Fern Torr would be a famous way of filling up the evening."

"O!" said Marian in a not very satisfied tone, "so she has a husband, has she? I fancied from your note that she only consisted of herself,"

"She consists of a son and daughters," said Selina.

"Her husband is dead, but the rest of the house you will presently see."

"Eh?" said Lord Marchmont, coming out of the other room where he had been writing, and greeting Marian.

"You don't mean that you have invited that young Faulkner?"

"You would, not have me leave out the only agreeable one of the party — something to sweeten the infliction."

Lord Marchmont smiled at the arch, bold, playful manner with which she looked up in his face, as if to defy him to be displeased; but still he was evidently vexed, and said, "It is hard upon Marian only to take her from Elliot Lyddell's society to bring her into Mr. Faulkner's."

"Indeed! but that is hard on Mr. Faulkner," said his wife. "As to worth, I suppose he and Marian's cousin are pretty much on a par, but it is but justice to say that he has considerably the advantage in externals."

"It cannot be helped now," said Lord Marchmont; "but I wish I had told you before, Selina. The esteem I had for that young man's father would make me still more reluctant to cultivate him, considering his present way of going on."

"Well, one invitation to dinner is not such a very agricultural proceeding, that you need waste such a quantity of virtuous indignation," said Selina; "I daresay he will not grow *very* much the faster for it."

The arrival of some of the party put a stop to the conversation, and presently Lady Julia Faulkner, Mr. and Miss Faulkner, were announced. The first was a fair, smooth, handsome matron, who looked as if she had never been preyed upon by either thought or care; her daughter was a well-dressed, fashionable young lady; and her son, so gentlemanlike and sensible looking, as to justify Lady Marchmont in saying that in externals he had the advantage of Elliot Lyddell. Marian sat next him at dinner, and though she meant to dislike him, she could not succeed in doing so; he talked with so much spirit and cleverness of the various exhibitions and other things, which are chiefly useful as food for conversation. Something too might be ascribed to the store of happiness within her, which would not let her be ungracious or unwilling to let herself be entertained, for on the whole, she had never been so well amused at a dinner party.

In the drawing-room the examination took place with which she had been threatened, but she had grown hardened to such things with time, and could endure them much better than she used to do. It was always the custom for her to outstay the guests, so as to talk them over with her cousins; and, on this occasion the first exclamation was, how very agreeable and clever Mr. Faulkner was.

"So much the worse," said Lord Marchmont gravely; "I think worse of him than I did before, for I find he has taken up Germanism."

Marian had some notion that Germanism meant that the foundations of his faith were unsettled, and she looked extremely horrified, but she had not time to dwell on the subject, for the carriage came to the door, and she was glad to be alone to hug herself with delight. The gas lamps looked as bright to her eyes as if there were an illumination specially got up in honour of her happiness, and the drive to Mr. Lyddell's was far too short to settle a quarter of what Agnes was to see and do.

It was almost four years since she had parted with her, but the correspondence had scarcely slackened, nor the earnestness of her affection and confidence diminished. There was no one, excepting Edmund, to whom she could look for counsel in the same manner, and the hope of long conversations with Mrs. Wortley was almost as delightful as the thought of seeing Agnes once more.

She had begged them to call the first thing, and accordingly soon after breakfast one fine Tuesday morning, a loud double-knock caused her heart to leap into her mouth, or rather her throat, and almost choke her. Mrs. Lyddell, Elliot, and Caroline were all present, and she wished them forty miles off, when the announcement was the very thing she wished to hear!

There they were, Mrs. Wortley giving that fond, motherly kiss, Agnes catching both hands, and kissing both cheeks, Mr. Wortley giving one hearty squeeze to her hand! There they really were, she was by Mrs. Wortley's side, their own familiar tones were in her ears! She hardly dared to look up, for fear Agnes should be altered, but no, she could not call her altered, though she was more formed, the features were less childish, and there was more thought, though not less life and light than of old, in the blue eyes. Indeed it came upon Marian by surprise, that she had not known before that Agnes was uncommonly pretty as well as loveable. She was surprised not to see her friend more shy, but able to answer Elliot's civilities with readiness and ease; whereas she who still felt stiff and awkward with a stranger, had supposed that such must be doubly the case with one who had lived so much less in the world.

That day was to be devoted by the Wortleys to visits and business, but they reckoned on having Marian to themselves all the next, and were to call for her early on their way to some of the sights of London. Mrs. Lyddell made them fix an early day for coming to dinner, and they took their leave, Marian feeling as if the visit had not been everything that she expected, and yet as if it was happiness even to know that the same city contained herself and them.

No sooner were they gone than the Lyddells began with one voice to admire Agnes, even Elliot was very much struck with her, and positively gained himself some degree of credit with Marian, by confirming her opinion of her friend's beauty. It was delightful indeed that Agnes should be something to be proud of; Marian would not have loved her one whit the less if she had been a plain, awkward country girl, but it was something to have her affection justified in their eyes, and to have no fear of Agnes being celebrated only for her cricket.

They called for Marian early the next morning, and now she received the real greeting, corresponding to her parting, as Mrs. Wortley's second daughter. Then began the inquiries for everything at Fern Torr, animate or inanimate, broken into by Agnes's exclamations of surprise at everything new and wonderful in the streets, a happy, but a most desultory conversation.

At last they got into a quiet street where Mr. and Mrs. Wortley went to choose a carpet, and the two girls were left to sit in the carriage.

"O Marian!" began Agnes, "so you have not quite lost your old self! I am glad to see how it all is at least, for I have something tangible to pity you for."

"I wonder what it is," said Marian, too happy for pity at that moment.

"O, my dear! that Mr. Elliot Lyddell!"

"He is hardly ever in my way," said Marian.

"And his sister! Her dress! What study it must have taken! In the extreme of fashion."

"Caroline's dress is not exactly what she would choose herself," said Marian.

"That must be only an excuse, Marian; for though you have a well-turned-out look, it is not as if you were in a book of fashions."

"I am not Mrs. Lyddell's daughter, and though I do expect a battle or two when I come out, it will not be a matter of obedience with me, as it is with Caroline."

"Is it very painful obedience?" said Agnes laughingly; "well, you do deserve credit for not being spoilt among such people."

"In the first place, how do you know they are 'such people?' and next, how do you know I am not spoilt?"

"You must be the greatest hypocrite in the world, if you are spoilt, to write me such letters, and sit so boldly looking me in the face. And as to their being 'such people,' have not I seen them, have not I heard them, and, above all, has not Mr. Arundel given me their full description?"

"But that was three years and a half ago," said Marian.

"And have they changed since then?" asked Agnes.

"I don't know."

"O how glad I am to hear that!" cried Agnes. "Never mind them; but to hear you say 'I don't know' in that old considering tone is proof enough to me that you are my own old Marian, which is all I care for."

"I don't —" began Marian; then stopping short and laughing, she added, "I mean I was thinking whether it is really so. Can any person live four years without changing? Especially at our age. What a little girl I was then!"

"Yes, to be sure, you have grown into a tall — yes, quite a tall woman, and you have got your black hair into a very pretty broad braid, and you wear a bracelet and carry a parasol, and don't let your veil stream down your back; I don't see much more alteration. Your eyes are as black and your face as white, and altogether you are quite as provoking as ever in never telling one anything that one wishes to know."

Marian gave a stiff smile, one which she had learnt in company, and grew frightened at herself to find that she was treating Agnes, as she treated the outer world. She did not know what to say; her love was deep, strong and warm within, but it was too soon to "rend the silken veil;" and this awkwardness, this consciousness of coldness was positive suffering. She was relieved that the return of Mr. and Mrs. Wortley put an end to the *tête-à-tête*, then shocked that it should be a relief; for, poor girl, her extreme embarrassment overpowering the happiness in her friend's presence, made her doubt whether it could be that her affection was really departing, a thought too dreadful to be dwelt upon.

Who would have told her that she should endure so much pain in her first drive with the Wortleys?

They went to call on Lady Marchmont that day, and, as Marian expected, did not find her at home. Agnes renewed the old lamentation that Marian could not live with her and thus avoid Mrs. Lyddell's finery and fashion. "Now why do you laugh, Marian? you don't mean that Selina Grenville can have turned into a fashionable lady? she was the simplest creature in the world."

"She is what she was then," said Marian; "but as to being fashionable — . My dear Agnes, you don't understand."

"We have not to reproach Marian for want of knowledge of the world now, Agnes," said Mr. Wortley, smiling at his daughter's bewildered look.

"Ah!" cried Marian, and there stopped, thinking how grievously she must be altered, since this was the reproach that the Lyddells used so often to make her. Some wonderful sight here engaged Agnes, and Marian's exclamation fell unheeded.

She spent a good many hours with the Wortleys while they were in London, but usually in the midst of confusion and bustle: Mr. and Mrs. Wortley were busy, and Agnes almost wild with the novelties around. Marian's heart ached as she recollected a saying which she had read, that a thread once broken can never be united again. Her greatest comfort was in the prospect of a visit to Fern Torr; for Mrs. Lyddell willingly consented to her accepting Mrs. Wortley's invitation to return with them, and to stay even to the end of her brother's holidays, which he was also to spend at *home*. She should know better there whether she was really changed; she could take it all up again there, and now she could afford to wait, and not feel the necessity of saying everything that would not be said in so short a time.

One thing was certain, she did not like to hear Agnes talk against the Lyddells. She could have done it herself; nay, she did so sometimes when with Lady Marchmont, but then that was only about "nonsense." She had lived with them too long, had shared in too many of their conversations and employments, was, in fact, too much one of the family, to like to hear them condemned. She thought it very strange, and she could not tell whether it was from having grown like them, or from a genuine dislike to injustice; at any rate it was this which convinced her that she had come to regard them in some degree as friends.

She wished them to appear to as much advantage as possible, but this they really seemed resolved not to do, at least not what was in her eyes and those of the Wortleys, to advantage. Mrs. Lyddell *would* have a grand dinner party to do honour to her friends, and the choice of company was not what she would have made. To make it worse, Elliot sat next Agnes, Walter was not at home, and the conversation was upon religious subjects, which had better not have been discussed at all in such a party, and which were viewed by most present, in the wrong way. All this, however, Marian could have endured, for she did not care to defend Mr. and Mrs. Lyddell or Elliot, individually, only when considered as forming part of "the Lyddells," but she really wished Agnes to like Caroline and Clara.

She did not know whether Agnes was not perverse about Caroline, whom she continued to call a mere fashionable young lady, not being able to find any other reproach than this vague one; but as to Clara, Marian herself could have found it in her heart to beat her when she made sillier speeches than usual in Agnes' hearing, and, above all, for having at this time a violent fit of her affection for Marian herself, whom she perseveringly called a dear girl, and followed about so closely as to be always in the way.

Marian would have been still more provoked with Clara, had Agnes not had forbearance enough to abstain from telling her all that Clara had said, when once, by some chance, left alone with her for ten minutes. After a great deal about her extreme friendship for "dearest Marian," she said, "Some people think her pretty, — do you, Miss Wortley?"

"Not exactly pretty," said Agnes, "but hers is a fine face."

"Ah! she has not colour enough to be pretty. She is much too pale, poor dear, but some people say that is aristocratic. And she is like her cousin, Lady Marchmont, the beauty. Do you know Lady Marchmont?"

"I used to know her as a girl."

"Ah! she is very handsome, and so much the fashion. It is such an advantage for Marian to be there, and I hope she will slyly bring us acquainted some of these days. But then all the Arundels are proud; Marian has a good deal of pride in her own way, though she is a dear girl!"

"Marian!" exclaimed Agnes.

"O yes! She is a dear girl, but every one in Wiltshire speaks of her pride; all our friends do, I assure you. I always defend her, of course, but every one remarks it."

Agnes was wondering whether simply to disbelieve anything so preposterous as that all Wiltshire should be remarking on poor Marian's pride, or whether to explain it by her well-known shyness, when Clara made another sudden transition. "Do you know Mr. Arundel?"

"O yes."

"Is not he a fine, distinguished looking man? We did admire

him so when he was here. I assure you we are all quite jealous of Marian. Miss Morley says there can be but one *dénouement*."

Here Marian came into the room, and Agnes proceeded to question within herself which was most wonderful, — the extreme folly of Clara, or of the governess.

Another vexation to Marian was the behaviour of Lady Marchmont. She herself was invited as often as usual to come to her cousin, but she could not spare a minute from her dear friends, and only was surprised and vexed that they were not included, and that Selina had not yet called upon them. She knew that one of her parties consisted of persons whom Mr. Wortley would have been particularly glad to meet, and she watched most anxiously for a card for him; she even went so far, as in her own note of refusal to give a very far distant hint, thinking that Selina only required to be put in mind of his being in London.

At last, only two days before they left town, Lady Marchmont left her card for Mrs. Wortley, but without asking if she was at home; and Marian, who was in the house at the time, felt the neglect most acutely. Mrs. Wortley saw the bright glow of red spread all over the pale check, and was heartily sorry on her account. Agnes broke out into exclamations that there must be a mistake, — the servants must have misunderstood, and she would have asked questions; but Marian said, in a voice of deep feeling, "No, Agnes, it is no mistake. You understand me now when I say Selina Marchmont is more of a fine lady than Mrs. Lyddell. But O, I never thought she would have neglected you!"

"Say no more, my dear," said Mrs. Wortley; "Lady Marchmont must have too many engagements to attend to us dull country folks. Indeed, it gives me no pain, my dear, except to see it grieve you. You know she has done her duty by us."

"Her duty by herself, she may think," said Marian, "in not doing what would be called rude, but not her duty by you; you, to whom all who ever — who ever loved *them*, owe so much."

The tears glittered in Marian's eyes, and her cheek was flushed.

"Marian, my dear, cool down a little," said Mrs. Wortley; "think how long it is since Lady Marchmont knew us, and recollect that the — the causes, which you think you have for caring for us, may not appear the same to her. She only thinks of us as dimly remembered neighbours of her cousin's, coming to London for a little while; she is full of engagements, and has no time for us, and just follows the fashions of other people."

"That is it," said Marian. "How shall I ever wish her good-bye in charity?"

They were interrupted; and it was not till Marian was gone that Agnes had the satisfaction of a full outbreak of indignation at all fine ladies, and of triumph in the impossibility of their ever spoiling her own dear Marian.

Marian had to spend the evening with the Marchmonts, and she was more constrained with them at first than she had ever been before. Yet it was not easy to continue constrained with Selina, who was perfectly unconscious that she had given any offence; and the feeling was quite removed by half an hour's play with little Willy, who was now promoted to be a drawing-room child for various short intervals of the day. He was under a nursery governess, who let his mamma have a little more property in him.

Selina asked about the intended journey, and thus renewed Marian's feeling of the wrongs of the Wortleys; but when Selina scolded her for not coming oftener, supposed she had been very happy, and envied her for going to dear old Fern Torr, Marian began to forgive, and did so quite when she wished she could have seen them, and lamented that she had been so much engaged. Three times she had gone out, fully meaning to call on them, and have a good long chat, but each time something delayed her; and the last, and fourth, she really was obliged to be at home early, and could not possibly make a call.

The charm of manner made all this appease Marian; but when the immediate spell of Selina's grace and caressing ways was removed, she valued it rightly, and thought, though with pain, of the expressive epithet, "fudge!" Could not Selina have gone to her aunt's old friends if she would? Had not Marian known her to take five times the trouble for her own gratification? Marian gained a first glimpse of the selfishness of refined exclusiveness, and doubted whether it had not been getting a hold of herself, when she had learnt of Selina to despise and neglect all that was unpleasing.

O the joy of knowing that she should turn her back on the great wicked world again, and measure herself by the old standard of home! And yet she trembled, lest she should find that the world had touched her more than she had thought.

CHAPTER X.

"Yes, friends may be kind, and vales may be green,
And brooks, may sparkle along between;
But it is not friendship's kindest look,
Nor loveliest vale, nor clearest brook,
That can tell the tale which is written for me
On each old face and well known tree."

R. H. FROUDE.

It was a happy day for both Agnes Wortley and Marian Arundel when they again entered Devonshire. Agnes seemed to feel her four weeks as serious an absence as Marian did her four years, and was even more rapturous in her exclamations at each object that showed her she was near home.

They walked up the last and steepest hill, or rather bounded along the well known side path, catching at the long trailing wreaths of the dogrose, peeping over the gates which broke the high hedge, where Marian, as she saw the moors, could only relieve her heart by pronouncing to herself those words of Manzoni's Lucia, *"Vedo i miei monti."* ("I see my own mountains.") She beheld the woods and the chimneys of the Manor House, but she shrank from looking at it, and gazed, as if she feared it was but a moment's vision, at the rough cottages, the smoke curling among the trees, the red limestone quarry, and the hills far away in the summer garb of golden furze. It was home, her heart was full, and Agnes respected her silence.

Down the hill, along the well-known paling, past the cottages, the dear old faces smiling welcome; the Church, always the same, the green rail of the Vicarage garden, the paint was the only thing new; the porch, with roses hanging thicker over it than ever; Ranger, David Chapple, Jane, the housemaid, all in ecstasy in their different ways.

That first evening was spent in visiting every nook of the garden with Agnes, and hearing the history of each little innovation; then, after a slight interval of sleepiness, came those fond, cordial "good nights," which dwell no where but at home.

She woke to the reality of a Fern Torr Sunday, not to shake off with disappointment and wearinesss, the dream of such a day. There was the pinkthorne, dressed in all its garlands, before her window, the dew lying heavy and silvery on the grass; the cart-horses enjoying their holiday in the meadow, the mass of blossom in the orchard, the sky above, all blueness, the air full of a delicious quietness, as if the sunshine itself was repose, Marian leant out at her window, and wondered if it was possible she should have been so long away, so familiar, so natural did it all seem.

The hurried breakfast, the walk to school, the school itself, how well she knew it all, and within the school how old a world it was, and yet how new! The benches, the books, the smiles, the curtsies, the very nosegays, redolent of southernwood, were unchanged, but all the great good girls of her day, the prime first class, where was it? Here was the first class still, Agnes' pride; but, behold, these are the little ones of her day, and the babies for whom she had made pink frocks and frilled caps, now stared up in her face responsible beings, who could say more than half the Catechism. Her own little pets of school-days were grown out of knowledge into the uninteresting time of life, the "old age of childhood," and looked as if they found it equally difficult to recognize "little Miss" in a lady taller than Miss Wortley. Next followed the walk to Church, full of meetings and greetings, admiration of her growth, and inquiries after Sir Gerald.

Yes, Marian did feel like the old self: her four years' absence was like a dream that had passed away, and was nothing to her; she could think only of home, home thoughts and home interests; the cares and the teasings, the amusements and the turmoils of Oakworthy and London, were as things far distant, which had never really concerned her, or belonged to some different state of existence. She was at home, as she continually said to herself; she felt as if she was in some way more in the presence of her parents, as if their influence was sheltering her, and shielding her from all external ill, as in the days of yore. Happy they who can return after four years' trial as Marian did.

She was preparing for Confirmation; for, to her great joy, she was in time to form one of Mr. Wortley's own flock, He gave her half an hour every other morning; and now it was that all the difficulties raised in her mind in arguments with Caroline, doubts with right or wrong, or questions why and wherefore, were either solved or smoothed down. Her principles were strengthened, her views were cleared up; she learnt the reasons of rules she had obeyed in ignorance, and perceived her own failures and their causes.

These were her graver hours. At other times she read, drew, and studied German with Agnes, who gladly availed herself of the aid of one well crammed by London masters, and who could not but allow, even to the credit of her enemies, that they had made Marian very accomplished.

There were long walks to every well-remembered hill and dell, with further expeditions planned against the return of the boys, and numerous visits to old friends at the cottages to present Marian's gifts, which had fairly overpowered Saunders' powers of packing. Delightful walks, how different from the parade on the chalk roads, over high hedges, through gaps doubly fenced with thorns, scrambling, at the risk of neck us well as of dress, over piles of fern and ivy-covered rocks, or hopping across brooks on extemporised stepping-stones, usually in the very thick of some *mauvais pas*, discussing some tremendous point of metaphysics or languages and breaking off in it to scream at the beauty of the view, or to pity a rent muslin.

Marian and Agnes talked considerably now, and, allowing for the difference in age, just as they used to do. Marian's fears of her own coldness and doubts of her confidence in Agnes had all melted in her native atmosphere, and were quite forgotten. She could speak of the Lyddells now, though still she did not find fault with them, nor make complaints; indeed, it was Agnes' abuse of them that made her first discover that she had a regard for them.

This prejudice, as she began to call it, seemed to her unaccountable, since she had never written complainingly, until she found at last, (which made her inclined to treat it with more respect,) that it was founded on what Edmund had reported. He had come to Fern Torr immediately after his visit to Oakworthy, very much out of spirits, and had poured out his anxieties to his friends, talking of Mr. and Mrs. Lyddell with less caution than he had used with Marian, and lamenting over the fate of his poor little cousins like something hopeless. Marian thought of Gerald, and her heart failed her, then she hoped again, for Gerald was coming home, and then she understood what Edmund had thought of it all, and knew that it was perfectly consistent with his last conversation with her. So she said that was four years ago, and that Edmund was very kind.

The time of Gerald's arrival came. Charles and James Wortley preceded him by about a fortnight, and all that Marian saw of them made her rejoice in such companionship for him. Mr. Wortley drove her to meet him at Exeter, and never was greeting more joyful. Lionel had sent her a message that Oakworthy would be as dull as ditch water without her, and if she did not come back before the end of the holidays, he should certainly be obliged to go back to Eton again to find something to do. Having delivered this message, Gerald made both his companions laugh by gazing about as if surprised to find Exeter still in the same place, and wondering at reading all the old names over the shops.

Marian was delighted that he recognised all the torrs on the drive home, and very proud of his height, his beauty, and his cordial, well-bred gentlemanlike manners, which gave the Wortleys general satisfaction.

The first thing he did was to go out and visit his old pony in the paddock, patting it very affectionately, though he seemed much surprised that it was so small.

In the evening they went to the Manor House. Marian had spent many hours there, sat in the empty rooms, wandered in the garden, and mused on past days, or dwelt on them with Agnes, and she had looked forward with great pleasure to having her brother there.

She wished to have had him alone, but he asked Agnes and the boys to come, and they all set out together up the rocky steps, Gerald far before the rest, and when Marian came up to him he was standing on the lawn, at the top of the steps, looking at the house.

"I thought it was larger," exclaimed he.

"But, Gerald, see how high the magnolia has grown, and how nice and smooth old Lapthorn keeps the lawn. Does it not look as if we had gone away only yesterday?"

"Yes, and there is the little larburnum that we planted. How it is grown! But how very small the house is."

By this time the door had been opened by the old housekeeper, and Marian, running up to her, exclaimed, "Here he is, Mrs. White! Come, come, Gerald, come and speak to Mrs. White!"

Gerald came, but with no readiness of manner. His "how d'ye do?" was shy and cold, and not at all answerable to her eager, almost tearful, "Pretty well, thank you, Sir. It is something to see you at home again, Sir Gerald; so tall, and looking so well. 'Tis almost old times again, to see you and Miss Marian."

He stood silent, and Agnes spoke, "Yes, Mrs. White, is not he grown? It does not seem to be so very long before we shall really have them here for good."

"Ah! Miss Wortley, that is what I have always wished to live for; I have always said, let me only live to see Sir Gerald come back, and find things in order as he left them, and then I would die contented."

"No, no, live to keep his house many more years," said Marian. "It is four years less now you know, Mrs. White; only eight more before we shall be able to live here. For, I suppose you would like to have me back too."

"I don't know Miss Marian; you will be married long before that, such a fine young lady as you are grown to be."

Marian laughed and passed on into the house, sorry that Gerald had taken no part in the conversation. They went into the drawing-room, that room where he had wept so bitterly the day before his departure. Again his observation was, "I thought this room was twice the size. And so low!"

"You have been looking in at the large end of a telescope lately, Gerald," said his sister with some sorrow in her tone, as she sat down on one of the brown holland muffled sofas, and looked up at her father's portrait, trying to find a likeness there to the face before her. There was the same high brow, the same dark eyes, the same straight features, the same bright open smile. Gerald was more like it, in some respects, than he had been, but there was a haughty, impetuous expression now and then on eye, brow, and lip, that found no parallel in the gentle countenance which, to Marian's present feelings, seemed to be turned towards him with an air of almost reproachful anxiety.

Perhaps he saw some of the sadness of her expression, and; always affectionate, wished to please her by manifesting a little more of the feelings which really still existed. He came and stood by her, and whispered a few caressing words, which almost compensated for the vexation his carelessness had occasioned. He looked earnestly at the picture for a few moments, then, turning away, suddenly exclaimed, "I should like to see the old dressing-room."

This was Lady Arundel's morning room, where many a lesson had been repeated, many a game played, and where, perhaps, more childish recollections centered than in any other part of the house. The brother and sister went thither alone, and much enjoyed looking into every well-known corner, and talking of the little events which had there taken place. This lasted for nearly a quarter of an hour, when they rejoined their companions to make the tour of the garden, &c. All was pleasant here, Gerald recollected every nook, and was delighted to find so much unchanged.

"Let us just look into the stable yard," said he, as they were coming away. It was locked, but a message to Mrs. White procured the key, and they entered the neat deserted court, without one straw to make it look inhabited, though the hutch where the rabbits had lived was still in its place; and even in one corner the reversed flower-pot, which Gerald well remembered to have brought there to mount upon, in order to make investigations into a blackbird's nest, in the ivy on the wall.

He now used the same flower-pot to enable him to peep in at the hazy window of the stable, and still more lamentable was his exclamation, "Can this be all! How very small!"

"Nothing but low and little, you discontented boy," said Agnes.

"Why, really, I could not believe it was on such a small scale," said Gerald. "Marian, now is it possible there can be only six stalls here?"

"Why, what would have been the use of more?" said Marian.

"Ah! why to be sure, there was no one to ride much," said Gerald. "But yet I can hardly imagine it! What could my father have done in his younger days? Only six stalls! And no loose box. Well, people had contracted notions in those days! And the yard so small! Why, the one at Oakworthy would make four of it."

"And you had really managed to persuade yourself that this was a grander place than Oakworthy?" said Marian.

Gerald made no answer; but after walking backwards till he had a full view of the stable and surrounding regions, broke out into the exclamation, "I see what is to be done! Take down that wall — let in a piece of the kitchen garden — get it levelled — and then extend it a little on the right side too. Yes, I see."

"You are not talking of spoiling this place!" cried Agnes, in dismay.

"Spoiling! only making it habitable," said Gerald. "How can a man live here with a stable with six stalls, and nothing like a kennel?"

The utter impossibility of such an existence was so strongly impressed on the mind of the young baronet, that as soon as tea was over he commenced a sketch of his future stables, adding various explanations for the benefit of Charles and James. There was almost a daily quarrel on the subject with Agnes, and much laughing on each side; but Marian, afraid of making him more determined, took no part in it.

Much might happen in eight years to make him change his mind, and this stable in the clouds might be endured, if everything else had been fully satisfactory.

Very happy were the boys next morning, setting off to the woods to study the localities of the game; very happy were they fishing and rabbit shooting; very happy, galloping over the country by turns on the two ponies; very happy were the whole party in pic-nic expeditions, and in merry evening sports; but these could not take up every hour and every minute; and Marian could not help observing, that while Charles and James could always find some work on which to be employed in the intervals, Gerald was idle and listless. There were hours in the morning when they had their Latin and Greek to study, while Gerald was usually loitering in the drawing-room. That he should voluntarily touch Latin or Greek in the holidays was perhaps more than mortal could expect; but that he should not read anything was disappointing. The vicarage afforded no periodical novels, no slang tales of low life, no manuals of sporting. The Waverley novels he had read long ago, and nothing of a more solid description would he touch; so his mornings were chiefly spent in drawing caricatures, and chattering to his sister and Agnes. He was indeed very amusing, but this was not all that could be desired. Now and then there were stories of feats which did not seem likely to be those of the best and wisest set of boys; and his idea of the life of a boy, if not of man, was plainly that it was to be spent in taking pleasure and shirking work. Then he took in a sporting paper, and used to entertain them with comments on the particulars of the races, and of bets, which no one in the house understood but himself; but these were never in the presence of either Mr. or Mrs. Wortley, where he was on his guard.

In these intervals of idleness, Marian tried to persuade him several times to write to Edmund, who would be glad to have a report fresh from home. He always said he would soon set about a letter, but the time never came, though she more than once arranged pen, paper, and ink in readiness for him. He had recently received a letter from his cousin, but he had torn it up, and could not remember anything about the contents.

Something between bashfulness and pride produced conduct which could not but appear like arrant haughtiness to the villagers, who had looked forward eagerly to seeing their young landlord. If Marian tried to bring him to speak to some poor old man, his answer was, "Give him this half-crown, then, that will do just as well!" and he walked off out of reach, while she remained to present the gift, and hear in answer, "Thank you kindly, Miss; I should like to see the young gentleman himself, but I daresay he does not like poor people."

If this was the feeling where there was half-a-crown to sweeten the neglect, what was it where such a propitiatory offering was out of the question, and where the original connection had been closer, among the old servants, the dependants and tenants? His lofty acknowledgment of their bows, — his short, reluctant "Good morning," when forced to speak, — and his willingness to escape from their presence, contrasted ill with the cordial greetings with which his cousin Edmund had always hailed each Fern Torr person as a friend. Indeed, "that nice young gentleman, Master Edmund," began to be recollected with regrets, which, had the Manor been a kingdom, might have amounted to treason towards the young heir.

Marian grieved at this behaviour, and would have attempted to argue him out of it, but he gave her scarcely any opportunity of a serious conversation; and Mr. Wortley gave him more than one hint, which, though be took it with perfect courtesy, never mended matters. Yet with all this, he was so agreeable, so good-natured and gentlemanlike, so pleasant a guest, and so affectionate a brother, that Mr. and Mrs. Wortley could not help liking him very much; and if they saw anything amiss, they did not pain his sister by speaking of it. Her misgivings were too vague and undetermined for her to be willing to consult Mr. Wortley; if she thought at one time that she would, she grew so frightened and reluctant whenever an occasion came, that she let it pass by; and she was divided between blame to herself for doing nothing, when a few words might be the rescue of her brother, and self-reproach for doing him cruel injustice.

Nay, she even defended him more than once, when Agnes was shocked. She protected a shirt, illustrated by his own hand, in marking-ink, with cricketers, which caused infinite scandal to the washerwomen of Fern Torr. She defended slang words, which Agnes, from not understanding them, fancied worse than they really were; and she never failed to say he did not mean to be unkind, whenever he was neglectful of the poor people. She was displeased with herself afterwards for speaking in favour of these things, for she well knew them to be only parts of the whole system which grieved her; but still she could not help it.

These thoughts were suspended by the solemn time approaching. Her confirmation-day came, and she stood among the maidens of her own home and village, who had been baptized in the same font, and shared with her the same instructions. Simultaneously with them she pronounced her vow; and perhaps it was a repining thought which crossed her mind, — "Why am I not like these, to remain in this peaceful nest, not sent forth to be wearied and tried by that glittering world of unrest, which I thus renounce?"

She knelt to receive the blessing, which brought with it the trust that the peace of that moment might dwell with her, refresh her, and shield her "as oft as sin and sorrow tire." And when her eye fell on her brother, it was with more hope, for now she could better pray for him. Whatever might happen, it could never hurt the memory of that awful yet soothing hour, nor of that first Communion when she knelt near her parents' graves between Mrs. Wortley and Agnes; the whole air filled with the prayers of those on earth and in heaven who loved her best; nor of her walk in the garden afterwards with Mr. Wortley, when he plainly spoke to her of her life as one of peculiar trial and temptation, and warned her how to be in the world, and yet not of the world.

The nest event of the visit to Fern Torr was Saunders' wedding. Saunders did not love Oakworthy, still less Mrs. Lyddell, and least of all Mrs. Price, the ladies' maid; and when she found herself at Fern Torr again, and heard Mr. David Chapple renew his tender speeches, the return thither became more and more difficult; and one day, while plaiting her young lady's hair, she communicated to her with a great gush of tears, that, though she could not bear to think of leaving her, and would not on any account cause her any inconvenience, she began to think it was time to think about her marriage.

It was a stroke to Marian to hear of losing any old familiar face, and her look of dismay was a great satisfaction to Saunders; but she could bear it better than she could once have done, and there were reasons which made a change not so very much to be regretted even by her. The quarrels between Saunders and the rest of the household were not agreeable, and what she now felt to be a serious evil, was that habit of complaining to her, and telling her stories against the family, of which Edmund had warned her long ago. She had tried to discourage it, but, once begun, it had never been entirely discontinued; and Marian felt it to be wrong in every way.

She made up her mind, therefore, with greater philosophy than could have been expected, to the loss of Saunders; and was further consoled by finding it gave hey an opportunity of promoting a nice young Fern Torr damsel, too delicate for hard work, who had been taught dressmaking, and whom Saunders undertook to instruct in the mysteries of the hair, quite sufficiently to carry her on till they went to London, and she could take lessons from some grand frizeur.

Mrs. Lyndell was written to, and gave her consent to the hiring of Fanny, and Marian and Agnes were so delighted at the opening thus made for her, that Saunders would have been jealous if she had not been too happily engaged in her own preparations.

As to Gerald he made a dreadful face when he first heard of

Saunders' intentions; but as her going made no difference to his comfort, he soon became resigned. David was an old acquaintance, whom he liked because he belonged to the genus groom; so he made no objection to his sister's attending the wedding. He presented the bride with a tea-set, splendid with gilding, and surprised every one by walking into Mr. Wortley's kitchen in the midst of the bridal entertainment, and proposing the health of the happy pair.

Marian was to return under Gerald's escort, at the end of the holidays. He was to go on to Eton, leaving her at the railway station, where she was to be met by the Lyddells' carriage. The last letter arrived, in which arrangements respecting time and train were to be finally confirmed. It was, as usual, from Caroline; and as she opened it, Marian gave a sudden start.

"Eh?" said Gerald, "whose mare's dead? Not Elliot's Queen Pomare, I hope!"

"No, but Miss Morley is going."

"O!" cried Gerald, "I hope she has been reading some more letters."

"Not quite," said Marian smiling.

"Well, but is it directly? I suppose you did not think she was to stay there for life? Has she been in any mischief, that you look so shocked?"

Marian really could not help discovering that she was not without tenderness of feeling for Miss Morley, and did not like to proclaim, in Caroline's strong and rather satirical language, across the breakfast table, that Mrs. Lyddell had discovered by accident that she and her pupil were in the habit of amusing themselves with novels which were far better unread. After reading quickly to the end of the letter, she answered, "O, she has been reading books with Clara that Mrs. Lyddell did not approve."

"A triumph! a triumph!" cried Agnes. "Now Marian will never attempt to defend Miss Morley again."

"What, not the poor unfortunate faithful? How can you think me so base?" returned Marian. "Besides, poor thing, she really is very kind-hearted, and has very little harm in her. I dare say it was more Clara's fault than hers,"

"Well done, Marian, striking right and left!" observed James Wortley.

"How long has Miss Morley been at Oakworthy?" asked Mrs. Wortley.

"She came about a year before we did," replied Marian.

"Her predecessor, Miss Cameron, must have been a very different person; Caroline and Walter always speak of her with such respect."

"Poor unfortunate!" broke out Gerald. "Well, if it had not been for Marian's letters, I should not have hated her so much. When one was making a row, she never did anything worse than say, 'Now Sir Gerald!'" which he gave with her peculiarly unauthoritative, piteous, imploring drawl.

"There was something in that title of 'poor unfortunate,' peculiarly appropriate," said Marian, laughing, "as I am afraid that it is now, poor thing. She is to leave Oakworthy immediately, and I do not know that she has any relation but an old aunt."

Mr. and Mrs. Wortley agreed with Marian that it was a melancholy case, but the others were too triumphant to be compassionate; and Gerald amused Agnes half the morning with ludicrous stories of her inefficiency.

Marian was thoughtful all day; and at last, when sitting alone with Mrs. Wortley and Agnes, exclaimed, "Poor Miss Morley! I really am very sorry for her; I did not know I liked her so well."

"Absence is the great charm with Marian," said Agnes, laughing; "we learn now what makes her so affectionate to us."

"No, but really, Agnes, when one has been living in constant intercourse for four years, and often receiving kindness from a person, is it possible to hear of her being sent away in disgrace and poverty without caring about it?"

"O yes; I know; after having lived in the same house with a kitchen poker for four years, you get so attached to it that it gives you a pang to part with it. No, but the comparison is no compliment to the poker; that is firm enough, at any rate, — a down cushion would be better."

"An attachment to a down cushion is nothing to be ashamed of, Agnes," said her mother.

"And Miss Morley did deserve some attachment, indeed," said Marian. "She was so ready to oblige, and she really did many and many a kind thing by the servants; and I believe she quite denied herself, for the sake of her old aunt. She was not fit for a governess, to be sure; but that was more her misfortune than her fault, poor thing."

"How do you make that out?" said Agnes.

"Why, she was obliged to get her own living; and what other way had she? She was educated for it, and had everything but the art of gaining authority."

"And high principle," said Mrs. Wortley.

"But," said Marian, growing eager in her defence, "she really did know right from wrong. She would remonstrate, and tell us things that were every word good and true, only she did it with so little force, that they were apt not to mind her; and then it was no wonder that she grew dispirited, and sunk into poor unfortunate."

"Yes," said Agnes, "I can understand it all; she was in a situation that she was not fit for, and failed."

"She would have been very different in another situation, most probably," said Mrs. Wortley, "where she and the children were not so much left to each other's mercy."

"Yes; Mrs. Lyddell never mended matters," said Marian. "She did not back up or strengthen her, but only frightened her, till she was quite as ready to conceal what was amiss as her pupils. And that intimacy with Clara was a very unlucky thing; it drew her down without drawing Clara up."

"I suppose that was the origin of the catastrophe," said Mrs. Wortley.

"I should think so; they have been more alone together lately, for I am sure this could never have happened when Caroline was in the schoolroom. And her making a friend of Clara was no wonder, so forlorn and solitary as she must have been." And Marian sighed with fellow-feeling for her.

"An intimate, not a friend," said Mrs. Wortley.

"And I could better fancy making a friend of Miss Lyddell," said Agnes. "I can't say my tête-à-tête with Miss Clara made me desire much more of her confidence."

"Clara is more caressing," said Marian. "I think I am most fond of her, though Caroline is — O! quite another thing. But what I wanted was to ask you, Mrs. Wortley, if you thought I might write to poor Miss Morley, and ask if there is anything I can do for her. I can't bear to think of her going away without wishing her good-bye, or showing any feeling for her in her distress."

"How very right and kind of you, Marian," exclaimed Agnes, "after all her injustice —"

"I do not think it would be advisable, my dear," said Mrs. Wortley; "it would seem like putting yourself in opposition to Mrs. Lyddell, and might be pledging yourself, in a manner, to recommend her, which, with your opinion of her, you could not well do."

"O, no, no, except in some particular case. Yes, I suppose you are right; but I don't feel happy to take no notice."

"Perhaps something may occur on your return, when you understand the matter more fully; or, at any rate, if you are writing to Oakworthy, you might send some message of farewell, kind remembrances, or love."

"Those are so unmeaning and conventional that I hate them," said Marian.

"Yes, but their want of meaning is their advantage here. They are merely kindly expressions of good will."

"And they will mean more from you," added Agnes, "as you never have the civility to use them on ordinary occasions."

"Well, I will take your advice," said Marian, "and thank you, Mrs. Wortley; I only wish —"

The wish ended in a sigh, as Marian sat down to commence — "My dear Caroline."

CHAPTER XI.

"But we are women when boys are but boys;
Heav'n gives us grace to ripen and grow wise,
Some six years earlier. I thank heav'n for it:
We grow upon the sunny side of the wall."

TAYLOR.

It certainly was quite involuntary on Agnes Wortley's part, but when the time came for returning to Oakworthy, Marian was conscious of more kindly and affectionate feelings towards it and its inhabitants than she had ever expected to entertain for them. She did not love Fern Torr or the Wortleys less; she had resumed her confidence and sympathy with Agnes, and felt the value of Mrs. Wortley more than ever; and it quite made her heart ache to think how long it would be before she saw another purple hill or dancing streamlet, and that she should not be there to see her dear old myrtle's full pride of blossom. But, on the other hand, her room at Oakworthy, with its treasures, was a sort of home; and she looked forward to it gladly, when once she was out of sight of the moors.

The train had stopped and gone on again from the last station before that where they were to leave it for Oakworthy, when Gerald, coming across to the seat by her side, said, "Marian, I say, can you lend me a couple of pounds?"

"Why, Gerald, what can you want with them?"

"Never mind; only be a good girl, and let me have them."

"You had plenty of money when you came to Fern Torr. How could you have got rid of it all?"

"Come, come, Marian, don't be tiresome. Haven't I had to give to all the old women in the place?"

"But do you really mean that you have no money?"

"O yes, I have some, but not what I want. Come, I know you keep California in your pocket. What harm can it do you?"

After all Marian's presents at Fern Torr, it was not quite as convenient, as Gerald fancied, to part with two pounds; but that was not the best motive to put forward, nor was it her reason for hesitating.

"I don't know whether it is right; that is the thing, Gerald."

"Right! why where is the right or wrong in it?"

"I am afraid it may do you harm," said she, in a trembling, doubtful voice.

"Stuff! I'll take care of that!"

"If you would only tell me what you want it for?"

"I tell you, Marian, I can't do without it; I don't know what I shall do, if you won't give it to me."

"Debts! O Gerald, you have not got into debt?"

"Well, and what do you look so scared about? Do you think they will kill me?"

"O, Gerald, Gerald, this proves it all."

"It? what?" said Gerald. "Come, don't be so like a girl! I have not been doing any thing wrong, I tell you, and it is all your fault if I can't get clear."

"With such an allowance as you have, O Gerald, how could you? And how could you throw about money at home, when you knew you were in debt?"

"You talk as if I had been ruining my wife and ten small children," cried Gerald, impatiently. "A fine fuss about making a few pounds stand over till next half. But you women go headlong at it, never see the rights of a thing. So, you won't? Well, it is your doing now!"

"I can't see any end to it," said Marian, reflectingly. "If I thought you would make a resolution — but you will be without money at all, and how are you to get through this half? O, Gerald! better write to Mr. Lyddell at once, and he will set you straight, and you can begin fresh."

Gerald made a face of utter contempt. The steam whistle was heard; they were stopping. "There is an end of it, then" said he, angrily. "I did not think you had been so ill-natured; it is all your fault, I tell you. I thought you cared for me."

This was dreadful; Marian's purse was in her hand, and she began "O Gerald dear, anything but that!" — when they found themselves close in front of the station, and Lionel pulling at the door of their carriage, and calling fiercely to the porter to unlock them.

Caroline was standing on the platform, and there was a tumult of greetings and inquiries for luggage to be taken out and put in. Gerald ran to see that his goods were separated from his sister's; Lionel shook hands with Marian, and scolded her for staying away all the holidays; roared to the porter that his portmanteau was for Slough, then turned again to say, "You've heard of poor unfortunate, Marian?"

The bell rang; Gerald ran back; Marian knew she was weak, but could not help it, — she squeezed the two sovereigns into his hand, and was comforted for the moment by his affectionate farewell. Lionel and he threw themselves into their carriage, and were whisked off.

"There!" said Caroline. "Now come along. O, I am so glad you are come; I have so much to say."

Marian could not dwell on Gerald; she put her arm within Caroline's, looked back to see Fanny safe under the care of an Oakworthy footman, and soon was in the carriage.

"Well, Caroline; and how is every one?"

"Pretty well, considering the revulsion of ideas we have all undergone. Poor Miss Morley left plenty of farewells for you. You can't think haw pleased she was with your message."

"Poor thing! Where is she?"

"At her aunt's; she went on Monday. Mamma was impatient to have it over. You know her ways."

Marian knew that this intimated that Caroline thought her mother had not been kind; and she doubted whether to continue her inquiries; but Caroline was too eager to tell, to wait for questions, and proceeded: — "There had been dissatisfaction for a long time, as I believe you may have guessed; mamma thought Clara backward, and wanting in what Miss Morley calls 'the solid;' and at last, coming suddenly into the schoolroom at twelve o'clock one fine day, she found reason good, for they were very comfortably reading M. Eugene Sue."

"O, Caroline, impossible!"

"Too possible," said Caroline, "though I would not believe it at first. However, they did not know what it was when they began, and were afterwards too much bewitched with the story to leave off; and as they felt it was wrong, they read it the more constantly to get it over faster."

"But how in the world could they get such a book?"

"From the circulating library. It appears that they found the evenings rather dull in London this spring, when we were all out, and so began a little secret hiring, which was continued at Oakworthy, and with a worse choice of books."

"That she should be so little to be trusted!"

"Nay, Marian, who could live with her half-an-hour in the schoolroom, and think she could?"

"Certainly, she often puzzled me when first I came."

"And you never saw the worst. You always kept order, after you came."

"O, Caroline, what nonsense!"

"Yes, indeed you did. I do assure you that, scores of times, the knowledge that your great eyes were wondering at me has kept me from bullying Miss Morley into letting me do what I knew to be wrong. I could persuade her and deceive myself, but I could not persuade you; and then all the rest went for nothing, because you were sure to be right."

"It is very easy to see the right for other people," said Marian, with rather a sad smile.

"Yes, only other people don't mind that, unless you do the right for yourself; and that is the thing in you, Marian. If you had said anything, I should not have minded it half so much; but your 'I don't know,' cut me home."

"I am sorry —"

"No, don't be sorry, for I am glad. If you had not come before all the good of Miss Cameron had gone off from me, what should I have been? O, Marian, I am very glad you are come back; I did not know I liked you half so well till you were gone."

"I am sure I might say the same" almost whispered Marian, in a choked tone, under her bonnet. Caroline caught it up eagerly, and seizing her by both hands, exclaimed, stooping forward to peep at her face, "Marian, Marian, do you say so? And are you really not so very miserable at coming back to us?"

A tear, one of Marian's very reluctant tears, actually rushed from her eye, and with a hard struggle to speak, she said, "Miserable! how can you say so? You are so very kind to me."

"And do you not hate us?" said Caroline, with, an arch look of delight, then softened into something of mournfulness. "Nay, I did not mean that; but you can bear to be with us after your own Agnes, — after those good people, — after such a home as Fern Torr?"

"O, Caroline, this is very unlike my first coming to you!"

"Yes, I know we were not kind; we were not as we ought to have been to you."

"No, no, no; I was stiff and disagreeable; I would not be pleased," said Marian, forgetting all coldness but her own.

"No wonder. O, Marian," and Caroline's voice trembled, "no one knows better than I do how much there is to be lamented in our ways of going on, — how different our house is from Fern Torr." Marian could not say no. "You were too good for us; you are still, I would not see you like us; but if we could make you comfortable enough to think Oakworthy not an exile, but something like a home, how glad I should be!"

Marian laid her hand on Caroline's arm; and, with an effort that cost her a spasm in her throat, she said, "You have!" Not another word could she get out; but this was enough. Caroline kissed her for the first time in her life, except at the formal partings at bed-time, and there were tears on both their faces. After a time, Caroline broke into the flood of thoughts in her cousin's mind, by saying, playfully, "When folks are missed, then they are mourned, people say; and I am sure you deserve the compliment, for till you were gone, I never knew your value. How many silly fancies of Clara's have flourished, for want of your indifference to put them down! How stupid it has been not to have you to read with, or talk to! How lonely the drawing-room has been, and nothing but nonsense if I went to the schoolroom. And then the boys, — Lionel has been so unruly there was no bearing it, and grumbling for you every day; and Johnny, — O, Marian, do you know it is settled that Johnny goes to sea, after all?"

"Johnny! I know he wished it, but I thought Mrs. Lyddell never would make up her mind to it."

"Ah! there have been storms in the higher quarters," said Caroline, with would-be gaiety. "You are very lucky to have been away all this time, for it has been by no means a serene sky. You know," she proceeded with gravity, "they say the times are bad; well, in the midst of papa's vexation at the tenants asking for a reduction of rent, in came a whole lot of Elliot's long bills, which made papa lecture Walter and me one whole evening on economy, and caused him to be extremely annoyed with everything and everybody, and to say mamma must give up her opposition to Johnny's being a sailor; and I never saw mamma take anything so really to heart. It has been very uncomfortable; and in the midst came this business of poor Miss Morley, who had rather harder measure in consequence."

"Poor little woman! Well, she was very good-natured," said Marian, glad to turn the conversation from this account of family matters, not given in the pleasantest style, but rather as if Caroline was trying to conceal her real feelings by an air of satire.

"She was like a child in authority. You see, we, who know her well, never think of blaming her as if she had originated the mischief; while mamma, who never did know her, cannot be persuaded that she simply yielded to Clara."

"That is not exactly the object one desires in a governess," said Marian. "Well, poor thing! and how is Clara? is she very sorry?"

"I really can hardly tell. I have been vexed with Clara myself, to tell you the truth; for I thought she acted shabbily. The blame passed over her, and lighted on Miss Morley; and she did not stretch out a hand to help her. Now Clara knew that it was wrong to read those books, just as well as you or I; indeed, it was all her doing; and I could not bear to see, her thinking herself innocent, and led into the scrape by Miss Morley. She did cry excessively, and was very unhappy when she found Miss Morley was really going, and the parting was heart-rending; but then the very next day, in spite of their confidential friendship, she began to disclose the poor woman's follies one after another, till I am quite tired of hearing of them. They must have grown much worse than they were in our time. I never knew then that she was always fancying people were in love with her."

"I wonder what she will do!"

"She would not be a bad governess where the mother looked after the children. Well, I hope she will soon get another situation, poor thing!"

"Yes, indeed, for I am afraid she never saved anything."

"O, no, she frittered all her money away, and always was poor at quarter-day; and she has only that old aunt to take care of her."

"Poor thing, poor thing! If she would but have been firmer. And is Clara to have another governess?"

"No, mamma thinks her too old; but I am sure I hope she is to develope more. I do not think you or I were like her at fifteen."

"I think," said Marian, meditatively, "that Miss Morley and Clara helped what — was not wise in each other."

"Yes, that is my hope, — that when Clara is out of her influence, she may grow wiser. People's minds do grow at different times, you know. Poor little Clara! I want Walter to talk to her, but it is hard to bring about; for they seem to have no common subject. Ours is a very odd household; we all go our own ways in our own worlds. Papa and mamma each have their way; and Elliot his way. Walter stands alone too; then I am a sort of connecting-link between the schoolroom set and mamma, — yes, and with Walter too: while the three boys are a party by themselves. O, Marian, no wonder you did not like us."

"Say no more of that, pray, Caroline."

She made no answer, but after a pause, suddenly exclaimed, "Nothing would matter, if it was not for Elliot. He is the root of all that has gone wrong."

"Is he at home?"

"No; he went last week, and the storm lulled then. O, Marian, I am weary of it all! But it is one comfort that you are come."

Caroline certainly looked very much harassed, and her words showed that every one had been out of temper, and she had been obliged to bear it all. Marian was very sorry, and felt quite fond of her, as she answered, with a kind tone, "Thank you."

"Walter has been the only comfort; but then he has been very unhappy too. I am afraid he knows more and worse of Elliot than he chooses to tell me. And then he is so busy, — going up for his degree, you know, after the vacation, and so nervous about it, that I have not liked to talk to him about anything tiresome, because, poor fellow, he is quite worried enough already. Well, but now tell me about pleasanter things — your pretty Agnes, how is she? and Gerald? — I wanted to have seen more of him. Was not he in glory?"

"O, yes," said Marian, as a pang shot through her at this recall of her anxieties.

"And tell me the whole story of Saunders' wedding."

The two cousins had so much to say, that the long reaches of white chalk road and the bare downs had hardly time to pain Marian's eye; and she was surprised so soon to find herself in the well-known street of Oakworthy.

It was not a hopeful prospect with which to return, after so happy a summer as she had spent; and yet a degree of trouble gave Marian a kindlier feeling towards the Lyddells. If it had not been for Gerald, she would have arrived at Oakworthy in a bright temper. Even now the discontent had been expelled by the dispositions fostered by Mr. Wortley; and if there was a weight on her, it was not a burthen of selfish repining, — the worst burthen of all. That Caroline had really missed her, — that Caroline loved her, — was a discovery that warmed her heart, and inclined her more than all before to look kindly on Oakworthy, when she drove up to the door, and met Clara in the hall.

Clara hung upon her, and overwhelmed her with kisses; Mrs. Lyddell received her just as she had done before; and Walter shook hands cordially, as if he was very glad to see her again. The talk went on about visits and engagements, and each moment made Marian feel that her Sunday world had passed from her, and her workday world begun again.

Clara came to her room with her, partly to see her new maid, and partly to talk with her about Miss Morley; but Marian, not wishing to have Fanny immediately astonished by her random way of talking, gave a sort of stern look and sign, which silenced poor Clara on that subject. There were plenty more, however, and she talked on fast; indeed, Marian had not two minutes alone that whole evening, till, somewhere towards half-past eleven, her cousins bade her a final good-night.

She had time at last to think over that parting with Gerald, which had hung heavily on her all this time, without her being able to enter upon the subject with herself. What did it mean? Was it so very bad a sign? Did it really confirm all her fears? or was it not possible that he might have got into some chance difficulty? Might he not be careless and extravagant, without being seriously in fault? Yes; but this was but of a piece with other things which she had observed. Alone, it might not have been so alarming; but even apart from this, she could not be quite happy about him, after all she had observed. And had she been weak? had she done what was bad for him? O, for some one to consult! — some one under whose charge to put him! Was it her own fault that she had missed the opportunity with Mr. Wortley!

To pray for him was all that could be done, and it in some degree stilled that aching feeling in her heart. Yet, whenever she woke in the night, she seemed to hear Caroline saying, "If it was not for Elliot!" with a foreboding that "If it was not for Gerald!" might be on her tongue in the same manner, for the rest of her life.

Every time Gerald's name was mentioned, there was a pang; every time she thought of him in solitude, the fear and anxiety gained strength. Consciousness of ignorance added to its poignancy; and young as she was, it would be hard to describe how much suffering she underwent in secret, night after night, as she lay awake, in her perplexed musings on that one absorbing thought. Yet they were like those vague nightly terrors of wolves, darkness, or mysterious horrors, from which little children often suffer so much, without revealing them, and entirely shake off by day; for Marian awoke in the morning to cheerfulness and activity, with spirits undepressed, full of interest in things around; and only when reminded of her fears, secretly wincing at the sudden throb of pain.

Marian's days were more at her own disposal than formerly. She might do as she pleased all the morning, — sit in her own room, and choose her own occupation; and she was just beginning to think over two or three bright plans of usefulness. She would make a series of copies, from prints, of Scripture subjects, for the Fern Torr children; she would translate some stories for them, and she had devised many other things to be done; when Caroline one day said to her, "Marian, I don't know if it is asking a great deal, but if you could sit with us sometimes in the morning, it would be a great gain. Mamma wants me to read with Clara. Now, you know I have no authority; and doing it for a lesson, as if it was for Clara's good, will only make her hate it, and pay no attention at all. But if we read together, as if it was for our own benefit, she will join in, and think it a womanly thing."

Marian smiled at the ingenuity of the scheme, such as she

would have been a great deal too awkward, as well as too straight-forward ever to devise. It was a case where "no" could not have been said, but there were many ways of acting a no; and Marian was so sorry to give up the Scripture drawings, the idea of which had greatly delighted her when proposed by Agnes, that she had it in her heart to have backed out of it as often as she could. A little thought, however, convinced her, that to help Caroline's plans for her sister's good was the foremost duty, that to avoid it would be positive wrong and unkindness; so she resolved to lend herself to it with all her might, even though Agnes might be disappointed.

And pray, why should Agnes be disappointed? Why were the drawing and reading incompatible? Marian had taught herself to think it impossible to do anything for Fern Torr, in public, for fear of being laughed at, or observed upon; and these drawings, which were of sacred subjects, and further involved some alterations of her own, would, she thought, be worse than any. She mused a long time whether this was right feeling or foolish bashfulness, and decided at last that it was a little of the former trying to justify a great deal of the latter, and that Caroline and Clara were not the same thing as Miss Morley and all the boys; so with an effort, which, considering the occasion, was almost absurd in its magni-tude, she brought her portfolio down, began to draw, and did not experience anything unpleasant in consequence. It was one of her first practical lessons in the fancifulness of her shyness. Her cousins took interest in what she was about, admired, and helped her to hunt up subjects to make her series complete; indeed the three girls were exceedingly comfortable together, and a pleasant, mutual good-feeling constantly grew between them. Clara was certainly becoming less childish and silly when no longer nomi-nally under the authority of Miss Morley, and the confidante of all her follies, but the companion of two sensible girls, young and bright enough to enter into all the liveliness about her that was not silliness and a great deal that was, and to drive away some of her nonsense by laughing at it.

The mornings were thus pleasant and satisfactory, the after-noons were less certain to be agreeable. If there was a ride, it was delightful, if a walk, it was all very well; but there was a third con-tingency, to which Marian had become liable, of being carried forth with her green card-case on a morning visiting expedition by Mrs. Lyddell, and this was one which required all her powers of resignation, though the misfortune was much more imaginary than real.

There were three chances of the way of spending the evening

too. The first, the family party alone, this was pretty well, and though not charming, was by far the best; Mrs. Lyddell's talk was agreeable, and to sit with Caroline, and perhaps with the addition of Walter, at the small table, working, reading, and talking, was as quiet and comfortable a way of passing the time as might be. A dinner party at home was next best, for she had her own quiet corners of conversation, and Walter would sometimes come and take shelter there too, and get into a talk, as well as if the room were empty of company, sometimes better, because his mother could not hear him, and he was never so backward in telling his real mind, as in her hearing. Worst of all was a party from home, where she knew few persons, and disliked all she knew.

Unhappily, this was generally her feeling towards all the neighbourhood; and though it may seem to be a strong expression, it is scarcely too much to say that in Marian's habitual frame she looked on every one that could be considered as company in the light of natural enemies, leagued to prevent her walks and rides, to tease her, and to spoil her evenings.

This was partly the result of her constitutional shyness, but it would have gone off, by this time, if she had not fostered it by imbibing Lady Marchmont's exclusiveness. Marian would have been shocked to realize how she despised and scorned her acquaintance — why? the answer would have been hard to find — because they were company — because they were the world — because they were Mrs. Lyddell's society — because she was superior? How or why? She disdained them all, without knowing it, and far less knowing why. She complied scrupulously with every rule of formal politeness, and had become a tolerable mistress, by rote, of such common-place small talk as served to fulfil her part, and make her not feel herself absurd, but this was all; she would not let herself be pleased or amused, she would not open her eyes to anything good or agreeable about the people, except a very few favoured ones, chiefly clergymen or their wives.

It was very wrong, it was Marian's one great fault at this period of her life, and it had the effect of making her almost disliked. Clara had scarcely said too much in telling Agnes that her pride was often remarked, for Mrs. Lyddell's neighbours were just the people to fancy pride where it was not, especially where the rank was superior to their own. Tall, handsome, and outwardly self-possessed, Miss Arundel did not gain credit, from superficial observers, for shyness, and was looked upon as a very haughty ungracious girl, while it was whispered that Mrs. Lyddell had had a great deal of trouble with her.

The autumn passed on in this manner, and towards its close, Elliot returned from shooting in Scotland, and announced that his friend, Mr. Faulkner, was coming to Oakworthy, to look at an estate, which was for sale in the neighbourhood.

Mrs. Lyddell was pleased, and questioned her son about Mr. Faulkner's thousands a-year; then turning to Marian, said,

"Surely, Marian, you know him; I heard of your meeting him and Lady Julia at Lady Marchmont's."

"Yes," said Marian, with her face of rigidity.

"Ah! yes, to be sure, he told me so," said Elliot.

"Any one but Marian would be impatient to know what he said of her," said Caroline.

"Do you want to know yourself, Caroline?" said Elliot; "shall I tell you?"

"Yes, do," said Caroline, in her curiosity, forgetting that Marian might be pained.

"Ah! you ought to be warned if you want to set your cap at him, for she has forestalled you. Let me see, what was it he said? O, that Lady Marchmont would scarcely be alone in her glory long, for, for such as liked the style of thing, her cousin was as perfect a piece of carving in white marble as he ever had seen."

White marble was certainly not the comparison for Marian's cheeks at that moment; it was pain and horror to her even to hear that she had been spoken of between Elliot and Mr. Faulkner, and to be told it in this manner, in public, was perfectly dreadful. She could neither sink under the table nor run away, so with crimson face and neck, she kept her post on the sofa, and every one saw she was intensely annoyed. Elliot, who had told it in a mischief-making spirit, fancying he should make his sister jealous, walked away, amusing himself with the notion that he had sown the dragon's teeth; Caroline was very sorry to have caused such painful blushes, yet was proud to hear of Marian's being admired; and Mrs. Lyddell said not a word, but worked on with a jerk at her thread, trying to persuade herself that she was not vexed that, as Elliot said, her daughter had been forestalled.

Marian did not recover herself sufficiently to say one word about Mr. Faulkner till she was in her own room, and then when Caroline came, to pity her for her blushes, and apologize for having occasioned them, she said, "O! how I wish he was not coming!"

"Why, don't you like him in return for his admiration?"

"He is a horrible man!" said Marian.

"Horrible, and why? What has he done to you? I am sure you

are very ungrateful."

"Don't talk of it," said Marian, blushing furiously again, then recollecting that she might give rise to a suspicion that he had already said something to her, she added, "I don't — I don't mean anything about that nonsense."

"Well, but what do you mean? Is it really anything more than his being Elliot's friend, and having dared to — ."

"No, but Caroline, don't say anything about it; it was what I heard about him at the Marchmonts."

"O what?"

"It does not seem fair to tell how they talked over their guests, so don't repeat it again, pray."

"You seem to find it like having a tooth drawn. Well! I am sworn to secrecy. I won't tell a living creature."

"I am sure I know hardly anything, only that Lord Marchmont thinks very badly of him, and was quite sorry he had been asked to dinner. And he spoke of his having taken up Germanism, and oh! Caroline, for a man's faith to be unsettled is the worst of all, for then there is nothing to fall back upon."

Caroline stood by Marian's fire, looking thoughtful for some moments. "Yes," she said, "you and Walter are in the same mind there, but it is not like what I was brought up to think. Miss Cameron used to teach us that the being in earnest in believing was the thing rather than the form of faith."

"O, Caroline, that cannot be right. We have been commanded to hold one form of faith, and it must be wrong to set up another and hold it."

"Yes, but if people are not clear that only one was given to every one, and that just as we say it is?"

"Then it is very bad of them!" said Marian indignantly, "for I am sure the Bible is quite clear — one faith — the form of sound words — the faith once delivered to the saints."

"I am quite clear about it," said Caroline.

"O, of course," said Marian, looking at her with a sort of alarm at her speaking of the possibility as regarded herself of not being clear.

"But if people are not clear, what are they to do?"

"I don't know," said Marian, quickly; "only I hope I shall never have anything to do with such people; I can't judge for them; I had rather not think about them; it is of no use."

"Of no use — what, not if you could do such a person good?"

"Only in this way," said Marian, taking up her Prayer Book, and turning to the Collect for Good Friday.

"Yes, but trying to convince?"

"I should be afraid."

"Afraid! Marian, I am sure nothing could hurt your faith."

"I would not try," said Marian, shaking her head sadly.

"But at that rate no one ever would be converted?"

"You forget that there are clergymen."

"Yes, but other people have done good."

"O yes, but not women by arguing. O no, no, Caroline, we never ought to put our weakness forward, as if it could guard the truth. You know the wrong side may find stronger arguments than we are able to do — mind I don't say than can be found — of course truth is the strongest of all, but we may be overpowered, though the truth is not. We women should not stand out to argue for the truth any more than we should stand out to fight as champions in the right cause."

"And is this the reason you never would argue?"

"I don't know — I mean no, it was only because I had nothing to say; I knew when a thing was right, but could not tell why, and the more you asked, the more I did not know."

"And do you know now?"

"Sometimes," said Marian, "not often, but Mr. Wortley taught me some things, and one grows up to others. But I could never explain even when I know."

"For instance —" said Caroline, laughing.

"O that came, I don't know how. Have I said so much?"

"A great deal that is very nice. Good night, Marian."

CHAPTER XII.

"She seemed some nymph in her sedan,
Apparelled in exactest sort,
And ready to be borne to court."

COWPER.

Mr. Faulkner came at the time appointed, and Caroline, who had kept Marian's counsel, according to promise, was very curious to see how they would behave towards each other. As to Marian, she was just what might be expected, — more cold, distant, and stately than she had ever been to the most vulgar of Mrs. Lyddell's acquaintance. She gave a chilling bend to repel his attempt at shaking hands, made replies of the shortest when he tried to talk to her, and would not look up, or put on the slightest air of interest, at all the entertaining stories he was telling at dinner.

The others were all extremely pleased with him. Elliot had never before brought home so agreeable a friend; a person who could talk of anything but hunting and racing was a new thing among his acquaintance, and every one was loud in his praise. Caroline, from having been prejudiced against him by Marian's history, was more surprised than the others: and scolded Marian, in the evening, for not having told them how very agreeable he was.

"I never can think any one agreeable when I know there is hollowness within," said Marian.

"I suppose Lord Marchmont knows," said Caroline, in a tone of annoyance and of a little doubt; and there the conversation ended.

Few people were ever more agreeable than Mr. Faulkner. He had read everything, travelled everywhere, and was full of conversation suited to every one. If Marain had not heard Lord Marchmont's account of him, she must have liked him; but knowing what she did, she could and would not: looking at him something as Madame Cottin's Matilde first looked at Malek Adel, and not suffering herself to lose any of her horror. For the first day or two her frigidity was something wonderful, as she found him inclined to make attempts to cultivate her acquaintance; but she thoroughly succeeded in repelling him. He left off trying to talk to her; and one day when they were obliged to go in to dinner together, only exchanged the fewest and most formal of words with her, and positively neglected her for his other neighbour.

After this, Marian did not quite so much overdo her stateliness. She could afford to be like herself with the others, even when he was in the room, though she never voluntarily took part in a conversation in which he was engaged, and her coldest air came over her whenever he approached. And it was well for her she could be so; for he stayed more than a fortnight, decided on buying the estate of High Down, and was asked to come again and make his head-quarters at Oakworthy, while superintending the alterations. All were sorry when he went; even the boys, whose first holiday week had been rendered very agreeable by his good nature. Johnny and Gerald vied with each other in his praise, heaping together a droll medley of schoolboy panegyrics; and Marian, not wishing to tell them of her objections, allowed that he had been very kind to them.

The Christmas holidays passed, and left no change in the impression on her mind regarding Gerald; only she heard no news of her two sovereigns, and he did not so much as give her the opportunity of speaking to him alone. The heartache was growing worse than ever, and she was beginning to have a sort of desperate feeling that she would — she would — do she knew not what — write to Mr. Wortley — write more strongly to Gerald than she had ever yet dared to do — when one morning, a foreign looking letter arrived, in handwriting she knew full well, though it had never before been addressed to herself. There was company staying in the house, and Marian was not sorry it was impossible to read it at the breakfast table. She did not know what she was eating or what she was saying, and ran away with it as soon as she could, to enjoy it in her own room. A letter from Edmund! Could it be possible, or could it — O disappointing thought! — be only some enclosure for her to forward. In alarm at the idea, she tore it open. A long letter, and quite certainly to herself; for there stood the three welcome words, "My dear Marian." She glanced hastily down the first page, to make sure that there was nothing the matter; but no, it was all right — he wrote in his own lively style. He began by saying it was so long since he had heard from England, that he was growing afraid he was forgotten, and felt very small when the post came in, and brought something for every one but him; and he was going to try a fresh person, since he was growing desperate, and had sent appeals in vain to all his correspondents. He asked many questions about home friends, and about Marian herself; and then told much to interest her about his own doings, his way of living, and his hunting expeditions, with all the strange wild beasts with which they had made him acquainted, and he concluded thus: — "I hope you will write soon, and that you will be able to give me a flourishing account of Gerald. His silence may mean nothing, but it may also mean so much, that to hear he is going on particularly well would be double satisfaction just at present. Therefore with a view to what passed in our last walk at Oakworthy, tell me if you are completely satisfied with regard to him."

It was a ray of light upon all Marian's perplexities; showing her what course to take, and filling her with hope. Her confidence in Edmund's power of setting everything right was still unchanged, and when Gerald's case was fully before him, he would know how to judge, and what to do; it would all be safe and off her mind. She felt sure that this had been the very reason of his writing; and full of gratitude, and infinitely relieved, she opened her desk, as if to answer was the easiest and most comfortable thing in the world.

She did not, however, get on quite as fast as she expected; she dreaded equally the saying too much, or too little, — the giving Edmund actually a bad impression of her poor Gerald, or letting him think that there was no cause for anxiety. Then she thought the best way would be merely to give the facts, and let him draw his own conclusions; but these facts were in themselves trifles light as air, and it seemed unkind to send them across half the world. She left off trying to write, and resolved to give herself time for consideration; but time only made her more perplexed. She waited a week, wrote at last, and as soon as her letter was fairly gone, thought of forty different ways of saying the thing better and more justly, dwelt again and again on each line that could convoy a false impression one way or the other, and reproached herself by turns for having spoken disadvantageously of her dear affectionate brother, and for not having let her cousin fairly see the full extent of the mischief. On the whole, however, she was much happier now that it was all in Edmund's hands; so much so, that when Mr. Faulkner came again, she could not be quite so stiff; and being entirely relieved from the fear of his taking notice of her, could do him the favour of laughing when he told anything amusing.

Winter and early spring came and went; the Easter holidays brought Gerald home, and she tried again in vain to get him to write to Edmund; but she could bear it better now that she had hopes.

They went to London, and Marian was carried into the midst of all the gaieties supposed to befit her age and situation. Mrs. Lyddell would have thought herself very far from "doing her justice," if she had not taken her to all the balls and parties in her way; and Marian was obliged to submit, and get into the carriage, when she had much rather have gone to bed.

She put off the expectation of much enjoyment till Lady Marchmont should come, and her arrival took place unusually late that season. She had not been well, and little Willie had been somewhat ailing; so that the bringing him into London air was put off as long as possible. It was not till the latter part of May that she came, as she had always promised to do, in time for Marian's presentation at court, on which both she and Mrs. Lyddell were bent; and Marian ready to endure it, by the help of a few romantic thoughts of loyalty. The day after Lady Marchmont arrived, she called at Mrs. Lyddell's and came in, as she generally did once in a year. After her visit was over, she asked Marian to come and take a drive, and no sooner where they in the carriage, than she exclaimed, "A nice looking girl, that Miss Lyddell! Is she the one who is to marry Mr. Faulkner?"

"O, Selina! how could you have heard such nonsense?"

"What, is it to be denied? It is not settled, then?"

"No, nor ever will be."

"Why, surely the man has been spending months at Oakworthy."

"Only weeks; besides, he was buying a house."

"A very proper preliminary to a wife."

"O, no, no it is impossible!"

"But why? Perhaps you know some good reason to the contrary; for I heard he admired you very much when he met you last year."

"Don't say such things, Selina. How could you fancy it possible, after all the horrid things Lord Marchmont said of him!"

"What is impossible, my dear? That he should think you very handsome?"

"Don't, Selina, pray don't! That any body good for any thing should ever marry him!"

"Any body good for any thing!" repeated Selina. "Well, granted, — and it is a considerable grant, — does that make the supposition out of the question?"

"Yes, as regards Caroline. O, Selina! you do not know Caroline, or you would not look so incredulous!"

"Time will show," said Lady Marchmont, gaily. "I reserve to myself the satisfaction of having known it beforehand."

"It never will be," said Marian. "And how is little Willie?"

"Very well, poor little man, if he would only grow, but he is so small, that I am fairly ashamed to show such a hop-o'-my-thumb. But he is coming out quite a genius; he reads as well as I do, and makes the wisest speeches."

And the history of his wise speeches occupied them for some time, with other matters, until just as their drive was nearly concluded, Selina exclaimed, "But all this time I have never asked you if you can throw any light on this extraordinary step of Edmund Arundel's?"

"What do you mean?" cried Marian.

"Have you not heard that he has exchanged, and is coming home? The most foolish thing, — just as he might have been sure of promotion. It is not likely to be health, for the climate agreed very well with him."

"Yes," assented Marian, wrapt in her own thoughts; "but did he write to you?"

"Not a word; we only saw it in the Gazette, and Lord Marchmont would hardly believe it could be he; but it was but too plain, — Lieutenant Edmund Gerald Arundel. It is very strange; he was not wont to do foolish things."

"No," said Marian, mechanically.

"And you know nothing about it? You know him better than we do. Ho seemed the very man for the Colonies, with no ties at home, unless — no, it is impossible — unless there could be a lady in the case."

"O, no!" replied Marian colouring so much at the secret consciousness of his motive, that Selina laughed, saying, "I could almost suspect you, in spite of your demureness, of being the very lady. However, I am glad you think there is no truth in my surmise, for he could not do a more absurd thing than marry. Only when a man gives up all his prospects in this way, there is nothing too preposterous to be expected to come next."

By this time they were at Mrs. Lyddell's door, and Marian gladly escaped, feeling stunned at the effect her letter had produced. How noble, how kind, how generous, how self-devoted Edmund was! this was the prominent thought. She knew him to be very fond and very proud of his regiment, to be much attached to several of his brother officers, and to have given them more of his affection than persons with home interests generally do; indeed, they had served him instead of home. All his success in life, and his hopes of promotion, given up too, — sacrifices which she could not estimate; and it was she who had caused them. She had thoughtlessly led him to do himself all this injury, out of his kindness and affection, and his sense of duty towards her and her brother. She was very unhappy when she thought of this; then came the bright ray of joy and relief in hope and confidence for Gerald, — Gerald saved, saved from corruption, ruin, from being like Elliot, from breaking her heart, made all that his father and mother would have made him, her pride, her delight, the glory and honour of Fern Torr, — O, joy, joy! And the mere seeing Edmund again, — joy, joy! Yes, the joy far predominated over the pain and regret; indeed, be the injury to himself what it might, who could be sorry that he had acted so nobly? Yes, Marian was happy; her eyes were bright, her smile frequent; she laughed with Clara, she romped with little Willie Marchmont, she was ungracious to none but Mr. Faulkner who came to the house so much, that she began to fear that Caroline might have the annoyance of an offer from him, more especially since he had made his mother and sister call on Mrs. Lyddell, and Miss Faulkner seemed to intend to be intimate.

The day of the drawing-room had come; Mrs. Lyddell and Caroline were going, and Marian was of course to go with Lady Marchmont. She had just been full dressed, and had come down stairs to wait for Lady Marchmont's carriage, when a step was heard approaching. She thought it was the servant, to announce it; it was the servant, but the announcement was not what she expected. It was "Mr. Arundel," — and Edmund stood before her, browner, thinner, older, but still Edmund himself.

She could not have spoken; she only held out her hand, and returned his strong pressure with all the force her soft fingers were capable of. Mrs. Lyddell spoke, he answered, explanations were given and received, and still she stood as if she was dreaming, until he turned to her, and said, "Well, Marian, these are transformations indeed?"

"I can't help it," said Marian.

"Do you think I want you to help it? I suppose I need not ask if the Marchmonts are in town?"

"Lady Marchmont presents Marian," said Mrs. Lyddell; "we expect her carriage every minute."

And just then the announcement really came.

"Her carriage, not herself?" said Edmund. "Well, I think I might go with you to her house, Marian, if your feathers are not ashamed of such shabby company."

"O, pray come!"

"And you will return to dinner, I hope, Mr. Arundel," said Mrs. Lyddell, "at half-past seven? Mr. Lyddell will be so glad to see you."

Edmund accepted the invitation, and the two cousins went down stairs together. As soon as they were in the carriage, Edmund said, "A lucky moment to come in. It is something to have seen you in all your splendour. You have grown into something magnificent!"

"All this finery makes me look taller than I really am."

"Nevertheless, however you may try to conceal it, I am afraid you have turned into the full grown cat. I saw it in your letter."

"O, Edmund, I am so sorry I wrote that letter."

"Why? Are you happier about Gerald?"

"No, I don't know that I am," said Marian, sighing; "but — but I little thought it would make so much difference to you. I did not know what I was doing."

"I am glad of it, or you would not have written so freely; though after all you could not have helped being like a sensible straightforward person."

"O, it is untold relief that you are come; and yet I must be sorry —"

"I won't have you sorry. No one should regret having told the honest truth. The fact is, I ought never to have gone. And poor Gerald?"

"I have no more to say, only vague fears. But now you are come, it is all right."

"Don't trust too much to me, Marian. Remember, it will be a generous thing in Gerald if he attends to me at all. He is not obliged to do so."

"You will — you must do everything. Gerald is as fond of you as ever, I know he is, though he would not write. O, I am glad! You heard of our delightful going home, I hope?"

"Yes. All well there?" said Edmund, hurriedly.

"Very well. Agnes is grown so tall, and it is so very nice there. The old Manor house —"

"Well," he broke in suddenly; "and how do you get on with Selina Marchmont."

"She is very, very kind. But O! here we are in her street, and I shall have no more of you today."

"Not at dinner?"

"O; it is a great, horrid party, as Mrs. Lyddell should have warned you."

"Could not I take you in to dinner?"

"I am afraid not. Mrs. Lyddell will never treat me as if I was at home, and I am afraid there is an honourable man that I must be bestowed on."

They had reached Lady Marchmont's door, and going up stairs, found her looking like a princess in a fairy tale, in her white plumes and her diamonds; and Willie, the smallest, most delicate, and prettiest of little boys, admiring the splendours of his papa's yeomanry uniform.

In spite of being considerably provoked with Edmund for having come home, Lord and Lady Marchmont welcomed him with as much warmth as if it was the most prudent thing he could have done. They insisted on his coming to stay at their house, and as it was full time to set off, left him to see about his worldly goods being transported thither.

"Has he told you his reason, Marian?" asked Selina, as soon as the two ladies and their trains were safely disposed of, in the carriage.

"I know them," said Marian, her colour rising, "and most noble they are; but I had rather let him tell you himself."

"Marian's discretion again," said Lord Marchmont, smiling.

"Only set me at rest on one point," said Selina; "it is no love affair, I hope?"

"No, indeed," said Marian; "or do you think he would have told me?"

Probably there were few young ladies who played their part that day in the drawing-room, that last remnant of the ancient state and majesty of our courts, with happier minds, or less intent on their own appearance, than Marian Arundel. She was very glad when the bustle and crowd were over, and she could be alone to enjoy the certainty that Edmund was really at home again.

He came according to promise that evening, but she could not have much conversation with him, as he was placed at a distance from her, the greater part of the time. He was not sorry to be thus able to watch her, though he did not see her in the point of view in which she pleased him best. She looked better now, he thought, than in the court dress; for the broad, simple, antique braids of her dark hair, only adorned by two large pearl pins, suited better than the plumes and lappets, with the cast of her classical features. All that he had thought promised beauty, as a child, had fulfilled the promise, and the countenance, the expression, would have been fine, seen on a much plainer face, and as she eat there, her black, shady eyes cast down, her dark pencilled eyebrows contrasting with her colourless cheek, and her plain white drapery in full folds, flowing round her, she might have been some majestic lady in a mysterious picture, who had stepped from her frame into a scene belonging to another age. She looked as if she was acting a tableau; she moved, indeed, and smiled, and spoke occasionally; but the queen-like deportment of her neck did not relax; her lips resumed their statue-like expression; there was no smile about the eye, no interest in the air. She was among the company, but not of them; neither shy nor formal, but as if she belonged to some other sphere, and had only come there by mistake. Edmund could have counted the times, for they were few enough, when her head bent forward with eagerness, and there was animation in her face.

How different from Caroline! her brightly coloured, blooming face sparkling with life and light; flowers among her light, shining hair; her dress of well-chosen, tasteful, brilliant tints, ornament, lace and ribbon, all well assorted in kind and quantity, her alert, lively movements carrying her from one group to another, with something pleasant and appropriate to say to all, bringing smiles and animation with her wherever she went. Not that Edmund did not prefer his cousin's severe simplicity, and admire it as something grand; but that stern grandeur was not all that fitted the place; and though he thought her beautiful, he was not satisfied.

Edmund had some talk with Mrs. Lyddell, who spoke of Gerald with great warmth; more, he thought, than she showed in the mention of Marian. He stayed till the last, and saw the relaxation of her grand company-face, before he wished them good night.

"Well," said Mrs. Lyddell, as the door closed behind him, and she lighted her candle, "Africa has not robbed Mr. Arundel of all his good looks. How old is he?"

"Nearly twenty-eight," said Marian.

"I am always forgetting that he is so young," said Mrs. Lyddell. "Well, good night. I wonder what brought him home?"

"I do not wonder, for it is plain enough," said Caroline, as the girls turned up their own staircase.

"Marian tries to look innocent," said Clara, laughing violently.

"I am sure I don't understand," said Marian.

"Now I am sure that is on purpose to make us explain," said Clara. "It is too bad, Marian; when he came straight to you, instead of going to Lady Marchmont."

"And the tête-à-tête in the carriage," said Caroline.

"Don't be so ridiculous," said Marian; "but I believe you like such jokes so well, that you would make them out of anything."

"I don't make a joke of it at all. I always thought it was with that very view, he was made your guardian."

"You very absurd persons, good night!" said Marian, shutting her door, and laughing to herself at such a very ludicrous idea as such a scheme on the part of her father.

These kind of jokes, of which some people are still very fond, may be very hurtful, since a young girl's inexperience may found far more upon them than the laughers ever intended. Caroline and Clara were not acting a kind part, though they were far from any unkind meaning. Marian had great susceptibility and deep affections; and had her mind been less strong, her happiness might have been seriously injured. Even if their observations had no real meaning, and no effect on her heart, yet they could not fail to occasion her many moments of embarrassment, and might interfere with her full, free confidence in her best and earliest friend.

In some degree they had this result. Marian began to be aware that her situation with Edmund was not without awkwardness, — that he was still a young man, and that she was now a young woman; and whilst shocked at herself, and disliking the moment that had opened the door to the thought, was obliged to consider how far there might be truth in the suggestion.

She was quite sure that she had influenced him strongly, quite sure that he regarded her with warm affection; she wished she was equally sure it was with a brother's love. Yes, she wished, for to think otherwise would lower him in her estimation. He was her first cousin, and if first cousins had better not marry he would never think of it; besides, the merit of his sacrificing all for Gerald's good would be lost, and his return would have been an act of self-gratification instead of self-devotion. No, she would not, could not believe any such thing; she was certain Edmund never would be so weak as to wish to do anything only doubtfully right, and thus, strangely enough, her full trust in the dignity of his character, prevented her from imagining him in love with her.

Still she knew her cousins were watching her, and this prevented her from ever meeting him in thorough comfort at Mr. Lyddell's; and even when at Lord Marchmont's, her maidenly reserve had been so far awakened as to make her shrink back from the full freedom of their former intercourse. This, however, was more in her feeling than in her manners, which, if they differed at all from what they were formerly, only seemed to be what naturally arose from her growth in years.

She observed that he was not in good spirits. It was not what others, not even Selina, could perceive, but Edmund and Marian had known each other too well and too long, not to read each other's faces, and know the meaning of each other's tones. She did not expect him to be as merry as in olden days at home, nor did she desire it; but there was more depression about him than she thought comfortable, and she was sure that it was an effort to him to talk in the lively way that had once been natural to him. She was afraid he felt the separation from his friends in his old regiment very severely, or else that he was very anxious about Gerald, and yet she had found out that the tenderest point of all was Fern Torr, for he either would not or could not speak of that, but always contrived to turn the conversation as soon as it was touched upon. She grieved over his unhappiness a great deal, and yet would not enter on any questioning, from an innate feeling, that it would not be becoming. He was only to stay a very short time in London, before joining his regiment at Portsmouth, and he meant to go and spend a day at Eton to see Gerald, but Lady Marchmont suddenly proposed that they should all go together; she said she must inspect Eton before Master Willie was ready to go, and that it would be a charming scheme to take Marian and surprise Gerald. Marian had a few secret doubts whether this was exactly the most suitable way of fulfilling Edmund's intentions, but it was so delightful a treat that she laid aside her scruples, and Selina coaxed her husband into finding a day to accompany them.

So one fine June morning, the day before Edmund's departure, they set off, Selina's high spirits and Marian's happiness giving the party a very joyous aspect. Father Thames looked as stately and silvery as ever, the playing fields smiled in the sunshine, and Windsor Castle looked down on them majestically. Marian felt it a holiday to have escaped from London into so fair a scene, and even if she had come for nothing else, would have been happy in beholding some of the most honoured spots in the broad realm of England.

She had many questions to ask, but Lord Marchmont was taken up with showing his old haunts to his wife, and she was walking some distance in front, with Edmund, on whose face there was an expression of melancholy thought that she would not disturb. He was an Etonian, and how fall of remembrances must all be around him.

Presently two or three boys met them running, and were passing them, when Marion exclaimed, "There is Lionel!" "Lyddell!" called Edmund, and one of them stopped, so taken by surprise that Marian was for a moment horrified by thinking she had mistaken him; but the next glance re-assured her, for she knew Lionel's way of standing, and his hat pulled far over his forehead.

"Lionel," said she, "where is Gerald?"

"Hallo! You here!" said he, wheeling round so that the light might not be in his eyes, and shading them with one hand while he tried to make out Edmund, and gave his other hand to Marian.

"How did you come here? Are any of the people at home here?"

"No, this is my cousin Edmund. I am come with the Marchmonts."

"You have quite forgotten me," said Edmund, shaking hands.

"Not if I could see you," said Lionel, frowning at the light, as he looked up.

"O, Lionel, how bad your eyes are!" exclaimed Marion.

"I have just been reading, and there is such a *hideous* sunshine today," said Lionel.

"And where is Gerald?"

"I'll go and fetch him."

"Where is he?"

"I'll find him," and off he ran, with a fresh pull of his hat over his forehead to keep off the hideous sunshine. The Marchmonts came up at the moment, and were told who he was, and that he was gone to find Gerald. Edmund asked what was the matter with his eyes.

"They are never very good," said Marian. "Reading and strong light always hurt them."

"Has he had any advice?"

"The surgeon at Oakworthy looked at them last Christmas, when the snow dazzled them, but he did not think there was much amiss with them. It was always so. But where can Gerald be?"

In the space of about five minutes, Gerald and Lionel appeared, and the former came up to them alone, with a look which had more of shyness than of pleasure, and his greeting, while more courteous, was less open and cordial than Lionel's had been. They all went together to the house of the boys' tutor, who had also been Edmund's; there was a great maze of talking and introductions: Lady Marchmont made herself very charming to the mistress of the house: Edmund and the tutor disappeared together, and did not come back till the others had nearly finished a most hospitable luncheon; after which the visitors set out to see all that there was time to see, and Marian caused Gerald to fetch Lionel to accompany them.

Lionel walked with Edmund and Marian, but Gerald on the other hand attached himself to Lord and Lady Marchmont, talking to them freely and pleasantly, answering Selina's questions, much to her amusement and satisfaction, and Lord Marchmont comparing notes with him, as old Etonians delight to do with "the sprightly race, disporting" for the time being, on the "margen green" of Father Thames. A particularly lively, pleasant, entertaining, well-mannered boy was Gerald, but, all the time, Marian was feeling that he was holding aloof both from her and Edmund, never allowing either of them the opportunity of speaking to him alone, for even a minute; and his manner, whenever Edmund either spoke to him or looked at him, was such as to betray to her that he was ill at ease.

Thus it was while they viewed the chapel, the court, with what Selina was pleased to call "Henry's holy shade," the upper school, the hundred steps, the terrace, and beautiful S. George's, with its gorgeous banners and carved stalls, and blazoned shields, that glimpse into the Gothic world of chivalry and romance; and in the midst of it that simple flat stone, which thrills the heart with a deep feeling at once of love, sorrow and reverence; that stone which recalls the desolate night which, in darkness and ruin, amid torn banners, and scutcheons riven, saw the Martyr king go white to his grave. Marian entered into all these things, in spite of her anxiety, for her mind was free enough to be open to external objects, now that her brother was in Edmund's hands, and she was relieved of that burthen of responsibility which had so pressed on her.

Such was their Eton day, and with no more satisfaction from Gerald did they part at the Slough station. The Marchmonts were loud in his praise, Marian sought the real opinion in Edmund's eyes, but he was leaning back, looking meditative, and when first he roused himself to enter into conversation, it was of Lionel and not of Gerald that he spoke.

"Do you say that any one has looked at that boy's eyes?"

"Yes, Mr. Wells, the Oakworthy apothecary."

"Do you know what is thought of him?"

"I don't know," said Marian considering. "He attends a good many people, I believe he is thought well of; but no one ever is ill at home, so I have no experience of him. Yes, he was called in once when we all had the measles, and last winter about Lionel's eyes. I am sure I don't know whether he is what you would call a good doctor or not; all I know is, that he is not at all like Dr. Oldham."

Edmund smiled. "Has Mrs. Lyddell not been uneasy?"

"O no!" said Marian. "No one ever troubles their head about Lionel, besides it was always so."

"Always how?"

"His eyes were always weak, and easily tired and dazzled, from the very first when I knew him. They don't look as if there was anything amiss with them, and so people don't suspect it."

"I think they do look very much amiss," said Edmund. "Do not you observe an indistinctness about the pupil, between it and the iris? Can you tell whether that was always the case?"

"I don't know, I see what you mean. I should say it had begun of late. Do you think it so bad a sign?" she asked anxiously.

"I am not sure; I only know if he belonged to me, I should not like it at all."

Marian pondered and feared, and considered if it would be possible to stir up Mrs. Lyddell; she herself was much startled, and rather indignant; but she doubted greatly whether poor Lionel was of sufficient importance in the family for any one to be very anxious on his account. In the meantime, she was extremely desirous of hearing what account Edmund had received from the tutor respecting her brother, but she had no opportunity till late in the evening, when he came and sat by her on the sofa, saying, "Now, Marian, I will answer your anxious eyes, though I am afraid I have nothing very satisfactory to tell you. I don't know that there is any positive harm — it is only the old story of a clever boy with too much money, and too much left to himself. Idleness and thoughtlessness."

"And what shall you do?"

"I don't know — I must think."

Whereupon they both sat silent.

"I shall see you again in the summer," said he.

"O yes — perhaps you will come in Gerald's holidays."

Another silence, then she said, "Do you think very badly of poor Lionel's eyes?"

"No, I don't say that, for I know nothing, only I wonder his family are not more anxious."

"I shall see if Mrs. Lyddell will believe there is cause for alarm."

The carriage was announced, she wished him good-bye again, thanked her cousins for her pleasant day, and departed, wondering to herself how it could have been a pleasant day, as after all it had been, in spite of doubt and anxiety and care.

She told Mrs. Lyddell when she came in, that she had seen Lionel.

"How were his eyes?" asked Caroline.

"I am afraid they were more dazzled than usual."

No one said anything, and after a pause she went on. "Edmund remarked a sort of indistinctness about the pupil, which he said was not a good sign."

"What was that?" said Mr. Lyddell looking up, and Marian, startled, yet glad to have attracted his notice, repeated what she had said. "Did not Wells look at his eyes last winter?" he said, turning to his wife.

"Yes, he said he could not see anything the matter with them — they must be spared — and he sent a mixture to bathe them. Lionel has been using it continually."

"How would it be to have him up here to see some one?" said Mr. Lyddell.

"Better wait for the holidays," answered his wife. "It would be the worst thing possible to set him thinking, about his eyes in the middle of the half-year. Little as he does now, it would soon be less, and his eyes have kept him back so much already that he really cannot afford to lose any more time."

There it ended, Mrs. Lyddell was not to be alarmed; she had been too long used to prosperity even to contemplate the possibility that harm should come nigh to her or to her dwelling. Mr. Lyddell, who left all family matters to her, forgot all about it, and though Marian talked Caroline into some fears on the subject, Caroline could do no more than she could herself.

CHAPTER XIII.

"*Benedict*. What, my dear Lady Disdain, are you yet living?"

"*Beatrice*. Is it possible Disdain should die while she has such meet food to feed her?"

Much Ado about Nothing.

The Lyddell family did not continue in London much longer; it had been a short season, and though the session of Parliament was not over, most of the ladies were taking flight into the country, before the end of June, — Mrs. Lyddell among the rest, — and her husband went backwards and forwards to London, as occasion called him.

The girls were glad to get into the country, but Marian soon found that she had not escaped either from gaieties, or from the objects of her aversion; for Mr. Faulkner brought his mother and sisters to High Down House, gave numerous parties there, and made a constant interchange of civilities with the family at Oakworthy. Archery was pretty much the fashion with the young ladies that year; it was a sport which Marian liked particularly, having often practised it with Edmund and Agnes, and her bow and arrows were always the first to be ready.

One day when Marian, Caroline, and Clara were shooting on the lawn at Oakworthy, Mr. and Miss Faulkner rode from High Down, came out on the lawn, and joined them. From that moment, any one could see the change that came over Marian. Instead of laughing and talking, teaching Clara, and paying only half attention to her own shooting, she now went on as if it was her sole object, and as if she had no other purpose in life. She fixed her arrows and twanged her string with a rigidity as if the target had been a deadly enemy, or her whole fate was concentrated in hitting the bull's eye; and when her arrows went straight to the mark, or at least much straighter than those of any one else, she never turned her head, or vouchsafed more than the briefest answer to the exclamations around.

The others were talking of archery in general and in particular, — just what, if it had not been Mr. Faulkner, would have delighted her; but she would not hear him. He might speak of the English long-bow, and the cloth yard-shaft, and the butts at which Elizabeth shot, and the dexterity required for hitting a deer, and of the long arrow of the Indian, and the Wourali reed of South America, — as long as he spoke it was nothing to her, let Caroline smile and answer, and appeal to her as much she would. Then came a talk about archery meetings and parties, in which at last they all grew so eager, that they stood still round the return target, and Marian could not shoot back again without perilling them; so she unstrung her bow, and stood apart with a stern face, which made her look a great deal more like Diana, than she by any means suspected or desired.

Two days after, there came a note from Miss Faulkner, — Julia, as she had requested to be called, — saying that her brother was so delighted with the archery schemes that had been discussed, that he could not give them up, and intended to give a grand fête at High Down, — archery in the morning, a ball in the evening, and all the ladies who liked, to be in costume. She ended by begging Caroline to come to luncheon that day, or the next, to enter into council on the subject. There was great delight; such an entertainment was quite a novelty in the neighbourhood, and the costume seemed to make it all the more charming in the eyes of Caroline, Clara, and their mother; all were talking at once, and wondering what it could or should be, while Marian went on reading imperturbably without one remark.

"It ought to be in Robin Hood's time, if only for the sake of Maid Marian," said Caroline. "She will be quite sure to win the prize."

"O yes, that she will," said Clara; "she shoots so much better than any one else."

"I shall not shoot in public," said Marian, looking up for a moment, and then going on with her book.

"You will do nothing to make yourself particular," said Mrs. Lyddell: "it will be very silly to set your face against this fête, when every one knows how fond you are of archery."

"We don't know anything yet about what is to be," said Caroline, quickly; and at that moment Elliot, coming in, offered to ride with her to High Down, whereupon she hastened to get ready. Such an obliging offer from her brother was certainly too uncommon a thing to be neglected, in spite of the unwonted graciousness and amiability which Elliot had for the last few weeks assumed towards her.

When she was gone, Marian and Clara resumed their ordinary occupations, and one of them at least troubled herself no more about the fête, until, shortly before dinner time, Elliot, Caroline, and Mr. Faulkner all rode up to the front door. Mr. Faulkner, it appeared, was come to dinner, and to carry on the consultation, since he was extremely eager about the scheme, and no time was to be lost in sending out the invitations. The Sherwood Forest plan had been talked over, and abandoned as too common-place. It was to be a Kenilworth fête; eight young ladies of Lady Julia's especial party were to appear in the morning in a pretty uniform dress, a little subdued from the days of the ruff and farthingale; and in the evening there was to be a regular Kenilworth quadrille, in which each lady or gentleman was to assume the dress of some character of Queen Elizabeth's court. In fact, as Mr. Faulkner said; —

> *"Gorgeous dames and statesmen bold*
> *In bearded majesty appear."*

Amy Robsart, Katherine Seymour, Anne Clifford, Frances Walsingham, Mildred Cecil, and other ladies of the time were mentioned, and then came the counting up of their eight living representatives, — the two Misses Faulkner, Caroline, yes, and Clara herself, who started and danced with ecstasy, then glanced entreatingly at her mother, who looked doubtful; Marian, two cousins of the Faulkners, who were always ready for anything, and a Miss Mordaunt, were reckoned up, and their dresses quickly discussed; but all the time Marian said not a word. She was thinking of the waste of time and consideration, the folly, levity and vanity, the throwing away of money, all this would occasion, and enjoying in her own mind the pleasure of resisting it *in toto*. She supposed she must go to the archery meeting, though why people could not be contented to shoot on their own lawns, instead of spoiling their pleasure by all this fuss, she could not guess; but make a show of herself and her shooting, be stared at by all the world, — that she would never do. Nor would she make a figure of herself at the ball, and spend the money which she wanted very much for her poor people and her books, now that her court dress and London finery had eaten up such an unconscionable share of her allowance. Increased as it was, she had never felt so poor as at present; she wanted Mrs. Jameson's "Sacred and Legendary Art" for herself, and there were all the presents to be sent to the old people at Fern Torr; and should these be given up for the sake of appearing as the fair Anne Clifford, or some such person, for one evening, during which she would be feeling most especially unnatural and uncomfortable? No indeed! and she trusted that she had a very good and sufficient defence against all such foolery, in the slight mourning which she was wearing for one of the Marchmont connection. True, she had thought of leaving it off next Sunday, but no matter; it would be such armour as was not to be lightly parted with; and if she went to the ball at all, it should never, never be as the heiress of the Cliffords, but as the faithful mourning relation of old Mr. Thomas Marchmont, her second cousin once removed, whom she had never beheld in her life, and who would have been dead at least nine weeks by the time it took place.

She said nothing about it in the drawing-room; but when they went up stairs, she told Caroline not to reckon upon her, for she should be in mourning, and could not wear a fancy dress. Caroline looked much vexed. "It was a great pity," she said, "and Julia Faulkner wished it to be all their own set. Besides, would not Marian shoot, — she who did it so well?"

"O, no, no, I could do no such thing with all those people staring."

"Not even for a silver arrow? You would be sure to win it."

"I should be ashamed of the very sight of it ever after. O no! I should like — at least I should not mind seeing it all as a spectator, but as to making a part of the show, never, never, Caroline!"

"Well, I know it is of no use to try to persuade you!" said Caroline, with a little annoyance in her tone. "Good night."

Lady Julia, with her son and daughter, came to call the next day. Marian thought herself fortunate in not being in the drawing-room. She put on her bonnet, slipped out at the garden door, and walked away with a book in her hand, to the remotest regions of the park, where she sat down under a thorn-tree, and read Schiller's Thirty Years' War with a sort of exemplary diligence and philosophy, till it was so late that she thought herself perfectly secure of the Faulkners' being gone. Yet she only just missed them, for their carriage was driving off at one door, as she reached the other.

"Where have you been, Marian?" was the first greeting.

"I have been walking to the old thorn."

"O, have you? We hunted for you everywhere in the house: we would hardly believe Fanny when she said you were gone out, for I knew you meant to walk with us."

"I thought you would be engaged so long that it was not worth while to wait for you."

"Well, but did you know you had missed the Faulkners?" said Clara.

"I knew they were here."

Every one understood this except Clara, and very little did it please Mrs. Lyddell or Caroline.

"Marian," said Mrs. Lyddell, "you really must not be so absurd about this matter. Your mourning is nothing. You need not be wearing it even now; and it will annoy Lady Julia, and put her to serious inconvenience, if you continue to refuse."

"I am sure I do not wish to inconvenience her," said Marian; "but there must be many young ladies who would be only too happy to take the part."

"Of course," said Mrs. Lyddell, "any one else would rejoice to be asked; but the point is, that it is so unpleasant to admit any thing of a stranger into the intimacy these things occasion."

"I am almost a stranger to them."

"Yes, but not to us, Marian," said Clara. "You have known them as long, or longer than we have; and you would look so very well. Lady Julia said herself that such a distinguished face and figure as yours would set the whole thing off to advantage."

Caroline well knew this was but the way to make Marian still more determined against it. She held her tongue through all the persuasions of her mother and Clara; and trusting a little, but not much, to the superior influence which she knew herself to possess, she followed Marian to her room, and began, — "Marian, are you still resolute against this unfortunate archery? because, if you do not really think it a matter of right and wrong, I should be very much obliged to you if you would only yield."

It was not so easy to withstand Caroline speaking in this way, as Mrs. Lyddell almost scolding and Clara talking nonsense; but Marian had made up her mind, and would not let herself be shaken. "I don't think I can," was her answer.

"Will you say whether you really think it wrong?"

"I don't know." Not her considering "I don't know," but the dry, provoking end-of-the-matter answer of half sullen days gone by.

"If you really thought it positively wrong," proceeded Caroline, "not another word would I say: but I don't see how you can without condemning all gaeties, and that I know you do not."

"I only think it a — a waste of time — a great deal of nonsense," said Marian, faltering for an answer; "and really I have spent so much money; I do not like to throw away any more."

"O, you do not know how we have settled that," said Caroline, beginning to be hopeful now that she had something tangible to attack. "The dresses for the morning will be nothing, — only a white skirt and green polka, which will do to wear for ever after, and a little ruff, very pretty, and no expense at all; and a little alteration will make our court dresses perfectly suitable for Queen

Elizabeth's ladies. You need not be at all afraid of being ruined."

Marian saw that, though there would be many a little expense to make a mickle one, yet it would still only cost her Mrs. Jameson, instead of the gifts to the poor people; but as this was what chiefly justified her in her own eyes, she would not admit the conviction, and answered, "Those things that are altered and adapted really are as costly in the end as if they were new altogether. Besides, I could not, I really could not shoot before such an assembly."

"I should so like to see you get the arrow."

"O Caroline, that would be worse than anything!"

"Well, then, don't get it; shoot as badly as you please: only do be kind and make one of us, or you will spoil the whole concern."

"How can that be? What difference can my dressing up or shooting make to any one?"

"Why, for one thing, if you are not one, as you must be, living with us and all, Julia will be obliged to ask that Miss Grimley; don't you know her?"

"What, that old young lady who has been figuring in the newspaper so long as getting all the archery prizes?"

"Yes, the veteran archer, as Elliot calls her; and Mr. Faulkner says, if she appears in character at all, it must be as Queen Elizabeth herself dancing a stately pavise to the sound of the little fiddle. She is some connection of theirs, and must be asked, if you will not take it; and she is almost as bad as Queen Elizabeth herself, and will give none of us any peace about the dresses, O Marian! Julia said she should esteem it as a real kindness from you if you would be Lady Anne, if only for the sake of keeping her out!"

"I think it would be very absurd for a person who hates the whole concern to be dragged in, for the sake of keeping out one who likes it!"

"Then you are still resolved? Well, I had not much expectation, but still I was half inclined to hope you would relent, if you did not think it a point of principle, when you knew that it would be a real favor to me."

"To you, Caroline! you do not care for such trumpery."

"I do care about seeing my friends mortified and vexed," said Caroline, mournfully.

"Your friends!" exclaimed Marian, in a voice of contempt.

"Yes, as much as kindness can make them."

"And esteem? O Caroline!"

"Kindness — readiness to oblige," repeated Caroline. "They are my friends, and I am very fond of them."

Caroline went away without another word, and Marian felt that her words implied that she preferred readiness to oblige, to rigid, unbending superiority in goodness. Marian felt it, and was disappointed in Caroline, and pleased to have kept her determination, without asking herself how far it was satisfied pride in obstinacy.

This was the last time for many weeks that Caroline lingered talking in Marian's room. The old chill had come on again. Both knew, though neither said so, that it was not so much because it was a display and expense that Marian refused, as because it was the Faulkners' party. If it had been Lady Marchmont's, it would have been very different. Now Caroline liked the Faulkners; they were all good natured, and much more agreeable than any others in the neighbourhood — than any, indeed, with whom she had yet been brought into close intercourse. She thought Marian was unjust and ungracious, both to them and to her; that she had been prejudiced from the first, and now was very decidedly making herself disagreeable by a rigidity in trifles, which was almost positive unkindness. Caroline's home, as has been shown, was neither a very happy, nor a very satisfactory one; so that of late she had learnt to look upon her brother Walter and Marian as her chief comforts, and was now much more hurt and disappointed at Marian's conduct than she was willing to show. It was particularly unfortunate just at this time, when there was so much to invite and gratify her at High Down, when she was in especial need of a true and affectionate friend and counsellor, and when Walter was absent, being engaged in preparing for his ordination, which was to take place in the course of the autumn.

Mrs. Lyddell was much displeased with Marian, and showed it by her coldness and formality; and Marian began to live more alone with herself, and at war with the outer world, than she had done even before Edmund's first visit five years ago. Caroline and Clara were a great deal with the Faulkners, either at High Down or at home. Clara was in a perfect transport at being admitted into the number of the archeresses, and had struck up one of her eternal friendships with Louisa, the second Miss Faulkner; and Marian might very fairly be provoked at seeing how entirely her mind was diverted from all the rationality which she and Caroline had been endeavouring — and as they had hoped, not without success — to infuse into her during the past year. To get Clara to settle quietly down to anything was an utter impossibility; her wisest employment was the study of Elizabethan costumes, her most earnest, the practice of archery. Now Marian always maintained that archery, on their own lawn, and among themselves, was a very pretty sport; and for the sake of consistency with her own principles, she very diligently shot whenever the Faulkners were not there, and did her very best, by precept and example, to make Clara fit her arrows to the string in her own direct and pur-pose-like way, draw the bow-string to her ear with a steady effort and aim, instead of a fitful jerk or twitch; and in fact shoot, if she was to shoot, like a sensible woman, who really intended damage to the target. Clara was very much obliged, and made some prog-ress; but Marian thus did herself little good with any one else, for her love of the sport, and her excellence at it, made her spirit of disdain all the more marked. Clara, was again, as in former times, her chief friend in the family; for Marian, after the first vexation, held her sense too cheap to blame her for her folly. It was the fault of the others that she had been put in the way of what could not fail to turn her head; so she listened, without showing many tokens of contempt, to her endless histories of dear Louisa, and all the plans at High Down, — of the witticisms that were perpe-trated, the anticipations of amusement and admiration, and of the tracasseries which Miss Grimley had not failed to occasion. Marian was often entertained, and Clara more than once hoped she was on the point of regretting that she was not one of the favoured eight; but nothing could be further from Marian's mind. She did not intend to absent herself either from the archery or from the ball, but she must wear her own character, and no other; and people were allowed to assume fancy dresses or not, just as suited their inclination, so that she was in no fear of rendering herself remarkable.

Caroline and Clara were to go to High Down two days before the great occasion, and stay till the day after; Marian to remain at Oakworthy. Just before they went, Clara danced into her room, saying, "Marian, do you know some of the officers at Portsmouth have been asked to the ball? You know there is a railroad all the way. I wonder if Mr. Arundel will be there?"

"Decidedly not," replied Marian.

"What, not when he knows what an attraction there will be?"

"Don't talk such nonsense, Clara; the idea of thinking a man would take such a journey for a ball! Well, I hope you will be very happy."

"O do come and see my dress, Marian, before it is packed up; it is on mamma's bed, and it is so beautiful!"

Marian came, and admired. Caroline was to be Amy Robsart, and Clara, Janet Foster; a part her mother had chosen for her, as more appropriate to a girl not yet come out. Certainly, Tony Foster would scarcely have recognized his demure little Puritan under the little lace hood, the purple bodice, and white skirt, at which Clara looked with such exultation; and Janet was further to be supposed to have taken possession of the Countess's orient neck-pearls, and was to wear them as the only ornament that could with any propriety be bestowed on her. It happened that Marian had a remarkably fine set of pearls. She had few jewels of any kind; but these had been her grandmother's, and there was some tradition belonging to them which no one ever could remember. Janet's necklace was so much less pretty, that Marian could not help exclaiming that Clara had better wear hers. Clara demurred, for she knew Marian relied on these pearls to help out a dress which had seen more than one London party; but it ended in Marian's having her own way, and being contemptuous at the gratitude with which her loan was received. Yet she was surprised to find that it was a relief to her that Mrs. Lyddell departed a little from her cold politeness, and showed herself really pleased and obliged.

Certainly, if Mrs. Lyddell had not in some degree relaxed, those two days would have been very forlorn. As it was, it was very odd to sit down to dinner with only Mr. and Mrs. Lyddell and Elliot, and to have no one but Mrs. Lyddell to speak to in the drawing-room. She was glad when the day came, to have it over; and she was not sufficiently hard-hearted to regret that it was as fine as could be wished. To High Down they went, and everything was just as Marian had expected, — every one walked about and idled, and wondered when the shooting would begin; and when it did begin, no one paid much attention to it except those who were interested in some of the competitors. Marian watched her pupil anxiously, and Clara, between excitement and nervousness, shot much worse than if she had been in the garden at home, and went so wide of the mark, that Marian was ashamed of her. Caroline did better, but not well; and the prize was of course borne off by Miss Grimley, who was popularly reported to have arrows enough to stock the quivers of two or three cupids.

Clara ran up to Marian, and walked with her a little while; telling her all that had come to pass during the last two days, — a great deal of bustle, and merriment, and nonsense, which Clara seemed to have enjoyed excessively, and of which Marian could have said, "Every one to his taste." Of Caroline she saw little or nothing; and after wandering about in the rear of Mrs. Lyddell, and exchanging a great many cold salutations, and colder sentences of small-talk, she was very glad to find herself once more in the carriage, though it was only to go home, dine and dress for the ball, and then High Down again.

She wore white, with jet ornaments, and a row of pearls round her hair, — the only thing that saved her from being rather shabbily dressed than otherwise. However, Mrs. Lyddell had long since announced that she had done saying anything about Marian's dress, and Fanny had not been a ladies' maid long enough to grow into a tyrant; so that she had her own way, and no one repeated to her, what she knew full well, that her white silk was yellow where it swept the ground, and the lace did not stand out as freshly as once it did.

Mrs. Lyddell and Elliot talked and laughed all the way, quizzing the company very sociably, and both appearing in the highest spirits. Mr. Lyddell was asleep in his corner; Marian with her forehead against the window, and her thoughts with Gerald. They reached High Down in the midst of a stream of carriages; and Marian, in her plain white, had to walk into the ball-room with Elliot, who had completed his offences in her eyes, by daring to assume the dress of Sir Philip Sidney. She soon, however, was free of him, for he liked her as little as she liked him, and moreover had to go and perform his part in the noted Kenilworth quadrille. Marian was left standing by Mrs. Lyddell, as she usually did, through the greater part of a ball; for as she never waltzed, there were few dances in which she could take a part. She had made half the Oakworthy neighbours afraid of her; and Mrs. Lyddell, having found that all activity in the way of being a useful chaperon was thrown away, had acquiesced in leaving her to herself, "doing her justice" sufficient by taking her to the ball.

Marian was entertained by the pageant, as she deemed it. It was a very pretty scene, with so many gay dresses, in the bright light; and it was amusing to recognise her acquaintances in the wonderful costumes some of them had seen fit to assume. She would have liked some one to laugh with, at a shepherdess dancing, crook and all; and she highly appreciated a good-natured old gentleman, who was willing to do anything, however absurd, that could please his friends, and had come out as my grave Lord Keeper himself, with

> "His bushy beard and shoe-strings green,
> His high-crowned hat and satin-doublet."

Caroline looked more like a beauty than she had ever seen her before. Her fair ringlets and white neck had a peculiar elegance, set off by the delicate fan-like ruff, and graceful head-gear of the Countess Amy. The only fault that Marian could find was, that poor Amy never could have looked as if she had so much mind as Caroline's countenance expressed. As to her partner, Marian did not behold him with very different feelings, from those with which she would have regarded the real Earl of Leicester, could she have had one peep at the actual pageant of Kenilworth, with its outward pomp, masking the breaking hearts beneath. Thereupon she fell deep into musings on "Kenilworth," which she had read at home, when, so young and unlearned in novels as not to have a guess at what would happen, when it was all a wonder and fairy-land of delight, and when poor Tressilian's name of Edmund had been his first charm in her eyes, even before she loved him for his deep character and melancholy fate. She thought how unlike all this common-place world was to the world it aped — how far these Raleighs and Sidneys were from being worthy to usurp the name even for one evening! and as to Tressilian, how impossible to see any face here that would even shadow her idea of him! And yet she did not know; she might have to change her mind. There actually was a countenance handsome, thoughtful, almost melancholy enough for Tressilian himself, with the deep dark eyes, pale, clear, sun-burnt, brown complexion, and jetty hair that befitted her hero; a short beard and dark dress would have completed him, but she almost thought it a pity that such a face should appear above a scarlet coat and gold epaulettes.

However, Tressilian had been moving towards the end of the room where she was standing, and was coming so near that she could not study him after the first; so she turned to speak to Miss Faulkner, who had finished her quadrille, and just as a polka was commencing, she was surprised by finding Tressilian himself standing by her, and asking to have the honour of dancing with her.

"Thank you, I don't dance the Polka," she replied; and as she spoke quick flashes of thought crossed her thus — "I have not been introduced to him — I have met him before — how horrid of Tressilian's face to talk of polkas — ha! it is Edmund!"

Edmund Arundel's eye it was that was glancing at her with a look of great amusement at her bewilderment.

"The next quadrille," he proceeded, in the same ceremonious voice.

"O Edmund, Edmund, I did not know you in the least! Who

would have thought of seeing you here?"

"Why not? Did you not know we were asked?"

"Asked? yes; but who would have come who could have helped it?"

"I wanted particularly to see you." Then, after speaking to Mrs. Lyddell, he turned to her again, and resumed, "But am I not to have the pleasure of dancing the next quadrille with you?"

"If it is any pleasure to you, I am sure you are very welcome."

"In the mean time, what is the meaning of your not being amongst the performers? You used to be a capital shot."

"I? O, of course I could not shoot before all the world."

"Well, I was in hopes my pupil had been doing me credit; so much so, that I tried very hard to make that lady with the silver arrow into you, and —" as Marian looked at Miss Grimley's thin, freckled face, and reddish, sandy locks, and could not help smiling, he continued, "when that would not quite do, I went on trying to turn each maid of honour into you, till, just as I gave you up, I saw young Dashwood fixed in contemplation; and well he might be, for there was something so majestic as could be nothing but Zenobia, Queen of the East, or Miss Arundel herself."

"Majestic! nonsense! nothing can feel less majestic."

"Then decidedly you are not what you seem."

"I was trying all the time to make you into Tressilian, only your red coat was in the way. You know I never saw you in it before."

"And so you have given up archery?"

"O, no! I shoot at home; only I cannot make a spectacle of myself, — I hate the whole thing so much."

"And you would not wear a fancy dress?"

"You see I am in mourning."

"Why, who is dead?"

"Don't you know? Old Mr. Thomas Marchmont."

"Yes, and his great-grandfather likewise! Well, you certainly are inclined to make the most of your connection with the peerage,"

"Edmund!" and for the first time Marian felt as if she had been making herself more foolish than magnanimous. He gave his arm and they walked along together. He presently began abruptly, "What I came here for was to consult you about a plan for Gerald. You see I shall never get at him unless I have him alone. Now I don't like to take him away from you for the holidays, but I do not see how it is to be managed otherwise."

"I don't do him any good now," said Marian sadly.

"What I thought of was this; I find I can get leave for two months this summer. Now suppose I was to take him to Marchmont's grouse shooting place in Scotland, and about among the Highlands and Islands. Perhaps the pleasure of that excursion would make up for the being carried off by an awful guardian, and those scrambles might bring him to the old footing with me."

"O it would be very nice to have him with you," said Marian; "but —"

"Well, what is the but?"

"I don't know, only would not taking him home be more likely to revive old associations than anything else?"

"No," answered Edmund most decidedly; then in a more hesitating manner, as if casting about for reasons, he added, "I mean he was at home last year — it would not appear so inviting as this expedition — it would be giving every one a great deal of trouble."

"To have the Manor House set to rights — yes — but just a week at the Parsonage — just to revive the old feelings with you. For you to teach him how to behave to the Fern Torr people."

"No," repeated Edmund, "it would not do."

He spoke in a manner that made Marian look up in his face with surprise, and exclaim as if hurt, "Then you are really casting off poor old Fern Torr."

The next moment she was sorry she had said so, for his namesake in "Kenilworth" could never have worn a more melancholy aspect than he, as he answered in a very low voice of deep feeling, "I am the last man in the world to be reproached with too little affection for Fern Torr."

Marian was grieved, surprised, confused, but she had no time to find an answer, for the quadrille was forming, Edmund began a search for *vis à vis*, and she found herself dancing before she had made up her mind what she should have said if she could have replied at once; but it was too late to return to the subject, and she thought it best to begin entirely another, by asking, the next time they were standing still, how he liked the officers of his new regiment.

"Very much, most of them," replied Edmund; "one or two are particularly nice people."

"Do you like any as well as Captain Gresham or —"

"New friends are not old ones," quickly answered Edmund.

"O no, but if you knew them as well, are there any equally worthy to be liked? I want you to be comfortable there very much, as it is all our fault."

"Don't say any more of that, Marian. Thank you, I am very comfortable — they are a very pleasant set."

"Are there any of them here?"

"Yes, three of them."

L'Eté cut short his speech, and when they paused again he began, "I mean you to dance with Dashwood — there that rosy tall boy standing partnerless behind the lady in a Swiss fly-away cap."

"O I see," said Marian.

"Yes, and don't be high and mighty with him."

"High and mighty, when I am only shy."

"Effects are seen, causes are not equally on the surface."

"O Edmund!"

"Well, he is a very nice right-minded boy, very shy himself; so don't be grand, for I have a great regard for him, and I want him to have a pleasant evening."

Marian was considerably frightened by being told to be agreeable, the thing which of all others she thought the most difficult; but she would attempt anything for the sake of obliging Edmund, and making no answer, consoled herself with thinking how far off the next quadrille was. In the mean time, whilst she danced in the most business-like and least pleasure-like way possible, she was pondering on what she had to say on her own account to her cousin, and when the quadrille was over and he took her to the supper room in quest of ices, she eagerly began, "Then you think me wrong about my fancy dress?"

"Shall I give your own favourite reply?"

"Don't you think it a good thing to avoid all this folly and expense?"

"And to prove Miss Arundel's lofty contempt for finery and foolery?"

"I do not want to set myself up, but how am I to help thinking all this nonsense?"

"A hard question, since no one attempts to say it is far otherwise; but after all, everything in this world is nonsense, except as a means of doing right or wrong."

"And you do not think I made this nonsense a means of doing right?"

"If it had been any body else, I should have admired, but I do not trust *you*. However I know nothing about it, I cannot judge of the amount of sacrifice. Cream ice or water ice?"

They could not converse any more just then, and in the next polka, Clara, who not being come out, was not well off for partners, was extremely honoured and delighted by being asked to dance by Mr. Arundel. When the turn of a quadrille came round again, Edmund, as good as his word, introduced to Marian his youthful ensign, and she, dreadfully afraid of not obeying Edmund by being agreeable to his friend, set herself to talk with all her might; told him what some of the costumes were intended to represent, speculated as to the others, found him very pleasant, and ended by making him consider his friend's cousin as delightful as she was handsome, and he had been very much impressed with her countenance. She saw Edmund was well pleased to see him looking animated and gratified, and the consequence was that she had to dance with another of his brother officers, and after all it had not been by any means such hard work to be amiable as she was apt to imagine. At any rate she never liked a ball so well, but then she had never met Edmund at any other, which might account for it. After the last quadrille, Mrs. Lyddell summoned her to come home, they took their leave of Caroline and Clara, whom Mrs. Lyddell promised to fetch tomorrow: Lady Julia was particularly full of empressement and affection, delighted that dear Caroline had been looking so lovely. She even came out with them to the cloak-room, where her son was assiduous in shawling Mrs. Lyddell, and all manner of civilities seemed to be passing among them in a low voice, while Edmund having disengaged Marian's shawl from the surrounding drapery, said, as he put it round her, "Then it is settled that I take Gerald and try to do for the best?"

"O if you are so kind —"

"Don's trust too much to it. I will try, which is all I can do."

"No one can do him any good if you cannot."

"Hush! And I must thank you for taking my scolding in such good part."

"I deserved it."

"I have since been thinking you are probably right. I am sure you are in the principle of the thing. It was the particular application that startled me."

Mrs. Lyddell moved on, the carriage was at the door, they were all in it, Elliot of course last, and as he threw himself back in his corner and the door was shut, he exclaimed in a satisfied tone, "Well! he is coming it pretty strong!" Who was coming what? thought Marian, but her suspense did not last long, for Mr. and Mrs. Lyddell both chimed in with exclamations of satisfaction which left no doubt that they were delighting themselves in the prospect of seeing Caroline mistress of High Down. Marian had been in some slight degree prepared for this, she knew Mr. and

Mrs. Lyddell would highly approve, nay, consider such a marriage as fulfilling their highest expectations, such an establishment as all that could be wished; and depending as she did on Caroline's principle and right feeling, she was sorry to think how much vexation and worrying was in store for her. As she sat disregarded and forgotten through that long dark drive, hearing all the eager gratulations and anticipations of her three companions, regarding a marriage which she could not think of without a sort of horror, how did she despise them, feel imprisoned, and long to make her escape. She had not the least doubt as to what Caroline would do; her rejection of such a man was a matter of certainty; but Marian was vexed with her for having allowed herself to become so intimate with the Faulkners, and thought she had brought on herself all the annoyances that would follow.

Tired, irritated, excited, Marian was very glad to escape from the carriage, wish the rest good night, and run up to her own room. She sat before her glass, slowly brushing out her long dark hair, and trying to bring home her feverish thoughts, and dwell on what had passed, especially with Edmund, on whom she had not yet had time to think, and of all those hints of his, as to her behaviour in this matter. Had he approved it or not? or would he if he had known all the circumstances? There was something that struck her a good deal in his saying "I cannot judge of the amount of sacrifice." Had it been a sacrifice to wear a plain dress, to abstain from archery? It would have been, to Clara, but was it to her? and as she looked at the two grey volumes, with their store of pretty engravings and pleasant reading which lay on her table, and thought that they were her own for life, and that Anne Clifford's dress would now be laid aside and useless for ever after the archery prize, if she had won it, would be worthless, and the admiration, had she valued it, passed from her ears, she could not feel, for one instant, that it had been a sacrifice. Then again came his words, "every thing in this world is nonsense, except as a means of doing right or wrong." Yes, pretty books, pleasant pictures, taste and intellect were in themselves as little precious as dress and finery, things as fleeting when compared with eternity, except so far as they trained the soul and the higher faculties which *might* endure for ever. She thought of "Whether there be prophecies, they shall fail, whether there be tongues, they shall cease, whether there be knowledge, it shall vanish away." All was a shadow except that charity which never faileth, a beautiful picture, even as a costly dress! the way we treat these things alone enduring. Her head throbbed as she tried to be certain as to whether she had acted right. If the dress had required the money set apart for the poor she would have been perfectly clear about it, but she knew it need not have done so. Would her vanity have been gratified? Decidedly not — admiration of her face was so distasteful to her proud shrinking bashfulness, that she felt it like an insult when reported to her, and could almost have wished not to be so handsome, if it had not been more agreeable to an artist-like eye to see a tolerable physiognomy in the glass, when obliged to look there, and besides she would not but be like the Arundels, and was well satisfied with the consciousness of having their features, as indeed she would have been if their noses had been turned up and their "foreheads villainous low." If *her* vanity was gratified, it was by standing apart from, and being able to look down on the rest of the world; and as Marian became conscious of this, her mind turned from it with the vexation of spirit, the disgust and sensation of dislike, and willingness to forget all about it, that every one is apt to feel with regard to a vanity passed away — something analogous to the contempt and dislike with which we turn from the withered shreds of tangible vanity, faded and crumpled artificial flowers, and tumbled gauze ribbon when disinterred from some dusty and forgotten corner. No feeling is much more unpleasant than the loathing of an old vanity; and though this of Marian's was not yet old, yet that touch of Edmund's which had shown her how he regarded her "high-and-mightiness," had made her very much ashamed of it. Then came the question whether it was, after all, self-will that had actuated her, pride and self-will, leading her contrary to every one's wishes, where she was not sure that she was fulfilling a duty. Again, on the other hand, there was this point about the Faulkner family, her dislike to them was founded on principle; indeed it was not dislike, for she allowed their agreeableness of manner, it was disapproval; it was determination not to enter into anything approaching to intimate acquaintance with a man whom she believed to be little better than an infidel. If Edmund knew this, would not he think her right? But then to be consistent, she should not have accepted his hospitality in any degree; she ought not to have gone to the ball, nor ever to have dined at his house. How far was she called on to set her face against him, how far was she independent, how far was obedience to the Lyddells a duty? This must be for a question for Edmund another time, and she hoped that Caroline's refusal would put an end to the intercourse. Nor were these all her reflections. She thought of Edmund and his kindness to Gerald, and the hopes, nay the confidence which it revived in her, setting her mind fully at rest about her precious brother, for in spite of Edmund's despondency, she could not help trusting entirely to the renewal of his influence; for who was like Edmund? Who so entirely treated, as well as spoke of, the world as nothing except as a means of doing right or wrong?

But then that he should be out of spirits, as she had more plainly than ever perceived tonight, in spite of the gaiety he had at first assumed, his manner of replying when she pressed him to go to Fern Torr, and his absolute avoidance of it, struck and puzzled her much as well as grieved her. She knew his loneliness, and could understand that he might be melancholy, but why he should shrink from the home he so loved was beyond what she could fathom.

She knew Clara would laugh at her for his having come so many miles on her account. Yes, quite sure that it was nonsense. Edmund had talked of coming to see her, so openly, he had laughed at and blamed her so uncompromisingly, that she had no doubt that he had not the least inclination to fall in love with her. She had the best of elder brothers in him, and he would take care of Gerald, and, happy in her confidence she fell asleep.

CHAPTER XIV.

"What is that which I should turn to, lighting upon days like
these?
Every door is barr'd with gold and opens but to golden keys.
*　 　*　 　*　 　*　 　*

"Yearning for the large excitement that the coming years
would yield,
Eager hearted as a boy when he first leaves his father's field."
TENNYSON.

Marian was not up much later than usual the next morning, but she had a long time to wait for the rest of the party. She read, wrote, drew, tried to busy herself as usual all the morning, but whether it was that she was tired with her ball, or that she was anxious about Caroline, she did not prosper very much, and grew restless and dissatisfied. She wished she knew whether she had done right, she wished she could feel that she had been kind and accommodating.

Her head was dull and heavy from the struggle to occupy herself when her mind was full, and after luncheon she tried to drive her stupidity away by a very long ride. Groom and horses were always at her service, as a part of Mrs. Lyddell's justice to her, and off she set, in search of breezes, to the highest and furthest downs, by her attainable. On she went, cantering fast, feeling her power over her spirited pony, letting the summer sun shine full on her face, and the wind, when she had ridden where she could meet it, stream in a soft ripple round her head, like the waves of the summer tide. She rode far enough to attain the object she had proposed to herself, namely, to look down on Salisbury spire, pointing up in its green valley with the fresh meadows around it, giving a sense of refreshment, repose and holy influence, which her eye carried to her mind. Good men had raised that pile, had knelt there, sung in praise there, and now lay asleep within its grey walls and shady cloisters; men and women who had been to the full as much wearied and perplexed with sin and worldliness around them as she could ever feel; they had struggled through, their worn and fainting hearts had rested there, and now their time of peace was come. Why should it not be so with her?

Ah! but things were changed; in their time there was energy; there were great crimes indeed, but the Church was active. The bad was very bad, but the good was very good, there were real broad questions then of right and wrong, not the coldness and frivolity, where all was so worthless that there was scarce a possibility of caring or seeing which part was the right.

No, Marian would not accuse the time in which she was born, and the station to which it had pleased God to call her. Mr. Wortley had warned her against that. She had a Church, the one true holy Catholic Church, as surely and truly, nay, the very same that those men of old had, and was as much bound to love it, serve it, fight for it in her own way, as ever they had felt themselves. Life, truth, goodness, there was still, she saw it, knew it, felt it in some; and though there was little of it in her immediate home, so little as to make her heart faint, she knew that

> *"Israel yet has thousands sealed*
> *Who to Baal never kneeled."*

If there was this frivolity, this deadness and chilliness about these present days, she knew it was a temptation long since prophesied of, as about to grow on the world "when, the love of many should wax cold," but the help and the hope were never to fail, and while she might but grasp after them, she had enough to do, and need not feel faint and weary.

Her ride had done her good, her sensation of bodily lassitude and mental stupidity had been driven off by the active exercise which had produced a more wholesome kind of fatigue, and the temper which tended to discontent had partly gone with them, partly been chased away by reflection in a right spirit. As she was entering the park, Elliot, also on horseback, came up in time to profit by the same opening of the gate.

"Are you but just come home, Marian?" said he, "I thought I was very late."

"I don't know what o'clock it is, but I see the sun is getting low."

"Have not you been at High Down?"

"No, I have been to Beacon Hill."

"To Beacon Hill! That *is* a ride! And you have not seen any of them since they came home?"

"No, I have been out all the afternoon."

"Well, I have a notion you will have something to hear. I dare say you have some idea. Catch a young lady not up to a thing like that."

A cold horror and disgust came over Marian, and she would not make a single inquiry, but Elliot went on.

"So you will ask no questions? I believe you are in the secret the whole time."

"No, I am not."

"No? You will never persuade me that you are not. Why, what else can you ladies sit up half the night talking about in your bed rooms?"

Marian despised him too much to deny.

"Then do you really mean to profess," said Elliot, turning full towards her, so as to look her in the face in what she deemed an impertinent way, "that you cannot guess the news that is waiting for you?"

For once in her life she could not say "I don't know," and her answer was a very cold "I believe I do;" while in the meantime she was almost feeling, and quite looking, as if she could have cut off his head. His disagreeableness was the one present pain, but behind it was undefined consternation, for she perceived that, at any rate, he did not think Caroline had refused Mr. Faulkner.

"You keep your congratulations till it is formally announced," said he maliciously, still looking at her, though few save himself could have failed to be abashed by the firm, severe expression of her dark eyes, and lips compressed into all the sternness of the Queen of Olympus.

Happily they were so close to the house that Marian, who would not deign a reply, could avoid him without absolute rudeness. She threw her rein to the groom, and sprung to the ground before Elliot had time to offer his assistance, then ran hastily across the hall just as Clara was coming out of the drawing-room.

"Why, Elliot!" cried Clara meeting her brother, "you have not been riding with Marian?"

"With Marian? No, I thank you! I only met with her at the gate, and have been spoiling your market."

"You don't mean that you have been telling her?" cried Clara; "O I wanted to have been first."

"Precious little thanks you'll get!" said Elliot; but Clara, without attending to him, flew up stairs after Marian, who had reached her room, and while Fanny was endeavouring to get her dressed in time for dinner, was trying to collect her dismayed thoughts. She would not believe Caroline so foolish, nay, so wicked as to accept him, yet if it could possibly be true, what in the world should she say or do which way should she look, or how should she answer? In the midst of her first confusion in danced Clara, with a face full of delight at having something to tell, then looking blank at Fanny's presence.

"Marian — my dear Marian — what do you think?" was her

first eager beginning, then changing into "How — how late you are — where have you been! I really thought you had been out with Elliot," and she laughed.

"I only fell in with him at the gate. I have been to Beacon Hill."

"Have you indeed? O I wish you had come with mamma! So Elliot has been provoking, and told you," she added, stopping there, and looking significant.

Marian glanced at Fanny, and shook her head. She was very glad she had such a protector, to give her time to collect her thoughts, but this was not easy, for Clara went rattling on in an eager discursive way about all sorts of things, the archery, the dancing, the partners, the dresses, hardly knowing what she said, nor Marian either, fidgeting about, trying to expedite the dressing, and looking most impatient, till at last Marian, anxious to know what had really taken place, pitying her eagerness, and willing to have it over, hurried the fastening of her dress, and arranging of her lace, and told Fanny to leave them.

"O Marian! Marian! what a shame of Elliot to have told you all about it. Did you expect it?"

"He only half told me," replied Marian, "but make haste, Clara, let me hear. Is Caroline really engaged?"

"Yes — yes — O yes! and every one is so delighted, Lady Julia, and Julia and Louisa, and all!"

"And she has accepted him?"

"O yes to be sure — at least — yes, only you know it is too soon to settle when they will be married. What a charming wedding it will be, won't it, Marian? — you and I find Julia and Louisa, and their cousins will be bridesmaids O! how delightful it will be. And then I shall come out."

"But Clara, Clara, don't be wild, do tell me all about it."

"Ah! you see you missed something by not coming to stay there as we did. And to tell you a great secret, Marian, Louisa says she really believes that it was you that her brother thought of, when he first accepted Elliot's invitation to come and stay here."

"Nonsense," said Marian, though her colour would rise.

"And he had not seen Caroline then, Louisa says," proceeded Clara, but there she got into an inextricable confusion, and was not speedy in stammering out of it, having suddenly remembered that it was no great compliment to tell Marian that Louisa had said how glad they all were that it was not Miss Arundel. Marian cut the hesitation short by saying, "You have not told me when it was settled, or how you heard it."

"It was settled last night after you were gone — in the conservatory — such a pretty place for a love affair, as Louisa says — at least I mean he asked her, but I don't think she gave him any real regular answer — no, certainly she did not."

"Did you know of it that evening?"

"O yes, Louisa and I had great fun in watching him all day, and all the day before, we saw it all quite plain."

"But did Caroline tell you that night?"

"Yes, of course she did. She could not have kept it from me, you know, for I began to laugh at her the minute we came up, and asked her if she had not been delightfully employed, and you should have seen what a colour she grew directly."

"And what did she say?" asked Marian very anxiously, almost hoping it might prove that Caroline's acceptance might have been taken for granted without having been really given.

"I don't exactly remember what she said, she was very grave and said it was no laughing matter, or something of that kind, and she walked up and down and begged me to be quiet and let her think."

"Well!"

"Then I begged her only to let me know if he had proposed, and what she had said, and she told me she had said nothing — she could not tell — she must have time, and then she leant her head against the side of the bed, and said she wished she knew what to do! And when I tried to cheer her up, and said how delightful it would be —"

"O Clara, how could you?" broke from Marian.

"Ah! I know you can't bear the Faulkners, but you must now, for they will be your cousins, you know, Marian. And I assure you I did not say anything silly, I said it was not only that Mr. Faulkner is handsome and rich, that would not be anything, you know, but he is so sensible and so agreeable, and kind, and good tempered, and we are all so fond of him, and the Faulkners all so fond of her, and it would be so very nice to have her close to us, and mamma would be so charmed. Well, poor dear girl, she did not sleep at all that night, and this morning she only wanted, if she could, to have sent a note for us to be sent for to come home to breakfast, but that could not be, you know, and when we came down, Lady Julia was so kind and affectionate, and kissed her and said she was tired, and took her to lie on the sofa, in the little boudoir. Lady Julia sat with her there first, and then Mr. Faulkner came, and stayed with her a long, long time."

"O!" sighed Marian, "was it settled then?"

"Not exactly settled, but somewhere about three o'clock, Mr.

Faulkner ordered his horse, and rode out to find papa, and then Caroline ran up to our room, and bolted the door, and said she could not let me in, but just then mamma came and went up to her, and it was all joy and congratulation through the whole house. Mr. Faulkner came back and papa with him. But dear me, there is the second bell! Come, Marian! O, I do so wish you had been there."

If Marian had been there, perhaps things would not have been exactly as they were at present, though this was very far from what Clara intended by her wish. Marian had done infinite mischief by the severity which had weakened the only home influence excepting Walter's which held Caroline to the right. Caroline respected her extremely, but the confidence and affection which had been growing up slowly but surely out of that root of esteem, had been grievously dulled and blighted, and at a most critical time. It had in fact been almost killed down to the ground, and though the root was a healthy one, and might yet shoot forth again, the opportunity had been missed when it might have been turned to good account.

Caroline knew Mr. Faulkner not to be a religious man, and her better principles warned her against him; but on the other hand she really liked his manners extremely, her heart was warmed towards him by his preference and expressions of affection, and she did not know whether she loved him already or not, or whether she should allow herself to love him, as he was sure she could do. She had been used to a world where the service of GOD was not the first object; she had always lived with men whose thoughts and time were otherwise engrossed, and though she might regret what she saw, her standard had been lowered, and she was far less inclined to hold aloof front one whom her conscience did not approve, than if she had been accustomed to see everything desirable in her own family; in those whom nature and duty obliged her to love and respect.

By the Faulkners she was greeted with such kindness as to win her heart, and she thought the power she would enjoy at High Down would enable her to set things on a footing there, on which she could never place them at home; she could not fail to be happy with Mr. Faulkner; she might work upon his mind, if he loved her as he said he did. Still there stood the great unanswerable obstacle, the three words, "It is wrong!" If she stood alone, if there was no family on either side, she could, she would refuse, but dismay seized on her when she thought of the displeasure, the persecution at home if she rejected him; on the other hand she shrank from ingratitude for the kindness of the Faulkners. There was Clara putting her in mind of all that could bias her in his favour, rejoicing already, saying how all the family would rejoice.

O that interval, that night! if Marian had but stood there with the grave, earnest, heartfelt voice that repelled all sophistry with the wonted "I don't know," if the dark eyes had been there to look with contempt on all but the "right," and to fill with tears, the more touching because so rare, as her tenderness, her deep feeling would have been called out by the sensation of seeing and aiding a friend to struggle nobly against a temptation, if Caroline had felt and seen the superiority, the loveableness of real, true, uncompromising regard for right, and right alone, if she had been by one touch made to partake of the horror Marian felt of any failure in faith, then all the innate strength and nobleness of her character might have been awakened, and she would have clung to "the right" at any cost, supported, carried through by Marian's approval and sympathy, keeping her up to feel that higher approval was with her.

But alas! alas! Marian was at a distance, and her image had at present connected itself with harshness and haughtiness. She might be good; but such goodness did not invite imitation; she did not appear half as agreeable as the Faulkners. Caroline turned away from the recollection of her, was all night and all the morning distressed, undecided, and vacillating; then came Lady Julia's affection, her lover pressing his suit, she hardly knew what she had said, but she found her consent was assumed, both families were rejoicing in it, she found herself considered to be engaged, and she returned home bewildered at all that had passed, flattered, almost intoxicated with the attention of various kinds paid her by every one, at High Down, and when her wonted dread of Marian's disapproving eye would return, hardening herself against it with the thought that Marian could not make every one as Utopian as her own Edmund and Fern Torr, that she was proud and determined in prejudice, and after all what right had she to interfere? Of Walter, Caroline did not dare to think.

Marian came down with Clara, wearing a rigid company countenance, expressing more of indifference than of anything else; she would not look at Caroline lest her eye should seem to judge her, and only by furtive glances perceived that she looked pale, worn and wearied. There was talk about the ball going on all dinner-time, but Caroline hardly put in a word, and Marian's were not many. Directly after dinner Caroline said she was tired, and should lie down till tea-time; she went and Mrs. Lyddell, taking Marian by the hand, exclaimed, "Now, Marian, I must be congratulated. I suppose Clara has told you all about it."

"Yes, Clara told me," said Marian, resolved not to offend except where she could not avoid it without sacrificing truth.

"You could scarcely be surprised," said Mrs. Lyddell. "It has been evident for a long time. Dear Caroline! Well, I am sure this is a satisfaction! Settled so near home, and family and connection exactly what could be wished; and so extremely fond of her."

"Yes, Lady Julia is very fond of her."

Mrs. Lyddell was too much rejoiced herself not to take sympathy for granted. The point, on which Caroline's scruples were founded, and which caused Marian's dislike, had never even occurred to her: she lived little, or rather not at all, in Marian's confidence, and really did not know that she disliked the Faulkners more than any one else, since her manners were so universally distant, that a little ungraciousness more or less was not very visible to a casual observer like Mrs. Lyddell. That same ordinary coldness and undemonstrativeness which had never thawed to Mrs. Lyddell was the reason that the entire absence of any expression of gladness or congratulation was not remarked, or at least only taken as her way, and besides at the bottom of her heart, Mrs. Lyddell was very much obliged to Marian for the repelling manner which had left the field to her daughter. So Marian got very well through half an hour's interview, without giving offence; but she feared the *tête-à-tête* with Caroline, and resolved as much as possible to avoid it, since she could do no good, and did not think it right to express her sentiments unless they were positively called for. Disappointed in Caroline, grieved, giving her up for lost, yet loving and pitying her, she had rather never meet her again, certainly not have any confidential intercourse with her.

She need not have feared: Caroline was quite as much inclined to avoid her as she could be to avoid Caroline; by mutual consent they shunned being left alone together, and talked of indifferent matters if they were, for there was not familiarity enough for silence. When with the others Caroline was the same as usual, lively, agreeable, obliging; perhaps, and Marian thought it strange, a shade gayer than her wont. In her behaviour to Mr. Faulkner every one agreed that she was exactly the right thing, quiet and sensible, and, as people said, "evidently so very much attached to him." Marian would have given worlds to know what was passing in her secret soul, but the right of reading there was gone. What did Walter think? To this also there was no answer; if he wrote, Marian heard nothing about his letter, and he did not come home. He was to be ordained in the autumn to a curacy in a large manufacturing town in the north of England, and in the meantime he was staying there with one of the other curates, helping in the schools, and learning something of the work before him. There was not a doubt in Marian's mind that his sister's engagement must be a great sorrow to him, and that this was the reason why he would not come home, even for a short visit. For Caroline, so really good, right thinking and excellent as she was, so far above the general tone of her family, wilfully to place herself in such a situation, to cast away all the high and true principles with which she had once been imbued, was too sad and grievous to be borne by one who loved her as Marian, did all the time, and how much worse it must be for her brother?

Yes, little did most of those who saw Marian's unmoved, marble countenance, and heard her stiff, formal words, guess at the intensity of feeling beneath, which to those who knew her best was betokened by that very severity; how acutely she was suffering for the future before Caroline, how strong were the impulses to plead with her once more, how sick and loathing her heart felt at the manner in which this hateful connection was treated by all around. If that reserve could, or ought to, have been broken, Marian would have astonished them all.

If her former anxieties about Gerald had been as of old, she really did not know how she could have endured them in addition to all this; but while she was at ease about him nothing could quite overwhelm her. And she was very happy about him; Mr. Lyddell had readily consented to the Highland plan, and Gerald was so enchanted that he forgot all his former fears of Edmund, saw in him only a fellow-sportsman, and when he wrote to tell his sister of the project, decorated his letter with a portrait of the holidays, every one of the thirty-seven days represented in a sort of succession of clouds one behind the other, in each of which Gerald was doing something delightful, — boating, shooting, bagging his game, and enjoying an infinite variety of sports, the invention and representation of which did considerable credit to his ingenuity. On the very day after the Eton election, he met Edmund in London, and they set off together to spend the time before the ecstatic twelfth of August in visits to the Trosachs, to Fingal's cave and every other Scottish wonder of note.

Lionel returned alone, and the first thing he said as he skimmed his hat across the hall table was, "There! thank goodness, I shan't touch a book again these five weeks!" Every one asked after his eyes, but they told their own story, for they were considerably inflamed, and so evidently out of order that Mrs. Lyddell herself grew anxious, and the apothecary, Mr. Wells, was sent for. He spoke of their having been over tried by the school work, advised complete rest, and sent his mixture to bathe them, which in a day or two reduced the inflammation, made them comfortable, and restored them to their ordinary appearance, so that all anxiety passed off again.

Marian, like the others, dismissed the fear, though a flash of apprehension now and then crossed her mind. She was more with Lionel than the others, they had always been great allies, and at present were more thrown together than had ever been the case before. Johnny had been appointed to a ship which was to sail from Plymouth in a very short time, and he only came home for two or three days, from the school where he had been prepared. Mr. Lyddell took him to London for his outfit, and then on to Plymouth; Mrs. Lyddell was extremely overset, more so than Marian had thought her capable of being, for Johnny was her favourite, she regarded him as a victim, and could not bear to expose him to all the perils of sea and climate.

Johnny however went to Plymouth, and then there was nothing to be desired but that he should soon sail, that his mother might settle her mind, for in the mean time she was nervously anxious and restless, and could scarcely give her attention to anything, not even to the Faulkners, far less to what Marian was observing from time to time about Lionel's eyes.

Now that John and Gerald were away, Lionel was deprived of his wonted companions: Elliot did not patronize him, and was besides too busy about the races to occasion on his own account any home sports in which Lionel might have taken a share, so that there was no companionship for him excepting with the young ladies. Caroline's and Clara's time was a great deal taken up with the Faulkners, and Marian and Lionel were thus left out by all and almost obliged to make a coalition.

Lionel haunted the drawing-room in the morning, either talking in the half-rhodomontade, half-in-earnest fashion of boys of sixteen, or listening if there was any reading aloud going forward. Clara's readings with Marian and Caroline had well-nigh fallen to the ground now, and Caroline almost always spent the morning in her own room, but Marian now and then caught Clara and managed to get her to do something rational. More often, however, the reading was on Marian's part to Lionel; he liked to hear her read scraps of any book she might have in hand, and she was very merciful to him in the selection, not being by any means too wise. She read him likewise the new numbers of the periodical tales, as well as the particulars of the rowing matches and cricket matches, overcoming for his sake her dislike to touching Elliot's sporting newspaper. Indeed she had not so forgotten her cricket as not to be very much interested, to enter into all his notes and comments, and to be as anxious for the success of Eton as he was himself, so that if she had been called to give an account of her whole morning's work for three days, she could have said nothing of it but that she had been studying the matches at Lord's.

In the afternoon, if Marian could escape from the drive in the carriage, they walked or rode together, the latter when it was not too bright a day, for Lionel avoided the sunshine like an owl; and when in their walks a sunny field, or piece of down had to be passed, he drew his hat down and came under the shelter of Marian's parasol, as if he fairly dreaded the glare. He was very apt too not to recognise people whom they met, and now and then made such strange mistakes about small objects near at hand, that though they were laughed at just at the moment, Marian thought them fearful signs when she recollected them afterwards, in that half-waking half-sleeping time when she had learnt to entertain herself with anxieties. Chess or backgammon was the great resource in the evening, when there was no dining out, and no grand dinner party, and the number of games Marian played with him were beyond all reckoning. He played, she thought, more by the touch than the eye, often feeling the head of a piece to satisfy himself whether it had the king's crown or the queen's round head, the bishop's mitre or the knight's ears, but he was so quick and ready that it was impossible to tell how far the defect of sight went, and she could not bear to ask or awaken his fears.

She did not think he had any; she did not believe that he had ever seen quite as well as other people, and therefore trusted to sight less than most; and his eyes had been so often ailing, and then better, that he was not likely to take alarm now. If he had, she believed he would have told her, for he was very confidential with her, and she often thought it a great pity that no one else had thought it worth while to enter into him enough to find out what a right-thinking, sensible boy he was, and how affectionate he would be if they would only let him. One day, when they had been taking a long ride together, he began talking about his intentions for the future. It arose out of some observation about the value of a tree in a new and an old country. Marian had been lamenting that no modern houses were ever built with the beautiful patterns of dark timbers, as we see them in old farm-houses; and Lionel answering that so much wood could never be afforded in England now.

"No, you must go to a primeval forest for that," said Marian; "and very stupid it is of the people in the colonies to build houses as bad or worse than ours, when they have all the materials for nothing."

"Well, I will build a famous house when I emigrate," said Lionel; "a regular model of an old English farm-house it shall be, — stout, and strong, and handsome, — just to put the people in mind that they do belong to an old country, after all."

"When you emigrate, Lionel?"

"Yes, I really have a great mind to do so, seriously, Marian," and he rode nearer to her. "I do think it would be the best thing I could do. Don't you think so?"

"I don't know," said Marian, considering, while his eager face was turned towards her.

"You see," Lionel continued, "we must all do something for ourselves; and I am sure my eyes will never be fit for study. To be a clergyman is out of the question for me, even if I was good enough; and so is the law —"

"Yes, yes, certainly."

"Well, then, there is only the army, and there one can't get on without money. Now you know Elliot has been a monstrous expense to my father of late, and the times have grown so bad, and everything altogether has gone wrong; so that I think the only thing for it would be for me to go off to some new part of the world, where, when I once had a start, my own head and hands would maintain me, — no thanks to anybody."

"I dare say it would," said Marian, rather sadly, "I am sure these are right grounds, Lionel; but it is a terrible severing of all home ties."

"O, but I should come back again. I should be an Englishman still, and come back when I had made my fortune."

"O, Lionel, don't be in a hurry to make a fortune; that spoils every one."

"No, no, I am not going to grasp and grub for money; I hate that. Only if the fortune comes, one does not know how, with cattle, or horses, or lands — O, Marian, think of being an Australian stockman, riding after those famous jockeys of wild bulls — hurra!" Lionel rose in his stirrups, and flourished his whip round his head, so as greatly to amaze his steed. "There is a life to lead in a great place bigger than all Europe, instead of being stifled up in this little bit of a poky England, every profession choke full of people!"

"Well done, Lionel, you do want a field indeed!"

"So I do. I hate to be fenced up, and in, every way. I should like to break out in some fresh place, and feel I had all the world before me! Then I'll tell you what, Marian," and he spoke with infinite relish, "suppose matters got a little worse here, and they were all of them really in distress!"

"O Lionel!"

"Well, but listen. Then I should like to come home with all this fortune that I had made somehow, and get them all on their legs again; buy back the estate, perhaps, and give it to papa again; and then — and then" — his voice quivered a little, and his eyes winked, as if the sun had dazzled them — "see if mamma would not think me worth something, after all!"

This was the only time Lionel had ever said a word to show that he was conscious of his mother's disregard of him; and the feeling it called up made Marian's heart so full that she could not reply. But he wanted no answer, and went on. "Would not that be worth living for, Marian? But, after all, that is all nonsense," he added, with a sigh; "at least it is all a chance. But what I really think is, that I should do much better for myself and every one else, in one of the colonies; and I have a great mind to speak to my father about it. By the by, I wish Mr. Arundel would come here when he has finished his journey with Gerald; I should like to talk to him about the Cape. I rather fancy the Cape, because of the lions; and one might have a chance of a row now and then with the Caffres."

Marian began telling all she could about the Cape, and from that time her *tête-à-têtes* with Lionel were chiefly spent in discussions upon the comparative merits of the colonies. One thing Lionel was resolved on. "I will go somewhere where there is a Church within a tolerable distance, — say twenty miles; that is a short one for a colony, you know, Marian; for I know I am such a wild fellow, that I should very soon forget everything good, if I had not something to put me in mind of it. Or, by the by, Marian, what would be jolly would be to get Walter to go; I dare say he would, if it was some place where they were very badly off indeed, with plenty of natives, and all very savage."

Marian understood quite well enough, to agree that it must be some place "very badly off indeed" to invite Walter, and Lionel greatly enjoyed the further arranging of plans for taking care of his intended chaplain, whom he meant to save from roughing it as much as possible. However, this might be regarded as a very aerial pinnacle of his castle, the first foundation of which was yet to be laid, by broaching the subject to his father. Lionel talked over the proposing it many times with his counsellor, and at length resolved upon it, with some slight hope that it might save his eyes from the suffering of another half year at Eton, which, as the holidays came nearer to an end, he began to dread.

"You see, Marian," he said, "I do not like to give out, when I can help it, for they think it shirking, and there was a time when I did shirk; but a great many times last half, I was nearly mad with the aching and smarting of my eyes after I had been reading. And all I did was by bits now and then; for if I went on long the letters danced, and there was a mist between me and them."

"I wish you would tell Mr. Lyddell; I am sure it is not fit to go on in such a way."

"I have told Wells," answered Lionel.

A pause — then Lionel said, "I believe papa is in the library; I'll go and speak to him about the emigration."

Marian was very anxious to hear the result of the conference, but she could not find out anything just at first as she had to drive out with Mrs. Lyddell and Caroline to make calls. In the evening, over the game at chess, Lionel told her that his father said he should talk to his mother about it; and two days after he came to her in the hall, saying, "Come and take a turn in the plantation walk, Marian; 'tis nice and shady there, and I have something to tell you."

The something was as follows: "Well, Marian, my father was very kind, paid something about its being a sensible notion, and that he would see about it."

"But are you to go back to Eton?"

"Yes, that must be; and I must scramble on as best I may. It will be better at first, after all this rest. It is something gained that the whole plan is not knocked on the head at once."

"Then he gives his consent?"

"Why, he says it will be time to think of it in a year or two, and I am too young as yet, which is true enough; only, I wish I was to be learning farming, instead of torturing my eyes with what will be no good out there. Then he said, as to giving up the army, I need not think that was necessary, because it was only that he did not want to have two sons in it, and now Johnny is otherwise disposed of; and, besides Mr. Faulkner had behaved in such a handsome way about Caroline's fortune.'

"O!" said Marian.

"Yes, I don't like that at all," said Lionel. "Johnny always was crazy to be a sailor, so he is all right, and that is not what I care for; but I don't want to be beholden to Mr. Faulkner. I had rather Caroline had her own money, and not that we should all profit by her making this grand marriage."

"I should quite feel with you."

"Marian, we have never talked that over; but I know you cannot bear the Faulkners."

"What is the use of asking me, Lionel?"

"O, I know you can't, as well as if you had said so; and I want to know how you could let Caroline go and do such a thing?"

"I? How could I help it?" said Marian smiling, at the boy's assuming that she had power of which she was far from being conscious. "Besides, I thought you liked Mr. Faulkner; you, all of you, did nothing but praise him at Christmas."

"I did at first, not at last," said Lionel. "Besides, liking a man to go out shooting with is not the same as liking him to marry one's sister."

"By no means!" cried Marian, emphatically. "But what made you think ill of him?"

"Things I heard him say to Elliot when we were out together."

"Did Gerald hear them?" asked Marian, very anxiously, as she remembered what a hero Mr. Faulkner was in her brother's estimation.

"No, I don't think he did. He certainly was not there the worst time of all, — the time that gave a meaning to all the rest. Don't you remember that day when Mr. Faulkner drove Elliot and me in his dog-cart to look at that horse at Salisbury? I am sure I never praised him after that day. He said what Elliot never would have said himself — never."

"How?" Marian could not help asking, though she doubted the next moment whether it was wise to have done so.

"Things about — about religion — the Bible," said Lionel, looking down and mumbling, as if it was with difficulty that he squeezed out the answer. "Now, you know, I have heard," he added, speaking more freely, "I have heard people make fun with a text or a name out of the Bible many a time; and though that is very bad of them, I think they don't mean much harm by it. Indeed, I have now and then done it myself, and should oftener, if I had not known how you hated it."

"It is a very wrong thing, but I see what you mean, — that some people do it from want of thought."

"Yes, just so; but that is a very different thing from almost quizzing the whole Bible, — at least talking as if it was an absurd thing to accept the whole of it, I do declare, Marian, he was worse when he began to praise it than he was before; for he talked of the Old Testament as if it was just like the Greek mythology, and then he compared it to Homer, and Æschylus, and the Koran. To be sure he did say it was better poetry and morality; but the idea of comparing it! I don't mean comparing as if it must be better, but as if it stood on the same ground."

"And did Elliot listen to all this?" said Marian, thinking the poison must have been in rather too intellectual a form for Elliot.

"He listened," said Lionel. "I don't think he would ever set up to say such things for himself; but I believe he rather liked hearing them said. I am quite sure this Faulkner will make him worse than he is already, for all this talk is a hundred times worse than going on in Elliot's way."

"To be sure it is — a thousand times!"

"But what I want to know is this, Marian? has Caroline got any notion of what sort of a man she has got? Because if she does it with her eyes open, it can't be helped; but if not, I think she ought to be warned; for I don't suppose the man is fool enough to talk in this way to her. Indeed, I think I heard him say that believing is all very well for women."

"Why don't you tell her, then?"

"That is the very thing I had on my mind all these holidays; but I know no one would ever listen to me. If Walter was here it would be a very different thing, for he is worth attending to, and Caroline knows that; though she thinks I have no sense at all but for mischief."

"She could not think so, if she heard you speak as you do now."

"Then there is another thing, Marian, and what makes it quite — at least very nearly out of the question; I don't believe they in the least reckoned on my hearing all this. You know the man is very good-natured; well, he took me up to go instead of his servant, and I was sitting back to back with them. I sometimes think my bad eyes have made my ears sharper, for I know I often hear when other people don't; and so I should not expect they supposed in the least that I was attending, though I did not miss a word, for I could not help hearing. Now, you see, I could not possibly go and betray him; and if you were not the safest person in the world, I would never have told you: only, if somebody could just give Caroline a hint that she is going to marry an infidel, it would be a pleasant thing."

"A pleasant thing!" repeated Marian. Then she paused, considering, and Lionel waited patiently while she did so, "I see," she said at last, "that you could hardly tell her of this conversation; and after all, Lionel, I believe we knew what was quite as bad of him from the first: this only proves it a little more fully."

"Did you?"

"Yes, Lord Marchmont told me something of it; and I mentioned it to Caroline before he came here at all."

"O, that is right!" said Lionel, greatly relieved, "then it is no concern of mine; though what can possess Caroline, I can't think. Is it love, I wonder?"

"I suppose so," said Marian, sighing.

"Well, it is a queer thing," said the boy. "I should have thought Caroline was one to care about such matters more than I, but perhaps she means to convert him. So! I did think Caroline was good for something, but it is no affair of mine; and I shall be all the more glad to get off to New Zealand to be out of the sight of it all."

"It is very sad indeed!" said Marian. "I am sure it will be nothing but wretchedness. Caroline can blind herself now, but that will not go on."

"And why can't you speak to her, and stop her? She used to mind you. Does she come and talk about this man as if he was perfection?"

"No," was the sorrowful reply. "She knew from the first my opinion of him, and we never have any talks now. We never have had one since she was first engaged."

"Whew!" whistled Lionel. "Then she does mean to go and do it, and no mistake! Then I've done with her, and shan't think about her any more than I can help. If she won't be warned, she must Lave her own way, and may marry the Grand Turk, if she likes it better." He whistled again, proposed a ride, and went to order the horses; while Marian, walking slowly to the house to prepare, did not so much grieve for Caroline, for that was an old accustomed sorrow, as marvel at the manner in which Lionel had spoken, and wonder where he had learnt the right views and excellent sense he had displayed. Far was she from guessing the value of such a steady witness to the truth as she had been from the first hour when Lionel had perceived and maintained "that she had no humbug in her;" how her cares for her brother had borne fruit in him; how he learnt from her to reverence goodness, and cleave to the right; and how he looked up to her, because her words were few, and her deeds consistent. More right in theory, than steady in practice was Lionel; very unformed, left untrained by those whose duty it was to watch him; but the seeds had been sown, and be his future life what it might, it could not but bear the impress of the years she had spent in the same family.

She knew nothing of all this; she only thought, as she watched his quick, bounding run, that he, the least regarded, was the flower of the flock, with principles as good as Walter's, and so much more manly and active. For Marian, with all her respect for Walter, could not help wishing, like the boys, that he had more life and spirit, and less timidity. A little mental courage would, she thought, have brought him to expostulate with Caroline, instead of keeping out of the way, and leaving her to her fate. Edmund would not have done so.

CHAPTER XV.

"It's hame, and it's hame, and it's hame."
                                        Cunningham.

Edmund and Gerald had promised to spend a few days at Oakworthy, before the one returned to Portsmouth and the other to Eton; but their plans were disconcerted by an event which, as Clara said, placed Marian in mourning in good earnest, namely, the death of her great aunt, old Mrs. Jessie Arundel, who had always lived at Torquay. For the last four or five years she had been almost imbecile, and so likely to die at any time, that, as it seemed for that very reason, every one took her death as a surprise when it really happened.

Edmund thought it right that both he and Gerald should attend her funeral. Lord Marchmont, whose wife stood in the same relationship to her, met them in London, and they all went together to Torquay, instead of making the intended visit to Oakworthy. Gerald was obliged to return to Eton on the following day, without coming to Oakworthy; but, to make up for it, he wrote to his Writer from Torquay, and his letter ended thus, — "Now I have a capital bit of news for you. Old aunt Jessie has done what I shall venerate her for ever after — left every scrap of her property to Edmund, except a legacy or two to her servants, a picture of my father to me, and some queer old-fashioned jewels to you and Selina. The will was made just after I was born; so it was to make up to Edmund for my cutting him out of Fern Torr. You may suppose how Lord Marchmont and I shook hands with him. It is somewhere about £20,000; there is good news for you! He is executor, and has got to be here a day or two longer; but Lord Marchmont and I set off by the first train tomorrow. I shall look out for Lionel, tell him, in case he is too blind to see me. Can't you come with him to the station, and have one moment's talk?"

This proved to be possible; and Marian, in the interval between the coming of the post and the setting off, had time, all the hurry of her dressing, to wonder if she ought to be very much rejoiced. She did not believe, that even wealth could spoil Edmund, but she did not think all this would be of much use to him. It did not give him a home, and in fact she thought it rather a creditable thing to be as poor as he had hitherto been. She had rather have heard of something to make him look less like Tressilian, than he had done the last time she had seen him.

She had a pleasant drive with Lionel, who was very glad of any good luck befalling Mr. Arundel, and presently, after some meditation, broke out as follows: — "My eyes! what miles and miles it would buy in Australia" and then proceeded to talk all the rest of the way about Australian bulls.

The meeting at the station was a bright one, though so short, as scarcely to be worth the journey, if the value of such moments were to be reckoned by their number. There was Lord Marchmont to be spoken to, as well as Gerald, which broke into the time. Gerald looked very happy and pleasant. He said Edmund was the best fellow in the world, and that he had been very happy — shot lots of things — he wished he could stop to tell about it. Then Marian hurried what she had to say, while Lionel was looking after his luggage. "Gerald, would you just try if you can do anything to spare Lionel's eyes? When you have the same things to do, could you not read to him, or something? they seem so much worse, and I am so afraid."

"I'll try," said Gerald, "but I don't think I can do much, and he will never give in."

The bell rang — Lionel ran up — she wished them good-bye, and drove home, happier than when last she parted there from Gerald, wondering what had happened in his journey with Edmund, and re-assured, by his free cordial tone. She took up a book and read all the way home.

The next thing that was heard of Edmund was in a note to Mr. Lyddell, saying that he should come and spend one night at Oakworthy, on his way to Portsmouth; that he hoped to arrive about one o'clock, and that he should bring Marian her aunt's legacy of the jewels. This was communicated to her by Mrs. Lyddell, and she could not discover from whence he wrote; she supposed from London, unless he was still detained in Devonshire. She looked forward greatly to his coming, as there was so much to hear about Gerald; and she felt, as if she wanted something pleasant, very much indeed; for, now that Lionel was gone, she found what a companion, interest, and occupation he had been, and missed him very much. The constraint with all the others, except Clara, was wearisome: and Clara, though never ceasing to talk, and very affectionately, was anything but a companion, while poor Caroline kept more than ever aloof, and had a flightiness of spirits — a sort of gaiety of manner — which, to Marian, seemed to be assumed. This was more especially the case, after there was an idea of fixing the marriage for some time in the autumn, and arrangements were talked over. Marian began to have little doubt that she was secretly unhappy, and grew more and more tender in feeling towards her; while, by an effect of contraries, her manner became more frigid and severe, in proportion to the warmth within.

Clara wondered a little what Mr. Arundel was coming for, and laughed and looked significant when Marian said she knew perfectly well; but Marian thought she knew so thoroughly as not to be in the least disconcerted, though Clara's glances were full upon her when he was announced. In he came, just at luncheon time; he shook hands with Marian with all his might, and one glance convinced her that he had not Tressilian's face — nay, that though the sun of Africa had left its traces, he was more like the Edmund of the olden time, than she had ever seen him since her father's death. There were a good many people at luncheon that day. Mr. Faulkner was there, and there were some visitors staying in the house. Edmund was a good way from her, and she could only hear his voice now and then in the buzz; but it was a very pleasant sound to hear, and when he laughed, it was his own natural, free, gay laugh, such as it used to be. She was sure he was very happy, and wondered if it was possible Aunt Jessie's fortune could have made him so, or whether it could all be the satisfaction of having set Gerald to rights.

As they rose to leave the dining room, he came to her, saying, "Marian, can you have a walk with me?"

"Oh, yes, I should like it of all things; I will be ready in one minute." And away she bounded, saying to Caroline, in the boldest and most innocent manner in the world, as if on purpose to show that she expected nothing, and would not be laughed at, that Edmund had asked her to walk with him. He waited for her in the hall, and they went out, she scarcely pausing till they were on the steps, to say, "Well, how did you get on with Gerald? I am sure you made him very happy."

"We got on famously. He is a very nice fellow; he only wanted a little stimulus the right way. He is thoroughly open and candid, and I have no fear but that he will do very well."

Marian could not speak for joy, and for gratitude to her cousin; and her heart throbbing with delight, she walked on, waiting for him to say something more on this most precious of all tidings. But when he spoke again, it was if he had done with the subject of Gerald. "Marian, I have something to tell you," He paused — she stood in suspense — he began again. "Marian, I am going to be married!"

"O!" and the inquiring, joyful, wondering, confident tone of that O, is what nothing can ever convey. Her eyes were turned full on him with the same eager curiosity, the same certainty, that he could not do other than the best. He did not speak; but the half smile on his lip was a full though mute reply to her confidence, that she had only to hear, in order to rejoice with all her heart; and he held out a note directed to her, in Agnes' writing!

Marian took it, but she was too wild, too delighted, too eager to look at him, and hear him, to be able to open it. "O Edmund!" was what she said now, and she caught hold of his hand for an ecstatic shake.

"Yes, thank you, yes. I said I must tell you myself, Marian — my sister."

"O, I never heard anything more delightful in my life," said Marian, with a sort of gasp, as soon as the overwhelming delight gave her breath. "O, Edmund, Edmund!"

"You have not read her note yet."

Marian tore it open, but there was scarcely any thing to read; it was only —

"Dearest Marian, — He will have a note to carry you, but I can't say anything for bewilderment. I know he will tell you all about it, so it is of no use my writing. Are not you sorry he should have a wife so far from good enough for him?
     "Your affectionate and most amazed
          "AGNES."

Marian held it up to him, smiling. "But of course you have seen it?"

"No, I have not; I suppose she thought I should not carry such nonsense."

"Well, I am sure there is no other person in all the wide world that I could have thought good enough for you. Agnes! Agnes! O, Edmund, I wish there was any way of not being quite choked with gladness!"

Edmund smiled, and perhaps he was "choked with gladness" beyond the power of speech; for the two cousins only proceeded to shake hands again. The next thing that was said was after an interval. "Marian, you remember our bargain six years ago? Have you grown so very fond of the Lyddells as to repent of it?"

"O, Edmund, you have not thought of that?"

"Have not we? It was one of the first things we did think of."

"I don't think I can bear to hear of much more happiness," said Marian, in almost a crying voice. "I am so glad for you that I can't be glad for myself yet. I can't take it all in; it is too good to be true!"

"Indeed it does seem so. But you agree? Agnes said I must make you agree first of all."

"Don't I? Only I want to enjoy it for you, — it is so beyond everything!"

"Well, wasn't I a wise man to say I would not miss the pleasure of telling you myself?"

"Then do tell me; do let us be rational, if we can. Then you came here from Fern Torr?"

"Yes. Did you not know that?"

"No. I did not hear where you wrote from. How long were you there?"

"I only went on Wednesday."

"Then it was only one whole day! How much you must have had to settle!"

"So much, that we settled scarcely anything."

"Then you don't know when it is to be?"

"No, and Mrs. Wortley talks of having time, — poor Mrs. Wortley, but I don't think I shall take her away far; I have some notion of looking out for some place close at hand."

"Just what we settled long ago. But O! begin and tell me all, Edmund, — as much as you like to tell me, at least. I want to know how you first came to think of it." Then, as he smiled, she added, "I mean, how long you have been thinking of it."

"If you mean how long with any hope, only since I knew of good aunt Jessie's consideration for me. How long it has been in my mind I cannot tell; certainly before I went to Africa. You see, Marian," he continued, as if he was apologising, "it was this which made me think it advisable for me to go, though, as I see now, it was not at all good for Gerald."

"What, — you mean — I am not sure that I understand —"

"Don't you see, Marian, feeling as I did, and knowing how out of the question it was for a penniless man like me, to think of marrying, — Agnes so young too, and I with everything to draw me to what had been my only home, — there was nothing to be done but to keep out of the way, to guard me against myself; and that was easier with seas between. I don't know whether I did right or not, but I hoped I did, because it cost me something; yet it was a forsaking of Gerald which might have done much harm, though I hope it has not, as it has turned out."

"I see it all!" said Marian, resting there, because she had not a word with which to express her honour of his noble conduct.

"You will forgive me now," he added, with a smile, "for what you thought my neglect of home."

"I am only afraid I must often have given you a great deal of pain," she almost whispered.

"Never, except when I thought it right to silence you. It was only too delightful to hear their very names. You might well tell me that she had grown prettier than ever."

On talked and walked the cousins, over the downs, which had certainly never been trodden by happier people. At last they recollected that they must return, if they wished to be in time for the post, and retraced their steps, talking as eagerly as ever. As they were coming near the house, Marian said, "Does Gerald know?"

"Not yet; I shall write to him tomorrow."

"Is it to be a secret? Of course I should say nothing about it while you are here, but may I mention it afterwards?"

"They said nothing about secrecy," said Edmund; "in fact I think attempting it, only results in making one look foolish. Yes, you are welcome to tell whom you please as soon as I am out of the way. I had rather the Lyddells know."

"Very well; indeed, I don't think I can keep it to myself, it is too much joy."

"Do you expect them to participate in your pleasure at making your escape from them?"

"There is no one to miss me, except, perhaps, Lionel, a little, when his eyes are bad. Caroline would once have cared, but that is over now, poor thing! There never was a time when I should have been more glad to get away. O, Edmund, if you would do one thing to oblige me, it would be, to have your wedding the same day as Caroline's, that I might not be obliged to be at it."

"At which?"

"O, you know!"

"Is it such a very bad affair?"

"O, I am very much grieved about it. The man has no religion at all, you know; at least, if he has any, it is all natural religion, — anything but the truth."

"Do you really mean that the family have accepted him, allowed this to go on, knowing such things of him?"

"I don't know how far they see it. I don't think they allow it to themselves, and I don't think they would understand some of it; as, for instance, when I heard him talking the other day as if he assumed that Christianity was only a development of people's tendency to believe, — as fleeting as other forms of faith. It was not very broadly stated, and I don't think I should have seen it, if it had not chimed in with something I had read; and, besides, I knew what was in the man."

"How do you know? Not from your own observation?"

"O, no, no; I liked him at first. I could have liked him very much, if Lord Marchmont had not told me about him, and then I had the key to him."

"And this poor Miss Lyddell?"

"She knew what I did," said Marian, sadly. "But he is very agreeable, — at least he is thought so, — and they all admired him so much, and paid such court to him, that — Yet I did think better things of Caroline. Lionel is the only one who has found him out, and he thinks of it just as I do, O, Edmund, I am sure you would like Lionel."

"How are his eyes?" asked Edmund, as they were coming under the portico, and could not talk of any of the more delicate subjects. "I thought Gerald gave a very bad account of them; indeed, I scarcely expected that he could have gone back to Eton."

"I sometimes think," almost whispered Marian, "that it is not he, poor boy, whose eyes are the worst in the house; but Mrs. Lyddell's head has been so full of Johnny, and Caroline, and all she has to do, that she will not see anything amiss with Lionel."

"He must be a boy of a great deal of resolution and principle, to have struggled on as he has clone, by Gerald's account. Ah! I meant to have told you about Gerald, but all our time is gone."

"Never mind, we can talk of him in the evening. There is a corner of mine where I always get out of the way of the people, and where I have had many a nice talk with Walter, or Lionel, under cover of Miss Grimley's music. Now where do you like to write your letter? If you had not rather do it in your own room, there is a nice quiet place in the old school-room, where I write mine, when the drawing-room is uninhabitable."

Edmund accepted the invitation, partly because he was just so shy of letting his own handwriting be seen in the address, that he meant to avail himself of Marian's cover. Just as Marian had finished a note, too joyous to have any sense in it, and containing a promise to write more sensibly tomorrow, had directed the cover, and told her cousin that he must wind up if he meant to catch the post, Clara opened the door, gazed, laughed, and was retiring in haste, when Marian, without a shade of the confusion Clara had hoped for, called her back. "Edmund came here to write a note," she said, "don't go away."

Edmund made some demonstration about intruding, and wrote the conclusion, at which nothing but some interruption would have made him arrive, put it into the envelope, gave it face downwards to Marian, and departed. Now Mrs. Lyddell and

Clara were both persuaded that Mr. Arundel had come for no other purpose than to propose to Marian; and they had been entertaining themselves during their drive with conversing on the subject; so that Clara was never more surprised and puzzled in her life than by seeing Marian stand there, smiling, and with beaming eyes, brighter than ever she had looked before, but without one particle of a blush, — white-faced as ever, only dancing first on one foot, then on the other, balancing her bonnet on one hand, and with the other holding the precious letter.

"Well, Marian!"

"Well!" Marian made a pirouette. "I must run and put this letter in the box." And so saying, away she ran down stairs, up again in a second; then meeting the astonished Clara at the head of the stairs, she took her round the waist, and fairly waltzed her to her own door, opened it, threw herself into a chair, exclaimed, "I beg your pardon, Clara; you'll think me mad, but I'll tell you all about it tomorrow."

Fanny was present, so Clara could do nothing but stare; and lateness, and a dinner-party necessitating a hasty toilette, she retreated, while Marian contained her raptures as best she could, and meditated on the delightful life she was to lead with Agnes and Edmund, in some cottage on the borders of Fern Torr. O happiness, such as she had never known, which seemed to bring back as much of her home as could ever return, — which would be everything for Gerald! Every care gone, Edmund happy, Gerald satisfactory, her own exile at an end. Her head almost swain round with happiness, and she wanted to turn to the glass, to persuade herself that she could be the same Marian Arundel, wide awake, and yet so very, very happy.

However, it was all future, as far as concerned herself; and that cares were in the world she was convinced, by her own pang at seeing Caroline, whom she overtook on her way down stairs. She had no disposition to whirl *her* round; but there was a softened feeling, belonging perhaps to the fulness of her own joy, that made her, as she came up with her, put her arm round her, as she had now and then walked with her in former days. Caroline looked in her face, and drew the arm closer without speaking. Their faces had always been unlike, but the contrast was stronger than ever. Marian, with those pale, regular features, plain dark hair, black eyes and eyebrows, with her mourning dress, and yet with a radiant, irrepressible joy and buoyancy all round and about her; while Caroline, with her small pretty features, rosy colour, blue eyes, glossy curls, her pink dress and gold bracelets, was in general air very different, and in countenance how much more; for the eyes were restless, the smile came rather as if it was called, than as if it resided naturally on her lip, — the colour of her cheeks, though bright, looked fixed and feverish; and now and then, there was a quiver about the whole face. How different from the secure expression of happiness, now and then illuminated, as it were, with some sudden flash of secret joy, which sat on Marian's broad, serene brow.

They entered the drawing-room together, and from that time Marian was outwardly her own stiff, distant self, till the promised time in the evening, when Edmund made his way to her in her corner, where he was greeted by a most sunny look. "Now for Gerald," said she.

Edmund had a great deal to tell about Gerald. He thought him, on the whole, a very nice, amiable, right-minded boy, who only wanted more training and watching than Mr. Lyddell would or could give. He had, after a time, been brought to be entirely open and confiding; and this, for which Edmund seemed to be really grateful to him, and to admire him, was the great point, he had made Edmund a friend, instead of looking at him as a guardian, — found that he could sympathize, and had ended by trusting and consulting him. Marian, though wondering how the reserve had ever been, conquered, felt the relief of knowing that all was safe now, and was not hurt by his confiding in any one but herself. Edmund really thought it was safe. "I believe I know the worst of him now, poor fellow," he said, smiling, "and the worst is not much. He has been going on in a careless, thoughtless way, out of high spirits and imitation, a good deal, and the consciousness made him keep back from you; he owns that, and is very sorry."

"Does he? dear Gerald!"

"He seemed to feel deeply that he had neglected you; but he said, and very truly, how much there had been against him, — no one, as he said, to make him mind; and the fellows would have laughed at him, if they had found out that he attended to his sister."

"Ah! Johnny sowed that mischief long ago!"

"I hope it is not weakness. I do not think it is; for there was manliness in confessing all, and he seemed to feel the folly strongly."

"Did he tell you about the debts?"

"Yes, and of his own accord. They are nothing in themselves; but he has been allowed too much money, has had little warning, and his title was against him too. So if we can break off the habit of extravagance, there is no great harm done. After all, you know, he is very young, and there is plenty of time to form his character. I am sure he has good dispositions of every kind, and if he has but resolution, he will be sure to do well,"

"I think there is resolution in his temper. Nothing shakes him when his mind is once made up."

So Marian was very well satisfied on the whole about her brother, and she might justly be so by Edmund's account. There was nothing to disturb her happiness, and she only doubted whether she should be able to sleep for it. Her brother restored, as well as everything else!

When bed-time came, Mrs. Lyddell looked at her, as if expecting something more to be said than "good night," but nothing came, — nothing but the dancing light in the eyes. Clara followed her to the room, and stood gazing at her. "Why, Marian," at last she said, "can't you tell me anything about it?"

"No; not till tomorrow."

"O, that is too bad, Marian, when you heard all I had to tell directly."

"I can't help it; I am not at liberty to tell other people's affairs."

"Don't look so grand, Marian, pray. I am sure I thought this was your own."

"So it is in a way."

"In a way? Why, Marian, what an extraordinary girl you are! not your own affair! Well, if you are impenetrable, I can't help it; but it is not kind, when we all want to congratulate you."

"Stop, stop, Clara!" exclaimed Marian, and now she did blush, "will you be satisfied if I tell you that it is not what you suppose? You shall hear what it is tomorrow, and then you will see what nonsense you have been talking."

"What?" cried Clara, "you are not —"

"Don't say it, pray don't! Never was any one further from it. Now do go to bed, Clara, for I cannot tell you a word more, and keep your curiosity at rest for tonight."

Marian took care not to be caught alone by Clara before breakfast the next morning, and almost immediately after breakfast, Edmund departed. Marian had been out into the hall with him to exchange some last words, and Mrs. Lyddell, meantime, was observing to Caroline that she never knew anything so strange; she thought it was due to herself, however unpleasant it might be, to claim some confidence from Miss Arundel, on such matters, while living under her care. Marian came back, however, with her innocent look of delight, — a look so unlike the bashfulness of a damsel in love, that Mrs. Lyddell felt again doubtful; and before she could speak, Marian had turned to Clara and said, "Now I will tell you what makes me so happy. Edmund and Agnes Wortley are engaged, and I am to go and live with them."

"Miss Wortley!" at once exclaimed Mrs. Lyddell and her daughters, in the extremity of surprise; and then Mrs. Lyddell and Clara asked all the usual questions in haste and eagerness, wondering within themselves most of all at Marian's full rejoicing, for till now they had never been able to see that Edmund was really to her only like an elder brother. Caroline scarcely spoke, only went on nervously with her work. At last, when some interruption had caused her mother and Clara to leave the room, she laid it down, looked at Marian for a moment or two, then said, in a trembling voice, "Dear Marian, I am glad you are so happy! I am glad you are to live with them!" then kissed her, and hastened away before she could answer or return the caress. Her handkerchief was raised as she closed the door. Marian sat and grieved, for well did she know all poor Caroline conveyed by that "I am glad you are to live with them." It meant that Caroline felt that she had given up the esteem and friendship in which they had lived, — that she thought her own home unfit for one brought from such a sphere as Fern Torr, — that she resigned all those plans for Clara's good, everything that had been valued between them, — that she looked not for happiness for herself, and though she had forfeited such affection as once had been hers, yet she still loved Marian. How could Marian rejoice so much, when such a fate was waiting for Caroline? Poor Caroline! she contrasted her feelings with those of Agnes, grieved again over her, and ended by blaming herself for all the coldness and severity of the last six weeks, requited as it was by so much kind, fond affection.

Yet Caroline was weakly, wilfully doing wrong. How should she behave rightly towards her? O, why would nothing happen to save her, and break off this mockery of a marriage? But as of this there seemed little hope, — as the Faulkners were at Oakworthy more than ever, and Mrs. Lyddell was talking in good earnest of wedding clothes, and bridesmaids, it was a comfort to have these better hopes to occupy herself with.

Especially did she enjoy the idea of Gerald's rejoicing, and it was very eagerly that she watched for his first letter of delight. It came as soon as heart could wish; but so mixed are joy and grief in this world, that even Gerald's letter could not convey unalloyed pleasure, but filled her with a fresh anxiety, — or more properly, strengthened and realized what had hitherto been but a vague terror.

"Eton, Sept. 14th.

"My dear Marian, — Never was anything better in this world than Edmund's plans. I give him infinite credit for them; and, as head of the family, he has my full consent. I wish they would go and live at the Manor House till I am of age, — that would be jolly! Lionel desires me to tell you that it is all very well, except your going from Oakworthy, and he shall go about the house like a mad fury," (here followed his portrait in the character,) "if you go before he is off after the blue wild beestes at the Cape. His eyes are very bad, and I wish you would tell Mrs. Lyddell about them; for I don't believe it is a bit of use his staying here, and though I am very glad to help him, doing all his work and my own too is more than I can stand. It is much worse than last half; then he could see to read, though it hurt him; now Greek or small print beats him entirely, and he cannot look out a word in the Lexicon. He does just manage to write, and he never forgets anything; so another fellow and I have dragged him through, this week. But it cannot go on so; and as he won't give up or complain, I will have something done about it, or he will blind himself outright before he has done. I cannot think how it is my tutor has not found it out, but I suppose it is that Lionel is so sharp, and has such a memory. Do speak to Mrs. Lyddell.

"Your affectionate brother,
"E. GERALD ARUNDEL"

Marian carried the letter at once to Mrs. Lyddell's dressing-room, but she found that Gerald had been mistaken in supposing the tutor had not observed Lionel's failing sight: for the same post had brought a letter from him, which had at length completely alarmed Mr. and Mrs. Lyddell, and the former was going at once to write to his son to meet him in London, where he intended to consult one of the first oculists.

This was a great relief. Mr. Lyddell set off, and the party at home comforted themselves with predictions that all would soon be remedied; Marian and Clara agreeing that it would be very pleasant to have Lionel at home to walk with them, and to be nursed.

Mr. Lyddell had been gone about two days; Caroline and Clara were at High Down, and Marian was returning from a solitary ramble in the park, enjoying her last letter from Agnes, when, as she crossed the lawn, she was startled by finding Lionel stretched on his face on the grass, just at the turn where some bushes concealed him from the windows. He lay flat, without his hat, his forehead resting on one arm; while with his hand he tore up daisies and grass, and threw them hastily over his shoulder, while his whole frame quivered in a convulsive agony of distress.

"Lionel! Lionel! you come home? What is the matter?" exclaimed she.

"Matter! matter enough, I think," said, or rather muttered Lionel; "There is an end of the Cape, or anything else."

"How are your eyes?" asked Marian, in consternation.

"Only I am blind for life!" answered Lionel; still hiding his face, and speaking in a sullen, defiant tone.

Marian, dreadfully shocked, almost beyond all power of speaking or moving, could only drop down sitting on the grass beside him, and take his hand.

"All neglect, too," he added; then vehemently, "I don't believe, no I don't, there is any pauper's son in the parish that would have been so used!"

Her voice was low with fright: "But, Lionel, what has happened? Let me see you. Is it worse? can't you see?"

"O yes, I can see now, after a fashion, at least, but that is soon to go, they say, and then — They have done it themselves, and they may have that satisfaction!" added he, with a fearful bitterness in his tone. "Elections, and parliament, and dinners, and that Faulkner, — that is what they have given my sight for." He withdrew his hand, and turned his shoulder from Marian, as if resolute not to be comforted; and again he shook with agony.

"O, don't say such dreadful things, dear Lionel! O, if I could but do anything for you!" she cried, in a tone of heartfelt grief, which seemed to soften the poor boy a little; for he twisted round, so that his face, still pillowed on one arm, was half raised to her, and she could see how flushed it was, and that the eyelids were inflamed, though not with tears, and the eyes themselves had not altered from their former appearance.

"'Tis not your fault," he said. "If my mother had cared for me one quarter —"

"Don't blame anybody, pray!" interrupted Marian: "it only makes it worse. Only tell me all about it. Did the occulist say —"

"Not to me," answered Lionel; "not the worst, at least. He examined my eyes very closely, and asked me all manner of questions about what I could see, and what I could not, and what things hurt them, and how long it had been going on, and how I had been using them. Then he told me that it was impossible for him to do anything for them as yet, till the disease had made more progress; that most likely I should quite lose my sight this winter, and then I must come to him again. So that was bad enough, but I could have made up my mind to that, and they sent me away. Then it seems that, after I was gone, he went on about it to papa, and told him that the mischief had been brewing time out of mind, and some time ago it might have been stopped; but all that straining of my eyes at Eton, last half, had done immense harm, and confirmed the disease; and it is of a kind that — that — there is no cure for!" He buried his face again.

"Did Mr. Lyddell tell you this?"

"No, he only told me we were to go home directly, and wrote to Gerald to send my things from Eton. He hardly spoke a word all the way, — only led me about, and poked me in and out of the carriage, as if I was blind already; it put me almost in a rage. Then as soon as we came home, — about half an hour ago, I should think, — he told it all straight out to my mother, did not mince matters, I assure you: indeed, I believe they both forgot I was there. They are apt to forget me, you know. He regularly stormed about the neglect, and told her it was all her fault; and while this was going on, I found I had heard the worst, and I did not want to be pitied, so I came out here. And so there is the whole story for you, Marian, and a pretty one it is! A fine sort of life I shall have instead —"

"Well but, Lionel," cried Marian, eagerly, "are you sure that he said *for certain* that it was hopeless? for it seems so odd that he should have told you one thing, and Mr. Lyddell another."

"Pshaw! I suppose he had got some consideration, and did not want to knock me down with the worst at once."

"I should think it was more comfortable to know the worst at once!" said Marian, meditatively, "so as to be able to settle one's mind to it."

"A pretty thing to settle one's mind to," said Lionel, "to know I must be a good-for-nothing, dependent wretch all my days! As well be a woman, or an idiot at once! There, I shall never see that tree green again; no, and spring — I have seen my last of that! and I may look my last at all your faces. Johnny I shall never see again."

He was crying bitterly now, — almost choking with tears; and Marian's were flowing too. She was much distressed at the present moment; for though the weeping was likely to relieve him, she feared it might be doing harm to his eyes, and she did not know in the least whether it ought to be checked, or, indeed, how to check it. Grieved and in great consternation she was, in truth, for she was very fond of Lionel, and full of such strong sympathy and compassion, as to be perfectly incapable of expressing it, in the slightest degree. But he knew her; she had been the only person who had ever been uneasy about his sight, and this went for a great deal with him: so that, with all her undemonstrativeness, there was no one whom he could have liked so well to have near him in that moment of dire despair. "O, I am so sorry!" expressed infinitely more than the simple words.

"You see, Marian," said he, raising himself, and struggling with the sobs of which he was ashamed, "I could bear it better if I had not had such a scheme for my life, and my father consenting too. Australia, and those wild cattle, and that glorious Bush life, always galloping in the plains; and now to be condemned to be moping about here, for ever, in darkness and helplessness. O, to think of the plans we have made, all come to an end for ever!" and again he was weeping violently.

"They might have been stopped otherwise," said Marian, catching at any possible idea that might answer, or seem to console him; "you know you might have been ill, or met with an accident, and had a great deal to suffer."

"I would suffer anything rather than lose my eyesight! You don't know what you are talking of."

"Then just suppose this complaint had come on, in some lonely place out in the wilds, with no one to take care of you."

"It would not, I should have had no Greek to put my eyes out."

"And after all, dear Lionel, you know —" there she was choked — "you know that —" and she was choked again — "you know where it comes from."

"I know what you mean," he said; "and if it did — But it is my mother's neglect; there is the bitterness of it. Why, you and my father tried to stir her up to it in the spring, and she would not; and then, when for very shame she must attend, what does she do but let me go muddling on with that old woman Wells! She has regularly thrown my sight away, as much as if she had pulled my eyes out and thrown them over the hedge."

"No one could ever have guessed —"

"I tell you she might have guessed. Any other mother in the world would have been frightened years ago, long before I went to school. If it had been Elliot or Johnny, wouldn't she have had half the doctors in London? but what did she ever trouble her head about *me*?"

"Now, Lionel, that must not be said. You know it is wrong, and I am sure you will see how sorry she is, and how it was really not having time."

"I dare say she is sorry — I should hope so — now it is too late, and she has done it."

"But why will you accuse any one?" said Marian, sorely perplexed, and secretly sharing all his indignation against Mrs. Lyddell. "You know it only embitters you and makes it all worse; and after all, even if man had actually done the mischief, it still would ultimately be sent from Heaven."

"I don't see that that makes it any better," murmured Lionel.

"O don't you, Lionel?" said she earnestly; "doesn't it make you sure it is for the best?"

"I don't know what I have done to be so punished," went on Lionel to himself; "I have not always been good, but I have tried, and more lately, to do right; there are many much less steady than I, who —"

"Yes, yes, Lionel, but perhaps it is not as good for them to be prosperous. Indeed, indeed I am quite sure, though I don't understand it all, or see the way, that if you will but bear it rightly, you will be glad, if not before, yet at least when you die, even of this terrible affliction."

"I almost wish I was dying now!" said Lionel gloomily, "if I could but die the last day that I am to see the sky and everything, instead of droning on in the dark, a burthen to myself and every one else, for I don't know how long, forty, fifty, sixty years perhaps. You know, Marian, I am only sixteen —"

There was a burst of tears again, and Marian felt herself an unsuccessful comforter, nor did she wonder at it, for she could not fancy that anything could relieve the sense of such a misfortune as poor Lionel's, except the really high source of consolation, and that as yet only by faith, which might make him take it on trust as the best in the end, though for the present he must feel all the misery. She had no time to answer him again, for the garden door opened, and at the sound he dashed away his tears, sprang to his feet, and assumed a firm, cold, would-be indifferent look, as Mrs. Lyddell came out and advanced towards them. Marian thought her looking flushed and agitated, and her voice certainly betrayed more emotion than had ever been shown in it, except when bidding Johnny farewell.

"Lionel, my dear, sitting on the damp grass? You will certainly catch cold! I have been searching for you everywhere, but I am glad you were with Marian. I wanted to ask you, my dear, whether you would like to have your own room or Walter's," added she, wandering on as if anxious to say what was kindest, yet dreading to come to the subject nearest their hearts.

"My own, thank you," bluntly answered Lionel, "I'll and unpack." He brushed hastily by her, and ran into the house up stairs, his roughness contrasting with her affectionate tone. She looked at Marian, and saw the trace of tears on her eyelids, and her own lip quivered while her eyes filled, and she said in a trembling voice, "Poor dear boy! has he been telling you? Does he know it all?"

"Yes," said Marian, anxiously, "but is it really so very bad? Is there no hope?"

"No hope? Who said so?" exclaimed Mrs. Lyddell quickly.

"He did," said Marian; "he said Mr. Lyddell told you so."

"Was he there?" exclaimed she: "Ah! that was Mr. Lyddell's strong way of putting things! So unfortunate — forgetting all about him. Poor fellow! I must go to him directly, and tell him it was no such thing."

"What? how? O do tell me!" cried Marian, turning and hurrying with her, and speaking with, such earnestness that Mrs. Lyddell could not doubt of her sympathy now. She slackened her pace, and explained that what the surgeon, had said was, that there was confirmed disease, and of a very serious character, but the precise nature could not be ascertained till it had made greater progress, and it was then possible that it might prove capable of removal.

Mrs. Lyddell was resolved that neither herself nor any one else should believe anything but what was most hopeful. She could not have borne it otherwise. She really was far from being indifferent to any of her children, though multiplicity of occupation, and thoughts, engaged on what she considered the welfare of the family, had prevented her from being properly attentive to all, and she was so accustomed to uninterrupted prosperity, as to have almost forgotten that there was such a thing as anxiety or misfortune. Lionel, neither the eldest nor the youngest, healthy, and independent, neither remarkable for beauty nor grace, just unruly enough to be provoking, and just steady enough to be no cause of anxiety, had been as much a cipher in the family as a One lively boy could be; but though slow to be roused into anxiety, she felt it with full force when it came, all the motherly affection, which while secure had appeared dormant, revived, she was dreadfully shocked, and would have been utterly overwhelmed by the accusation of neglect, had it not been for her sanguine spirit. In this temper she represented all to Marian in the most cheering light, and hastened up stairs to do the same to Lionel. Marian, relieved and hopeful, was waiting to collect some properties of hers, to carry to her room, when she met Mr. Lyddell. She went up to greet him, and thinking that he looked very mournful, there was more cordiality and fellow-feeling in her way of addressing him than ever there had been before, though she simply said "Good morning" and shook hands.

"You have heard about it, Marian?" said he. "Has he been with you, poor fellow?"

"Yes," said Marian, "he is in his own room now."

"Ah! you spoke long ago," said Mr. Lyddell; "I wish we had attended to you."

"It was Edmund who remarked it," said she.

"Ay, ay, and senseless it was not to attend. Then it seems that something might have been done, at any rate he would not have gone on injuring them with his work at Eton, but now it is as good as a lost case. Poor fellow!"

"O!" exclaimed Marian, thrown back again, "I thought there was a hope that it might not prove to be the worst."

"There is just a shade of chance that it may turn out otherwise, and that, your mother — Mrs. Lyddell I mean — takes hold of, but I have not the slightest hope. The surgeon said, it had all the appearance of a confirmed case, such as cannot be removed."

Marian stood aghast, and Mr. Lyddell, with a sort of groan, most painful to hear, passed her, and shut himself into his study. The only thing she could think of doing, was to pour out her dismay and compassion in a letter to Gerald, and she repaired to the schoolroom for the purpose of writing, but she had not been there long, before Lionel came in, and sat down astride on the music-stool, just as he used to do, but with a very different expression of countenance from the wild, reckless spirit of merriment which used to possess him. He sat and meditated for a little while, then exclaimed, "Marian, whom have you seen since I left you?"

"Nobody but Mr. and Mrs. Lyddell."

"Did you hear papa say anything about it?"

"Yes, a little."

"Did he say what the doctor thought of it?"

"Yes."

"Tell me the very words," and he leant his elbows on the table, looking at her fixedly.

"Ah! Lionel, can you bear it? They are so very sad."

"Tell me them, I say."

Marian looked down, as if she could not bear to meet his countenance, and faltered as she repeated them.

"Ay!" said Lionel, springing up, and flinging himself round passionately, "I knew it was humbug all the time!"

"What? How? O Lionel, what have I done?"

"As if I was a fool or a baby, to be fed with false hopes," proceeded Lionel, sitting down, and hiding his face on his crossed arms on the table; "she might have let that alone, she has done me mischief enough already."

"Lionel," said Marian, firmly and gravely, for she was really shocked at his tone, "you must not come to me, if it is to speak in such a manner of your mother."

"Very well," said Lionel coldly, rising up to leave the room, then pausing just as his hand was on the door, "I thought *you* did feel for me, Marian."

"O Lionel, dear Lionel," and she sprang to him, to lead him back to his seat, but he still retained his hold of the lock and would not move; "you know" — her tears were flowing — "you know how I grieve for you; but if you are in trouble, that ought not to make you do wrong," He was turning the lock, and hardened his face, but Marian went on, "Don't go, Lionel, only hear me. Mrs. Lyddell is very unhappy about you, and I am sure you must see yourself, that if she blames herself for any want of care, her only comfort must be in hoping for the best, making the most of this little ray."

"Then *you* think there is a ray!" interrupted Lionel.

"So far as that nothing is certain, but I am afraid it is so slight, that you had much better not trust to it, but settle your mind to bear whatever may come."

"Very easy talking! If you had but to do it!" cried Lionel, impetuously wrenching the door open in spite of her gentle resistance, and running off determinately, leaving her, poor girl, in great despair, at having so completely failed either in comforting, softening, or bringing him to any kind of resigned feeling, having besides vexed him, made him think her unkind; and though this was unintentional, and might be better for him, just contradicted what his mother wished him to believe.

Her distress was too great even for writing to Gerald, and she walked up and down, thinking what to do, longing to find him some better comforter, and offering up many a prayer for him, till at last she heard Caroline and Clara come home, and remembering that happen what might, she must dress for dinner, up she went, heavily and sorrowfully.

As soon as she was dressed, she went to Clara's room, feeling that this would be but kind. Clara was not there, and she hesitated whether to go on to Caroline's, once her frequent resort. At that instant, however, both sisters came up together, and hastened to her. "O Marian Marian!" exclaimed Clara.

"You know all about it, I suppose," said Caroline.

"Yea, indeed I do."

"Come in here," said Caroline opening her door; "I want to know about him, poor fellow, and how he bears it. Have you seen anything of him?"

Marian told all she could, without betraying what was confidential, and did her best to soften Lionel's conduct, by which his sisters evidently had been disappointed, saying that he had scarcely chosen to speak to them. Marian explained what was on her mind, how she had, without intending it, flatly contradicted Mrs. Lyddell's cheering assurances, regretting it much, as injustice towards Mrs. Lyddell, but of this, Caroline thought little.

"Mamma is always sanguine," she said, "and it was only her colouring that made Lionel think her account hopeful. It must be better for him, poor fellow, to know the truth, than to have his mind unsettled with vain hopes. O dear! O dear! how sad it is, and at his age too! It breaks one's heart to think of it."

All coldness and distance had left Caroline's manner in speaking to Marian, and this was a great comfort, in the midst of their troubles.

A very uncomfortable time it was, which thus commenced. Lionel was a good boy on the whole, with right principles, and some seriousness of mind, but he was far too undisciplined to meet patiently such a trial as this. He had pride, and a high spirit, and this made him assume a bearing, which was a good deal admired in the family, trying to carry it off with a high hand, never openly uttering a word of complaint, and seeming as if he would rather die than directly express the miserable despairing feelings within, though, poor boy, he little knew how evidently they showed themselves in his gloomy silence, his outbreaks of temper, and his almost desperate, defiant spirit of independence.

His father and mother, not understanding him in the least, managed, in the revulsion of feeling which made him now the first object in the family, to try his temper perpetually. He had in former times, missed their demonstrations of affection, though healthy, high-spirited, and by no means sentimental, the craving had been only occasional, he had done very well without them, and had gained habits of freedom incompatible with being petted. He had never been used to be interfered with, and could not understand it at all; and that remembrance of past neglect embittered all his feelings.

Mr. Lyddell had just found out, as Marian had thought long ago, that Lionel was the flower of his flock, the one of his sons, who alone united spirit and steadiness, for the emigration scheme had shown a degree of sense, enterprise, and consideration which had at the time pleased and surprised him, and now added much to his sense of the promise lost. He laid all the blame of the neglect on his wife, but he did not lament it the less keenly. His extreme kindness and solicitude for the boy, were, to those who compared them with his general character, quite affecting, but unluckily they displayed themselves is a way which harassed Lionel very much, for he treated him as if he fancied him completely blind already, cautioned him, guided him, and looked anxious, if he did but walk across the garden alone; whilst Lionel, who could see quite well enough for all ordinary purposes, was teased, reminded of his troubles, and vexed above measure by having notice attracted to his defect of sight.

In the main, however, he owned that his father was kind, and sorry for him, though each particular instance annoyed him; but it was much worse with his mother, for her petting was more minute, more constant, and such as would have been worrying to any boy in full health, even if it had not, as in poor Lionel's case, been connected with the dark future, and with a past, which had sadly soured him against her. He was always rough and morose with her, rebelling against her care, never wakening into affection, or showing pleasure in what she proposed, though she continued to press on him her attention, with uunwearied assiduity.

His sisters were treated much in the same manner; Clara made him cross with over care, and Caroline, though showing better judgment, and much real tact and affection, was also kept at a distance, and often harshly answered. Marian too, was quite sufficiently like a sister to come in for many an unreasonable fit of rudeness, and temper when it was perfectly impossible to find any means of pleasing him.

Indeed such unoccupied days as his were in themselves a trial of good humour. Idleness was very pleasant in the holidays, but his was too active a spirit to bear it for long together, especially when it left room for such anticipations as those for which his hopes of a Bush life were exchanged, Yet he treated offers of reading to him as insults, and far less would he endure to learn any occupation that might serve him when his sight should be quite gone; he professed to hate music, and lounged about disconsolately in the house or garden. Now and then, if he found the young ladies reading on their own account, he would be beguiled into listening and being amused, and their ingenuity was often exercised in appearing to be doing it naturally, and he sometimes took part in conversation, and thus had his attention withdrawn from his misfortune; but it was not often that his moodiness of manner could be charmed away, unless strangers were present, when he thought it a point of honour to seem at his ease and merry.

After luncheon, he liked best to ride, but against this, Mr. and Mrs. Lyddell set their faces, persuaded that it must be very dangerous. This, Lionel thought the height of unkindness; he could ride just as safely as in the holidays; and it was too cruel to make him give up the one pleasure he best liked, while he was still able to enjoy it, and though not sufficiently familiar with them to attempt any remonstrance, he became doubly discontented and sullen. He would not walk with the girls, but wandered far away over the downs by himself, often not coming back till very late, and till both his parents had been in some alarm. At last, after about a week, Marian ventured to expostulate; she prevailed, and he was allowed to resume his rides, under a restriction that it must never be alone. Now, taking a servant with him was an avowal of his misfortune which he never would endure; so Marian, who never in her life was afraid of what any horse could do, became his companion, and rode out with him a good deal, feeling him indeed a charge, but not nearly so heavy a one as her cousins fancied.

Still, though not afraid of accidents to him or to herself, these rides were almost a subject of dread to Marian, daily as was their occurrence, for it was then that poor Lionel made up for the reserve he exercised with all the rest. If she could have done him any good, it would have been a different thing, but surely, the world did not contain, as she thought, a worse comforter than herself; for day after day, answer as she would, came the same sad strain of regrets, and laments over vanished plans, repelling every attempt at leading him to resignation, and only varied by the different moods in which he would sometimes look on his case as hopeless, and sometimes be angry with her for assuming that it was so. Still worse were the complaints of his parents, in which he would indulge after each fresh provocation, or rather, what he thought so, though she never gave him the least encouragement to talk in this manner, argued for them, and often blamed him; yet do what she would, he never was convinced. The same battle on some other ground was sure to recur, often the next day, and Marian, right as she knew she was, never felt as if she had the victory; for five times out of six, it was in a surly, impatient manner that he turned away from her, as they dismounted. She often wondered whether she ought to let him go on thus, whether it was right in her, if it did him harm, by confirming all his unpleasant feelings, or whether it might not be worse for him to let them rankle in his heart instead of pouring them out. It seemed too unkind to silence him, when he fancied such talk a comfort, and she was the only person in his confidence, yet what was right? what was good for him? Her head ached with the self debate; she felt positively worn and depressed, with the continued useless, harassing conversations; she knew he was beyond her management, yet, with all her doubts, she was too tender-hearted to vex him; she let him go on and only combated each point, instead of refusing to listen.

Why would not Walter come home, the only true comforter Lionel was likely to find, whom he really respected and loved? Walter was by this time ordained, yet he did not propose coming home; indeed Marian had not even heard whether he had written, and she was inclined to think he could not have been informed of the state of things at home.

At length, when Lionel had been at home nearly a month, there came one morning a letter directed to him. His mother and Clara both offered to read it for him, but he gruffly refused, glanced it over, and put it in his pocket. He loitered through the morning, and rode with Marian in the afternoon. As they happened to meet with some entertaining subject of conversation, the ride was more cheerful than usual, and she hoped she had escaped the ordinary discussion; but when he helped her to dismount under the portico, he said, "Don't go in just yet. Come and take a turn in the plantations."

Her heart sank at the task that was coming, but she would not disappoint him, and gathering up her habit, she followed his quick steps. As soon as they were out of sight of the house, he produced the letter, saying, "Here, read me this."

"O! I was in hopes that you could."

"I thought I could at first, but it was only 'my dear Lionel,' that I could read. It was all haze after that. There is a step In these three weeks," he added in a voice meant to be manly and careless. "Come, let us hear. 'Tis from Walter, is not it?"

The letter had been written on first receiving intelligence of Lionel's condition, which had been communicated by his father when he had to write about something else. Marian, as she read, rejoiced in the letter, it was so exactly what she wanted to have said, and yet never could venture on, about regarding the affliction as a cross, and bending to bear it patiently. She had often felt that here was the best relief, but she had never dared to set it openly before Lionel, fearing that her awkwardness, and his way-wardness, might lead to his saying something scornful, which would be worse than all. Here it was put before him in just the right way, and one to which he must attend, and she watched eagerly for some token of the way in which he took it.

He made no remark, however, seeming to hear it as a matter of course that Walter would say something of the kind. After asking if she was certain she had read all, and pointing to a few crossed lines at the head of the first page, to make sure that she had not missed them, he only said, "Then there is not a word about coming. Well, I do think he might come when he knows that after this time I shall never be able to see him."

"I don't suppose he thinks of that," said Marian — "I mean perhaps he would not think of your caring for the mere *sight* of him as a pleasure."

"He does not know then," said Lionel, "I am trying to learn all your faces, and I don't think I shall forget them."

"I am sure if he guessed you wished for him he would come that instant."

"I am not going to ask him," said Lionel proudly.

"What, I really think, is the reason of his stayin away," said Marian, hesitating, "is about Mr. Faulkner. I think more espe-cially now he is a Clergyman, he will not have anything to do with him."

"Ay, ay," said Lionel, "that is a reason good for something. I only should like to do the same, except that if I was Walter I would have done more long ago, instead of just keeping out of the way, and told Caroline it was a regular shame, and she ought not to be taken in with his fine speeches, and balls, and stuff."

"I don't know —" said Marian.

"What don't you know?"

"How far even Walter would be authorised to interfere about what Mr. and Mrs. Lyddell approve."

"Don't talk nonsense, Marian. If a thing is right, it is right, if it is wrong, it's wrong, and all the world ought to try to prevent it. I know I would, if anybody would mind me, for it makes me sick to see that man come into the room, and the fuss mamma makes with him. I think he grows worse. I declare I'd as soon see her marry Julian the Apostate! I am so glad he is gone to those races. I should like to ask Caroline what sort of happiness she expects with a man that talks of the Bible as if it was no better than the

Iliad! I only wish he would talk so to her, perhaps that would shock her."

"I don't think she is very happy," said Marian.

"I am sure she ought not to be," was the answer.

"The more talk there has been of fixing the day the more unhappy she has looked," said Marian. "You know she has begged the Faulkners to let it be put off a little longer, because she could not bear that it should be while you are in this doubtful state."

"I did not know it," said Lionel, "and much good does it do me! A nice life I shall have with no one but Clara to speak to! And when is your marriage, Marian? Mr. Arundel's, I mean, for that is as bad."

"O that will not be till next summer," said Marian: "Mrs. Wortley wishes Agnes to be twenty-one first, and Edmund has to build a house."

And Marian was ready to forgive them for the delay when she saw how glad it made Lionel look. Yes, rejoiced as she must be to escape from Oakworthy, she could not go without a chequered feeling. If she was adroit at managing people, she would make Clara take the place she held now with Lionel, which would be good for both, but she was far too clumsy to bring that about; and O! what a refuge Fern Torr would be after all this harassing life! It would be better for Lionel not to have her to divert his confidence from his own family, and at any rate she should be there to help him through this sad autumn of uncertainty. Then would come the peace, rest, and guidance she had longed for all her life, in her own home, and that hope might well cheer her through life.

CHAPTER XVI.

"The brass, by long attrition tried,
Placed by the purer metal's side,
Displays at length a dingy hue,
That proves its former claim untrue;
So time's discerning hand hath art
To set the good and ill apart."

Lionel's affliction had certainly tended to lessen the gulf which the engagement with Mr. Faulkner had made between Caroline and Marian. Caroline was very anxious about her brother, and knowing that Marian had his confidence, was continually coming to her for reports of his state of mind and spirits, and with despairing questions as to what was likely to please him, — questions which Marian was quite unqualified to answer, and which were curious, since she had no tact, and Caroline had a great deal.

Thus it came to pass, that nightly sittings by each other's bedroom fire were renewed, and long consultations took place, always at first about Lionel, but sometimes branching to things in general, even as in the olden time. Caroline was, however, very unlike what she had been a year ago, when as Marian full well remembered, they had first talked of Mr. Faulkner's visit. She was gayer in public, but her spirits were very low when alone with Marian; and now and then the conversation flagged, till she sat for full half an hour, her head on her hand, without a word. At first she would try to excuse such a reverie, by calling herself very tired; but as days went on, and it recurred, she smiled as she woke from it, and told Marian "it was such repose to be with a person who would let her be silent."

There was much confidence in such silence. Marian began to grow even more sorry for her than at first, because it was impossible to continue to be angry; and tried in every way to show her kindness, becoming, unconsciously, much more demonstrative in affection than ever she had been before. On the day on which Lionel received the letter mentioned at the end of the last chapter, Caroline came into Marian's room at dressing-time; and after lingering about a little, she said, "Could Lionel read that letter to day?"

Marian shook her head sadly.

"He brought it to you, then?" sighed Caroline, "Ah! I saw who it came from."

She looked wistfully at Marian, as if longing to hear something of the letter, though she would not ask; and Marian, though much touched, was determined against saying one word about it, however indifferent, as she felt that, without Lionel's consent, she ought to be as mute as the paper it was written upon. Caroline paused, then continued, "Do you think he will ask you to write his answer for him?"

"No, I think not. You know he wrote a note to Gerald in one of my letters the other day. I dare say he will always be able to write; Mrs. Wortley has a blind friend who does."

Caroline did not answer, but gazed at the fire for almost ten minutes. At last she said, "Poor Walter! I wonder what he is doing."

"I am sure he must be making himself very useful," said Marian.

"That is one thing we may be sure of," said Caroline, smiling mournfully. "Walter is excellent wherever he is; but O, Marian," continued she, in a voice of inexpressible sadness, "who would have told me, a year ago, that all I should hear of Walter's ordination would be in the newspaper?"

Marian could make no answer but some sound expressive of sorrow.

"He has only written to me once since — since June!" proceeded Caroline, in the same utterly dejected tone.

Then Walter had remonstrated, which was a great comfort to Marian, by restoring him to his place in her estimation. Still she maintained her expressive silence, and Caroline went on after another interval. "You and he have been consistent from the first, Marian."

At that moment Fanny came in, and no more could be said, for Marian was obliged to dress for dinner in a hurry. She took an opportunity of saying to Lionel that evening, something about the pleasure it would give Caroline if he would tell her about his letter.

"What! you have been telling her about it?" said he, in a tone of great vexation; "that is always the way with women — no trusting them!"

"No, indeed, Lionel, I said not one word; but she saw it was Walter's writing."

"And you went and told her I could not read it?"

"If she asked me, what could I do but speak the truth?" said Marian gently; but he only made an impatient exclamation.

"I gave not the least hint of what it was about," added Marian, pleadingly. "Of course I could not think of that, nor she either; but she looked as if she did so long for some news of Walter: she has not heard from him since the summer."

"That is her own fault," said Lionel, in his surly voice.

"That only makes it the worse for her. She is so much out of spirits, Lionel; and if you would only tell her that part about his schools and his lodging, I am sure she would be so much obliged to you."

"I shan't do any such thing," was his reply; "I always keep my letters to myself, and I wish you would not talk about me."

He turned sharply away, and crossed the room; but his temper was not improved by the consequences of his stumbling over a footstool which had been left full in the way, and in rather a dark place, where it would have been a trap for any one. He recovered in an instant without falling; so that it would not have signified if Mr. and Mrs. Lyddell had not both been startled. The former issued an edict that no stumbling-block should be left in the way, and the latter entered upon an investigation as to who had been the delinquent in the present case, so as to make a great deal of discussion of the very worst kind for Lionel.

Thenceforth the evening was uncomfortable. Marian felt as if she was guilty of all, and was extremely provoked with herself for that blundering way of driving at her point, which made things worse when she most wanted to set them right. She had not comforted Caroline, and she had led poor Lionel to fancy his confidence betrayed, and himself discussed and — as he would call it — gossiped about. No wonder he looked as if she had been injuring him; yet, unjust as it was, she had only her own mal-adroitness to blame. A person of tact would have smoothed it all at once, instead of ruffling everything up.

The tact Marian longed for is a natural talent; the consideration, the delicacy of feeling, that she really had, were a part of her sterling goodness, such as may be acquired by all; and her thorough truth, trustiness, kindness, and above all her single-mindedness, had a value, where she was really known, which weighed down, in the long run, all that was involuntarily against her in manner, and won her not only esteem, but such warm affection, such thorough reliance, as neither she herself, nor those who felt it could fathom. Tact is an excellent thing, but genuine love to our neighbour, seeking to show true kindness, delicacy, and consideration, — striving in fact to do as it would be done by, — is as much more precious, as a spiritual gift is than a natural quality.

That very night, as Marian was sitting in her own room in her dressing-gown, pondering on these unfortunate blunders, there was a knock at her door, and in came Caroline. Sitting down by the fire, she held out a letter on two or three sheets of closely written notepaper. "Read that, Marian," said she, turning her face straight, to the fire as she gave it.

It was from Walter, and the date showed that it had been written, immediately on receiving the announcement of Caroline's engagement. It was grave, earnest, and affectionate; not accusing Mr. Faulkner of anything, not positively objecting to him, but reminding Caroline of the solemnity of the duties she was about to undertake, and of the extreme danger of allowing herself to be so attracted by agreeableness of manner, or led on by the opinion of those around her, as to forget that the connection she was about to form was to last for life, and that she must be responsible for the influence her husband would exercise on her life here, and therefore on her life hereafter. He said he was sure she could not enter lightly on such an engagement, and therefore trusted that her own mind was thoroughly convinced that she had chosen one who would be a guide, an aid, and a support in the path that all were treading.

It was exactly Walter's way, as Marian well knew, to manage to say, in his simple, and as he thought, guarded manner of representing things, what to sharper people had very much the air of irony; and as she gave back the letter, her observation, as the first that would occur, was, "It is very like Walter."

"Very," said Caroline.

"Did you answer him?"

"I wrote again, but — but" — her voice began to fail — "it was not an answer. I would not seem to understand him. I wrote a lively, careless sort of letter, and only said papa and mamma were delighted, or something of that kind. And O, Marian, Marian, he has never written to me again, and I have deserved it." She burst into tears.

"But why don't you write now? He must be very anxious to hear of Lionel, and there is no one to tell him."

"I cannot," she replied; "I cannot, while — while he thinks of me as he must — as he ought!" She wept bitterly, and Marian stood by perplexed and distressed. "Dear Caroline," was the utmost that she could say.

"Marian!" cried Caroline, looking up for a moment, then hiding her face again — "I would give anything in the world that he had been at home last summer; or that you had slept at High Down that night."

A flash of hope and joy came across Marian. "If you think so," she began, but Caroline cut her short. "I know what you mean, but that it? impossible, quite Impossible — decidedly so," she added, as if these assurances were to strengthen her own belief in its impossibility, and not arguing, from a consciousness that her friend would overthrow every one of her arguments. "I don't know what made me come to you, and tease you," said she, rising and taking her letter; "good night."

"Tease me! O, Caroline, Caroline, you know —"

What she knew was lost in a most affectionate embrace; but Caroline would not stay any longer, and left Marian as usual, regretting everything that had passed.

The nest night, however, Caroline came again, as if there was some irresistible spell that drew her to Marian. It was Sunday, and Marian had long since observed that on such days Caroline was always most out of spirits. She sat down, and let a long time pass without talking; but at last she said, "Marian, it is very kind in you to let me come and sit here. You cannot — no — you will never know how wretched I am."

"My dear, dear Caroline, if I could but do anything for you! but," she proceeded, gathering resolution from her day's reflections, "you are the only person who can do anything for yourself."

"Impossible!" repeated Caroline.

Marian was not exactly silenced, but involved in deep considerations as to the propriety of interfering, and whether attempting to persuade Caroline would be doing evil that good might come. Before she had made up her mind, — as, indeed, how could she in five minutes come to a conclusion to which hours of previous perplexity had failed to bring her? — Caroline spoke again, "If it had but never begun! but now it has, it must go on."

"I don't know —"

"It must, I tell you!" repeated Caroline. "If it had all to begin over again, it would be very different. O, if it was but this time last year!"

"But Caroline, Caroline," repeated Marian, carried away by the thought that rose to her lips, "only think; you say now if it was this time last year — now, while you can escape. Shall not you say so all the more when it is really too late, — when you will wish you had drawn back now?"

"You have no right to say I should wish, that!" said Caroline, offended. "You don't know what the love is that you are holding so cheaply."

"I beg your pardon, Caroline," and Marian was thrown into herself again; but she thought a little longer, and seeing that Caroline was still waiting and musing, she ventured on saying, in a timid voice, "Somehow, I think, it would seem to me that the more affection there was, the more painful it would all be."

"You are right there, Marian," exclaimed Caroline, in a voice of acute feeling.

It was a strange question that Marian next asked abruptly, on an impulse sudden at the moment, though it was what she had long eagerly desired to know. "Do you love him after all?"

Caroline did not seem vexed by the inquiry, but went on speaking rather as if she was examining herself as to the answer, — "Love him? I don't know; sometimes I think I do, sometimes I think not. It is not as people in books love, and — and it can't be as your Agnes must love Mr. Arundel."

A most emphatic "O no!" escaped from Marian, she hardly knew how, as if it was profanation to compare Mr. Faulkner to Edmund; and perhaps the strongest proof that Caroline's was not a real attachment, was that she let it pass. "But then," pursued she warmly, "I am sure he is attached to me — yes, very much — and — well, and I am glad to see him come into the room; I like to walk with him. There is no one — no — no one in the whole world whom I like so well. All my doubts and fears go away at the first sound of his voice, and I am quite happy then. O, Marian, that surely is love?"

"I don't know," said Marian; "I can't fancy love that has not begun with esteem, with looking up,"

"I do look up!" said Caroline, eagerly. "He is so clever, so sensible, has such a mind."

"I did not mean looking up intellectually,"

"Ah! you can live in that way," said Caroline, quickly; "your own people are all of *that sort*. But you know I should never have had any one at all to love, if I had begun looking for *that kind of thing*, even at home."

Too true, thought Marian, while she answered, "It is a different thing where you have to begin afresh, and take it voluntarily upon you."

"Voluntarily!" repeated Caroline; "I am sure my will had very little to do with it. I found myself in the midst of it, without knowing how, before I had made up my mind one way or the other. O, Marian! if you had but been with me that morning."

"Would that have prevented you?"

"I do really believe it would. You would have looked as if you thought it so impossible, that I should have been strengthened up to do something they could not have taken for consent. I'll tell you all about it, Marian, from the beginning, and you will see how little free will I had in it, and how distracted I am now."

Caroline went through the whole story, incoherently, and often only half expressing her sentiments, and passing over what Marian knew already. It seemed that she had been pleased with Mr. Faulkner's agreeableness, flattered by his attention, and entered upon the same sort of intercourse with him as with any other pleasant acquaintance. It would never have been her way, brought up as she had been, to shrink from him with such shuddering aversion as Marian did, simply from what she had heard of his opinions. He was so agreeable, that it was just as well quite to forget that, or only half to believe it. Then came the growing perceptions of his intentions towards her, and of her mother's triumph in them. But this was not till the archery arrangements were so far advanced, that she could not have drawn back from them; and she was, besides, in a whirl of gaiety and excitement that left little time for serious thought: that she put off till his offer should be made, if it was really coming. It came, and when she did not expect it. She knew not what to do she was too confused for consideration. The next day was bewilderment, and in the evening she found herself engaged. The new sensation given her by her lover's affection, her genuine admiration of his personal superiority, and wonder at herself for having attracted such a man, — her gratitude to his family for their kindness, the triumph of her parents, — all formed such a mixture of pleasurable, almost intoxicating feelings, as at first to giddy her, (or, as the French will express it, *l'ètourdir*,) as to what she had done, and what she was about to do. Marian's grave, still face, and omission of one congratulatory, even of one sympathetic word, were indeed witnesses; but the impression of her unaccommodating ways was then recent, and Caroline thought of her as one who showed goodness to be unpleasing and impracticable, and looked on her silent disapproval as part of that system of severity in which, she was consistent, but which her conduct only proved to be absurd and unreasonable.

In the same spirit Caroline disregarded Walter's letter, — only a letter, which could therefore be laid aside, and which, in truth, did not say all he meant as forcibly or as well as it might have been said, since, as every one knew, Walter was more good than clever. A tenderness of feeling, reminding her that Walter loved her, would not let her destroy the letter, or be offended; but she intrenched herself in her parents' satisfaction, and being resolved not to attend to it, she would not seem to understand it. So time passed; at first she was really not exactly happy, but possessing what passed very well for happiness with herself and every one else; then came a time when an effort became necessary to persuade herself that she was so. It was not that Mr. Faulkner showed his character more openly, or startled her with any such plain expressions as had so much shocked Lionel; for he held that most subtle and perilous of all views partaking of unbelief, — that Christianity was the best and most beautiful form of religion yet promulgated, that it was all very well now for women and weak-minded people, and it was a step to some wonderful perfectibility, which was a sort of worship of an essence of beauty and intellect.

He did not say such things to her, but they were the principles on which all his sentiments were founded: and as she knew him mire and more intimately, compared and discussed their tastes and likings, and the grounds on which they were formed, there were tokens, which could not help now and then showing themselves, of those opinions of which Marian had warned her.

Very slow was she to admit the conviction, for she was growing much attached to him; and whenever he praised the beauty, the poetry, the morality, the majesty of anything belonging to religion, she caught at it and silenced all her doubts with it, — hoped she had silenced them for ever, — but the perception would return that it was only the beauty that he praised, because it was beauty, and struck him as such. Shade upon shade, imperceptible in itself, but each tint adding to its depth, the cloud of misgiving darkened, and though she tried to fight it off, — though she told herself it was too late, — though she was very angry with herself for it, there it still hung; and the ever-present consciousness of Marian's disapproval heightened it, till in impatient moods she began to dislike Marian, and wish her out of the house,

Then came the news of Edmund Arundel's engagement, rousing Marian into such a glow of warm-hearted delight, as to waken Caroline to a complete sense of her power of affection, as well as of the contrast of the manner in which she regarded the prospects of her two friends. Caroline grew more unhappy, and strove both against her own growing wretchedness, and an almost magnetic attraction, which drew her to impart it all to Marian, in spite of the chill with which it would be first met, and of the advice which could never be taken; whilst a yearning, longing desire for the long-suspended intercourse with Walter, and a sense of his displeasure, formed no slight portion of her miserable feelings. The arrangements for her marriage she looked on as part of her destiny, — at any rate, they occupied her mind; and there would be an end, after that, of these dreadful and vain doubts.

In the midst of all this, poor Lionel's threatened misfortune gave Caroline, as it were, a glimpse down a long dark road, where nothing had ever yet caused her to look; yet who could say whether it might not be her's to tread it? Affliction, sickness, sorrow, death, certain at last, — there was but one stay in them; and what if she should lose it, — if she was losing it already? I She thought of bearing them with *him*, — of the hollowness, the fallacy, the utter misery of trying to be sustained by aught that had not its foundations firmly fixed beyond the grave, — of not looking as sorrow as fatherly chastisement. (Caroline hardly yet entered into its still higher claim,) or at death as the gate of life. And O! if she loved him as her husband, what would it be to see him die, thinking, or even having thought, as he too surely did? All the train of fallacies about sincerity rather than forms of faith, — all the hopes that he might yet be brought to see the truth, and that she might be the means, were only soporifics for a moment, which failed to still the ever growing agony. She knew there was nothing in them, and that they were only extenuations; but still, amid all her unhappiness, there was a resolution to persevere, a want of moral courage which determined her to go on, and enter on such a life as this, rather than go through all that would ensue on an attempt to break off the match. Thus, though her reluctance was increasing, and she now sought to put off the decisive day, instead of precipitating it, as at first, all she attempted was to have the wedding deferred in consequence of her brother's condition; and though, logically taken, there was no great reason in the request, every one agreed it was a very amiable feeling, and so her desire was complied with. She would have avoided Marian more than ever, but this could hardly be, now that her cousin was in fuller sympathy, with all the family than she had ever been before; and little as was her immediate power with Lionel, Caroline would have given worlds even for that. Thus, as has been shown, the old sympathy grew up again; the root, blighted months ago, shot out once more, and at last accident and impulse led Caroline to do what she had little expected ever to have done, — to pour out all her griefs, cares, and doubts to Marian, knowing all the time what she would say, and resolved against her advice, yet irresistibly impelled to go on, as if talking would relieve her of her burthen, and resting on the solid, firm truth of that deep love, which manifested itself by few tokens indeed, but those were of extreme worth.

The confession was a perplexity and a sorrow to Marian while it was being made, though she was very glad it had been done; and how intense were the affection and compassion for Caroline that filled her heart is beyond all power of narration. She answered with earnest sympathy, at each step helped out the broken words, and showed her comprehension of the pauses. She was a perfect listener in all but one respect; she would not give the counsel Caroline wanted; and she would not have been Marian, she would not have had her own reality and bracing severity, if she had. She could not cheer Caroline up, bid her banish fear, and look forward to happiness; she could not even tell her there was no help for it: she only said, "I don't know," and sat considering whenever Caroline reiterated that it was impossible, and too late.

Some power those "I don't knows" had beyond eloquence; for when Caroline had seven times fully proved how entirely out of the question any attempt to escape from her destiny would be, she ended by asking, in quite a different tone, "What would you have me do?"

The reply was, of course, "I don't know;" but this was immediately followed by a repetition of the former counsel, "Write to Walter."

Caroline could not — would not; it would be of no use: poor Walter should not be tormented. If, in his strict sense of right, he chose to come and try, as he would think, to save her, there would be nothing but uproar and confusion in the family; and to think of him, with his timidity, bringing his father's anger on himself for her sake, seemed to her at the moment beyond all things dreadful. No, no, no, it was utterly impossible; and therewith the fire being out, and the clock striking two, Caroline thanked Marian for her kindness, said it was all of no use, kissed her, and bade her good night.

Marian thought no good was done, and only made herself very unhappy at seeing her led, by weakness, to sacrifice herself against her better judgment. The next night, Caroline came again, and the conversation was resumed, or rather gone over again, with no more satisfactory result than before; and so it was the next, and the next. To be comforter and adviser sounds like a delightful privilege, and so, thought Marian, it would be, if one could only do it; but to have all the opportunity, — to have people coming for comfort, and not in the least be able to afford it, neither to relieve them, nor to be sure that she had not done them harm was to the highest degree painful and unsatisfactory. And from Lionel's repinings to Caroline's doubts, she went, suffering for each, equally unable to console either, and wondering which was the saddest case. Lionel's was, she thought, far the best, if he would but perceive it; but then Caroline's might yet be remedied, if she had but strength for one struggle. All that Marian could do without mistrust, was to pray for them both, and to pray that she might not be the means of doing them harm.

She saw how wrong it would be in her, personally to interfere between Caroline and her parents' wishes; and it was this that made her adhere to that one piece of advice, that Walter should be written to, since on his judgment and sense of right there was the most absolute reliance; and, both as brother and Clergyman, he was by far the most proper person for Caroline to consult, or to act for her.

For three days, however, it was all in vain, Caroline would not write; and she began to despair, and to grow angry with the feebleness that would not take one step in the right direction. On the fourth, Caroline, who the night before had seemed as averse as ever, showed her, as she crossed the hall on the way to luncheon, a letter directed to the Reverend Walter Lyddell. Her heart leapt, but as she smiled satisfaction, she saw Caroline's face so wan, dejected, and miserable, that she could not make herself too happy. There were other doubts, now that this point was gained, as to how Walter might be able to manage Caroline, — whether he would lead her to the right, or unconsciously turn her to the wrong, by his want of skilfulness; what might be his idea of her duty to her parents, or to her promise; whether he might think it right to take upon himself to advise, or whether either he or his sister, when it came to the point, would have nerve enough to excite their father's displeasure.

The only thing Marian thought at all favourable, was that Elliot and Mr. Faulkner were both at Newmarket, and there was no present appearance of their coming home. Elliot was likely to make more opposition than any one else, and Mr. Faulkner's influence was of course to be dreaded. Indeed, had he been at hand, believing, as Caroline did, in his affection for her, it was most probable that she would never have spoken of her misgivings at all, and very possibly have hardly acknowledged them to herself.

Caroline's letter had been written on Thursday. It was Monday, and no answer had come, which caused her to look more worn and dispirited than before, unable even to keep up the appearance of cheerfulness which she had hitherto assumed when with the rest of the family. It was a cold, gloomy, wintry day, with gusts of sleety rain, and no one chose to attempt going out, except Marian and Lionel, the former of whom was a systematic despiser of weather, and never was hurt by anything but staying in-doors, while the latter would rather have done anything than idle away a whole afternoon as well as a morning in the drawing-room. Even they thought it too bad for riding; so after making the circuit of the park, they went into the town, where Lionel wanted to buy a silk handkerchief. He had been told the day before that his neck-tie was growing unfit to be seen, he did not choose to ask any one to get one for him, and it was against his will that he was obliged to take Marian to secure him from buying "any thing awful," as he expressed it.

The purchase prospered very well, Lionel hoped that the shopman had not found out how entirely he trusted to his companion for the choice, and was proud that his old precaution of substituting a key for a slider at the gold end of his purse, had saved him from making any mistakes about the money. They were walking away, arm in arm; it was not yet necessary to guide him, but Marian thought, beginning now would soften the first commencement of dependence. And, indeed, even in the holidays Lionel, in his first tail-coat, had been well-pleased to find himself man enough to have his arm taken by a young lady.

A carriage was passing. "There is Walter!" joyfully exclaimed Marian, as she saw the well-known spectacled face peering from the window of one of the carriages from the Great Western Station.

"Walter! what, come at last?" cried Lionel, looking up and frowning in that painful way that had become habitual to him when he strained his eyes to see distinctly. Walter had at the same moment spied them, stopped, thrown the door open, sprung out, and was shaking hands with them, but scarcely speaking. He turned again to order the driver to go on and set his things down at the house, and then joined his brother and cousin, looting very anxiously at Lionel, whose arm Marian had quitted, and still keeping silence. Marian on her side was very glad; but at the same time almost overcome by the thought of what this return home must be to Walter, and feeling a strange, solemn sensation at first meeting her cousin and companion, after he had become in an especial manner the servant of the Most High. He was Walter still, Walter with his near-sighted eyes, and nervous manner, yet he was so much more, and his clerical dress would not let her forget it for a moment.

Lionel was the most unembarrassed of the three, he was very glad to meet his brother, and wishing to show that he could bear his troubles manfully, he spoke joyously, "So you have thought better of it and come at last, Walter; I hope it is for a good long time."

"Only till Saturday," was Walter's answer.

"Well, that is something, only I can't think why you did not come before."

Walter murmured something about having been much occupied, and then seemed to be watching Lionel too intently to say any more. Marian thought the brothers would get on much better without her, and, coming to a cottage, said she wanted to speak to somebody in it. "O Marian, we will wait for you," said Walter, with a pleading look, and she saw from his agitated, fidgeting manner, that he was excessively nervous at the notion of being left to take care of Lionel back to the house.

"Very well," she said, "I will not be a moment;" and delivering her message, which had been only devised as an excuse, she walked on with them, in a sort of despair as to Walter's being of any use. "If he is afraid to walk home with Lionel," thought she, "what will it be about stirring up his father? Why cannot people have a little courage?" She consoled herself by remembering that Walter could not know the degree of Lionel's blindness, and probably thought it worse than it yet was; but even if it had been total, she could not see that he need have been afraid of guiding him in the street and through the park. If it was the additional nervousness, of disliking to begin on so painful a subject, that she thought worse than all. Marian being by no means troubled with nerves herself, had little toleration for women who had them; and none at all for men. She thought the case lost, and half repented of her advice to write to Walter, yet she did not know what else she could possibly have said. Lionel talked on, told who was at home, and what every one was about, and when Johnny had last been heard of, all in a bright, lively tone, not exactly assumed, for he was much cheered by his brother's arrival, and yet partly from the wonted desire of showing himself happy. Walter did not make much reply, but when Lionel after saying Elliot was at Newmarket, added, "And Mr. Faulkner is there too, so you won't have the pleasure of an introduction," he started, and Marian saw the trembling of his lips.

Thus they reached the house, and Lionel dashed forward In his own headlong way before them, to announce Walter's coming. Then Walter looked at Marian, saying, "Then it is not so bad yet?"

"O no, it is only that he cannot see anything distinctly; he cannot bear not to be independent."

They were entering the hall by this time, and his mother and sisters had come out to meet Walter, Caroline very white and trembling, and holding by the back of a chair instead of coming forward; Mrs. Lyddell kissed him, and seemed more affectionate than usual, for it had been a great pleasure to her to see Lionel rush in with that animated face, and a shout such as he used to get into disgrace for.

Nothing came to pass that evening, there were no private conferences, and there was nothing remarkable, excepting that Lionel was quite merry and talkative, and Caroline more silent than ever, seeming hardly to attend even when Walter was sitting between her and Clara, talking to Marian and Lionel about the beautiful arrangements of Church and school in his new curacy. At night she was in such a terrible agitation, walking up and down the rooms so restless and wretched that Marian, seriously afraid she would be quite ill the next day, persuaded her with great difficulty, to go to bed, and did not leave her till very late at night, when she had read her to sleep.

It was a, great relief to find her pretty well in the morning, at least with nothing worse than a headache. She and Walter both disappeared after breakfast, and did not come down till luncheon time, when she looked so ill that Mrs. Lyddell was alarmed and insisted on her lying down and keeping quiet. Then Mrs. Lyddell said that Walter ought to go and call on Lady Julia Faulkner, and offered to take him there. Marian looked at him by stealth, and could have gasped for breath, for by what he did now, she thought she could see what line he would take.

"Thank you," he said, or rather hesitated, "but don't let me interrupt your plans. I thought I heard something about — about. Salisbury. I have something to do there."

"The girls did talk of wanting to go," said Mrs. Lyddell. "Did not you, Marian or Clara, which was it?"

"My watch wants to have something done to it," put in Lionel, whose father had given him a repeater, which of course began its career by doing anything but going properly.

"Well, perhaps it will he as well to go to Salisbury today, as Caroline has this headache. She never likes going there, and she may be able to go with us to High Down tomorrow."

So it was settled, and they left the luncheon table. Marian happened to be the last lady, and whether it was fancy or not she was not sure, but she thought she heard on Walter's lips, a self-reproachful whisper of "Coward."

The expedition to Salisbury, in which Marian was obliged to take part, prevented her from seeing anything of Caroline till the evening, and then as soon as Clara was out of the way Caroline rose up, caught hold of her hand, and exclaimed, "O, Marian, what have you made me do?" then walked about in a paroxysm of distress, almost terrible to witness.

"Caroline, dearest, O don't!" cried Marian quite frightened; "do try to be calm! O what is it?"

"O it will all be misery!" said Caroline, sitting down and clasping her hands over her face, "I little knew what it would be when you made me write to Walter. He says it would be wickedness — yes, those were his words — he called it wickedness in me to go on with it, as I feel now!"

"And you mean to —"

"I cannot tell — I don't know — he must do as he pleases; O it will make me wild! He must do as he pleases, for I must be wretched either way,"

"Dear Caroline — but O! how much better to be unhappy for the sake of doing right than when —"

"Yes, yes — so he said — but O! the horror. It kills me even to think of what it will be! O, Marian, Marian —"

"It will be over in time," said Marian; "but O! I am glad you have made up your mind —"

"No, I have not — at least I must, I suppose — for after what Walter said I can't go on. Walter's words would be a dagger — O! I don't know what they would be, all the rest of my life if I did. No — you and Walter must have your own way; I am too wretched already to care what becomes of inc. But he — O Marian, I never can —"

"If it is right you can," said Marian.

"You can, but you don't know what you say to me," said Caroline. "Right has never been to me what it is to you."

"Yes, indeed it has, dear Caroline, or you would not be making this struggle now. Indeed there must be strength in you, or you would have gone on without faltering."

"Walter said he should never have spoken one word after that first letter, if I had not begun," said Caroline; "but when he saw my mind misgave me, and I wanted help, he thought it his duty to come and set it all before me. O, Marian, he said dreadful things; I did not think Walter could have been so cruel. O, such things! He made me look at the Marriage Service, and say how I could answer those things; and he talked about death and the Last Day. He said it would be a presumptuous sin, and a profaning of the holy ordinance for me to come to it, knowing and thinking and feeling as I do. O what things he said! and yet he was very kind to me."

"Well, and —"

"I left it all to him. I knew it would be misery, and I did not care in what way; but then, Marian, O! worse than all, he said it must be my own doing."

"I suppose it must."

"He said he would help me; but I was the only person who had a right to do anything! O, Marian, Marian, I wish I could die."

"It will be over in time!" repeated Marian.

"Yes, but it will not be over. Mamma, papa, O I shall be reproached with it for ever; I shall know I have made *him* unhappy. O would that I could begin all over again!"

"You will have comfort at last in having been strong. The greater the effort the nobler it is! O, Caroline, do only hold out nobly. It is so glorious to have something to suffer for the sake of doing right!"

"Glorious!" murmured Caroline, her desponding gaze raised to contemplate the grand head, fine brow, firm lips, and dark glancing eye, turned up for a moment in the enthusiastic spirit of self-devotion. That look, unknowing as was Marian that she wore it, penetrated into Caroline's soul, and warmed her too with the temper of martyrdom. "Glorious;" she repeated a second time, and the tone was not so broken and hopeless as before.

"To be sure it is!" said Marian, going on with her own thoughts, "and it is so seldom people can ever partake of it, in ever so slight a degree, in these days; I always think it so beautiful where the account is given of the Apostles' great joy when they found a persecution was really going to begin."

"Persecution — yes, real persecution."

"And every suffering for the sake of the truth, for conscience' sake, must partake a little of that, I suppose," said Marian reverently.

There they were interrupted by Clara, who came to call Marian down stairs. Caroline came too, which the others had not expected. She was more calm and composed, and her headache was supposed by her mother to account for her want of spirits. She went to bed early, begging Marian to come and visit her when she came up. Marian contrived to do so as soon as possible, and found her already in bed, quiet and comfortable. "Marian," she said, "I have made up my mind. Now read to me, if you please."

She was worn out with agitation and sleeplessness, and soothed with having come to a determination, she soon fell asleep, and Marian went to her own room, wondering over the part

Walter had acted, and what he might be going to do next, whether he had led or driven his sister, and how far the courage of principle would avail to subdue natural timidity.

Caroline was pretty well the next morning, but the time was broken up in various ways, so that it was not till the afternoon that she could see Walter again in private. Lionel was considerably disconcerted when he found himself left to Marian. He had no notion of what was going on, had believed Walter's return to be entirely on his account, and was much disappointed at not having more of his company; for though both had been of the party to Salisbury, one had been outside the carriage and the other inside, so that they had not seen much of each other, and this morning had been interrupted. He was so much vexed and inclined to be hurt, by what he felt as a slight on his brother's part, that Marian could not resist telling him what she knew would console him. "I don't think you will mind it, Lionel, when you know why it is that Caroline wants him."

"Ha?" said Lionel, "you don't mean that she has thought better of it, and is going to send Julian the Apostate to the right about. Eh? You don't say so. Well, then there is some good in Caroline after all! But then what should she want of Walter?"

"To help her, to advise her."

"Well, if she likes, but I can't see what advice she wants. She has only got to make him a curtsey and say, 'Very much obliged to you, sir, but I had rather be excused.'"

Marian could not help laughing, in spite of her deep feeling on the matter, and Lionel, who had acted the voice and the curtsey, laughed too, and then perhaps ashamed of making fun of such an affair, added, "It is the best news I have heard this long time. What, and that is what she has been so dismal about these last few days, is it?"

"Yes, she has been very unhappy indeed. It is a terrible struggle."

"What? she likes him, does she? Poor Cary! After all I am glad she is coming right again, she is very good natured, and a great deal too good for Ju — . Ah! you won't have him called so, I know. They have taken a good time for it now he is away and Elliot too, but what a tremendous row there will be about it. Mamma thought it was such a speculation for Caroline."

"Yes, I am afraid she will have a great deal to go through."

"Yes," said Lionel, pondering gravely for some minutes; then asking "What is going to be done?"

"I don't know in the least; I believe she is settling with Walter today."

"Then nobody knows about it yet?"

There was no more to do but to have the satisfaction of talking over the engagement together, an occupation which put Lionel into particularly good spirits, and made their walk very pleasant. In the next glimpse which Marian had of Caroline, she learnt that Walter had undertaken to speak to his father that very evening. Caroline looked ghastly white as she said so in a whisper, but her dreadful agitation seemed to have left her; she had evidently quite made up her mind, though she said she believed it would never have been done if it had rested with her to begin by telling either of her parents. Both she and Marian knew that nothing but a spirit of moral heroism could have braced Walter to bear the first brunt of his father's wrath, and she was very much shocked at her own weakness in suffering it, but still it was much in her to allow it to be done.

That the conversation had taken place at night, when all the rest had retired, was evident to Marian when they met the nest morning from the very dark, severe loots of Mr Lyddell, from his wife's impatient angry manner, and sharper, louder voice. Walter was almost absolutely silent, Caroline went through the forms of breakfast as if she was in a dream, Lionel frowned, fidgeted, and tried with all his might, poor boy, to scan the faces which were daily growing more obscure to his vision; even Clara saw something was wrong, and glanced from one to the other in a puzzled, alarmed manner When they left the dining-room, Marian heard Mrs. Lyddell say, "Caroline, I want you." She flew up to her own room, and hiding her face, as she knelt down, she entreated earnestly that her poor Caroline might have steadfastness to go through this fearful trial. She was interrupted by Clara, begging to know what was the matter, if anything was wrong about Mr. Faulkner; she thought Lionel knew, but when she him be would do nothing but crow like a cock. Marian would have been glad if she could have made any equally convenient demonstration instead of an answer, but she could only say that she had heard nothing of Mr. Faulkner, and could not tell Clara anything about the matter.

"Do you know anything?" said Clara.

"I do know."

"Ah! you are in all Caroline's secrets now, and that is very odd; you who used to hate the Faulkners. Well, but are not you coming down?"

In spite of his cock-crowings, Lionel was very anxious, and

when in the course of that long desultory forlorn morning he was left alone with Marian, he earnestly asked her what she knew. "Nothing" was her answer.

"O if Caroline will but hold out!" he exclaimed, "that will be what I call being good for something! I hope mamma won't be desperately angry, for that I could stand less than anything, it goes on so much longer with her than with papa."

"She will be very much disappointed. O how I wish I knew what is happening!"

It was a long time before any intelligence could be gained: Mrs. Lyddell was very much flushed, and looked extremely displeased when she came down, hardly speaking to any one but Lionel, and glancing most sternly at Marian, Caroline did not come down at all, and when Marian was going up stairs after luncheon, Mrs. Lyddell said with extreme coldness, "Do not go to Caroline, if you please, I wish her to be left quiet."

Marian was in great consternation, since it was evident that Mrs. Lyddell perceived how her influence had been exerted, and was very much offended, indeed it was no wonder that she should be. Nothing but "very well" could be said so she quietly prepared to go out. Lionel had his brother this afternoon and did not want her, so she had only Clara for her companion full of surmises and of excitement. When she came in and was on her way to her room, Caroline opened her door. "Marian! O will you not come to me?" cried she imploringly.

Marian could not but comply, indeed she had no hesitation, for she thought Mrs. Lyddell's injunction only applied to the time before she went out.

"O, cheer me up, comfort me, Marian!" said Caroline, drawing her cousin's arm round her waist, "I do want it so much!"

"You are going on bravely then!" said Marian, caressing her.

"Bravely!" sighed Caroline; "No, indeed, but I have held firmly so far! I could not but stand by poor Walter, you know, when he confronted it all for me! I could not say much — I could only cry — but I took care they should not think I consented again."

"And is Mrs. Lyddell very much displeased?"

"O, don't speak of it, Marian. I cannot bear it."

The door opened and Mrs. Lyddell entered, and the air of indignant surprise on seeing Marian called for an answer: "I beg your pardon, I thought you only meant me not to go to Caroline just after luncheon," said Marian.

"I wish matters, such as we have been discussing, to be confined entirely to our own family," replied Mrs. Lyddell, too angry not to say something, yet too much afraid of Marian not to say it very courteously.

"Mamma!" said Caroline eagerly, "only hear me. I assure you that not one word did Marian ever say to me till I voluntarily went to her a week ago, because I was so very miserable I could bear it no longer."

"I should have thought your mother the proper person to go to in such a case. Miss Arundel's sentiments had so long been visible, that you could have no doubt of the advice you would receive from her."

"Mrs. Lyddell," said Marian, collecting herself, and speaking slowly, "I am very sorry I have appeared to act a part which I know must seem unjustifiable. I never spoke to — to Caroline" (the remembrance of Lionel prevented her from saying to any one) "of my opinion of this engagement, after it was formed, till she came to me for advice, in her distress. I could not speak against my conscience, and I tried not to forget what was due to you. I only begged her to write to her brother as the fittest person to help her, as being a clergyman. I beg your pardon for having acted against your wishes." So saying, Marian went out, surprised and alarmed at finding herself in open opposition to Mrs. Lyddell, and bewildered as to how she ought to have acted. Her comfort was in looking forward to the refuge at Fern Torr, and she smiled as she compared Mrs. Lyddell with her other guardian's future wife.

Mrs. Lyddell wished her at Fern Torr fully as much as she did. She had already become jealous of Lionel's preference, and it was too galling to find the affection of her children stolen from her by that cold, pale, proud, unprepossessing girl. Had the love been on the part of Elliot or Walter, Mrs. Lyddell would hardly have regretted it, considering Miss Arundel's large fortune and high connexions; but nothing was less probable than this, and Marian's influence over Caroline was at present, in Mrs. Lyddell's eyes, only a source of mischief.

Lionel was alone in the drawing-room, and met Marian eagerly inquiring "What news?"

"I have hardly seen her. Has Walter told you nothing?"

"No; he thinks I don't know, and I was not going to let on that you told me. Is she steady?"

"Yes, so far."

"That is right," said Lionel, thoughtfully, "I am very sorry for her, but I shall think the better of her ever after."

"Have you been out with Walter?"

"Yes, we have had a very nice talk."

Here Walter came down, and began to talk to Marian about schools and lending libraries.

It was a strange state of things, with all those different pairs of confidential friends. Both Marian and Walter were the stay and support of Caroline and Lionel; yet, though acting in concert, and perfectly agreed, not saying a word in confidence to each other on either head. Neither did Walter speak of Caroline to Lionel, nor Lionel, though much interested for her, speak to her of his affairs or her own. Clara indeed bestowed her communications on every one, but she got nothing in return that was satisfactory. Marian was the central point with all except Walter, but the fulness of her heart was bestowed elsewhere. And, alas! none saw so little of those young hearts as the parents, who had never earned their confidence; so that when they turn to them, it was from duty, as to rulers, not as to counsellors and friends.

Very sore was Marian's heart that night, when she felt it her duty to bid Caroline good night in Mrs. Lyddell's hearing, in spite of the piteous, imploring glance turned upon her. Might not her support make all the difference now? she thought. No; shame on her for thinking that she could do more good than He to whose hands Caroline was trusted! Folly, to dream that her awkward, blundering words could be more help than the prayers she could pour out alone!

Yet all these consolations could not prevent poor Marian from being very miserable, under the dread that Caroline thought her unkind, and felt herself deserted, after being involved in all this suffering. And O, should she fail! Walter must go on Saturday, and then she would be left to fight her battle alone.

On the Friday the whole house knew what was going on. Mr. Lyddell himself had a conversation with Caroline, but nothing of it transpired. It only was evident that she still continued in the same mind, and she looked more wretched than ever. Marian was anxious to show her affection and sympathy in her manner, but her anxiety only made her cold, and dry, and awkward. Clara was excited and puzzled, Walter was hardly spoken to by father or mother; and when at breakfast on Saturday he spoke of his departure, the silence that he encountered seemed to express that he had much better not have come home at all.

Marian felt fierce with indignation, and Lionel, perhaps by way of effusion of the same feeling, dashed his chair away from the table, and called out, "Mind you come back again as soon as ever you can."

But the dead silence that followed was more painful and marked than it had been before.

CHAPTER XVII.

"The flowers do fade, and wanton fields,
To wayward winter reckoning yields,
A honey tongue, a heart of gall
Is fancy's spring, but sorrow's fall."
                              SIR W. RALEIGH.

The Sunday after Walter's departure was a very uncomfortable and melancholy day. It was very sad to see poor Caroline looking wan and suffering, and turning now and then a wistful appealing glance at Marian, as if intreating for the help which must not be afforded to her; and then at each meeting and parting, Marian was dissatisfied with herself for having been rendered stiff and dry instead of tender and consoling, by the very wish to be affectionate, which prevented her from being at ease. She heard from Clara that Caroline's great desire was to be allowed to write to Mr. Faulkner on the subject before she saw him again, whilst he was still in London, and that it was this which her parents so strongly opposed, convinced that a meeting with him would renew all her feelings of attachment. Marian dreaded the same, for she could not think Caroline's resolution sufficient to hold out in sight of his affection, and of his prepossessing qualities, and at the same time, every day that the engagement continued made it more difficult to break it off.

One comfort was, however, that Lionel's anxiety and interest in Caroline's affairs, were drawing his attention from his own trouble, and he was much less irritable and unhappy than before. Perhaps this might have been in part owing to his conversations with Walter, who could venture on giving him more lessons on the right principle of endurance than Marian had ever dared to put before him. She was more pleased than she had been for a long time, when as they were walking together in the plantations, after evening service, he said with some abruptness and yet with some hesitation, "Marian, didn't you once read something with Gerald in the morning?"

"Yes," said Marian, sure of what the something meant.

"Do you do it still by yourself?"

"Yes."

"Then I wish — Would you mind reading to me?"

"The Psalms and Lessons? O, Lionel, I should be so glad I Only could you get up in time? for I don't know when to do it except before breakfast."

"To be sure I could get up in time. I only lie in bed because there is nothing to do, and nobody to speak to."

"Well then, will you meet me in the schoolroom at eight o'clock in the morning?"

"Very well."

No more was said, but Lionel kept his appointment. It was, as Marian guessed a recommendation of his brother's. Walter had asked him to get one of his sisters to read to him, and Lionel had made the request to Marian, as his real sister, though he had never told Walter whether he meant to take his advice.

The next Sunday, Marian, on coming down after dressing for dinner, was surprised to find Elliot standing by the fire. He just inclined his bead, and moved his lips by way of greeting.

"When did you come home?" said she drily.

"Half-an-hour ago."

The answer was brief and with no encouragement to say more. She thought he looked dark and moody, and, taking up a book, was silent. The next time the door opened, it was Lionel who entered. He frowned and gazed up, perceiving the figure but not able to make it out. "Ha, Lionel! How d'ye do?" said Elliot in a short, gruff, indifferent voice; without moving or attempting to shake hands, without any token that he thought of Lionel's misfortune.

Lionel's equally indifferent tone, "How d'ye do?" was sign enough to Marian that he was hurt. He came and sat by her, talked fast and low, and laughed several times in the constrained manner he used to put on by way of bravado; Elliot all the time taking no notice. The others soon made their appearance. Mr. and Mrs. Lyddell had seen him before, and to his sisters his greeting was much in the same style, hardly vouchsafing any recognition of Caroline at all.

The cloud was thicker and darker than ever all dinner time. Mr. and Mrs. Lyddell tried in vain to talk, he answered them in a short snappish way which he was apt to assume whenever his father made any attempt to check his extravagance.

The ladies and Lionel were glad to get into the drawing-room, and leave him and his father to themselves. Tea came and they did not appear, ten o'clock struck, half-past, and they came not. The ladies were putting away their books, and thinking of wishing good night when suddenly the door was thrown open, and in tramped Mr. Lyddell, red with passion, while behind him came Elliot, with less of violence, but with a dark scowl of resentment on his downcast and always unpleasant face.

"Caroline!" began Mr. Lyddell, in a voice of thunder, and great was the alarm of all, for her sake, as she turned pale and trembled. "Caroline! You have my full consent to do as you please. You may break with Faulkner tomorrow, if you like!"

Some discovery! thought Marian, transfixed with wonder and hope; Caroline sat still but for her trembling, her face bent down, and her hands nervously clasped together.

"Now, sir," proceeded Mr. Lyddell, turning round on Elliot, "you see if I am the tyrant you would make me. You see if I am going to force my daughter into a marriage against her wish — sacrifice my whole family because I have an ill-conditioned scamp of a good-for-nothing son. You see."

"I do see, sir," muttered Elliot; "and you'll see whether you like the consequences."

Marian thought she had better be out of this family scene, and had her hand on the door, but Mr. Lyddell called out "Stay here! Marian! I don't care if all the world heard me. He thinks he can threaten me into tyranny over her inclinations, and I tell him she is as free as air! I vow —"

"Mr. Lyddell! do consider, do think," expostulated his wife; "I daresay Elliot was a little too vehement a partizan for his friend —"

"Friend! Pshaw! He care for his friend!" said Mr. Lyddell scornfully. "'Tis for himself he is a partizan, I tell you. Nothing else does he care a straw for. 'Tis for nothing but the saving of her fortune that he would have me persecute his sister into this marriage! Aye! he has the face to tell me so! and what more do you think he comes and says to me! Why! that Lionel will be nothing but a burthen for ever! A pretty pass things are come to when he speaks after that fashion of his own brother! He cared for his friend, indeed!"

"No one ever thought of compelling Caroline," pleaded Mrs. Lyddell.

"But I tell you he did," interrupted her husband. "I told him I was very sorry, but I could not help it; if she would have her own way, I could not make her marry the man against her will, and he answers in his sneering way that it is all nonsense, he would be bound to make her give up in no time — any man could bring a girl to reason. As if I was to persecute my daughter to force her into what she tells me is against her conscience. Better too much conscience than none at all, I tell you, Master Elliot."

"We had better bring this scene to an end, sir," said Elliot sullenly. "We understand each other."

So saying, he took up his candle and flung out of the room. The girls were but too glad to escape, and Lionel followed them, leaving Mr. and Mrs. Lyddell to themselves.

Caroline and Clara both were trembling like aspen leaves, each threw an arm round Marian's waist, and leant against her as soon as they were out of the room. She had been startled and trembling before, but their fright seemed to give her firmness; and it was well, for Caroline's knees shook so much, and she was so nervous that she could hardly have reached her room without support. Clara began to exclaim, but Marian stopped her, made her fetch some camphor julep, helped Caroline to undress, and put her to bed. Caroline hardly spoke all the time, but as Marian bent over her to kiss her, and wish her good night, she whispered, "I may soon be able to have you again, dear Marian!"

Marian went to bed, wondering at all that had passed, indignant with Elliot, pleased with Mr. Lyddell, hopeful for Caroline, and cheered by finding that she had not been thought unkind.

She heard doors opened and shut, and the trampling of feet the next morning, and when Lionel met her in the schoolroom for their reading, he told her that be had been overtaken by Elliot running down stairs at full speed; and had only just time to clear out of his way. "And hark! is not there something at the front door? Look out, Marian."

Marian looked from the window. "Yes! It is his dog-cart. Can he be going away, Lionel?"

"Going off in a rage!" said Lionel, looking grave; "I thought there was mischief in his voice last night."

"Yes, there is his portmanteau," said Marian, in a tone of consternation; for little as she liked Elliot, it was too shocking to see a son thus leave his father's roof.

"It is a pretty piece of work," said Lionel. "He has been coming it a little too strong for my father, it seems! Well, poor Caroline will be let alone, that is one good thing; but I am afraid he will go and get into some tremendous scrape, if it is only for the sake of spiting my father."

"It is very dreadful!" said Marian, sighing.

"I am very glad my father was so angry, though!" said Lionel. "Wanting him to drive poor Caroline into it by unkindness! That was a little too bad!"

"Yes, indeed," said Marian. "But O! here he comes out of the door with his cigar. He is getting in! There he goes! O, Lionel!"

They both were silent for some little time. Then Marian took up the prayer-book, and began the Psalm, and when she heard

Lionel's voice join in the Doxology, a thrill came home to her, making her feel that blindness might yet be indeed the blessing to him that faith taught her to know it must be. How much better to be thus than like his brother.

When they met the others at breakfast, it proved that they alone knew of the departure; Mr. Lyddell interrogated Elliot's servant, and heard from him that he had orders to follow his master to Paris as soon as he had packed up his goods. This was all that could be learnt, and all that Marian could make out as to what had passed, was that he had been strongly averse to Caroline's engagement being broken off, that he had tried to induce his father to insist upon it, and to drive her to overcome her reluctance by what could be only understood as domestic persecution, and that in short he had allowed his unfeeling selfishness to appear to such a degree, that it had positively revolted his father, whose displeasure had long been excited by the extravagance that had been causing serious inconvenience, and who instantly, while under the influence of his first indignation, resolved to show that he would not be domineered over, nor sacrifice the rest of the family to the extravagance which he had already too freely supplied.

Mr. Lyddell had given his consent while angry, and he could not retract it when he was cool. Caroline therefore might write her letter as soon as she pleased. She had nothing to dread from him; indeed, as if out of opposition to Elliot, he was kinder to her than he had ever been before, called her "my dear" more than once, and observed on her pale looks. Her mother spoke little to her, and that little was cold and unkind, while she looked so vexed and unhappy that even Marian had some feeling for her, and what must it have been for her own daughter? However, all open opposition was withdrawn, and Caroline had only herself to struggle with. There was no reason why she should not once more seek comfort from Marian, yet all that day she kept at a distance, and it was not till the next evening that she came into Marian's room, and sinking into a chair, murmured, "I have done it."

"Written your letter?"

"Sent it."

"O, I am so glad!"

"Glad?"

"Yes, but you will be glad when it is over."

"O!" sighed Caroline, incredulously. "You know nothing about it. Marian."

"Every one must be glad to have done right," said Marian, firmly.

"O what a week it has been! And I have sown dissension in the family! And no one can tell what may be the consequence with Elliot! And he will be unhappy! O! Marian — I wish — I wish you had let me go on my own way and be miserable alone," added she with a kind of anger.

"It was your own doing," said Marian gently; "you felt it to be right. Only worse misery could come of your going on, for that would have been positive wrong; now it must and will get better."

"I don't know," sighed Caroline. "I never knew till now how much I cared for him! O, Marian!" and she burst into a hearty fit of crying.

Marian was perplexed, as she always was when any one cried, and stood without a word till Caroline had relieved herself by tears, and began to speak again. It was very sad and melancholy, and it was very difficult to find anything to answer; Marian could see no consolation but that "it was right," and that did not seem to have much effect on Caroline; while, added to the former trouble of renouncing the man who loved her, and of grieving her parents, there was the dread of what Elliot might do in his anger.

However, the being able to pour everything out to so true a friend was more of a comfort than anything that, could have been said to her. She told Marian that she had gone through the conversations with her father and mother better than she could have thought possible. She could not desert poor Walter, that was one thing that helped her, she must stand by him, and papa was not half so angry as she expected. It seemed as if her strength had grown with each occasion for it. The first effort of writing to Walter had cost her most of all, then the allowing him to break the matter to her father had been dreadful; but after all, the conferences with her parents, singly and together, had not been as bad as the fear of them, and Marian tried to persuade her that it would be the same when she saw Mr. Faulkner, but poor Caroline shook her head, and said Marian knew nothing about it. And Marian was much of the same opinion, and held her peace, but before the end of the conversation she had the great pleasure of hearing Caroline say, "The thought of being able to have you again has been the one great help to me through all!"

Two days after this, as Marian and Lionel were going out riding together, Marian exclaimed, "I do believe that is Mr. Faulkner!"

"Where?"

"Riding on the Salisbury road," said Marian; "I am sure it is his horse."

"Don't let us meet him! can't we get out of the way?" said Lionel. "Aren't we somewhere near the thorny lane?"

"No, but we might ride off on the Down. Only take care, Lionel; you had better keep close to me," said Marian, much more unwilling to meet Mr. Faulkner than to conduct Lionel through the ups and downs of the green, chalky common.

She watched and guided his pony up the bank and upon the Down, and on they trotted fast, for Marian was actuated by a very undignified fit of terror lest she should meet Mr. Faulkner, towards whom she felt positively guilty, nor did she wish to be seen fleeing from him.

"We must be out of sight of the road by this time, aren't we?" said Lionel.

"I don't know," Marian turned her head to see. At that moment Lionel's pony stepped into a hole, stumbled, and when she looked back again, there was Lionel on the ground. Her head swam with fear, but the next moment Lionel was on his feet and laughing.

"Not hurt, Lionel! are you sure?"

"Not a bit! Is that Sorrel?"

Sorrel was rushing off with his bridle loose, and Marian began to dread having Mr. Faulkner's assistance in catching him. "Stand still, Lionel!" she called, and then riding between Sorrel and the road, she managed to turn him towards a long hedge that crossed the Down, saw him stop to eat a tuft of grass, made a grasp at his bridle, but failed, while he dashed off across the Down, happily not towards the road.

She called to Lionel, told him of her ill success, and begged him not to move, while she again pursued the runaway, and a long dance he led her, far out of sight of Lionel. Once she had considerable hopes, when she came in sight of a shepherd boy, who stood in amaze at the lady in chase of the runaway steed, then came up with a run to cut off its course, but so awkwardly that the pony was still more frightened, and galloped off in another direction faster than ever! Poor Marian! However after full half an hour, she succeeded in hunting him into a narrow place between two fields, ending in a gate, caught safely hold of the rein, kept it fast, and at length led Sorrel back in triumph to the spot where poor Lionel stood still patiently. She called out to him as soon as she came near enough to make her voice heard, and he answered, and walked forward to meet the dark shapes, which were all that he could see.

Marian feared that he would be very much mortified at having been obliged to remain thus helpless, while a girl was doing what he would have so much enjoyed, and she looked anxiously at his face, alas! she could look there now without his knowing it. It was disconsolate, but the look was not bitter. She held Sorrel while he mounted, and she then apologized for having been so long, and said she feared he had thought she had forgotten him. He made not much reply, did not even ask how she had managed to catch the pony. Marian conducted him safely into the road before she would speak again. He did, however, congratulate himself on not having been obliged to be beholden to Mr. Faulkner for catching the pony, as well as on Sorrel's not having gone home to tell the tale himself.

"Yes, indeed, they would have been terribly frightened," said Marian.

"Ay, and if they once knew of my tumble, they would never let us go out riding again."

"But, Lionel, we must tell," said Marian.

"Just like a girl!" grumbled Lionel. "Then there's an end of all our rides, and all the comfort that I have in life."

"I don't know," said Marian. "At any rate I can't ride with you, I should not think it right, unless Mr. Lyddell knew of this fall. It is my concern and not yours, for it was all through my carelessness."

"You go on just as if you were a child still," said Lionel, still cross.

"Well, Lionel, I believe the only way is to manage ourselves as if we were children still."

"All very fine," was Lionel's surly answer, and they rode on, while Marian was very unhappy. She blamed herself for having given way to a foolish fit of nervous bashfulness, which had led to what might have been a serious accident to her especial charge. It had further made a very unpleasant confession needful, and Lionel's vexation and irritation seemed to have overcome all his late improvement. The thought of what poor Caroline was going through was enough to stifle everything else, and Marian wondered at herself, as for a sort of unkindness, in having been so fully occupied as to have had no time for anxiety.

Both had been very silent ever since Lionel's reply, until Marian asked him to strike his repeater. It was half-past five, and they turned homewards, taking a bye road so as to avoid meeting Mr. Faulkner. And now Lionel began to talk of Caroline, and wonder how she had sped. He seemed to throw off his own private troubles as he talked of hers, and his fit of petulance was melting fast away. At last he made up his mind to inquire how she had caught Sorrel, and was positively interested in the narration, laughing at the idea of the scrape they would have been in if Sorrel had made his way to the road, and Mr. Faulkner had caught him.

He said no more about the confession, but it was evident that he had conquered his annoyance sooner than he had ever done before. Marian had not theorized on the matter, but if she had she could not have judged better, for Lionel was far better dealt with by being bold and uncompromising. It was very strange to have this concern of their own so much on their minds when Caroline's fate was at its crisis, yet perhaps it was good for Marian to be thus occupied, since she was apt to suffer very much from anxiety, as persons of her calm and reserved demeanour often do. A sickening, throbbing, trembling feeling came over her, making her temples beat and her hands cold, as she came into the house, expecting to hear whether Caroline had endured and been true to herself, and it was well she had not had longer to suffer from it.

No one was in the drawing-room, and she ran as fast as her trembling knees would allow to Caroline's room, knocked, received no answer, opened the door, and saw Caroline stretched out on her bed, in a state best described by the French word *anéantissement*, for it was not fainting, but the sort of prostration consequent on the completion of an effort for which she had wound herself up. She was very pale, her eyes were shut, and her breath came short. Marian stood watching her in alarm, wondering whether to speak, and how. At last Caroline looked up, held out her hand, and drew Marian down on her knees till her face was level with hers, then put her arm round her neck.

"Dear Caroline!" said Marian, though it was not easy to say anything, "you will be happier now."

A more caressing person would have been much more at ease herself and given more comfort to Caroline, that must be confessed, but as there was no one else to be had, Marian was obliged to do her best, and this was to kiss Caroline timidly and say, "I am so glad you have done right."

But Caroline only hid her face at the word *glad* and murmured, "You never did him justice! You never did!"

"If it had not been for the want of that one thing he would have been all right," said Marian.

"O, he is very noble! he has such a mind! such — such — O, he loved me so much," and Caroline fell into a paroxysm of silent misery. Marian began to dread lest the parting had not been final, and though doubtful whether she ought to ask, could not help saying, "But is it over?"

"Yes, yes; you have your wish, Marian. It is done! He is angry with me now! It is over, and I am wretched for life!"

"Not so wretched as if you had done wrong." said Marian. Caroline did not turn away this time, and Marian gathered courage to say, "You have persevered, and now there will be comfort. There will always be comfort in knowing you have tried to do right. Walter will be so glad, and so will Lionel."

"Lionel," repeated Caroline.

"Yes, he has been very anxious about you."

"Poor boy!" sighed Caroline. "Well, Marian, there is one thing still to be done. Only one, and it is all that I shall live for. I shall devote myself to him, if I can but do anything to please him, and make him care for me when you are gone. It will be my one object."

"Yes," said Marian, "it will be very good for you both."

They were interrupted by Clara, who came in, dressed for dinner, pitying Caroline, and telling Marian it was very late. Caroline sat up, but she had a violent nervous headache, and they both persuaded her to lie down again.

Marian ran off to dress, and though the dinner-bell rang in the midst of her hurried toilette, came back to look at Caroline, beg her to keep quiet, and promise to come up as soon as dinner was over. As she went down, the other trouble of having to confess their adventure came over her, but she was resolute, in spite of the want of favour with which she knew she was regarded.

Want of favour, evident from the scrupulous formality with which she was treated; for if she had been like a daughter of the house, as she ought to have been, would they have waited dinner for her, and let her find them all looking uncomfortable and expectant in the drawing-room? They went into the dining-room; there was a silent, formal dinner, nothing like a family party. As soon as the servants had left the room. Marian quailing secretly, not from fear of Mr. and Mrs. Lyddell, but lest Lionel should lose his rides, began, "I have a confession to make, Mr. Lyddell," and told the story of the accident, explaining how it was entirely caused by her carelessness.

Exclamations and inquiries arose, and Mrs. Lyddell certified herself by several questions that Lionel had not been hurt, but not one of them was addressed to Marian. It was as if this was only one among many injuries, too frequent for a reproach more or less to be needed. Mr. Lyddell did not take it half so much to heart, and no prohibition against future rides was issued, for the truth was that no one liked to mortify Lionel. It was exactly one of the cases in which the whole danger is not conquered, because it melts at the very aspect of moral courage.

It was not comfortable to have to walk away to Caroline, knowing how much she had displeased Mrs. Lyddell; but it must be done, and it was, at least, agreeable to leave these cold looks. She found Caroline better, and able to tell her something of what had passed. At first Mr. Faulkner would not believe her to be in earnest, and had imagined this was a way of showing her displeasure at his long absence, or some trifling "lovers' quarrel;" but when he found that she really meant what she said, and her tears and stifled whispers alike announced her adherence to what she had expressed in her letter, he became extremely angry, thought himself, (as indeed he might with some justice) very ill-used, and though he had retained his gentlemanlike manner and language, had pretty plainly expressed that Miss Lyddell should have known her own mind. Poor Caroline wept bitterly, beseeching that they might not part in anger, but he disavowed all irritation, and took a cold, courteous leave, which wounded her more than all.

Marian could not easily sympathise with regrets for such a lover, but she liked to magnify the sacrifice in order to admire it more, and greatly rejoiced in being able to give full admiration to one whom she had learnt to love so heartily as Caroline. Such a triumph over natural timidity and feebleness of character was indeed a great and gallant thing, and Marian used to muse and wonder at it in her solitary hours. There was still much to suffer externally as well as internally; there was the return of letters and presents, with all their associations; there was the feeling of the pain and offence given to Lady Julia and her daughters; there was the perception of the opinions of the world, and the certainty that all the gossips of the neighbourhood were busy with their conjectures; there was the continued anxiety about Elliot, and the marked vexation and displeasure of Mrs. Lyddell, who treated Caroline as one who had disappointed all her best hopes.

Under all this there was only Marian to sustain Caroline, and their friendship was an additional offence. Marian knew that Mrs. Lyddell regarded her as the head of a hostile party, and a sower of dissension in the family, by no means an agreeable footing on which to stand; but the only way, was to appear completely unconscious, and behave as far as possible as usual. She was grateful to them for making it no worse, and still more for not having objected to her continuing her rides with Lionel, from whom, it may well be believed, she scarcely ever took her eyes, from the time his foot was in the stirrup.

Lionel was triumphant at the dismissal of "Julian the apostate," but he was disappointed to find that Caroline did not recover her spirits "now she had had her own way, and got rid of the man." He did not like to have her presence announced by a sigh, and to hear the subdued, dejected tone of her voice, and he used to wonder over it with Marian, who laughed at him for fancying it was such an easy matter to part with a lover, yet agreed that it was hard to understand how there could be love where there was no esteem. Lionel used to consult her as to what was to be done to cheer his sister, since his mother would only make everything worse and he could not bear her continued melancholy.

"I do believe, Lionel," said Marian, "that you could do more for her than any body else. If you would but sometimes let her do things for you, ask her to help you, as — as you ask me."

Lionel would not take the suggestion as she wished. "I thought you liked to help me," said he, in a somewhat offended tone.

"O, don't I?" cried Marian, eagerly; "but so does every one, if you would only allow them."

Lionel flourished the little switch in his hand till it made an ill-tempered *swish!* and Marian knew that he thought her ungrateful for the exclusive preference with which he honoured her.

"She is your sister," she added.

"Very well," said Lionel, crossly shaking off her arm, "I shall know what to be at, if you are tired of helping me."

He could not see the tears in her eyes, and though she was extremely grieved, her voice did not betray how strong her feeling was. "Tired! O Lionel, how can you think it? But would it not be better to learn to depend less on me against I go away?"

"Ay, and glad enough you'll be to go."

"For all but your sake and poor Caroline's," said Marian. "Mrs. Lyddell does not like to have me here."

"It would not be fair to want to keep you," said Lionel, "but —"

"I should have much more comfort in going if I thought you and Caroline were helping each other," said Marian. "I know she wants to make you her first object."

Lionel made no answer nor any change in his ways for some days, yet sometimes it seemed, as if when he thought of it, he was more willing to allow Caroline to do him some of the small services which his fast increasing blindness rendered necessary.

Caroline being more dexterous and neat-handed than Marian, did them well, and then Marian was vexed with herself for a few feelings like annoyance at not being equally necessary to Lionel, but she persevered, encouraged by seeing the comfort that each approach on his part seemed to give his sister. It was the hardest thing Marian had ever had to do, to give up the being first with him, as she must cease to be when the natural affection of the brother and sister was called into play. But it was right, and she would bear it. She thought it right as well as very pleasant to accept an invitation from the Wortleys to come and spend the Christmas holidays with them, joining her brother on the railroad, and meeting Edmund at Fern Torr. The repose would be beyond everything delightful, and no less so, the being in a house where her presence was welcome to every member of the family. Besides, she longed to see and to talk to Agnes, and the more she thought of her promised visit the more she enjoyed it.

Caroline and Lionel both were very sorry to part with her, and jointly and separately lamented her going; but Caroline blamed herself for selfishness in wishing to keep her, and perceived that it would be a good thing that her brother should begin to be weaned from his sole dependance upon her, while Lionel seemed half afraid to trust her to depart, lest she should never return, and insisted on half a dozen promises that she would come back at the end of Gerald's holidays.

CHAPTER XVIII.

"They made a famous procession
My good little women and men;
Such a sight was never seen before
And never will again."

SOUTHEY.

A division of a first-class carriage, occupied only by Gerald, received Marian at the station, and first she had to be shown the
hat, cloak, and umbrella with which he had constructed an effigy,
which, as he firmly believed, had frightened away all who had
thought of taking a seat in it.

"Thinking you a mad monkey, and that your keeper," said
Marian, looking proudly at the handsome face and dancing black
eyes of her beautiful brother. "Why! how you are grown, Gerald!
Do stand up, and let me see if you are not taller than I am."

"No, not quite so tall, unless it is your bonnet," said Gerald,
after craning up his neck in vain.

"At any rate, you are taller than Lionel. He only comes up to
my ear," said Marian.

"Poor Lionel! How are his eyes?"

"O Gerald, it is very sad. He has very little sight left. I believe
he finds his way about quite by feeling now. It has grown worse so
much faster in these last three weeks."

"Poor fellow! What can he do all day?"

A long description followed, and then Gerald wanted to hear
all about Caroline, and what Marian thought fit to tell him,
together with his comments, lasted till, in spite of his effigy, a lady
made an entrance, and for some time Gerald was reduced to
silence, and as he sat on the same side, to making horrible side-
long scowls at her, out of her sight, which sorely tried his sister's
propriety of countenance.

The tongues of two such happy people could not long, however, continue tied, and presently Gerald rattled off into a history
of his sporting adventures in Scotland, as if he would detail every
shot. The narration was endless, and very tiresome it would have
been to any woman but a sister, and a sister who had so much of
the hunter spirit in her as Marian; but she listened and sympathised with all her heart and soul, and understood why such a shot
was a good one, and why such another failed, and was absorbed in
the interest of the attempt to recover a wounded bird when the
retriever was stupid, long after the intruder had made her exit,

and they might have returned to matters touching her more closely, though regarded by Gerald as hardly equal in importance to roe deer, salmon, and grouse.

They were on Devonshire ground before they ever began to rejoice over Edmund's engagement, and from thence to talk of Edmund himself. Gerald pronounced many an eulogium on him, in which praises of his excellence as a fisherman and sportsman were strangely mixed with a real genuine appreciation of his goodness and superiority.

"'Tis a capital thing that he is come home to stay," said Gerald, heartily.

"Isn't it?"

"I like him specially," said Gerald. "Do you know he showed me some of my father's letters."

"Did he indeed?"

"That he did. It was before I was born, when he thought he was going to have Fern Torr and all, he had rather an idle fit, and these were what papa wrote to him."

"Was Edmund ever idle?" exclaimed Marian, falling into a reverie of wonder whether this did not make it more hopeful for Gerald.

"I am very glad he has got this money," proceeded Gerald. "I only wish it was more. One letter he showed me that was best of all. It was from my father when I was born. You can't think what a nice letter it was. There was something about its being a disappointment to him — to Edmund, I mean, but how papa cared for him as much as ever, and thought after all it might be better for him in the end. And then, Marian, papa said he could hardly expect to live till I was grown up, and he asked Edmund to be my godfather, and said he trusted to him to be like an elder brother to us."

"That he is!" murmured Marian.

"Edmund said he wished me to read it that I might not think him interfering."

"You never could have thought so!"

"I don't know. I could not have stood it from some people, but I could see the sense of what Edmund said."

Without entering into particulars, Gerald was now all freedom and openness, casting quite away the restraint that had so long grieved his sister. How happy she was!

Mr. Wortley himself met them at Exeter, and in spite of the early darkness of the winter day, Charles and James met them at the foot of Blackstone hill, and Edmund and Agnes were a little further on.

What a happy greeting it was! Marian and Gerald would jump out and walk home with them, the boys ran and called in the dark, the stars came out overhead, the tall hedges kept out all the glimmering light, splashes alone made them aware of the puddles; but on the happy party tramped, all talking an unmitigated flow of merry nonsense, laughing and enjoying it, all the more the darker and stranger it grew, and merrier than all, when they got home, at Mrs. Wortley's dismay at their having dragged Marian a mile and a half, in the dark and dirt, after her long journey. "Pretty guardians to have the care of her!"

All the evening again there was nothing but fun and joyousness, fun of the brightest, happiest kind, positively wild in the three boys, and Edmund not much less so, the girls weary with laughing, and contributing their share to the sport. A person must have lived like Marian, pent up by formalities and the certainty of being disliked, to know what was the enjoyment of the perfect liberty and absence from constraint, the thorough home-like feeling of every one loving and understanding each other, which existed at Fern Torr. How delightful it was to have no heart achings for Gerald, to see Edmund just like his old self, and the dear Agnes, so very lovely and bright! so very unlike her only former experience of betrothed lovers. It was no small happiness to the Fern Torr party to have one so prized and loved as Marian to rejoice with them, indeed, all this evening every one was too joyous to dwell on any of the causes of their felicity, it was nothing but high spirits, and unreflective mirth.

When they had bidden each other good night, and were gone up stairs, there was more of gravity and thought. Marian and Agnes could have sat up talking half the night, if Mrs. Wortley would have allowed them, but she said Marian must have time to rest, and ruthlessly condemned her to bed.

Never did Marian spend so happy a Christmas. There was plenty of depth and earnestness in her *tête-à-têtes* with Agnes, when they talked over the wonders that had happened to them both, and always ended by returning to recollections of happy old days before Marian left Fern Torr, when Edmund had been the prime mover of every delightful adventure. Marian was as good as a sister to each of the lovers, so heartily did she help each one to admire the other. Or when they were "lovering," as the boys chose to call their interminable wanderings in the manor gardens, Marian used to be extremely happy with Mrs. Wortley, talking over the history of the engagement, and settling how and when the love began. Mr. Wortley suggested that the first attraction had been Agnes' unmitigated horror of the Lyddells, which he declared had won Mr. Arundel's heart, though he never owned how much he participated in it. It needs not to be stated how Edmund's noble behaviour was appreciated, more especially after the new lights which Marian was able to throw upon it.

Then came the discussion of the plans for the house which Edmund was to build, on a farm, which had come into the market at the very nick of time, just on the other side of the hill, and in Fern Torr parish. Marian and Gerald were taken the first day to look and advise whether the new house should be on the old site, or under the shelter of a great old slate quarry, crested with a wood, a beautiful view spread before it, and capacities for making the loveliest garden that was ever seen.

Edmund sketched house and garden in every possible point of view, each prettier than the other, and all the young gave their voices eagerly for the quarry, while the old protested on the difficulty of getting so far up the hill, and suggested damp. But the young carried the day, and the plans were drawn and debated on a dozen times in twenty-four hours, always including the prettiest of little sitting-rooms for Marian, with a window opening into the garden, and a door into the drawing-room, and then came letters to architects and calculations with builders, and reckonings that the house should be habitable by next September, and Mr. Wortley laughing at their credulity for expecting it.

Marian was surprised to find how far away and secondary seemed the thoughts that had of late engrossed her entirely. She wondered to discover how little her mind had been occupied with Caroline and Lionel, fond as she was of them and very anxious about them. This was so very different a world! and she felt so much more as if she belonged to it. She obtained from Agnes some admiration for Caroline's conduct, though in somewhat of the "better late than never" style, and at the price of warm abuse of the parents, in which Marian was not indisposed to join.

Caroline wrote nearly every day, saying that she missed Marian dreadfully, and that her letters were the only comfort she had; she would not wish her back again, for that would be selfish, but it would be a joyful day when she returned. These constant letters, which Marian always kept to herself, rather surprised the Wortleys, but Edmund could better guess at her position. "Depend upon it," he said to Agnes, "it is she who has saved Miss Lyddell."

"O, Edmund! do you think so? I wanted to have thought so,

but she says it was the brother."

"He took the steps which would not have become Marian, but Walter Lyddell could never have moved without his sister, and where could she have found the principle but in Marian? I see now that her perseverance in right is beginning to tell on those around her, in spite of all untoward circumstances."

"I don't know anything like Marian!" said Agnes. "How very fine her countenance is!"

"That steadfast brow and lip."

"I saw her yesterday standing on the edge of a rock looking out on the view, and she was like some statue of Fortitude."

"Yes, Marian is a grand creature," said Edmund; "so strong and firm, yet with such feminine, retiring strength. There are still prejudices and little roughnesses, but I doubt whether they have not been her safeguard, outworks to secure the building, and I think they are disappearing with the occasion."

"Ah! papa and mamma think her very much softened down."

"She has had a very hard part to act, and her shyness and rigidity have been great helps to her, but I am glad to see them wearing away, and especially pleasant it is to see her expand and show her true self here."

"And to know she may soon be free of them all for ever!" said Agnes.

The time when Marian was to be free of them for ever, as Agnes said, was to be the next summer. Edmund and Agnes were to be married in July, Marian would then come to Fern Torr, and comfort Mrs. Wortley for losing her daughter, till the holidays began, when Edmund and Agnes would return, and some undefined scheme of delight was to be settled on for Gerald's holidays, until the house should be ready. Gerald was in the meantime very agreeable and satisfactory on the whole. He was too busy drawing varieties of stables for Edmund, to talk about his own, and marvellous were the portraits of the inhabitants with which he would decorate Edmund's elevations, whenever he found them straying about the room. Very mischievous indeed was the young gentleman, and Marian considered him to have been "a great deal too bad" when on a neat, finished plan, just prepared to be sent to the builder, she found unmistakeable likenesses of the whole Wortley family, herself and Gerald, assembled round a great bowl of punch, large enough to drown them all, drinking to the health of Edmund and Agnes, who were riding in at the gate, pillion fashion, supposed to be returning after the honey moon, which in one corner of the picture was represented in a most waning state, but the man in the moon squinting down at them with a peculiarly benignant expression of countenance.

Marian was very angry, but Edmund and Agnes would do nothing but laugh, though the whole plan had to be drawn over again, and Edmund was kept at work with ruler, scale, and compasses the whole evening, Marian scolding Gerald all the time, and Edmund too, for spoiling him, thinking her cousin the most heroically good natured and good tempered man in the world to bear with such an idle monkey, and laugh at the waste of time and trouble; and getting at last a glimmering perception that these tricks, thus met, were the greatest proof of good understanding and friendship. It ended in Gerald's inking in the plan, of his own free will, and very neatly, and getting up at six, the next morning, to ride to Exeter, in the dark cold misty December twilight, to take it to the builder, that no time might be lost; indeed, as he boasted, it was there a quarter of an hour before it would have come by post, as it would have done had it gone yesterday.

Gerald's studies were not extensive, but Edmund, by some magic secret, unknown to Marian, made him read history to himself for a short space every morning. The sporting paper had disappeared, and nothing was heard of Elliot or of Queen Pomare, while though he could not yet go the length of talking to the poor people himself, he stood by very civilly while Edmund talked to them.

The first ten days of Marian's stay had thus passed, when Caroline one day mentioned in her letter that mamma had a regularly bad influenza cold, and was quite laid up. It was aggravated, Caroline said, by the distress they were all in about Elliot. "But you will hear enough of this when you come back," wrote she, "so I will not grieve you with it now; though it is an additional load upon my mind — an additional offence, I fear, in poor mamma's eyes, since all this would not have come to light had I persisted. But you must not think I am repenting, for I never was further from regretting what I have done. The different spirit in which I could come to this Christmas feast, is a blessing to be purchased at any price, even at such wretchedness as it has been this autumn; and most earnestly do I thank you, dearest Marian. I can thank you by letter, though we never can speak of such things. Yes, I thank you. I regret nothing but my previous folly and weakness, and bitterly do I suffer for them; though all is better now, and Christmas has brought me peace and calm. It is as if the storm was lulled at last, and nothing left but dreariness, and the longing to be at rest. How bright the world was before me not a year ago! and now how worn out it seems, — only three comforts left in it, you, and Walter, and poor Lionel. For Lionel is a comfort; he is very kind and considerate, and, I do believe, softens mamma towards me. I suppose it is best for us that our hearts should have no home but one above; and if I was sure it was not disgust and disappointment, I should hope I was seeking one there; for I know the only feeling of rest and refreshment is in turning thither, and surely that must come from the FATHER, Who is ready to receive me. But I must leave off, for mamma is too unwell to be long left.

"Your most affectionate
        "CAROLINE LYDDELL."

After this, the letters, hitherto constant, ceased entirely, and Marian grew very uneasy. Her mother had died of influenza, so that the name gave her a fatal impression; and she dreaded to hear that Mrs. Lyddell was very ill, or that Caroline was ill herself. Another week, and at length she heard from Clara, in answer to a letter of inquiry, and to fix the day of her return.

"Oakworthy, Jan. 7th.
"MY DEAR MARIAN, — Caroline desires me to write to tell you, with her love, that she has this horrid influenza, and has been in bed since Monday. She is very feverish, and her throat so sore that she can hardly speak or swallow. Sarah sat up with her last night, and I think she is a little better this morning. Mamma is better, but only gets up for a little while in the evening, and cannot leave her room. I wish you were at home, for I don't know what to do: I am running backwards and forwards between the two rooms all day, and poor Lionel is so forlorn and solitary down stairs, with only papa. There! — that great blot was a tear, for I am so worn out with fatigue and nursing, that I am almost overcome. This winter I was to have come out, — how very different! I forgot to tell you, after all, that the carriage shall meet you, as you mention, on the 15th. I wish it was directly; they will be all well by the time you come. But it is so very forlorn, and I am so nervous; so excuse this scrawl.

"Your affectionate cousin,
        "CLARA LYDDELL."

As soon as Marian read this letter, she gave it to Edmund, saying, "I think I had better go home."

"O, Marian, you must not cheat us!" cried Agnes.

"I think they would be very glad of you," said Edmund, and

withal Marian's mind was made up, and she withstood all the persuasions of Gerald and Agnes that it was nothing — nonsense — only Clara's dismality — they would laugh at her for coming for nothing. No; Marian knew she was no nurse, but she could not bear to think of Lionel left to his blindness and helplessness, still less of Caroline, ill, and with no one to cheer her. She was sure she was wanted by those two at least, and she resolved that she would be at Oakworthy tomorrow evening, wrote notice of her intention to Clara, and prepared for her journey, giving up that precious last week, so prized because it was the last. She could go alone with her maid; there was no use in spoiling Gerald's holidays; so he would stay for all the delights that she gave up, ruining all by her absence, as every one declared.

Agnes grumbled and scolded her to her face, but made up for it out of hearing, by admiring her more than ever. Mr. and Mrs. Wortley gave her silent approval, and the boys would not wish her a pleasant journey. She was ready early the next morning, and once more left Fern Torr, bright with the promise that, when she was there next, it would be no more a guest.

She prosperously arrived at the station nearest Oakworthy, and soon saw the servant waiting for her. "Is Miss Lyddell better?"

"A little better than last night, ma'am. Mr. Lionel is in the carriage."

Marian had not at all expected any one to meet her, especially Lionel, coming all this distance in silence and darkness. She hastened to the carriage, and saw him leaning forward, listening for her. His face lighted up at her, "Well, Lionel," and he fairly hurt her, by the tightness of his grasp, when once he had met her hand. "So, you're come! What a time it has been since you went! Now you are come, I don't care."

"And how are you?" she asked anxiously.

"Bad enough to be going back to the oculist next week," he answered; "I can't even see the light."

A long silence; then, "How is Caroline?"

"Pretty much the same; it is a bad, feverish cold, and shocking throat. She breathes as if she was half stifled, and can hardly speak."

"I suppose she has Mr. Wells?"

"Yes, two or three times a day,"

"And Mrs. Lyddell is better?"

"Better, but not out of her room. It has been a tolerable state of things of late. Not a creature to speak to, except, now and then, Clara coming down to maunder and sigh over all she has to do, and my father, who has been thoroughly in a rage about Elliot. Do you know about all that, Marian?"

"No," she answered.

"It is out now, why he was so set upon Caroline's marriage, he had got Faulkner to back a bill for him; you don't know what that means, I suppose," said Lionel, with his old superior manner; — "made him engage that the money Elliot borrowed should be paid. There was to be some shuffle between them about her fortune it seems; so after the engagement was off, when the bill became due, Faulkner sent the holder of it to my father for the money and the news of this set on all the other creditors. No end of bills coming in, and he has been pretty nearly crazy among them; says we shall be beggars, and I don't know what all! I vow, it is my old plan coming right!" cried Lionel vehemently. "If the man in London can but set my eyes to rights, I'd be off to Australia tomorrow, instead of staying here to make all worse. Well, it's no use thinking of it: if ever I make my fortune now, it will be with a dog in a string, and a hat in his mouth."

"But go on, Lionel; are the debts so very bad?"

"I believe they are indeed, and no one knows the worst of them yet. No wonder Elliot was off to Paris in such a hurry, like a coward as he is, no one knows how he is ever to come back! And worst of all is to have mamma going about saying 'tis Caroline's fault! Hadn't I rather come to the hat and dog in good earnest than to see her marry that man? Why, Marian, he is actually engaged to Miss Dashwood! What do you say to that? To the Radical Dashwood's daughter that behaved so shamefully to papa!"

"The daughter?"

"No, the man. Fit company for the apostate, isn't it? He had better have begun with her. Fine love his must have been. Only six weeks. Should not that cure Caroline?"

"Has she heard it?"

"No, we have only known it since she was ill, and Clara thought she had better not tell her."

"Very right of Clara," said Marian; "but I think she will be glad, when she is well enough to be told."

Fast and eagerly did Marian and Lionel talk all the way, sometimes gravely and sorrowfully about Elliot and Caroline, sometimes cheerfully about Fern Torr, Edmund, and Gerald, of whom Lionel wanted much to hear. He clapped his hands, and danced himself up and down with ecstasy at the history of Gerald's embellishments of the plans, vowed that Gerald was a Trojan, and that it was as good as Beauty and the Beast, and seemed to be enjoying a perfect holiday in having some one to speak to again. "But," he said, "what a horrid bore it must have been to you to come away!"

"I thought I might be some help to Clara."

"Did she make you think Caroline so very ill? Mr. Wells says it is only a very bad cold. But I am very glad you are come."

Clara met Marian in the hall. "O Marian, I am glad you are come, but I am sorry you came home in such a hurry. Mamma says there was no occasion, and that I need not have frightened you, for it is only a bad attack of influenza."

"Then I hope Caroline Is better."

"Yes, rather, and she will be so glad to see you. Come to her at once, won't you? she heard the carriage, and is watching for you."

Marian hastily followed Clara to Caroline's room. In a few seconds both Caroline's arms were thrown round her neck, and a burning feverish face pressed to hers, then as she raised herself again, one of her hands still held fast, and Caroline lay looking up to her with an expression of relief and comfort. "Thank you," she murmured, in a hoarse low painful whisper, the sound of which gave an impression of dismay to Marian. Caroline was far worse than she had been prepared to sec her. That loud, oppressed, gasping breathing, the burning fever of hands and cheek, the parched lips, — this was far more than ordinary influenza. Marian stood watching her a little while; speaking now and then, until she closed her eyes in weariness, not for sleep, when she was about to leave the room, but Caroline looked up again anxiously and restlessly, and tried to say, "Come back."

"Yes, I'll come in a moment," said Marian, "I'll only just take off my bonnet, and go and see Mrs. Lyddell, if I may."

"O, yes, she is up, she knows you are come," said Clara, and Marian was presently knocking at Mrs. Lyddell's door.

She found her sitting by the fire in a large easy chair, in her dressing-gown and shawl, and was surprised at the first sight of her too, for that very weakening complaint, the influenza, had made a great change in her, perhaps assisted by all that she had gone through during the last summer and autumn, beginning with the parting with John, the grief and anxiety for Lionel, the disappointment and warfare with Caroline, and worse than all, the discoveries respecting her eldest and favourite son. She looked a dozen years older, all the clearness of her complexion was gone, and the colouring that remained, as if ingrained, was worse than paleness; her hand shook with weakness, and the only trace of her prompt, decided activity was in the nervous agitation of her movements, and the querulous sharpness of her tones, as if her weakness was irritating to her.

"Marian, how are you? I am sorry you have cut short your visit to come back to a sick house. I am afraid Clara has been alarming you needlessly."

"I am very sorry to find you so unwell," said Marian; "I thought Clara would want some help."

"Thank you, it was very kind," said Mrs. Lyddell, rather sharply, as if her thanks were only for form's sake. "Have you seen Caroline?"

"Yes, and I am afraid she is very ill. Such a terrible oppression on her breath."

"Ah! so Clara says. Mr. Wells has been applying mustard poultices."

"Have you had no further advice?" said Marian.

"No. He managed me very well; he is perfectly competent to attend an influenza such as this — a very simple affair."

Mrs. Lyddell was evidently under the unreasonable infatuation that so many people are subject to, who will go on trusting their favourite apothecary, in spite of proofs that he is not to be trusted; but Marian, in her short life, had heard a good deal of doctors, and whether reasonably or not, had imbibed a distrust of country practitioners, which Lionel's misfortune had not tended to remove in Mr. Wells' case. Indeed, she had a particular dislike to the man, with his soft manner, love of set speeches and fine words, and resolution not to own that anything was the matter. There were stories abroad in the neighbourhood of his treating cases wrongly because he would not own they were beyond his skill.

"Mrs. Lyddell," said she, very earnestly, "I do believe that Caroline is very ill. I think her throat is in a very alarming state, and I should not be at all satisfied to go on with no further advice."

Mrs. Lyddell made some answer about girls being easily frightened, and Marian went back to Caroline, very unhappy and anxious, and trying to find comfort by telling herself that the cure does not depend alone on the physician.

However, the words she had spoken were not without effect. Mrs. Lyddell's answer had been prompted by her first impulse of dislike and opposition, as if Marian was taking still further upon her; but she became very anxious when left alone. She thought that Marian's fresh eye might be better able to judge of the degree of Caroline's illness; she remembered how she had reproached herself about Lionel, and at last worked herself into such a state of alarm and anxiety, that though she had not yet walked further than to the window, she rose, left her room, and presently was by her daughter's bed-side.

There needed no more to convince her that Caroline was excessively ill, and quick and prompt as ever, her first measure was to send Clara for her father, and hold a consultation with him outside the door; a message was despatched to hasten Mr. Wells, and the result was that a physician was sent for. Marian, who had all this time been watching the severe suffering, unable to do the least thing to alleviate it, was almost as glad as if she had been told of Caroline's certain recovery. She had again to tell herself not to put her trust in physicians.

CHAPTER XIX.

"Preach, read, and study as we will,
Death is the mighty teacher still."

Baptistery.

Caroline continued very ill all the evening, hardly able to to look up, and every attempt to speak or swallow causing her great pain. Her mother would not leave her again, and sat watching her, and she smiled, and gave a pleased look of surprise at her kindness, which she had so long missed; but her chief comfort seemed to be in Marian's presence. She followed her about the room with her eyes, and was uneasy whenever she fancied that she was going out of the room.

She was not told that the physician was coming till he was actually in the house, and then she gave Marian a quick, sharp look of alarmed inquiry; but Marian was not able to answer, as she had to leave her to his visit. When it was over, and Marian returned, while Mrs. Lyddell went to hear his opinion, Caroline was striving hard to speak. Marian bent over her, and at last heard one word gasped out — "Walter."

"Yes, I will tell Mr. Lyddell; he shall be sent for, dearest," said Marian; and Caroline seemed satisfied.

It was long before Marian had an opportunity of hearing what the physician's opinion had been, and there was little comfort in it. It was a very severe case of inflammation in the windpipe, and the only hope of subduing it was in instant recourse to strong remedies. How badly it was thought of she saw plainly enough, without words, in Mr. Lyddell's restless, hasty manner, and in the exertions which Mrs. Lyddell was allowed to make, at a time when she ought to have been in her bed. The worst sign of all was, it seemed to her, that as soon as she mentioned Caroline's wish to see Walter, Mr. Lyddell took measures for sending a letter at once by the railroad, instead of waiting for the post, which would have made a delay of two days.

Lionel sat meanwhile, by himself in the drawing room, or was found wandering on the stairs, anxiously listening. Marian came on him once, and had exclaimed at finding him in the dark, before she remembered that it made no difference to him. She was in haste to fetch something for Caroline and could do nothing for him but say the sad words, "No better."

All night Mrs. Lyddell and Marian stayed with Caroline; the one because she could not bear to go, the other because she could not be spared. Mrs. Lyddell would not acknowledge the extent of the danger to herself, far less allow any hint of it to come to Caroline; and for this Marian was sorry, though she was sure that Caroline was conscious of it herself; but with Mrs. Lyddell always present, it was impossible to read any of the things that would have been the only support at such a time. Poor Caroline could not speak to ask for them, and as if her mother feared they would bring death, she seemed to be watching Marian jealously to prevent the least approach to them.

It was a terrible night; the applications did nothing but cause suffering, instead of removing the disorder, — the oppression grew more and more severe, — each breath more painful; the two watchers hardly dared to meet each other's eyes, and Caroline was in too much pain, too oppressed and overwhelmed, to give any token how far the mind and thought was awake within her. Such another day succeeded, every hour extinguishing some faint hope, and bringing the dread certainty more fully upon them. There was little or nothing to be done: they could only watch the sufferer, and try to glean her wishes from her looks; but these usually expressed more of pain than aught else, and no one could tell whether the ear and thought were free. One, at least, who sat beside her prayed fervently, and trusted in hope and love; holding fast by the certainty that Caroline had embraced the good part, and given up the allurements of the world, in health, for the sake of the treasure to which she was hastening. That last letter of her's was surely a proof that she was ready; and who could wish to detain that worn, harassed spirit from the repose where earthly cares shall "cease from troubling, and where the weary are at rest?" Yet how Marian loved and clung to her, and felt as if she could never bear to part, and lose the affection that had been so long kept off by her own repulsive demeanour, but that was so ardent and unreserved! How grievous to think of the blooming, life-like creature that she was so lately, now so suddenly cut down!

Hour after hour went by, bringing no change for the better. Day had faded into twilight, and twilight became night. Midnight had come, and Marian was still sitting, as she had done for more than an hour, holding up the faint head; for Caroline could no longer breathe in a recumbent posture, and sat partly supported on pillows, partly resting on Marian's shoulder. Her eyes were shut, and she seemed unconscious; it might be that she slept, but the features were full of suffering, and Marian could feel each of her breaths, gasping and convulsive. Her mother hung over her, feeling her pulse, sometimes sitting, sometimes standing, or walking to the foot of the bed to speak to Mr. Lyddell, or to the apothecary, in the restless misery of despair. Mr. Lyddell came in and out, unable to bear the sight, yet unable to stay away. Clara had been too much overcome, and growing hysterical, had been sent away, and advised to go to bed. Lionel, too, had been sent to bed, but his room was in the same passage, and he lay with his door open, catching, with his quickened ears, at every sound in the sick room, and hearing each word of the hushed conferences that took place outside.

A fresh tread was in the house — on the stairs — in the passage; Lionel's heart could not help bounding at it, as it came so softly along. It was the tread of the brother who, for his effort of courage and principle had been allowed to leave home like an exile, and treated as an offender. Lionel heard his father's step coming to meet him: how would they meet? He could hear the movement as their hands grasped together, and then Mr. Lyddell's smothered, choked whisper, "Only just in time, Walter! she won't know you. Come!"

"Is it so?" said Walter, in a low tone, as of one extremely choked and overwhelmed.

A sort of sob came before the answer, "Going fast."

The steps moved on; Lionel could not stay where he was, dressed himself, and felt his way to the sick room. He heard the stifled breathings: he felt onward, — found he had hold of the bed-post, and leant against it, unheeded by all, so intently were all watching Caroline.

"Speak to her," was the first thing he heard whispered by the doctor.

"Caroline!" said Walter's trembling voice, "dear Caroline!"

Poor Lionel could not see how, at the call, the dark blue eyes once more opened, and looked up in Walter's face; he only heard the steadier tone in which the brother said the ministerial words, "Peace be with this house!"

The solemn calmness of the tone came gently and soothingly upon Lionel's ear; and withal there spread over Caroline's face a gleam of joy, and then a quiet stillness, as of a freedom from suffering. There was an interval — a gasp — another interval — another gasp — a pause —

Marian's voice was the first, and very low and awe-struck. "It has been without a struggle."

A slight cry from his mother, and a confused movement, as if they were lifting something — steps — he stood still, and the next moment felt Marian's hand on his arm. "Mrs. Lyddell has fainted," said she, in explanation; "Mr. Lyddell and Walter are taking her to her own room,"

Lionel clasped Marian's hand very tight, and each felt how the other was trembling. "We must come away," said Marian; then hesitating, and with a quivering whisper, she said, "Would you like to kiss her?"

"Yes, let me!"

It was strange to guide the blind brother to kiss the white brow of the dead sister. Marian's throat was aching to such a degree with intense feeling, that she could hardly utter a word; but Lionel, who could not see, must hear. "She looks so calm, so sweet," said Marian struggling, "but I must go to your mother. Let me take you to your room; I'll send Walter to you. Lionel, Lionel, indeed she is happy!" said Marian, earnestly, while Lionel burst into a flood of tears, wholesome tears, as she led him from the room.

She thought Walter would be the greatest comfort to him; and recollecting Mrs. Lyddell had no woman with her but her maid, she told Lionel she must go to his mother, ran down, and met Walter waiting in the dressing-room. "Is she recovering?"

"A little."

"Will you go to Lionel?"

"This instant, but —" and he looked at her earnestly.

"Yes, yes," said she hastily, "it is all right and beautiful. Here's her last letter; I've been reading it all day. Take it; you'll see how —"

Marian's voice broke down, and she hastened to the open door of Mrs. Lyddell's room. There was something for her to do in attempting to restore her, for the maid was not helpful; and Mr. Lyddell stood at the foot of the bed, as if all his powers were paralysed. Mr. Wells wanted assistance; for Mrs. Lyddell, exhausted by watching and her previous weakness, was in so sinking and depressed a state, as to need the greatest care.

Marian was employed in attending her till towards morning, when she sank into a sleep. "You had better go to bed," said Mr. Lyddell, very kindly, as Marian at length turned away from her, and stood by the fireside, where he was sitting in the armchair, his hands over his forehead "I must not let you overwork yourself."

"O, I am not tired, if I can be of any use."

"No, no, rest now, thank you," said he, in a broken, dejected tone.

She went, and again found Walter in the outer room, watching for tidings of his mother. "Asleep," she said. "Lionel?"

"Asleep too, I hope. You are going to bed?"

"Yes, thank you; but Clara —"

"I will go to Clara the first thing in the morning. I shall sit up on my father's account. Don't you think of it, — sleep as long as you can; you have had watching enough."

"I have been so glad," Marian said, in a tear-stilled whisper.

"You cannot tell how I have longed to thank you, Marian, for what you have been to her:" said Walter, speaking from the fulness of heart, which overcame his natural reserve and bashfulness. "You are thanked enough by our present feelings on the subject, — by that letter: — may I keep it a little longer?"

"O yes, yes!" cried Marian, hastily, disclaiming in her heart all his thanks, though unable to do so with her lips.

"It takes away all regret for the briefness of the illness," added Walter, as if the speaking of it was a satisfaction he could hardly relinquish.

"I am sure she thought much; no one can tell what passed," said Marian, in a low, broken murmur.

"Little did I think last summer —" said Walter, aloud to himself. "Yes, this is best, far best, if one could but feel it so!"

Marian thought the same, and, like him, could not feel it; but unable to express herself, she simply said, as soon as her tears would let her, "Good-night," and went up to her own room.

Fatigue came on her now. When she took off the dress she had worn since leaving Fern Torr, she found her limbs stiff and aching, and her head dizzy with weariness. She could hardly get through the operation of undressing; and when she tried to say her prayers, they would not come. She could only go through the LORD'S Prayer; and too worn out to be shocked at herself more than in a dull way, scarcely even alive to the recollection of what had happened, she laid herself down on the bed, which seemed strangely soft, but for a long time was too tired to sleep. With confused thoughts and exhausted spirits, she kept on feeling as if her aching limbs belonged to somebody else, and going off into odd, dreamy vagaries, each more uncomfortable than the last, — ever and anon waking into a moment's remembrance that Caroline was dead, wondering at herself for being so dull as only to think it strange, then losing the consciousness again. At last the light of morning made her perceptions clearer. Fanny knocked at her door, and brought her a cup of tea. She heard that all was quiet, — said she would get up; but with that resolution she suddenly became more easy, and while believing she was getting up, fell into a sound sleep.

She awoke refreshed, and entirely herself again, though feeling stunned and bewildered by the all-pervading thought. Caroline dead! It seemed as if it was not otherwise with the rest of the family. Her illness had been so short, that there had been no time to grow familiar with the idea of her danger; and it was the first death in the household that had hitherto been so strong and confident in health, — the first touch that taught them how little the world they loved was an abiding-place. So sudden had been the stroke, that they seemed to pause and stand aghast under it, scarcely conscious how deep the wound might be. Her father went about the house, bowed down and stricken with grief, his tones low, sorrowful, and so gentle when speaking to his children, or to Marian, that they could scarcely be recognised as the same voice; but, without a word, so far as Marian, Clara, or Lionel knew, of his daughter, or of his own feelings. Her mother, already very weak, and suffering most acutely from the remembrance of the coldness with which she had treated her during the last autumn, became so seriously unwell, between a return of influenza, and her extreme depression and nervous hysterical agitation, that Marian and Clara were almost entirely occupied in nursing her, and trying to soothe her. In this work they were little successful. Marian had no hold on her affection, no power of talking soothingly, though most anxious to do what she could, and distressed excessively by her inability to be a comfort in the painful scenes which she was obliged to witness. She almost thought her presence made things worse, and that Mrs. Lyddell wished her away; but poor Clara was so entirely helpless and frightened, clung to her in so imploring a way, and was so incapable, from the restraint that had always subsisted between her and her mother, of saying anything to comfort her, or assuming any direction, that Marian was obliged, for her sake, to be almost always in the room. The only thing Marian could do in the way of consolation was to read aloud; she could not talk of the great thankfulness, peace, and hope which she felt herself, to Mrs. Lyddell, though she could have done so a little, with time, to Lionel, or even Clara; she could only read, and whether this did any good, she knew not. At any rate, it was what she ought to do; and the sound of the voice going on continuously had certainly a calming effect. Walter used daily to come and read, but this she did not seem to like, though she never made any objection; and there was so much reason for guarding against agitation and excitement, that he, never familiar with her, could not venture to attempt speaking to her on the subject of which all their hearts were full. It was only Mr. Lyddell who had any real serviceable influence with her. Her hysterical attacks never came on in his presence, and a few affectionate words or demonstrations from him would soothe the very worst of them. Marian saw so much real tenderness in his character, that she positively began to feel considerable affection for him.

Clara was entirely bewildered and frightened, hardly yet realizing that she had lost her sister; perplexed and alarmed about her mother, suddenly thrust forward, from being an unregarded child, into having all the responsibilities of the eldest daughter of a sick mother on her hands, she could only depend upon Marian, and hang on her for direction, assistance, and consolation, — say "yes" to whatever she suggested, and set about it; and whenever she felt lonely, sisterless, and wretched, lean on her, pour out her grief, and feel that she had a kind listener, though only a monosyllabic answerer. She used to have great fits of crying at night, when they passed Caroline's door; and more than once she was so inconsolable, that Marian was obliged to come and stay in her room, and sleep all night with her arm clinging round her. Altogether, it was very desolate and perplexing; and Marian was grieved at herself for dwelling more on this, and on the loss of her dear companion and friend, than on the hope and happiness that ought to occupy her. How different in the two deaths she had known before, where there was none of this weary, harassed, doubtful, careworn feeling; only the sorrow, bitter indeed as it was, of the parting, but with time and scope for dwelling on all thoughts of comfort, when they would come.

Lionel had his brother, and was thus in the best hands; and she saw very little of him except at meal-times, when all were silent and subdued.

So passed the week before the funeral. Only the gentlemen attended it; Marian and Clara stayed with Mrs. Lyddell, who went through the time better than they had ventured to hope. She was altogether improved, and was able to sit up a little in the evening. Lionel was to go the next day to London, to be seen by the oculist; and her sanguine mind was fastening itself on the hope of his recovery; and though there was too much danger that she was only hoping in order to be the more disappointed, yet the present relief was great.

Marian and Clara went down to dinner somewhat cheered, and hoping to carry satisfaction with them; but there was a deeper despondency in Mr. Lyddell's air than ever. He scarcely seemed to know what he was doing; and when at last dinner was over, he rose up, stood by the fire a moment, coughed, said to Walter, "You tell them," and ran upstairs.

There was a silence: each of the three dreaded to ask what was the matter; Walter did not know how to begin. Marian began to think it was some family misfortune, better mentioned in her absence, and was rising to go away; but Walter exclaimed, "No, don't go, Marian; all the world must know it soon, I fear."

"Not Johnny!" cried Clara. "O, Walter, Walter, don't let it be Johnny!"

"No," said Lionel; "I know it is something more about Elliot. Is it very bad indeed, Walter?"

"Very; I do not think he is going to tell my mother the full extent. There was a letter from Paris this morning, from Captain Evans, saying he thought it right that my father should be warned that Elliot is going on there in his old way, and worse still, is reported to be on the brink of a ruinous marriage."

Clara was the first to break the silence of consternation. "Marriage! and now! a Frenchwoman! O Walter, Walter it can't be true! he can't do it now, at any rate!"

"There is some hope that this may make a delay: it is the one chance that my father trusts to," said Walter. "The history seems to be this, as far as I can understand. When the discovery of all these debts came on my father, he wrote Elliot a very indignant letter, refusing to be answerable for any of them except that which Faulkner had guaranteed which of course he paid at once. This letter seems to have stirred Elliot up into a fit of passion; he went on more recklessly than ever, and now is getting drawn into this miserable connection."

"Yes, just like Elliot!" said Lionel. "And what is papa going to do?"

"He means to go to Paris at once, sacrifice any thing, pay all the debts at any cost, if he can only bring Elliot back with him, and save him from ruining himself entirely."

"But he is not going to tell mamma about the marriage, I hope?" said Clara.

"No, he will leave her to think it is only the old story, and that he wants to see if anything can be done about the debts. There is a hope that the news he must have had by this time may have checked him."

"Perhaps it may be bringing him home," said Marian.

"No, I fear he is too much involved to venture to England."

Again following a silence; no one could think of anything consoling to suggest; all were unwilling to heap censure upon one who deserved it but too richly. Only Lionel was heard to give a sort of groan, find after a time Clara asked, "Is it a Frenchwoman?"

"Yes," said Walter; "a person connected with the theatres."

The four again sat in mournful silence.

"I suppose," said Lionel at length, "that my going to London had better be put off till he comes back."

"No," said Walter, "he wishes that to be done at once. We are all three to go to London tomorrow, as was settled before; he will go with you to see the oculist, and on to Dover by the night-train; and if the oculist wishes to keep you, I shall stay with you in London till he comes back, or till my mother and the rest can come."

"Thank you," said Lionel, sighing; "I wish I could help it! Is not it leaving a pretty state of things behind us, though? not that we are any great good to the ladies to be sure!"

"Yes, it is leaving you at a very sad time," said Walter, looking at the two girls, "but we are hardly able to be of much use to my mother, and if there was any prospect of your improvement, that they all say would do her more good than anything else. However, my father said that must be according to your feelings, Clara and Marian, if you were afraid to be left with the charge of her, I would remain."

One of Walter's awkward ways of putting the question, and it instantly suggested to Clara to be afraid.

"I am sure I shan't know what to do. Only think, Marian, for us to be left — what should we do if mamma was to get suddenly worse? We should have no one to help us, I shall be in such a ner-vous state, I could do no good."

"No, no, Clara, you won't," said Marian, whilst Walter had begun to look in consternation at Clara. "Nobody ever has nerves when there is anything to be done. You know Mrs. Lyddell is much better."

"O but she will be so very unhappy and excited about papa's being gone, and I am sure I shall never be able to conceal from her all this dreadful business about Elliot."

"Yes, you will," said Marian quietly. "We shall do very well indeed, it cannot be for long, and if we wanted him we could get Walter home in a few hours' time. If he can send us good news of Lionel, it will help us much more than his staying here could do."

"If dear Caroline," — and Clara burst into a fit of weeping, which obliged her to leave the room. Every one was feeling the same thing, that Caroline, with her energy, good sense, and the power she had once possessed with her mother, would have made all easy, and the sense of missing her had come strongly upon them all. Marian followed Clara to her own room, let her lean upon her and cry, wept with her, joined in saying how grievous the loss was, and how much they had loved her, and how they should want her every day and every hour, then called hack the remembrance that Caroline had not been happy here, and had longed for rest, and it was come to her, and they must not be selfish, but there Clara cried more, saying that Marian never knew what a sister was, and it was unkind to wish her to be glad.

"I don't know," said Marian, pausing as her tears flowed fast, "I have known death, Clara."

"You weren't glad!" said Clara passionately.

"I don't know," she said thinking, and speaking with difficulty. "Not then, not always now, O no! But I always knew I ought to be glad, for dear papa had suffered so much, I could not wish it to be going on still — no, no. And dear mamma, when he was gone, it was a sad world for her, she could only have wished to stay for our sakes. Yet, after the first, I always felt it was right, and so will you too, Clara, in time."

"If she was but here to help me!" sobbed Clara.

"We must try," said Marian, "we can't be as useful and ready as she was, but we will do our very best. I am sure Mrs. Lyddell likes to have you sit with her."

"Did you think so?" said Clara, ready to be cheered by any token, of preference.

"Yes, I saw how glad she was to have you instead of me, when you came in from the garden."

Clara looked pleased.

"You will sit with her, and read to her, and I can help you when you have too much on your hands at once. You see it is a great comfort to Mr. Lyddell to have you to leave her with."

The being made important was a great thing with Clara, and she was quite reconciled to the prospect of her charge by the time they had to go down stairs to tea.

After tea Marian was left alone with Lionel, while Clara was with her mother; and Walter in consultation with Mr. Lyddell, for here at least was one benefit, that Walter seemed to have taken his proper place, and to be a real comfort and help to his father in a way he had never hoped for.

"You've cheered up Clara, I hear in her voice," said Lionel.

"O yes, we shall do very well."

"Do you mind it, Marian?" said he, turning his ear towards her, as if to judge by the minute intonations of her answer, as people do by the expression of the countenance.

Her reply was brave, "No, not at all."

"Are you sure?"

"Yes. I don't see what would be gained by keeping you and Walter here. She does not depend on Walter as she does on your father, and all that is required we can do as well without Walter in the house. It would be nonsense to keep you merely for the feel of having some one, and for the rest, I am sure Clara will be the better for being thrust forward, and made useful."

"Very well. I should not in the least mind waiting, for I have not much hope myself, but it is just as well for oneself and every one else to be put out of one's misery as soon as possible, and settle down into it."

Marian remembered how differently he had spoken half a year ago, when the danger first broke on him, and looking up she saw his steadfast though mournful face. She spoke her thought.

"It has been a great thing to have this long preparation."

"Yes, I am glad of it, though I have been a great plague and nuisance to every one, especially to you, Marian. I know what you're going to say, so let alone that. I wish — . But no use talking of that, she was very kind and we got very comfortable together after you were gone, Marian, and I like to remember that."

"Ah! I was sure you would. And Walter read you what she said about you?"

"Yes, I wish — I little knew" — then suddenly "Marian, I'll tell you something: one morning when you were gone, she had to read a bit of a chapter in the Gospel about the healing the blind man, and you can't think how hard she tried to get through it without breaking down, but she could not. She cried at last, as if she could not help it, and then she got up, and came and kissed me, and I felt her tears on my face. I didn't know what to say, but that's what I like to remember."

"And the Church-going on Christmas day," whispered Marian.

"Ay, she led me up," said Lionel.

"Everything is so very comforting," said Marian.

"So Walter says."

"Lionel, do you remember the print you and Gerald gave me long ago of S. Margaret walking through the dark wood of this world, and subduing the dragon? I am sure she is like it. She had all this world before her, and she chose vexation and trouble instead of doing wrong! O Lionel, it is very noble!"

"That it is," said Lionel, "only things never seem so at the time. I wish they did, but. I am glad my father saw it all right before, and said he was glad she had given him up."

"Yes, that is a comfort."

"My poor father!" said Lionel presently, "I never guessed he cared so much about — things. Do you know, Marian, I think even if I do get back my eyes, I could not go after the Australian bulls, unless 'twas the only way of getting a living."

"I am glad you have put them out of your head," said Marian, smiling sadly.

"Ay, I was very mad upon them once," said Lionel, "but I see that eyes or no eyes, we must set ourselves in earnest to be some sort of comfort to them, and if Johnny is to be always at sea, I had better not be on the other side of the world. If I am to see, why then it is all right; if not, I'll do the best I can at home."

"That's right, Lionel."

"I can do a good deal already, I am no trouble to any one, am I? I can go all over the house and park by myself, and find all my own goods without any one's help, and I'll do more in time, so as to be no bother to any one, and I do believe now they like to have me at home. Don't you remember, Marian," and he lowered his voice confidentially, one reason why I wanted to go to Australia, and make a fortune?"

"Yes," said Marian, knowing that he meant his vision of winning love from his parents.

"Well, I think," said he, "that being blind has answered as well."

A silence, then he went on, "I know what you meant now about a time when I might he glad to have been blind. If Caroline had married that man, she would not have died as happily as that, and there was an end of all the trouble and vexation; so there will be an end to my blindness some time or other, and it will keep me out of lots of mischief. I don't mean that there is not plenty of opportunity of doing wrong as it is," he added, "but not so much. Better be blind than like Elliot, and perhaps I might have come to that."

"O Lionel, it is such a comfort you can speak so!"

"I've tried it now, and 'tis not so very bad," said Lionel, turning with an odd mixture of smile and sadness, "besides I saw almost the last of her face, and I should only miss her the more like her voice. I have got her face stored up with all of yours. You know I shan't see when any of you grow old and ugly, Marian. Well, and after all I am glad it is to be settled now, I don't think I shall mind it near so much as I should another time, now I have just heard all that over her grave. I got Walter to read it to me all over again when we came home. It has been very nice to have Walter."

Marian guessed how Walter had strengthened and helped him, and she judged rightly, but she did not know how silently he listened to all Walter's talkings and readings, unable to pour out his full feeling to any one but herself.

The others came in from their different quarters, it was late, and Marian was about to wish good night, when Walter in a low hurried voice said to her and Clara, "Don't go yet, my father wishes to have prayers."

A moment more and the servants came in, all were kneeling, and Marian's tears of thankful joy were streaming fast as Walter read an evening prayer. Was not Caroline glad? was the thought, as she recollected that first morning, when all had seemed to her childish mind so dreary and unhallowed, and when Caroline had lamented the omission. Yes! was not Caroline glad, now that one of the dearest wishes of her heart had been gained? Was she not glad of this first token that trouble had brought a change over her father?

Each fresh petition brought such a gush of earnest softened tears that Marian's face bore evident traces of them, when she rose up, and had to wish Mr. Lyddell good night. She did not speak, but held out her hand. He spoke with difficulty, "My dear," he said, "I have wished to thank you, but I cannot otherwise than by leaving more on your hands. Walter has told you how it is with us. You are kind enough to help Clara. I don't know what we should do without you. I rely on your judgment entirely."

"I'll do my best," said Marian, "I am glad to be of use."

"You were *her* best friend," said Mr. Lyddell hastily. "Well, good night, thank you, my dear," and he kissed her forehead, as though she had been his own daughter.

CHAPTER XX.

"Let us be patient. These severe afflictions
Not from the ground arise
But oftentimes celestial benedictions
Assume this dark disguise.

"We see but dimly through the mists and vapours
Amid these earthly damps
What seems to us but sad funereal tapers
May be heaven's distant lamps."

LONGFELLOW.

There were morning prayers before the hurried breakfast, which was interspersed with numerous directions about what was to be done for Mrs. Lyddell, and what letters were to be sent after Mr. Lyddell. Lionel was grave and silent, as became one whose fate was in the balance, without either shrinking or bravado; but somewhat as if he was more inclined, than had been the case last night, to hope for a favorable result. With heartfelt prayers did Marian watch him as be crossed the hall and entered the carriage, calling out a cheerful good-bye, — prayers that, if it were the will of Heaven, his affliction might be removed; but that if not, help might be given him to turn it into a blessing, as he seemed almost to be beginning to do. His father, too, — little had Marian ever thought to feel for him the affectionate compassion and sympathy, of which she was now sensible, as she responded to his kind, fatherly farewell, and thought of what he must be feeling; obliged to leave his wife in so anxious and suffering a state; his daughter, the pride of the family, removed so suddenly; his most promising son probably blind for life; his eldest, a grief, pain, and shame to them all. Marian must pray for him too, that he might be supported and aided through these most bitter trials, and that the work which they had begun in him might go on and be perfected; that these troubles, grievous as they were, might in his ease also turn to blessings.

The occupation of the two girls was all day the care of Mrs. Lyddell. She was not worse, as far as bodily ailments went; the attack of cold, brought on by leaving her room to attend on Caroline, had gone off, and her strength was in some degree returning; but she was restless, excited, irritable, and with an inability to restrain herself, that was more alarming than Marian liked to own to herself, far less to Clara.

She insisted on getting up at an earlier hour than she had hitherto attempted; she was worn out and wearied with dressing; she was impatient and vexed with Clara, for some mistake about her pillows; and the trembling of her hand, as she was eating some broth, was uncontrollable. The broth was not what she liked, and she would send for the housekeeper, to reprove her about it; asked questions about the arrangements, found them not as she wished; spoke sharply, said no one took heed to anything while she was ill, and then burst into a fit of weeping at the thought of the daughter who would have been able to supply her place.

This spent itself, (for the girls were unable to do anything effectual in soothing it away); the doctors made their daily visit, and cheered her up a little. The consequence of this exhilaration was, that she began talking about Lionel, and anticipating his perfect recovery; arranging how they were all to go and join him in London, and working herself up to a state of great excitement; pettish with Marian for not being able to answer her hopefully, and at last, hysterically laughing at the picture she drew of Lionel with restored sight.

Marian asked if she would be read to, and took up a serious book, with which she had put her to sleep two or three times before, but nothing of the kind would she hear; and as the best chance of at least quieting her, Marian went on a voyage of discovery among the club books down stairs, and brought up a book of travels, and a novel. Mrs. Lyddell chose the novel; it was a very exciting story, and caught the attention of all three. Marian grew eager about it, and was well pleased to go on; and so it occupied them most of the afternoon and evening, driving out a great deal of care, as Marian could not help gratefully acknowledging, though she would willingly have had space to work out with herself the question, whether care had best be driven out or grappled with. Mrs. Lyddell was indeed in no state to grapple with it, and there was nothing to be done but to take the best present means of distracting her attention; yet it was to be feared that, though put aside, the enemy was not conquered, — and might there not be worse to come?

It was about half-past seven and the two girls were drinking tea with Mrs. Lyddell in her room. She was just beginning to make herself unhappy about Mr. Lyddell's late journey and nightvoyage, when there was a tap at the door, and on the answer, "Come in!" it opened, and Lionel stood there.

There was a sudden exclamation: they all three sprang up and looked at him, but alas! it was still by feeling that he came forward, though his countenance was cheerful, and there was a smile upon his lips.

"Well, mamma," he said, in a brave, almost a lively tone, "you must be content to have me at home." And in answer to their broken, half expressed interrogations, "No, he can't do any thing for me; so it was not worth while to stay any longer in London. How are you this evening, mamma?"

He was guiding himself towards her chair, one hand on the table; she threw herself forward to meet him, flung her arms round his neck and sobbed, "My boy, my poor dear boy! O Lionel! it has been all my fault and neglect!"

"No, no, don't — don't say that, mamma!" said Lionel, extremely distressed by her weeping, and not knowing where to rest her, as she hung with her whole weight abandoned on him. Marian and Clara were obliged to help him, and seat her in her chair again; while she still wept piteously, and poor Lionel stood, hearing the sobs, and very much grieved. "Ought I not to have told her?" said he to Marian. "I thought if she saw I could bear it, it would be better than writing."

"Yes, yes, you did quite right; she will be better presently."

She was soon better, and leaning back on her pillows exhausted, looked up at the fine tall boy before her, the glow of youth and health on his face, spirit and enterprise in every feature, — but those large blue eyes, bright as they were, for ever darkened and useless.

"O Lionel!" she sighed again.

"The man behaved very well," said Lionel; "he did not plague me at all. He only pulled up my eyelids — so — and studied them, and I suppose he gave some sign to my father, for I heard him make a noise that showed me how I was; so I asked. He told me there was not a chance, and made me understand the rights of it; and so here I am. Never mind, mamma, there was a tendency to it all my life, and nothing would have stopped it in the end; and now I know what it is, I have no doubt but I shall do very well. I mean to be like the blind man that unharnessed all the horses in the middle of the night, when the coach was upset, and no one else was of any use."

He stopped once or twice in his harangue, to judge how his mother was, by her breathings; and he spoke with a smile and look of resolution and eagerness, as he concluded with another "Never mind, mamma, for I don't." She took hold of his hand, and pressed it, too much overcome to speak.

"Is papa gone?" asked Clara.

"Yes." And Lionel proceeded to give a message which he had sent back.

"And where's Walter?"

"In the drawing-room."

More people were already in the room than Marian thought good for Mrs. Lyddell; and understanding Clara's wishes, she went down to speak to Walter, to carry a message that his mother would see him after tea, and to arrange for a substantial supper for the two youths, who had had no dinner.

Walter was waiting anxiously to know how his mother had endured the tidings.

"She was very much, overcome at first," said Marian; "but now she has had a good cry, she will be more likely to go to sleep quietly. Poor Lionel! he did it admirably."

"It has been his chief thought," said Walter. "He begged to come home at once, saying it would be the best way to have it over before night; it would save all hoping and worrying, about him; and the instant we arrived, he ran straight up stairs."

Walter and Marian were not familiar enough to say it to each other, but both were comparing his present conduct with his former bitterness of spirit against his mother. Death, sorrow, anxiety, and illness had drawn close the cords of love, and opened the well-springs of affection, so long choked up and soured by neglect and worldly care.

"How did he bear it at the first?"

"Bravely; he had wound himself up. He was flushing and turning pale all through the journey; but when once he came to the door, he was as calm and steady as possible. My father was much more agitated; he would lead Lionel himself, and very nearly threw him down the steps. You should have seen how Lionel never flinched, — did not let one feature quiver while he was being turned round to the light and examined. We saw how it was by the doctor's face, but Lionel spoke first, as — no, more steadily, than I can tell it, 'There is nothing to be done, then?' — attended more firmly to the explanation of the causes than we could, spoke as freely as if it had been about some indifferent case. The doctor was quite struck with it. He shook hands with him when he went, and kept me a moment after, to say, of all the many cases he had seen, he had never known greater resolution, — never seen any one he had been more sorry for. However, it was not only that, — that might have been the pride of firmness; but it has been the same all along. He set himself to cheer my father, who was very much overcome; and ever since has been telling me of all his schemes for employment, and arranging how to spare my mother as much as possible. Yes, he is a fine fellow!" said Walter, stopping with a heavy sigh.

"I am sure he will make himself happy," said Marian earnestly; "you don't know how many resources he has, and you see how wonderfully independent he is already."

"Yes," said Walter, sadly; "but though I know it is all right — to see what he might have been! But that is mere nonsense," he added, catching himself up; "we should never have known what was in him; and perhaps he would have been very different."

Not a word expressed of Walter's sincere thankfulness for the change that affliction was bringing on them.

Lionel came down presently, Marian presided at their tea, and would have enjoyed it very much, if she had not been sorry Clara should not be relieved from her harassing attendance up stairs. But her mother could not spare her, and perhaps the being positively useful, and pulled by force out of her childishness, was the best thing for her.

"Marian, I hope you will be able to ride with me tomorrow, if mamma does not want you?" said Lionel.

Walter looked full of inquiry and consternation.

"If we can manage it," said Marian, cheerfully; though now that the custom had been disused for a time, she did not like the notion quite so well as before; since she could not now even figure to herself that Lionel guided himself at all, He had said it chiefly for the purpose of asserting his intention of continuing the practice, and was quite satisfied by her answer.

Walter went up stairs to his mother shortly after, and Lionel was left alone with Marian.

"I am sure I hope it won't hurt her," said he; "I thought it was best to have it out at once."

"Much the best, since it was to come."

"Yes," he said, pausing for some space, then exclaiming, "I don't know, though! I thought it would be better to know the worst, and have one's mind made up; but I don't think 'tis more comfortable, after all. I should like to get back that little spark of hope I had this morning! O, Marian, there was one time when the sun shone out full, and so warm, exactly on my face, and some one in the train said it was a glorious winter day. It was close by Slough; I knew we were in sight of the castle, and perhaps one might see the chapel, and the trees in the playing-fields. I thought soon, I might be seeing it all again: and I vow, Marian, I could have leaped from here to Windsor at the bare thought. It was being a great fool, to be sure; but as we came back, I was half glad it was dark, so that nobody else could see it."

"Yet I am sure your last half year at Eton was no happy time; you went through a great deal."

"I'd do it all again, if I could see as much as I did then," said Lionel. "I don't mind it so much in general now; I get on much better than I thought I should, and it is not nearly as bad now I am quite in the dark, and wake up to it, as when the glimmer of light was going. I can do very well, except when a great gush — I don't know what to call it — great rush of remembering the sky and all sorts of things comes on me, and I know it is to be darkness always. Then! — but it is all nonsense talking of it. I shall get the better of that, some day or other, I suppose. But I did not think, yesterday, that the being sure of it would be half so bad!"

"You braced yourself yesterday, and that helped you today."

"Yes; and then there was my father, — he has enough to vex him, without knowing all this. And, after all, it is nothing; I've got plenty to do, and I'll manage it capitally. I'll tell you what, Marian, if mamma can spare you, we'll ride to Salisbury, and get some of that good twine, and I'll make Gerald the fishing-net you said he wanted."

Lionel had hitherto never consented to learn to net.

Mrs. Lyddell was better the next day, and all was quiet and prosperous, so that Walter could write a satisfactory account to his father. Clara had a good walk with her brothers in the morning, and in the afternoon the ride took effect: Marian came into Mrs. Lyddell's room in her habit, and gave notice, "we are going to ride," so much as if it was a matter of course that Mrs. Lyddell asked no questions, and feared no dangers. Walter went with them, and Marian could have wished him away, for he was so anxious and nervous as very nearly to make her the same, and though he said nothing of his anxieties, Lionel found them out, and told him in his old gruff way that there was nothing to be in a taking about; indeed, Lionel was the more inclined to be adventurous in order to show himself entirely at his ease.

However, nothing went wrong, and Marian and he both felt it a point gained that their riding together was established. A few days passed on quietly and gravely, a pause of waiting and suspense. Mrs. Lyddell, though less ill, was not materially improved as regarded the excitability of her spirits. She would be excessively depressed at one time, at another in such high spirits as were much more alarming. Sometimes she would talk about their being all ruined and undone, and go on rapidly to say they must give up the house in London, retrench, live on nothing; at others she anticipated Mr. Lyddell's bringing Elliot back, all his debts paid, to live at home and be a comfort, or some friend was to give Walter a great living, or Clara was to come out, and to be presented in the summer. At the same time the fretful irritability of nerve and temper continued, and any unusual excitement, the talking a little longer in her room, a letter, or a little disappointment, would keep her awake all night. One thing, however, seemed certain, that Lionel's presence had some of the same power over her as her husband's; she was too much occupied with watching him, to work herself into her anxious excited moods, and now that he had grown more familiar with her, his cheerful lively way of speaking always refreshed and pleased her. He would come in, in a glow of bright health, from a quick walk or ride in the clear frosty air, and show such genuine pleasure and animation as must console those who were grieving for his privation; he would undertake her messages, and find things in a wonderful manner, and he liked to listen to the reading aloud that always went on in her room. When Lionel came in, Marian and Clara always felt relieved from half their present care.

At last came a letter from Mr. Lyddell to Walter. The worst of his fears were fulfilled. Elliot was actually married, and report had not exaggerated the disgrace of the connection. Mr. Lyddell had not chosen to see him, and intended to be at home, by the end of the next day, after they would receive the letter.

It was a great shock, but perhaps none of the four young people had such lively hopes of Elliot as to be very much overwhelmed by the disappointment, as far as he was individually concerned. He had never been a kind elder brother to Clara or Lionel, and it was only Walter who could have any of those recollections of a childhood spent together, which would make the loss of intercourse personally painful. They had all been brought up to a sort of loyal feeling towards Elliot as the eldest, and to think his extravagance almost a matter of course, but only the tie of blood, and sympathy for their parents could cause them any acute pain on his account.

For their parents they were greatly grieved, for Elliot had with all his faults, been their especial pride and hope, and the effect on Mrs. Lyddell in her present state was very much to be apprehended. It was a comfort however that it was decided in full council that they might put off the evil day of telling her, for there was no occasion that she should be informed till her husband returned. He came the next day, and very worn down, broken and oldened did he look, as he returned to his mourning household. Not a word did he say in public of the object of his journey, and all that transpired to Marian, through Lionel, who heard it from Walter, was "that it was as bad as bad could be; it was thought Elliot had done it out of spite, at any rate he was never likely to bring his wife to England." Neither did Mrs. Lyddell speak of it, and Marian only knew that she had been informed of it, by the increased excitability and irritation of her nerves. Poor Clara underwent plenty of scolding, for she was the only victim, since Mrs. Lyddell's continuous dislike to Marian kept her on her ordinary terms of ceremony, scarcely ever asking her to do her any service, thanking her scrupulously, and never finding fault to her face.

Marian was at first very sorry for Clara, who was bewildered, and disconcerted, but after a day or two, things seemed to right themselves wonderfully. Clara grew used to the fretfulness, and was no longer frightened by it, nor made unhappy, but learnt how to meet it and smooth it down without being hurt by it. It was surely the instinct of natural affection, for inferior in every way as she was to Marian, yet in her mother's sick room she suddenly acquired all the tact, power, and management that Marian failed in. Hitherto she had been childish and astray, as if she wanted her vocation; now she had found it, and settled admirably into it, acquiring a sense, energy, and activity that no one could have supposed her capable of.

Outside that room, she was the same Clara still, without much either of rational tastes or conversation, afraid of her father, and not much of a companion to her brother, helpless in everything that did not regard her mother, and clinging to Marian for help and direction, Marian must speak for her, tell her what to say if she had to write a note, take the responsibility of every arrangement. Nothing was much harder than to shove Clara forward into becoming the ostensible lady of the house, as it seemed as if she must continue for some time to come, since the doctors spoke of the most absolute rest and freedom from excitement being necessary to restore her mother's shattered health and spirits. She was to see no visitors, be soothed as much as possible, have no cares or anxieties brought to her, be only moderately occupied and amused, or the nervous attacks would return. Marian had a suspicion that they feared for her mind. She became stronger, was able to rise earlier, and to drive out in the carriage, but she never dined with the family, and remained in her sitting room up stairs, with Clara for her regular attendant, and visits from the rest.

Walter returned to his curacy as soon as he could be spared, and Lionel became, as usual, chiefly dependent on Marian, who read to him, walked with him, rode with him, assisted him in his contrivances for helping himself, and was his constant guide and companion; doing at the same time all she could for Clara's service, but keeping in the back ground and making Clara do all the representative part for herself.

They missed Caroline every hour of the day, far more since they had settled into an every-day course of habits and most especially in the evening and at meal times. There always used to be so much conversation going on at dinner and now no one seemed to say anything; Clara sat at the head of the table in awe of her father, Lionel and Marian did not feel disposed to talk in their own way before him there never had been any freedom of intercourse, and nobody knew how to begin.

Marian thought the silent party very sad and forlorn for poor Mr. Lyddell, and that it must remind him grievously of the state of his family. Some one must talk, but how were they ever to begin? She was the worst person in the world to do it, yet try she must.

She began talking over the ride they had taken that day, but Clara was not at her ease enough to ask questions, or make observations, Lionel did not second her, and Mr. Lyddell said no more than "O." Another day she tried giving a history of a call that had been made by some of their neighbors, but nobody would be interested. How could she be so stupid? She almost dreaded dinner time. At last one day, she luckily cast her eyes on the newspaper, and it is a melancholy truth that the sight of a horrid murder gave her a certain degree of satisfaction! She began about it at dinner, when every one talked about it, every one had some view as to the perpetrator, and it really carried them through all dinner time without one dreary tract of silence, and served them on a second day.

A second day and a third, for more intelligence came out, and then luckily for her, came a revolution, next a dreadful accident, and at last the habit of talking became so well established that there was no need to look for topics in the newspaper. It was without an effort that she could originate a remark addressed to Mr. Lyddell. Lionel began to shake off his old schoolboy reserves, and rattle on freely. Clara grew more at ease, and Mr. Lyddell began to be entertained, to be drawn into the conversation, and to narrate his day's doings, just as of old when his wife was there, pleased with their interest in them, making explanations, and diverted with Lionel's merry comments.

It was however dreary and uncomfortable, with all these vague anxieties for Mrs. Lyddell, and with the whole house in the unsettled state consequent on missing its moving power. The servants had been used to depend on her, and could not go on without her; they teased Clara, and Clara teased Marian about them, no one knew what to do, nor what authority to assume, and the petty vexations were endless that were borne by the two girls rather than annoy Mr. Lyddell; perplexities, doubts whether they were doing what was wise or right by the house or by the servants; Marian's good sense making her judge the right, but her awkwardness, and Clara's incapacity, breaking down in the execution; continual worry and no dignity in it.

The loss of Caroline as a companion was severely felt. Marian had not been fully conscious how very closely entwined their hearts had been, how necessary they had grown to each other even before those latter days of full confidence. Every pursuit was mixed up with Caroline, every walk recalled her, every annoyance would have given way at her light touch. There was no one left with whom Marian could have anything like the conversations they had been used to enjoy from almost the earliest days of her coming to Oakworthy. Lionel was indeed a very agreeable companion, nay more, a friend, full of right feeling, principle, good sense, thought, and liveliness; but a younger boy could never make up for the loss of such a friend of her own sex. Each evening as she sat over the fire in her room, her heart ached with longing for Caroline's tap at the door, or with the wish to go and knock at hers, and then the thrill at thinking that there was only gloom and vacancy in her room. Had they but found each other out before! But oh! how much better to think of her as she did of her own parents, added to her store in Paradise, than to see her the wife of that man, unhappy as she must have been unless she had lost all that was excellent and hopeful.

These thoughts would comfort Marian when she went up to bed, harassed, weary, disgusted with cares and vexations, and craving for rest and sympathy. She thought of the home that awaited her at Fern Torr, the hope that had carried her through last autumn, but withal came a dim vague perception that a great sacrifice might be before her. Would it be right to seek her own happiness and repose there, and leave the Lyddells to their present distress? She did not think she was of much use, Clara was all-sufficient for her mother, and Marian was rather less liked by Mrs. Lyddell than formerly; but as a support to Clara, as a companion to Lionel, and as some one to talk to Mr. Lyddell, she was not absolutely useless. She had no doubt Clara and Lionel would miss her sadly, indeed it would be unkind to leave them, it would be positively wrong to forsake them when she was of some value, and go where she could not suppose herself to be actually wanted, though she might be loved and cherished. Yet to give up that beloved hope! The vision that had delighted her from the first years of her orphanhood; the hope become tangible beyond all expectations, the wish of her heart. To give up home, Edmund and Agnes, for this weary life! How could she? But it was not worth while to think about it yet, things might change, before they were ready for her, Mrs. Lyddell might recover, Clara and Lionel might grow sufficient for each other, anything might, would or should happen, rather than she would give up her beloved hope of the home she longed for, especially now the house was actually building, and each letter brought her accounts of its progress.

CHAPTER XXI.

"Perchance it was ours on life's journey to enter
Some path through whose shadows no lovelight was thrown,
With heart that could breast the fierce storms of its winter,
And gather the wealth of its harvest alone;
It is well there are stars in bright heaven to guide us
To heights we ne'er dreamt of, — but oh, to forget
The fortunes that bar, and the gulfs that divide us
From paths that looked lovely, with some we have met."

F. BROWNE.

Many weeks had passed away, and nothing had changed, in any material way, since the spring. Mrs. Lyddell's condition was still unsatisfactory, and she seemed to be settling into a confirmed state of ill health, and almost of hypochondriacism. So many shocks, following each other in such quick succession, on a person entirely unprepared by nature, experience or self-regulation, had entirely broken her down, and shattered her nerves and spirits in a manner which she seemed less and less like to recover. She was only able to rise late in the day, take a short drive, and after dining in her own room, come down in the evening, if they were alone, and it was a good day with her.

No change, neither sea air, nor London advice, had made much difference, and her condition had become so habitual, that her family had ceased to expect any considerable amendment; and it was likely that Clara would, for many years, have full employment as her companion and attendant. Lionel was perfectly, hopelessly blind, but growing reconciled to his misfortune, and habituated to the privation, as well as resigned in will. His natural character, of a high-spirited, joyous, enterprising boy, showed itself still in his independence and fearlessness, joined to cheerfulness, and enlivened the house. He had even gone the length of talking freely and drolly to his father, and Mr. Lyddell had learnt to smile, and even laugh at his fun.

There had been fears that the removal to London, for the session of Parliament, would be a great privation to him, since he would miss the wandering about the downs by himself, and the riding with Marian; but his temper and spirits did not fail. He walked every day with her, and was entertained with all he heard, both by his own quick ears, and by her description. They went to exhibitions, where she saw for him, and there were lectures, readings, and other oral amusements, to which his father, or some good-natured friend, would take him. He began to acquire a taste for music, which he had hitherto never cared to hear, and concerts became a great delight to him: though he had not the correct ear, and admirable appreciation of music, that often, in blind persons, seems like a compensation for the loss of the pleasures of the eye.

Lady Marchmont became very kind to him. She was thoroughly good natured, and the sight of the blind youth, whose arm Marian held as they walked together, stirred all her kindly feelings. He was gentlemanlike and pleasant looking, and his manner, now divested of schoolboy *brusquerie*, was frank and confiding. Selina was disposed to like him, and to be interested in him. She found, too, that Marian did not like to go out when his amusement was not provided for; so at first for Marian's sake, then for his own, she made him join them when they went to concerts, or to any other amusement that could gratify him. Her bright liveliness and spirited way of talking, won him; and it delighted Marian to see what great friends they became, even to the length of laughing over the old Wreath of Beauty story together. And when at length she was brought, of her own accord, in some degree to patronise Clara, it was a triumph indeed; and Mrs. Lyddell was more obliged to Marian than for all the real benefits she had conferred, when she saw Clara dressed to go to a party at Lady Marchmont's.

All this time Marian was becoming more and more a prey to that secret doubt, whether it might not be a duty to give up her cherished hope of a home at Fern Torr. She did not see how she could be spared. Clara was an admirable attendant on her mother, and was becoming a better mistress of the house; but she was not able to be at the same time a companion to her father and Lionel, and, poor girl, she would be very forlorn and much at a loss, without Marian's elder sisterhood; for the sense of help and reliance that Marian's presence gave her was little less. For her to go away, would be to bring home to Clara the loss of Caroline more than she had ever been left to feel it.

Yet, on the other hand, Clara was no companion. They talked, indeed, but they never discussed, — never had any interchange of higher sympathies or reflections; it was not getting beyond the immediate matter in hand; and often Marian, would be sensible that, if her own pleasure were consulted, a walk or ride, with her thoughts free to range in meditation or day-dream, was preferable to Clara's chatter.

Her own pleasure, — that she enjoyed but little, and less now than ever, for her time was never her own. There was Lionel on her hands almost every day, to be read to, or walked with; and if he went out with his father, or spent an hour in his mother's room, there was Clara wanting her quite as much, for gossip, exercise, or consultation. Mrs. Lyddell, too, must be visited; for though Marian was not the most beloved, or most welcome person in the world, yet a change of society and conversation was desirable, both for her sake and Clara's; so more than two hours every day were spent in her sitting-room. Then, in the evening, Marian's thoughts and ears must be free for Mr. Lyddell and Lionel. All her own pursuits were at an end, she had hardly touched a pencil the whole year, nor opened a German book, nor indeed any book, excepting what she read to Lionel, and these were many. She was very seldom able to enjoy the luxury of being alone; she could hardly even write her letters, except by sitting up for them; and even the valuable hour before midnight was not certain to be her own, for if Clara had no other time to pour out her cares, she used to come then, and linger in her cousin's room, reiterating petty perplexities, endless in detail.

How delightful to escape from all this, to quietness, peace, freedom from her own cares and other people's, — Fern Torr air and scenery, Edmund and Agnes for companions, and liberty to teach school children, go about among her own people, do good in her own way, and enjoy her own studies. It was like a captive longing to be set free, — a wanderer in sight of home.

But the captive paused on the threshold of the dungeon; the wanderer stood still on the brow of the last hill. Marian paced up and down her own room, and thought and reasoned half aloud, —

> "Sweet is the smile of home, the mutual look,
> When hearts are of each other sure;
> Sweet all the joys that crown the household nook,
> The haunt of all affections pure:
> Yet in the world even these abide, and we
> Above the world our calling boast."

"And I am making them the world, if for their sake I give up what my conscience calls on me to do. I know, though I do little good here, my going away would make them more uncomfortable. Have I any right to seek my pleasure? But I should do more good there; I should go to school, read to the poor people, go to Church in the week, be more improved myself. O that home of peace and joy! And Gerald — my first duty is to him. But what harm would it do him? I could go home for his holidays. I must not deceive myself; I have been put in the way of positive duties here, or rather, ways of being useful have grown up round me. Is it right to run away from them, — poor Lionel, poor Clara! Would not every weary hour of Lionel's — every time Clara was teased, and teased her father, — be my fault? But how Edmund and Agnes will be disappointed! — they who will have been throwing away so much kind care! O you goose of a Marian! are you going to fancy it is for your sake that they mean to marry? don't you think they can do very well without you? How very silly to be sorry that it must be so! — how very, very silly! And even Gerald will marry one of these days, and will not want me; and shall I always be alone then? For as to that other sort of affection, I am sure it is quite certain that I can never care for any body enough to marry, — never half as well as for Gerald. No, no one will ever love me as I do others; every one has some one nearer to them; a lonely life, and never a home! Well, then there is a home somewhere else, and those who made my earthly home are waiting for me there, in the Land of the Leal."

Such was the tenor of Marian's oft-repeated musings. The practical result was a resolution to consult Edmund when she should go to Fern Torr to his wedding, early in August. She could not write her pros and cons, but to Edmund she could tell them, and trust to him as a just and impartial judge; and if Agnes was angry, it would serve them, thought Marian, smiling, for a quarrel, for they won't have many other chances of one.

However, the time drew on when, behold, every one's calculations were disturbed by a sudden dissolution of Parliament. Hitherto such events had not made much difference to the Lyddells; as Mr. Lyddell's election had been, for the last twenty years, unopposed; and the only doubt at present was, whether he thought it worth while to stand again, considering that he was growing old and weary of business, and besides could not well afford the London house.

He had been hinting something of the kind to Lionel and Marian in the evening, as a matter under consideration and they had heard it with joy, when the next morning made a sudden change in affairs, by bringing tidings that Mr. Faulkner was soliciting the votes of Mr. Lyddell's constituents on the opposite interest, taking the wrong side of the question, — a most important one, upon which the dissolution had taken place.

Here was indignation indeed. There was something so unfeeling in such a proceeding, on his part, that the mildest word spoken against him was Marian's, and that was "atrocious." To give up was one thing, to be thus turned out was quite another; and it was clearly right to the moral sense, as well as satisfactory to the indignant temper, that Mr. Lyddell should oppose "to the last gasp," as the furious Lionel expressed it, one who espoused principles so pernicious both in politics and religion. One thing was certain, that nobody would ever wish again that Caroline had married him. Ill as Mr. Lyddell could afford the expense of a contested election, his blood was up, and he was determined not to yield an inch. Never had Marian believed she could grow so vehement about anything that concerned him, but now her whole soul seemed to be in his success. He had always been on the right side; and now that a steadily growing sense of religion was influencing all his actions, he was just the fit person for his position, and Marian could, on principle, wish earnestly to see him retain it, for his own sake, as well as to keep out Mr. Faulkner. But, alas! poor Marian, that the ministers should have chosen this precise time, so as just to bring the election the very week of Edmund's wedding!

What was to be done? Mrs. Lyddell could not believe that an election would go on right without dinner-parties of every visitable individual in the county; and how was Clara to manage them all? Mrs. Lyddell's only experiment, in coming into the room when there was company, had done her so much harm, that it was not on any account to be repeated; and her restlessness and anxiety, — her persuasion that nothing could be done well in which she was not concerned, — made the keeping her quiet a more anxious business than even the receiving company. There was Mr. Lyddell wanting to have lists written, and needing all sorts of small helps to which he had been used from his active wife; everything came on the two girls, and Marian did not see how she could be spared even for the three days it would take to go to the wedding.

Perhaps that excitement about the election would have somewhat dulled the acuteness of the sacrifice, if it had not been for what was to come after it. The die must be cast without consultation with Edmund; she must write and tell them that their kind design for her was in vain.

Gerald was at Oakworthy for the first week of his holidays, and he was the only person she could call to hold council with her. She had some difficulty in catching him; for he was galloping about with messages all day, figuring to himself that he produced a grand effect in the canvass, — making caricatures, describing them to Lionel, and conducting him wherever he was not expected to be seen. However, catch him she did, at bed-time, and pulling him into her room, propounded her difficulty.

"Gerald, I don't see how I am ever to manage to go with you to their wedding."

"Ha? don't you? Well, it would be a pity to lose the nomination-day, and the show of hands; I should travel all night to be in time, but you could not, I suppose?"

"I? why you don't think I should go to it?"

"Lionel will — I am to take care of Lionel. Can't you go? What a bore it must be to be a woman! Well, then, why don't you come to the wedding?"

"Because I think Clara will get into such a fuss, if there is no one to help her at the dinner the evening before. There is Mrs. Pringle coming to dine and sleep, so it can't be only a gentleman's party: and there is so much to do."

"Whew! it will be very stupid of you not to come; and how Agnes will scold! But I suppose yen can't be everywhere. One would give up something for the sake of beating such a rogue as that Faulkner."

"If we were but sure of doing it."

"Sure! Why we shall smash him to shivers, if one fortieth part of the people are but as good as their word. Did I tell you, Marian, how I answered that old farmer today?" &c., &c., all which Marian had to hear, before she could get him back to the matter in hand.

"I am almost sorry to give up those three days," he said, "though it is for their wedding; but you see, Marian," and the boy spoke with his air of consequence, "I think it is expected of me, and they would all be disappointed. It would not look as if it was well between Edmund and mo, if I was not present; but you can please yourself, you know."

"Yes, yes, you could not stay away," said Marian; "I should be very sorry that you should. You must go."

"And if I come away that afternoon, I may be back by the mail train by one at night, and be in time for the show of hands. Hurrah! I've a'mind to write to Jemmy, to buy up all the rotten eggs in Fern Torr."

"You wild animal! But do be sensible a little while, Gerald, for I have something serious to ask your advice upon."

"Well," — and all the wisdom of sixteen was at her service.

"I want to know what you think about my living here, or at Fern Torr?"

"Hollo! why I thought it was settled long ago that you were to live at the Quarry with them."

"So it was; but I don't know whether I am not more wanted here than there."

"You don't mean that that have changed their mind, and don't want to have you?"

"Not a bit — O dear, no! but I think, somehow, Clara and Lionel find me of more use than they would."

"To be sure, this place would be in a pretty tolerable sort of a mess without you. I don't know how any of them would get on."

"Well, then, I wanted your opinion, Gerald; I had better tell Edmund and Agnes that I ought to stay on here."

"But what am I to do? I mean to be at Fern Torr in the holidays, I assure you, except a week or two, just to see Lionel; and I don't mean to have my holidays without you, I declare!"

"O, I hope always to come home for them."

"Why, then, if I have you when I am at home, I don't care, — I mean —" said Gerald, conscious of the egotism he was committing, "I mean you don't like it half so well, do you?"

"O no — I mean — I don't know —"

"Which do you mean?"

"I don't know — at least, of course, I had rather be with Edmund and Agnes than anybody else, except you; but then, if I was thinking Lionel had no one to read to him, or to ride with, or that Mrs. Lyddell was worse, and Clara unhappy, I could hardly enjoy it."

"You would not think so much about it if you were away from them."

"Perhaps not, but it would be the same, and it would haunt me at night."

"But, Marian, you can't give up Edmund and Agnes now they have built a room for you."

"I must have it when I come for your holidays."

"Well, you must do as you please," said Gerald.

"And you won't be vexed?"

"Vexed! Why should I? It is nothing to me, if I have you when I am at home; and, indeed, I don't see what poor Lionel would do without you. I suppose it is the best way, since you like it; only you must settle it with Agnes your own way. I shall tell her it is not my fault. Won't she be in a rage, that's all!"

With which sentence Sir Gerald's acquiescence was conveyed, with little perception of the struggle in his sister's mind, and of the pain and grief it was to her to write to her cousin and friend, begging them to release her from her promise.

As to the rest of the house, they never appeared to think at all about her quitting them; or if Clara and Lionel did, perchance, remember that it had been spoken of, they hoped it had blown over, and dreaded the revival of the idea too much to refer to it. Not one of the whole family guessed that to them was sacrificed the most treasured project of Marian's life.

She had made up her mind, but she could not bear to write to tell her friend that her plans were frustrated; so it was to Edmund that she wrote the full detail of her reasons and regrets, begging him to forgive her, and to make her peace with Agnes; while she begged Mrs. Wortley to excuse her for missing the wedding.

Edmund's answer was just what she wished, and indeed expected. "You are right," he said, "and it is of no use to tell you how sorry we are. It is impossible to be so selfish as to wish you to act otherwise, and in process of time you may perhaps obtain Agnes' pardon: in the mean time we never walk to the Quarry, without her abusing you for giving so much trouble for nothing. I would only advise one thing, namely, that you make no promise nor engagement respecting your place of residence, since circumstances may alter; and you had better not feel yourself bound. With this proviso we resign you to your own judgment, and to the place where you seem indeed at present to be most wanted."

So wrote Edmund: Agnes did not write at all. Marian announced that she had given up going to the wedding. Clara was sorry she should miss it, but could not guess how she should have managed without her; and no one else had leisure to think at all, or else considered it quite as a matter of course that site should not go away when she was wanted.

If any one had, seven years, or even one year ago, told Marian how she would spend that bridal day, her incredulity would have been complete. So absorbed was she in Mr. Lyddell's election affairs that she hardly had time to think about it, between hopes and alarms, doubts and intelligence, visitors and preparations, notes to be written and papers to be found, Clara to be helped, Mrs. Lyddell to be kept quiet, Lionel's news to hear, the dinner party to be entertained. Very differently had Marian now learnt to sit in company from former days. She had a motive now, in the wish to help Clara, and all her distant coldness had melted into a quiet, kind, obliging manner, which had taught her to take genuine interest even in common-place people, and caused it to be said that Miss Arundel had ceased to be shy and haughty. It was all one whirl, leaving no time for sitting down, and still less for musing. Lionel went indeed with his father to the committee-room, and was there half the day; for his services were wonderful, and particularly his memory for names and places, to which Mr. Lyddell declared he would rather trust than to any memorandum. He was thus out of Marian's way all the morning, but there was enough to occupy her without him, and in the afternoon he came home, full of news, and especially full of glory, in a conquest of his own, a doubtful voter, whom he had recollected, and undertaken to secure, had made the servant drive him round that way, canvassed on his own account, and obtained a promise, extracted as Marian suspected, by admiration of the blind young gentleman's high spirit and independence.

Mr. Lyddell was particularly delighted; when became home very late, just before the eight o'clock dinner, he came up into his wife's room, and told her the whole story, told Marian all over again on the stairs, and told it a third time to some of the dinner guests, before Lionel came down. Marian saw he valued that vote above all the rest.

Busy as the day had been, Marian was resolved to sit up till her brother's return at two o'clock in the morning, to hear his tidings, and she expected to enjoy the space for thinking; but the thoughts would not be settled, and instead of dwelling on Edmund and Agnes, she found herself continually going back to the voters' list, and counting up the forces on each side. Then she grew sleepy, and fell into a long musing dream of shapeless fancies, woke herself, tried to write to Agnes, and went off into her former vision of felicity in the house at the Quarry, which she indulged in, forgetting that she had renounced it. At last came the sounds of a carriage, and of opening doors. She met Gerald on the stairs, but he was sleepy and would say little. "It had all gone off very well — yes — nobody cried — he had a bit of wedding-cake for her, and here was a note, she should hear all about it another time;" — yawn, and he shut himself into his own room. That was all Marian obtained by her vigil. You, there was the note, put in with the wedding cards.

> "MY DEAR MARIAN, — I can't relieve my mind by scolding you, and I don't know what else you have a right to expect after the way you have treated us. They tell me I must write, and I have not a word to say, though I always promised you should have the first letter from
> "Your affectionate cousin,
> "AGNES ARUNDEL."

Wild as ever, thought Marian, as a little disappointed, she laid down the note, but she understood how Agnes had felt obliged to write, in hurry and agitation, and just because she felt deeply, had been unable to express herself otherwise than what some people would call foolishly and unsuitably.

There was not much more of the wedding to be heard from Gerald the next morning, for he was full of the nomination, and proud of having Lionel under his especial charge.

This day was as wild a bustle as the former one, and there was still more excitement in the evening. Of course the show of hands had been in favour of Mr. Faulkner, of course he and his proposer and seconder had behaved one only more disgracefully than the other, of course the rabble bad behaved shamefully, and the boys were almost beside themselves with wrath; and besides the details of all these matters-of-course, the boys had adventures of their own, for somehow Gerald and Lionel had been left in the midst of a vituperative mob, out of which Gerald had brought off his companion in a most spirited and successful way, without letting any one discover Lionel's blindness, which would have been the most efficient protection for both. Again and again Marian was told of the gallant way in which both boys had conducted themselves, and proud and pleased was she.

Mr. Lyddell lost his seat, and the boys were half mad, a hundred times more concerned than he was himself, while Marian moralized to herself on why it was allowed to happen that he should be set aside from public life, just when he would have begun to act on truly sound principles. And yet perhaps the leisure he thus obtained, and the seclusion from the whirl of politics were the very things he needed, to draw him entirely apart from the world which had so long engrossed him.

It was about sis weeks after this that Mr. and Mrs. Edmund Arundel, in acceptance of a warm invitation from Mr. Lyddell, were driving along the white road leading to Oakworthy, after a very pleasant visit to the Marchmonts, when Selina had treated Agnes so affectionately, as to cause her to forget all past neglect, and had, as Edmund said, scaled their friendship, by raving at Marian's decision, "It was too bad," said she, "when they had given up London, — the only thing that made it tolerable."

To which, however, Agnes did not quite agree.

"And now," said she, "I shall see whether Marian is happy."

"I don't believe you wish her to be so," said Edmund.

"No, I am not quite so spiteful," rejoined Agnes, "but in order to forgive her, I must think it a very great sacrifice."

"And have a marvellously high estimate of our two selves,"

said Edmund.

"What do I see?" said Agnes. "Look at those two people riding on the down up there against the sky, don't you see their figures? It is a lady. Gould it be Marian? No, she is riding so close to the other — he can't be a servant."

"Lionel, I suspect," said Edmund.

"The poor blind boy! O surely she does not ride alone with him! O what a pretty cantering on the turf. It is really Marian, I see now. How I do like to see her ride."

A moment or two more, and descending from the high green slope, the two riders were on the road meeting the carriage. Marian looked her best on horseback, with her excellent seat, and easy, fearless manner, her little hat and feathers became her fine features, and the air and exercise gave them animation, which made her more like a picture of Velasquez and less like a Grecian statue than she was at any other time. Lionel rode almost close to her, a bright glow of sunshine on his lively face, and a dexterity and quickness in his whole air that made Agnes hesitate for a second or two, whether he could really be the blind youth. A joyous "How d'ye do?" was called out on each side. "Well, Lionel," then said Edmund, "are you quite well?"

"O yes, thank you," replied a gay voice, "we thought we would see if we could not meet you."

"We rode over the down," said Marian, "and we are going back the same way. We shall be at home as soon as you are. Goodbye. To the right, Lionel."

And they were seen trotting up the hill again, then as the carriage came in sight of the front door, there was Lionel jumping Marian down from her saddle. Agnes did not know how to believe that he could not see, as she watched his upright bearing, and rapid, fearless step, so unlike the groping ways of persons who have lost their sight later in life.

Clara presently came down, and Agnes was struck with her more thoughtful face, and collected manner, so unlike the giddy child she had last seen, not intellectual indeed, but quiet, lady-like, and sensible. And as to Mr. Lyddell, he looked so worn and so much older, so subdued in manner, and so free from those over civilities of former times, that Agnes made up her mind that he must not be hated.

Of Mrs. Lyddell she saw very little, only sitting in her room for an hour each morning, as a visitor, but it was evident she was very much out of health, and a great charge to them all. Agnes could be sorry for her, but could not like her while she did not speak more cordially of Marian. All praise of her had something forced and against the grain, and Agnes thought her intensely ungrateful.

Lionel interested Agnes extremely, with his happy, independent ways, unrepining temper and spirit of enterprise. He was always eager about some contrivance of his own, and just at this time it was wood-carving. His left hand showed as much sticking-plaster as skin, and he used to come into the drawing-room with it wrapped up in his handkerchief and say, "Here's another, Marian," when Marian very quietly produced her sticking-plaster, as if it was quite an ordinary matter; nay, would not follow up the suggestion that he should not have so sharp a knife, saying that it was much better to cut one's finger with a sharp knife than a blunt one. He had cut about twenty bits of wood to waste, to say nothing of hands, but he persevered with amusing energy, and before the end of the visit had achieved a capital old man's head for the top of a walking stick, which he presented to Edmund. He promised Agnes a set of silk winders, and in the mean time made great friends with her, getting her to tell him about her brother's sporting adventures, and in return making himself very amusing with relations out of his sailor brother's letters. Johnny had been concerned in the great exploit of climbing the Peter Bottle mountain, and Lionel was as proud of it as if he had done it himself, making Marian show everybody a drawing which Gerald had made of the appearance that Johnny must have cut, standing on one leg on the highest stone. They were also struck with the change in the manner in which Walter was regarded, and the pride and affection with which all the family spoke of his doings at his curacy.

But that Marian, though not prominent, and apparently merely a guest, was necessary to the comfort of each member of the family, was a thing that at the end of a fortnight, Agnes could not deny. Nor could she attempt to make up a case to show that she and her husband were equally in want of her.

"So, Marian," said she, as they parted, "I forgive you on condition of your spending Christmas with us."

"And I ought to forgive you," said Edmund, "in consideration of the fulfilment of my prediction that you would not be able to leave the Lyddells when I was ready to receive you."

Marian smiled, and watched them from the door. As they lost sight of the house, Edmund turned to his wife, saying, "How little we are fit to order events! Here, Agnes, I looked back at this house six years ago in a sort of despair. I was ready to reproach Providence, to reproach everything. I thought I saw my uncle's children in the way to be ruined, all his work undone, and there was I, unable to act, and yet with the responsibility of the care of them. I tell you, Agnes, I never was so wretched in my life. And yet what short-sightedness! There has Marian been, placed, like a witness of the truth, calm, firm, constant, guarding herself and her brother first, and then softening, and winning all that came under her influence."

"Oh! but, Edmund, your coming home saved Gerald," said the wife, who could not see her husband's credit given away even to Marian.

"I brought the experience and authority that she could not have, but vain would have been my attempts without the sense of right she had always kept up in his mind. Trouble has done much for those Lyddells, but I don't believe that without her, it would have had that effect: When I remember what Mr. Lyddell was, his carelessness, the painful manner in which he used to talk; when I see him now, when I think of what that poor Caroline was saved from, when I see the alteration in Clara, and watch that blind boy, then I see indeed that our little Marian, whom we thought thrown away and spoilt, was sent there to be a blessing. If she had been naturally a winning, gentle, persuasive person, I should have thought less of the wonder; but in her it is the simple force of goodness, undecorated. I once feared the constant opposition in which she lived, would harden her, but instead, she has softened, sweetened, and lost all that was hard and haughty in her ways, when it was no longer needed for a protection. Selina Marchmont has failed too in giving her the exclusive spirit which I once feared for her. It is as if she had a spell for passing through the world unscathed."

"And you think she is happy?"

"As happy as those that never look for their happiness in this world."

Agnes sighed. "My vision has always been," said she, "to see Marian as happy as — ourselves."

"She may be yet," said Edmund smiling, "but she has the best sort of happiness. She is in less danger of clinging to this world than we are. And somehow she gives me the impression of one too high and noble to seek her happiness in the way in which most people look for it. Yes, we ourselves, Agnes, we have a nest and home in this world; she stands above it, and her only relation with it is to make others happy."

"She little thinks how we talk of her," said Agnes. "And still stranger it is, that with the reverence I have for her, I can play with her and scold her."

A silence; ending with Agnes repeating,

"GOOD LORD, through this world's troubled way
Thy children's course secure;
And lead them onward day by day,
Kindly like Thee and pure.

"Be theirs to do Thy work of love,
All erring souls to win;
Amid a sinful world to move,
Yet give no smile to sin."

www.ingramcontent.com/pod-product-compliance
Lightning Source LLC
Chambersburg PA
CBHW032208030726
47494CB00020B/722